SITE UNSEEN

NANCE NEWMAN

Praise for the work of Nance Newman

Stone Cold Secrets

With a fast-paced and engrossing storyline and some real doozies of twists that throw out wonderful spanners, Newman delivers a read worth picking up and savoring. Very highly recommended.

-Readers' Favorite

Stone Cold Secrets is one book readers won't quickly forget. Filled with thrills, chills, and mysterious characters, it has all the ingredients for an exciting, page-turning read. If you are one that's drawn to tales of complex love filled with damning and dangerous secrets, then you won't want to miss this unforgettable journey.

-Women Using Words

It's difficult to talk about this story without giving away crucial hints about the very twisty and surprisingly dangerous mystery. The author made my head spin after every one of my guesses about what was happening, much less whodunnit, turned out to be totally incorrect. None of the characters are exactly what you might think, and I was impressed with how far the author strayed from every expectation. 16 Best Sapphic Books of 2024 List.

-TheLesbianReview.com

The book is gripping and hard to put down once the twists start coming. The story is suspenseful and full of intrigue. To tell more would spoil the story.

- Kaye C., *NetGalley*

A totally engrossing book that will keep you glued to the pages. So many twists and turns, with an intricate story that the author keeps a tight rein on and maintains coherency throughout. Thoroughly enjoyable.

-Sandy J., NetGalley

Other Bella Books from Nance Newman

Stone Cold Secrets

About the Author

I firmly believe that you should never give up on your dreams. And I never will.

I worked at Eastman Kodak in Motion Picture film for over twenty years before the company started to downgrade. I then moved to education, working as a teacher and then in the school bus industry (and yes, I drove a big yellow bus once or twice!)

I have always been a writer. Since high school, I have written songs, novels, short stories, and journals. I love many genres and have dabbled in stories in magical realism, paranormal mysteries, lesbian urban dystopian, lesbian fiction and now lesbian domestic psychological thriller. I am now writing full time.

I live in upstate New York with my two rescue dogs, Ela, a miniature Australian Shepard/Corgi/Pomeranian mix who survived the Puerto Rican hurricanes. She didn't respond to any commands when I brought her home, but after a friend asked if she barked in Spanish, we started our journey together where I taught her English, and she taught me Spanish (at least enough to understand each other). My other dog is Misty, a poodle/Pomeranian mix rescued from a puppy mill. I love dogs—they are true companions.

I enjoy being active outdoors and partake in many activities, including kayaking, biking, hiking and gardening. I play the guitar and love to sing. I also love movies—lots and lots of movies.

But most of all, I love to write and bring my imagination to life on the written page.

And some day, I just might write about a big yellow school bus!

SITE UNSEEN

NANCE NEWMAN

BELLA
BOOKS

Bella Books, Inc.
P.O. Box 10543
Tallahassee, FL 32302

First Edition - 2026

Editor: Cath Walker
Cover Designer: Kayla Mancuso

ISBN: 978-1-64247-674-3

PUBLISHER'S NOTE

Acknowledgments

Thank you to my publisher and all the hardworking people behind the scenes for getting my book out to the readers.

To the Readers—thank you for going on this journey in the outdoors with me.

To De and Marsha—thank you for all the fun years of camping and the ones to come.

Dedication

I dedicate this book to my mother.
I wish you were here to see this!

In every walk with nature one receives
far more than he seeks.

–John Muir

PROLOGUE

The state of the body lying at the bottom of the gorge was not a surprise. I mean, anyone who fell from that height onto solid rock two hundred feet below would not land in a normal position. Definitely not on all fours like a cat and then walk away, or even two legs, for that matter.

The force of the fall would shatter the leg bones into hundreds of pieces if someone tried to land on their feet. But no human would try that. Even the thought of it would be sheer stupidity. A fall like that would force the body to hit in a supine position face up or face down, most likely shattering every bone in the body and crushing the skull. And that's what it looked like as I surveyed the battered body lying in blood diluted with the water running from Upper Taughannock Falls.

I think the shock upon seeing the mangled body made me wonder why anyone would get close enough to topple over the edge. Topple. What a strange word to describe a fall from such a height in a place where most people would not even contemplate the thought of trying such a daredevil feat. No, a daredevil would string a wire across from one side of the gorge to the other and try traversing it. Even so, no one could survive a fall like that.

Therefore, my logical mind deduced it had to be a suicide or a murder. Or an accident. I think the shock upon seeing the mangled woman's body on my first day as a rookie policewoman in the city of Ithaca made these crazy thoughts go through my head. It was a horrible way to die.

The forensics team had already determined it was a female, a young female—late teenager or young adult. And that news made me feel faint. And it made me want to quit my job. Why then, you ask, was I there? I had recently graduated from the Ithaca Police Academy, and it was just my luck as a rookie policewoman, that this was my first deceased-person case.

The thought that ran through my head as I took in the scene was it might also be my last. The violence of this woman's death enraged me and sent the deepest sorrow coursing through my veins. As a cop, I knew it could have been a suicide, but that didn't lessen my anger. I had a hard time understanding why someone would end their life, and in that way. How could someone want their loved ones to see them in that condition, knowing they would die inside themselves?

I stood in the back, behind the throng of Ithaca police personnel. I didn't want to see the body. It repulsed me and since I was a rookie under Officer Mac Taylor, it was better if I stayed out of the way, in the background.

So, as I looked everywhere but at the body, my question was: did this person…strike that…did this woman want to end her life? Or did someone end it for her? Or was she careless and jumped the barrier chain-link fence that was supposed to keep people from getting too close to the edge and got…too close to the edge. So maybe an accident. It happened.

Taughannock Upper Falls Park was closed while we gathered clues in the gorge as well as from above. They found footprints to match the woman's sneakers, suggesting the spot where she went over the ledge. Once the medical examiner finished inspecting the body, the female was carefully placed into a black postmortem bag. I cringed as I watched because this poor woman's body was so mangled and broken, I had a hard time looking at her remains. They struggled to get her parts into the body bag and then onto a backboard. The bag looked more like a regular kitchen trash bag with a normal week's buildup of garbage from a family of four.

The whole process of moving her body into the postmortem bag and fixing the backboard underneath, reminded me of cracking an egg into a frying pan and after it's cooked, tipping the pan and letting it slide onto a plate. To this day, that particular image still made me want to vomit whenever it entered my mind. It was a long time before I ate fried eggs again. My eyes focused on the cadaver pouch as the ME zipped it up. The sound of the zipper threads seemed louder than it really was as each metallic tooth of the zipper connected with its counterpart like a hammer hitting an anvil. I turned away quickly, hoping to stop the noise by putting my hands over my ears or at least hide myself from others at the possible upchuck of my breakfast. Neither would have looked good for a rookie, even if it was her first actual death scene, so I stood stoically.

Without looking, I knew when they were placing the body on a gurney. I heard the body bag rustle and the plopping sound of the backboard landing on the plastic-covered mattress. When I heard wheels running over the stone bed of the creek with the sound of the rushing water, I looked up. The gurney opened a path in the water like Poseidon opening a path in the ocean.

Would I be able to do this job?

I heard whispers amongst my uniformed colleagues and the detectives as they speculated on the cause of death. If it was a suicide, they feared this could be the start of another rash of people taking their own life by jumping into a gorge. The rate of suicides among college students had increased, starting in the 1970s. For whatever reason, students from the Ithaca's two universities decided the only way that they could solve their problems was to toss themselves into one of the famous gorges off of one of several bridges on the college campuses. Between 1990 and 2010, twenty-seven people had suicided that way. There had also been deaths from jumps or falls in different places in the Upper Taughannock State Park, but they were either accidental or from recreational jumps into the deeper pools of water below. But this young woman's death was the first of its kind in that part of the state park, speculating that it may not have been a suicide.

Suicide. Murder. Accident. It didn't matter to me. Although they taught you about these things in the Academy, it didn't become real until you stood at the bottom of a gorge looking at a young female body. I wondered when the faint red color—the mixing of her blood with the creek water—would reach the top of the falls spilling into the water below. It was no surprise when I heard a policeman say they would close lower Taughannock Falls for that very reason and it would remain closed for a day or two until the water was clear again.

"Moore, let's go."

I turned to see Officer Mac Taylor, my mentor, waiting impatiently for me. I could tell he wasn't happy having a woman as his first rookie. Or maybe he just didn't like me. Or maybe he saw the beads of sweat on my forehead, and the green tint to my skin as I fought to keep the bile down while I contemplated whether I was going to cut it as a cop or become a waitress. I knew after my first day with him when I overheard him tell another cop that women weren't good enough to be cops that the next six months with this man would be brutal in more ways than one.

I took one last look around, and just as I turned to leave with him, I noticed something caught in a clump of weeds in the water. I walked over to a thin gold, chained bracelet tangled in strands of wet grass and mud. A small charm dangled from the chain, swaying back and forth with the downward flow of the water in the current. I began to sway with it.

"Come on, Moore, get your ass in gear," I heard him shout to me. "What is it now?" he yelled in total exasperation when I didn't move.

"I found something, sir," I said, struggling to speak.

I heard him call for the forensics team, telling them *he* found something. *He.* Found something. That was yet another clue among so many that had stared me in the face since I began working with him. I should have quit then and there.

The other officers approached, standing focused on the piece of jewelry sparkling in the rays of sunshine. Even though my commanding officer and the forensic team crowded me out of the way, I managed to make out the shape of the charm, a tiny image of Tinkerbell. I fought to keep the tears back as I watched the item be photographed, picked up with tweezers and placed in a clear-plastic evidence bag.

I was so close to losing the contents of my stomach.

The condition of the body, the smashed head and face, would make it impossible to identify the body without forensic testing. I wasn't even sure dental records would be helpful as her teeth appeared to be shattered, but now *I* knew. There was no need for me to tell them who I knew it was. It would only open a door I did not want, and I could not open.

Tinkerbell. I fought harder to keep the tears from rolling down my cheeks by wiping them with my sleeve. My head pounded, and I bounced back and forth between feeling faint, and wanting to vomit, but I couldn't do either. I was a cop. Cops weren't supposed to faint or vomit at a crime/suicide scene.

The Tinkerbell charm told me who she was. It said, at the very least, she was young at heart, a believer in magic—not the fantasy kind of magic, but the magic of life and love, and she *was* so full of life and love. Yet, the one thing she needed, represented by this bangle, was hope. Hope for dreams to come true, for the wonderful life she had planned, for luck and love. She had had it. Once. But she had lost hope in the few moments before her body took the plunge.

I thought my heart would explode through my chest like in the movie *Alien* when I realized that either she thought she had no hope and that was why she jumped, or she realized seconds before someone pushed her over the edge that hope was gone.

I felt like I was lying on the gurney with her as my heart broke into a million pieces. I knew then there was nothing more devastating than to lose all hope. She had died without it.

Now, I would live without it.

CHAPTER ONE

"Blake, wait, don't open the slide-out yet. You forgot to lower the stabilizers," I heard Myra yell from outside.

"Crap," I muttered under my breath. I had arrived at Rock Creek Campground in the late afternoon and still had to unpack. I had planned on carrying everything into the trailer and unpacking it after I had the trailer set up. It was a system that I went over and over in my mind. That was how I worked. I was a big planner, and I thought I had this thoroughly and logically organized on paper. But when I jumped the gun to do something out of impatience—like pushing the button to extend the slide-out before I had time to put the stabilizers in place—my planning skills went right out the window.

I had a good explanation for my momentary stupidity. This was the first time I had opened my trailer for seasonal camping. In fact, it was the first trailer I owned. I had read the manual over and over, taken notes, and made my plan, but now I had to admit that I didn't really know what I was doing. I had to accept I still needed help.

Enter Myra Lewis, my second-best friend who was the master at opening trailers, closing trailers, and of how the workings of the tin cans, well, worked. Even though I was a cop, and systems worked for me (in the judicial, crime kind of way), I felt somewhat at a loss on the whole cranking-before-opening, septic-hose-attaches-here, open-this-valve-and-that-valve camping thing. It was all Greek to me. Obviously, studying the manual hadn't done me much good. I guess I had to see it done to learn how it was done.

Myra Lewis owned a very successful contracting company that she built from scratch. Her employees were all women, making us doubly proud of her accomplishment. She'd worked hard for many years to make the company the financial success it was, and because of that, she could now work remotely from the campground in the summers. She handled the financials, and contracts for the clients, and assigned the work to her contractors.

Myra didn't do the manual labor anymore, but she inspected every job her workers completed. Sometimes, she visited sites when there were problems, and at the very least, she stepped in when she didn't have enough employees for a job, or when her friends (like us) required something to be fixed or we requested she build something for us...like a deck on our trailer.

Myra spent most of her days on her computer and phone, but she made sure to take one or two days off during the week to spend with us, along with the weekends. While Myra worked, her wife, Jen Anderson, played housewife, gardener, errand runner, and anything else she felt was needed to keep Myra happy at home while working. That was the advantage of being an elementary school teacher—summers off!

I went outside to the back where Myra stood, grinning at me with her trademark lopsided grin, and opened the compartment where I stored the crank. I had come before the season began and placed pieces of two-by-six short planks into the compartments to be used beneath the stabilizers. This would keep them from sinking when the ground got saturated on rainy days. Annoyed, I pulled everything out. One day, I would get this right so I could do it by myself without breaking something that would be too expensive to fix, and then I'd have to dip into Mabel's savings.

Mabel was my dog—half poodle, half Pomeranian with two very large blue-brown eyes. A rescue, who had spent the first seven years in a crate having one batch of puppies after the other in a disgusting puppy mill. She was the sweetest dog you could ever meet.

After hearing about the horrific conditions the breeding dogs were kept in, I researched and read everything about these dogs that I could find. The literature said she would be so unstable that I'd need to fit her for a white coat, but Mabel was gentle, meek, mild, and as time went by, the puppyhood she had been refused during the first years of her life began to surface. She would explore, want to play, and loved to cuddle with her two moms. But, like most small rescue dogs, Mabel had to have her teeth cleaned because of total medical and dental neglect that was common for so many of these animals. The cost was outlandish, so I started a savings account for her in case something else major came along that could cause a big dent in my retirement savings. It was a good thing because soon after her dental surgery, she needed knee surgery for a luxating patella, and I saw another dent in my savings. I increased the monthly amount I put into her account and by the time she was ten years old, I often joked that she would be financially better off in her retirement than I would be in mine.

I placed a piece of wood on the ground where each leg of the stabilizer would land and then turned the crank to bring it down. Maybe in time, the setup would become natural to me. After all, I'd only be doing it twice a year—once when I opened the trailer in the late spring and then again in the fall when I closed it. Which reminded me…

"You know, Myra," I said as I cranked. "You'll have to help me close it too."

"Yeah, yeah, yeah. Keep cranking." She chuckled. Her arms folded, she watched me like a teacher grading a final. It was a warm day and there were beads of sweat dripping from beneath her short brown hair. She was an inch taller than me and that inch contained a whole lot of tenacity.

I had Covid to thank for all of this. Like for so many, Covid had shut down the possibility of traveling on vacation for a few years, especially if you had anxiety about catching the disease like I did. I was getting close to that magic age when you retire and you can do whatever you want while adding a greater risk of catching a myriad of illnesses—the worst at that time being Covid.

I watched both parents of my friend Steph die from it. Others spent time in the hospital, some on ventilators, and others ended up with long-term Covid. It totally freaked me out. I wore the mask, always positioned myself more than six feet away from other people, and ordered things online to stay out of stores. I was very cautious to the point of obsessive, so I began to relax a little and not be so worried about getting sick. And then, despite all my overzealous cleaning and other precautions, I got it.

I won't go into details because who wants to hear about your bout with Covid? What I will say is I was scared again and found myself struggling to stay off the anal train I had been on before catching the disease. Me. A cop. Getting scared. Kind of sad because I wasn't scared of your average break-in criminal or a gang shooting. I was afraid of dying from something unseen that attacked my body, and I had no control over. So, when I finally got to the other side of one very nasty illness, I was ready to retire at the ripe young age of fifty-seven, from my job as a criminal profiler.

My friends suggested it was time to go camping, hoping it would relieve my stress, and it might possibly do that since this would not be the tent-kind of camping where you sit cramped in a nylon box on rainy days getting bored and feeling a chilly dampness seeping into every pore of your body. No. I had already been that route and now I wanted a bed, a toilet, air-conditioning and heat—everything a trailer had to offer. They called it glamping.

So, I bought a twenty-nine-foot trailer built for two (which worked for me since there was only…me. I'll get to that in a minute). It was made with living space and comfort in mind. I also wanted to spend my summers in an area that offered lots to do. I didn't want to travel too far from home in case I needed to get back for something. I looked at many campgrounds, but nothing came close to the campground south of Ithaca, where my friends also had their trailers.

Back where I had spent my first days as a policewoman.

I had spent some extremely difficult years in Ithaca, but the beauty and splendor of the countryside were hard to refuse. Another plus was the close proximity to over one hundred and fifty waterfalls and more wineries, breweries, and distilleries than you could visit in one summer.

But the number one reason I was going to try Rock Creek Campground was that my closest friends were there. I promised myself if it became too hard for me, I would find another spot. Make new friends if I had to. But I knew it wouldn't because the campground was far enough away from the small city that I wouldn't have to be reminded of those rookie years every day. There would also be no reason to go to the center of the metropolitan area where the police station was if I didn't want to. The newer, main drag on the south edge of town had everything one needed: restaurants and big chain stores of every kind.

After I walked off my rookie job in 1993, I spent the next thirty years in Rochester as a member of the RPD profiling criminals. I didn't want to just quit. I wanted to stay in law enforcement because I came from a long line of cops and I needed and wanted to carry on the tradition.

My father always wanted a boy who would one day follow in his footsteps. But you don't always get what you want and he ended up with a girl. I never knew of my father's disappointment until my mother cried the day I told her I wanted to attend the police academy when I was older. She said my father would be so pleased and proud, and how he always hoped he'd have a son who would become a policeman like him. My heart sank, but it never hit bottom, because then she said, "But, he will be on top of the moon that his daughter, who he loves more than life, will be the one to follow him in his footsteps."

It had taken me a long time to reach my full potential as a criminal profiler, but I worked hard to attain my Bachelor in Criminology and Masters in Applied Behavior Analysis. I was proud of my accomplishments and the job that I did. I also worked hard to tuck the memories of my years on the Ithaca police force back into the recesses of my mind, vowing never to let them run my life.

Soon after I took the position, I met my ex-wife, Tess Angler (ex is the key factor here). She worked for the largest health insurance company in the city. We met at a local bar and over a couple of martinis, we found we had a lot in common. She was of average height, average weight with curves in all the right places. Her skin was soft, her shoulder-length auburn hair shone in the sun and her baby-blue eyes had magical sparkles in them when she smiled. It may not have been love at first sight, but it was close.

Throughout our relationship, we actually found ourselves spending many weekends in the Finger Lakes area hiking, biking, kayaking, wine tasting, festival going…well, you get the picture. She met my friends. They took an instant like to her and she to them. We took the time to explore the many breathtaking waterfalls near Ithaca, doing enough hiking to help keep us physically fit in our younger years. So, it wasn't just the presence of my friends at Rock Creek Campground that persuaded me to plop a trailer on a campsite at the age of fifty-eight, but the attachment I had to the area over many years. I also knew there were other lesbian and gay couples included in the eighty seasonal campers. So, good and bad.

"Are you done yet?" I heard Myra call out from the other side of the trailer.

"Just about. I'll be right over to do that side."

"Good. Jen is going to wonder what's taking me so long."

When I got to the other side, I saw her checking the seals to the slide-out.

"Did I ruin them?"

"No, no. The trailer is brand new. They can take a misfire." She laughed. "Just don't do it again. But remember to grease these once or twice during the summer."

"I promise. The first thing I'll do tonight when I'm sitting in my recliner is write down everything we've done and what I need to do." I turned the crank for the next stabilizer. "Do you gals want to come over for cocktails later?"

"Don't you have a lot of unpacking to do?" She stood with her arms folded in that teacher inspecting their students' work pose once again. At that moment, I didn't know why but I felt so inadequate and contemplated whether I should go back to police work where my cup runneth over with confidence. It was only a trailer, for God's sake. Then again, I was never good at mechanics. Except for guns. I was very good at shooting a gun, cleaning a gun and taking it apart and putting it back together. But that wouldn't help me here.

I placed another piece of wood under the stabilizer and stood waiting for my master to give me approval. When I thought I had the trailer at a good height to keep it stabilized and level, I stood and said, "How's it look, Obi-Wan?"

"You're such a goof. Stay here and I'll go check the level." Seconds later I heard, "You're good. Now you can open your slide-out."

She was waiting inside for me. I stepped in and pushed the button on the control panel that said "Slide-out Extend." I was like a little kid at Christmas watching the ten-foot-long section of my trailer extend to the outside world.

"Wow. It's so much bigger now!" I exclaimed, with giddiness. "Why would you not have slide-outs?" I turned my body and sidestepped up and down the length of the trailer, acting like I was sandwiched between walls. Then I walked up and down like I was outside with no walls around me whatsoever. "Now which would you choose?"

Myra laughed as she shook her head. "I get your point. They do make a difference. Sometimes, Blake, I can't believe you were a policewoman. Okay, let's finish the rest and I'll go ask Jen if she wants a drink."

We hooked up the sewer, placing wood under the long, hard plastic hose to keep the drainage on a downward slant. She showed me where the drainage levers were and gave me a quick explanation of which one to open first when draining the tanks and how often I should do it. Then we attached the water hose and the electrical cord.

"Thank God, I came early for the Internet guys. I'll have TV tonight along with a flushing toilet, running water, and electricity. What more could a gal ask for?" I exclaimed. Then I gave her a big grateful hug and went inside to get Mabel. I was anxious to get unpacked, but first I needed to take her for a quick walk. Settling in would have to wait a bit longer.

As I walked my dog, I introduced myself to people who interacted with me and waved at the rest. Campers were a friendly bunch, so it didn't surprise me that everyone I saw stopped to welcome me. That's what Jen and Myra had told me. They also said I would have no problem fitting in since I already knew a lot of the seasonal campers from having stayed with my friends over many a summer.

I was back in my trailer deciding which cupboard to put the box of Cheerios in when I heard a voice outside.

"Well, if it isn't the newbie camper. It's me, Steph." She opened the door and let herself in. "How's it going?"

"Don't you know it's not safe to just walk into somebody's box?" I said as I shut the cupboard door.

"That's why I announced myself."

I walked over to her and hugged her fiercely. We had been friends since childhood, and she was the tightest connection I had to Ithaca. We lived next to each other as kids, went to the same high school, and played on several sports teams together, but when we left college, we went different ways. Kind of. She headed to a university to begin work on her medical degree when I entered the police academy. Her dream was to become a medical examiner.

Neither of us knew that the other was studying a field in the same line of work. So when I saw Steph at that first dead body scene I investigated with my mentor, it was a shock. Part of me wanted to hug her because of the excitement of seeing each other after so many years, but I couldn't. I was a rookie and she was doing summer intern work under the medical examiner. Being the professionals that we were, we simply nodded to each other, but picked up our friendship as if we had never gone our separate ways until discussions over that poor dead woman at the bottom of the gorge. Disagreements on what happened to her and why I seemed to care so much made her wonder if there was more to it. I said there wasn't, but that I didn't think she killed herself. Steph believed she did and we drifted away from each other once again. I saw her now and then in the summer months on cases involving dead people, and we would politely acknowledge each other. Then I left. Went to Rochester and married a wonderful woman.

Years later, she contacted me and we put our friendship back together. We promised each other to leave the years in Ithaca behind us. Where they belonged. After that, she was the best friend anyone could ever have. She was always there when I needed her—even when Tess left me for another woman.

"How about a margarita? I've gotten to be an expert at making them."

"Wow," she said, sitting on the recliner. "Happy hour before five. Retirement *has* changed you." She chuckled. "Oh, and I love your trailer."

"Right? Isn't it great? I'm so excited to start this summer."

"Then get those margaritas going and I'll meet you outside."

"I haven't set up any of the outdoor stuff yet."

"Where's your chairs? I'll do it while you make the drinks."

"Chairs are under the trailer next to an outdoor rug. Myra promised me she'd help me get a deck built. Until then, it's the ground."

"Works for me. Just put the awning out. The sun is warm."

"Got it."

Steph went outside, and I pushed the button on the control panel that read "Awning Extend." I was in love with the control panel. It explained things in such easy terms. Gone were the days of cranking out the awnings or slide-outs. While I stood there pushing the button, a thought struck me. Maybe I should have bought a trailer with electric leveling. Maybe next trailer.

I mixed the ingredients: tequila, lime juice, Cointreau, and fresh raspberries floating on top into two glasses of crushed ice. Steph had the rug down, and two chairs and a small table set up. I placed the glasses on the table and hooked Mabel to a long lead that I connected to the picnic table. But instead of wandering, my small dog, who lived for routine and repetition, lay down on the outdoor rug that was made of waterproof, plastic material, and I imagined not very comfortable to lie on. So, I pulled out the small bed I purchased specifically for Mabel's camping comfort from a storage compartment. She hopped right in and wagged her tail.

"Nothing like spoiling your dog," Steph said, chuckling. She leaned down and scratched my dog's ears. "Well, Mabel, what do you think about camping?"

She lifted her head and gazed her sad eyes on Steph, who laughed out loud at the sight of my sweet girl's facial expression. Whether she was happy or sad, her eyes were always pitifully sorrowful.

"She's not sure what to make of it," I said. 'It's not home, or the routine we had when I was working. She had a hard time when Tess left and when I retired. We've only had a few months for her to get used to all of that. Now we have this. Been a lot of changes for her."

"A lot for you too, but you'll both settle in."

"We will," I chuckled. "Right about the time we have to close up and go back to Rochester."

We laughed and then discussed the Memorial Weekend events at the campground and the seasonal camper gatherings.

"So, is everyone pretty open to us gay women?"

"Yes, they are. I think there is one gay couple and three or four other lesbian couples and they all get along with the heterosexuals."

I laughed at her joke.

"You and I, however"—she tipped her drink in my direction as if toasting—"are the only singles."

"Oh God. The last thing I want is for people to try to fix me up. I'm so done with that."

"There are some single men here, and the last thing you want will probably be the first thing that happens to you since you're fresh meat."

I slapped her arm. "Oh, my God. You're so crass."

"Maybe so, but it's true. All the older couples here, who, by the way, are not a lot older than us, feel that everyone should have someone. They went hog wild with me the first year I was here. It took a lot of no's for them to finally get the message."

"What message were you trying to convey?"

"The *I'm not interested* message."

"Not the *I'm a lesbian and don't do men* message?"

"Well, here's the thing. Everyone here accepts us and treats us like everyone else."

I snorted. "As long as they don't have to talk about it or see it."

Steph raised her glass again. "Ding, ding, ding. You win the prize." She set it down without taking a sip.

"I know things have changed since we were in college and first coming out, but sometimes, it doesn't seem like it's changed at all."

"I don't think that's true. Things have changed. So what if there are still those who don't like us? There are still people who don't like people of color, people of certain religions, or Democrats." Steph said the last word with a twinkle in her eye. "If you don't put your way of life out there on the stage for all to see, you'll be okay."

"Really?" I shook my head. "I don't know if I should call you a diplomat or just naïve."

"What's that supposed to mean?"

"In today's world, there is no fucking way you can appease everyone." My response may have sounded angry, but I was trying to sound humorous. We had been over this so many times before it seemed more like a joke. "Come on, Steph. You know that. It's been that way since the beginning of human existence and will be that way until the end of human existence. So why bother? No matter what you do, there will always be someone in this campground who won't like two women together in a trailer. Or two men, for that matter. Or a single woman or a Jewish man. You won't be able to change that with your diplomacy, so we might as well be ourselves and deal with whatever they want to throw at us."

"When did you become so cynical? Oh wait, don't answer that. Must have been those years on the police force. Good thing you moved out of patrol early and into a desk job. I can't imagine how you'd be if you stayed on the streets."

I glared at her. She knew I didn't like to talk about my time working with the IPD. During those years, I never admitted to anyone that

I couldn't stomach the violence or the stupid and evil people that committed it and the failure of our system to put an end to it. When I finally accepted that it would never go away (both my stomach issues and the societal issues), I took a desk job in Rochester. And even though the societal issues didn't go away, my stomach issues did. It was a way for me to attack the evil without having to see it up close and personal. Still, there were days when profiling a criminal made my stomach churn.

Yet, here I was saying we had to put ourselves out there no matter what people thought of us. The problem was, although I truly believed it, I had difficulty doing it. Steph was right on one thing. Putting yourself out there was just asking for trouble, but as human beings, I truly believed we had a right to do that without being persecuted, and I knew why it was hard.

"The police department didn't do that to me," I answered her. "Criminals did. I thought you knew that by now."

"Yeah, you could help from the back seat."

"Ouch." I didn't get angry, but the hurt had been with me from the first time we had this same argument.

"Sorry," she said, like she did every other time. "But don't you think it's a little hypocritical? As a lesbian, you say we should be out front on the stage, yet in the criminal world, you took a back seat. I'm just saying that we don't have to flaunt it. Heterosexuals don't flaunt their relationships."

I shot her a sideways glance. "Really? They don't hide them either."

"Right. We don't have to hide, just not set off fireworks every time we walk by. Besides, in campgrounds, everyone keeps their relationships inside their trailers. It's been that way since the dawn of camping." She winked.

"Fine, fine, fine. I won't hug you unless we are inside with the shades down and the door closed. Does that make you happy?"

"Just because it's the way I want to be doesn't mean I'm happy about it. But I appreciate the effort."

My next statement would have been, "If it doesn't make you happy, then why do you do it?" But like I said, we had been down this road many times before and I knew the destination. The saying, "If you keep doing what you've always done, you'll always get what you always got," was very apropos in this case. So, I closed my mouth and swallowed my sentence.

We sat in silence for a few minutes, and I realized it was more the sun that was making my body heated than the argument we had had so many times and would probably have again. The sun was at an angle that the awning wasn't shading out. "I'm going to drop that side of the awning. I'm getting warm. Aren't you? Besides, I heard it might rain later this afternoon."

"Sounds like a good idea. You want to make sure you've got it at an angle for the water to run off. Or just put it in when you're done using it," Steph said.

I got up to lower one end of the awning and heard the one voice that had brought terror to me every time it had bellowed at me in the past. The only voice that made me feel like I was on an ancient torture device—like the one where your arms and legs are tied down and someone is turning a wheel that stretches your joints until the ligaments and tendons snap. A rack. Yeah, that's what they called it.

Officer Mac Taylor was my torture device.

Memories of my calling him The Rack when I was off duty rushed back, and I swallowed hard to keep them at bay.

I heard the familiar deep, baleful voice exclaim, "Well, I'll be a monkey's uncle!"

CHAPTER TWO

Something in the tone and mocking attitude that exuded from the statement made my stomach churn like it did back when I was a rookie officer under his tutelage. I turned to see a man in his late sixties, grayish hair around the temples that betrayed a once-full head of black hair. Bushy eyebrows dipped toward each other, hiding dark-brown eyes that always seemed to have only one expression—loathing and imperiousness. Thin lips stretched straighter than a ruler brought memories of Officer Taylor bellowing, making me shrink into the background. I had never seen his lips in any other shape. No frown, no smile, no nothing. Just straight like he had practiced this look for years as his *you'll never know what I'm thinking* mien.

After six months of training with him, I learned it was also his look of loathing for me.

He was sitting in a golf cart, one arm draped lazily over the steering wheel, the other on his knee. "Never in my life did I think I'd see Officer Squeamish again. I thought you ran scared to some city for a desk job 'cause you couldn't take real work."

If ever there was a time I wish I had my gun in my hand, this moment was one of them. I'd shoot that hateful grin right off his face, leaving a big open hole of shock.

"Well, well, if it isn't the illustrious Officer Taylor. Still up to your old harassing ways?" I heard Steph cut in.

She had come over to stand next to me and that put a smile on my face. I knew she wouldn't put an arm around me to show solidarity for lesbians, but I hoped she might just for support because she knew the most about my time with this bastard. I would have loved it if she had done so to shove my lifestyle and my beliefs down his throat. But she didn't. Instead, she goaded him. Therefore, I had to join in the fun.

"So, what are you doing here? In a golf cart, no less? Got a license to drive that thing?" My attempt at cracking a joke was poorly received. It didn't surprise me. It was a poor joke.

He snickered, sat up straight, and announced as if he were king of the jungle, "I own the place. I was looking for something to do when I retire, and stumbled on this gem. And before you ask, no, I'm not retiring yet, but I'm close. I just couldn't pass this up. If you run it right, it's a cash cow. And I plan on doing just that. Running it right." His grin said it all. My old nemesis was going to change the campground from a quiet democracy to a dictatorship.

He wouldn't be able to stand retirement without people to boss around, I thought to myself. I folded my arms as if that action would stop me from saying something I would regret. I already regretted my lame attempt at sarcasm, but I didn't want to regret any further interaction with whom I remembered to be a very vile and contemptible man.

I had spent four years at IPD with Officer Taylor speaking down to me, making me the scapegoat for his blunders and mistakes, ordering me into a dumpster for evidence that wasn't there, sending his friends into the locker room when I was there alone to accost me, whispering in their ears about my lifestyle. He reported to my superiors that he felt my work was subpar, and at his encouragement, other officers would target me, one of whom tried to rape me and got away with it. Memories of Mac Taylor swept the range of nasty things done to me as a rookie under his tutelage, thus my name for him—Officer Nasty. I had tucked it all well away. Hearing him, seeing him at this campground had brought them all flooding back. The memories ran like a soap opera where someone was dying and they put all the pertinent scenes of their life together in one montage.

My next words could make my life at the campground, um... difficult or not.

So, wondering about the previous owners, I asked, "What happened to Randy and Phyllis?"

"In his words, Randy was sick and tired of catering to a *certain kind of folk*." He winked, but not directly at me. His one-eyed gesture was definitely aimed at my friend, thus indirectly at me. "I don't cater to anyone."

Steph shot me a sideways glance as if to say, "See what I mean?"

"This is my friend Steph. She has a trailer on the other side of the field."

He flashed her an obnoxious male smile. "Yeah. I know her."

What an idiot I was. Of course, he would know her. He was on the Ithaca police force. She was the IPD medical examiner. Duh was the appropriate word going through my head at that moment. I was not helping myself where Mac was concerned, as evidenced by his snicker.

He studied Steph like a man who was sizing up his next female experience.

I almost gagged. "Most cops here know me," she pointed out.

Another "duh" resonated in my brain. I knew she was trying to help, but I had already looked stupid to Mac. We had never talked about who she did and didn't know in the police department. Except for the captain. We were both friends with Maddie Spinner.

"Yeah. Great," he muttered under his breath.

Steph was about to say something, but I shooshed her as inconspicuously as I could with a nudge and then said to Officer Taylor, "I never took you to be the camping kind of guy. So what do you go by around here, Officer Taylor? Lord and Laird of Rock Creek Campground?"

He studied me a moment, as if deciding whether or not I was going to be one of those problem campers. His following smile was far from genuine. "Mac will do just fine. I'm the new owner. Or did you forget that already? Early dementia?" He chuckled. "As I said, I own the place and I'm gonna make it great."

Talk about being vague and elusive. "So what changes are you going to make as the new owner?" I asked with no sarcasm, because I really wanted to know.

"My office staff will be sending out an email on the new rules and regulations, as well as a calendar of events for the season. Look for it. I gotta be on my way. Things to take care of, you know." He turned on the motor and said, "See ya round, Officer Squeamish," laughing as he drove away. He sounded like Vincent Price in Michael Jackson's "Thriller" video.

"Real nice of Randy and Phyllis to let us know they sold the place, let alone who they sold it to," Steph said. We watched him drive down the dirt road toward the barn where the mowers, bobcats, tools, and whatever else needed to run a campground were stored.

"And if what he said was true, it's kind of sad that they left because of a certain clientele." I finger-quoted *a certain clientele.* "I thought they liked all of us."

She turned to me with the *I told you so* look on her face, so she didn't have to say it.

"Just because Mac said that doesn't mean they really said it. You know as well as I do how he can be. He probably made it up."

Steph turned her head to look out over the field that stretched out between our trailers. "They've never acted that way, and were always very nice to us. They didn't give anyone a hard time. Even so, it would have been nice for them to tell us they were selling." She put a hand on my shoulder. "As far as selling to Mac. Don't take it too personally. They wouldn't have known the connection between you and him. If they did, I really don't think they would have sold to him. They know you from all the times you visited us here, and they also knew you were going to be a seasonal."

We watched the elaborate golf cart make its way down the dirt road. I expected him to be hosing it off when he got back to the main house, which I assumed he would live in like the previous owners. It was a large Colonial painted brown. I thought the color was chosen to make it look more rustic, but it only made it look worn and old. The building was situated at the entrance to the campground, with a two-lane dirt road running alongside it that opened up to a parking lot. The camp store was attached to the back of the house. Across from the parking lot was another very large one-story building with a stage and a connecting kitchen and bathrooms used for group events. The pool was on the other side of this building.

"You're right. I've never discussed those years on the force with Officer Nasty with anyone other than my close friends. But even if Randy and Phyllis knew, they probably would have sold it to him anyway. Kind of hard to sell campgrounds, don't you think? You wouldn't want to turn down an offer."

Relenting, Steph spoke softly, "God, I hope we don't have to look for another campground."

"I just got here. I hope not either," I answered. "Let's see how it goes. If he's still working as a cop, I imagine we'll only see him on the weekends. I can live with that."

"And if you can't?"

"I'll go home on weekends." Upon hearing familiar voices near our campsite, I turned to see who it was and then looked at Steph. "I've got good friends here. I'd hate to leave that, especially if none of you are willing to go to another campground. But"—I paused for emphasis—"I'm going to keep my options open."

Her returned smile was more of a sympathetic sadness that I knew was sweet and understanding on her part, but it pissed me off because it was about something that happened long ago, and that I thought had been put to bed. Now, instead of filtering into my dreams every once in a while, there was a strong possibility it was going to stare me down even when I was awake.

"I never took you for a brown-noser," Jen chided as she and Myra approached. "Rubbing elbows with the new owner? Did he give you a discount on your site? I met him the other day," Jen continued as they watched the high-end golf cart that screamed "I am lord, king, and president" jostle down the dirt and stone road. "He's creepy. How do you know him?"

"I think it's happy hour," Steph interrupted. "Blake made me a delicious margarita. Maybe if you ask nice she'll make you one and then she can fill you in?"

"If you don't want one, I've also got beer and mixers," I informed my friends. I noticed Steph's glass was still half full. "Can I get you another one?" I asked her.

"I'm good," she replied.

"We'll take your specialty drink," Myra answered. "Have you got any other chairs? I'll set them up."

"In my shed," I answered while walking toward my camper.

Myra looked around. "What shed?"

"Why the one under the trailer, of course," I said, and then went inside to make the drinks.

"When we build that woman a deck, I think we need to do a shed as well," I heard Myra tell the others while I was inside.

"I'd be a fool to refuse that offer," I yelled out so they could hear me, followed by their laughter.

"You've got the ears of a bat," I heard Jen say.

"Not hard to hear outside when you live in a tin can," I replied. They sat waiting for my specialty drink, which I had boasted about many times. I wondered if it was as good as I thought it was because Steph hadn't drunk much of hers. I shrugged my shoulders. It didn't matter as long as they pretended to like it.

After teasing oohs and ahhs over the delectable refreshments, we talked about my miserable years working under the new owner of the campground, and how it might be awkward for me. Actually, only Steph and Tess knew the complete story. Jen and Myra had only heard part of it. They knew who he was and that he had not been a nice officer. However, I never elaborated on the specifics of how he treated me and the difficulties I had working with him. Some things were better left unsaid. I had to let them form their own opinions of the new owner and, by Jen's reference to Mac being creepy, I surmised their judgment of him would be pretty close to mine.

"Holy shit. I can't believe the new owner of this place is the same crappy officer you worked with," Myra said. "Are you going to be okay with him here?"

"I'll have to be," I answered. "I already paid for the site, and for reasons I won't list, I don't think he would give me a refund."

I had my reasons for not telling Jen and Myra everything about my years with Mac despite how long we had been friends. What bothered me was now that Mac was the owner of the campground they resided in, they might want to know more about what happened. Especially if this man decided to take up his old crusade and make my life miserable once again. Even though I wasn't working for him, I knew he might already be looking for ways to make my first summer as a seasonal camper at *his* campground a very miserable one.

I wasn't stupid enough to think there wouldn't come a time when I couldn't keep it from them any longer. The more that jackass was around, the more likely the rage that had been bottled up inside me for years would explode. My friends wouldn't understand because I rarely acted that way. And unless I could steer clear of Officer Taylor, they might see another side of me I wasn't proud of. Anger and I never did well together.

His mission in life when he was my mentor was to make my life a living hell. To this day, I had no idea why, he just seemed to get his jollies from it. Now that he owned the campground where I was to spend the summers with my friends, I was pretty sure my presence would give him a new lease on life that would only worsen when he retired. He would never let me be. He never could when I was a policewoman under his direction. Because of Officer Taylor, I believed people like him rarely changed.

"What exactly did he do to receive such animosity from you?" Jen asked, holding out her glass to me for a refill.

I enjoyed being here with my friends. More days than not, someone announced it was cocktail time (we at least waited until afternoon), and we would sit with our drinks and talk away the hours. Our discussions ran from personal to current events to politics and any subject in between. Each topic discussed had all kinds of points of view that every one of us pondered over and respected, whether we agreed or disagreed. It was stimulating, bonding, and full of affirmations that we were no longer in the background but at the forefront of our lives. Still, I kept the Mac secrets to myself.

Now the time had come when I couldn't hide everything from my friends anymore. "So, the little things included making me work more hours than any other officer. He always gave me the dirtiest of jobs, like climbing into a dumpster to look for evidence. That would have been okay because it was my job, except he only did it when he knew there wasn't anything there or the forensics team had already removed it. However, he always knew when the garbage was smelly, gooey, and would make me extremely uncomfortable, at which point he would have a good laugh at my expense." I sighed, remembering one such forage into a back-alley bin filled with dead rats. He seemed to know which bins had the most vile garbage in them, and I felt like a dog getting sprayed by a skunk. The smell was hard to get off me.

"That's crappy. Didn't you report him?"

"Back then, most of the police force was men, and they were either like him or turned their backs the other way. It would have done me more harm than good to report him. Thank God things are different now. Men have a little more respect for their female coworkers. Today, if they had a commanding officer who treated them like he did me, they could report him and something would be done. It just wasn't that way back then."

Myra held up her glass. "Here's to our generation for paving the way for the younger women of today. We sure put up with a lot not only as lesbians but as women."

Steph shot her a glance.

"Oops sorry. Too loud," Myra said with a snicker.

Although Jen understood Steph's point of view of staying in the shadows, Myra did not and took every opportunity to take a jab at Steph. I directed a disciplinary look in Myra's direction before she took it too far. She tipped her drink toward me in acknowledgment, smiled, and took a long sip to keep herself from saying anything else.

Still, Myra *and* Jen giggled, and Steph, being as good-natured as she was, chuckled in such a way you knew she was aware of each verbal statement, eye roll, and chuckle made in her direction and what it meant. I told Steph once that she didn't have to take the digs. It was up to her how she wanted to deal with it. "Besides," I explained. "What's a little jocularity among friends." But every once in a while, I had to give Myra one of my disciplinary looks. It was an agreed-upon signal between her and me that worked most of the time.

So, four friends lifted their glasses in salute because we knew Myra's toast was full of truth. We knew what it had been like in the '70s, '80s, and even the '90s, not just for lesbians, but for all women. Today, it was better, but we recognized we still had a long way to go.

"So, what are you going to do about the new owner?" Steph asked.

"Hopefully, if I steer clear of him, he'll do the same with me."

"He's never seemed the type to just let something go," she mumbled.

"You're right. I'd like to think he's gotten better over the years. Besides, there's nothing left for him to hang on to. We haven't seen each other since I left Ithaca thirty years ago."

"I don't know," Myra spoke up. "Creepy guys like that don't change."

Then Jen, who we knew believed all people could change if they really wanted to (which was a great way to be if you taught little children), said just that, followed by Steph who had to put her two cents in. "I agree with Myra. Misogynistic pricks like that don't change and it's because they don't want to. I think they get off on being assholes."

Steph's proclamation surprised me. She didn't have constant direct contact with Officer Taylor, but from conversations we had over the years, I knew she watched him. I wondered what she had seen that made her feel that way about him. She wasn't one to dishonor her fellow officers in any way, no matter how bad they were. But her words told me otherwise, however, she would never admit it.

We all laughed, but underneath there was a tone of uncertainty and mistrust in the evolution of man that we had discussed many times before. Myra and I believed agression seemed to stay in their DNA. We felt that many men had overcome the pull to the dark side, but there were still some that just couldn't see their way out of the blackness. At that moment, I think the four women, including Jen, seated on folding chairs on a plastic rug outside of my camper were thinking the same thing. That Officer Nasty might be one of those men. I really hoped we were wrong.

So, I did the only thing I could do. Change the subject. "What are we doing for dinner?" I inquired.

"First night has always been hamburgers," Jen offered. "Blake, since you just got here, why don't we have dinner at our place? We've got plenty of hamburgers already thawed. Myra can get the grill going. We've also got macaroni salad."

Steph sat up straight. "The kind with the big pasta?"

"Steph," I said. "Put the drool back in your mouth."

She slurped and then swallowed. "Uh, sorry."

We burst out laughing. I, for one, was glad for the change of subject.

"And as we are the sugar goddesses, I made dessert for tonight, hoping we would eat dinner together," I added.

"Oh, oh, is it that blueberry cobbler thing you made last year?" Steph's eyes were wide like a child seeing all the presents under a tree on Christmas morning.

"Have you eaten today, Steph?" I asked, laughing harder. "And yes, it is."

"I've got baked beans. Not homemade and not green. The barbecue canned kind." Steph looked at me and confessed, "And no, I haven't eaten much today."

"Okay. It's settled," Myra said. "Meet you all at our place."

"Leave your glasses. I'll take care of them," I said.

Myra and Jen crossed the field that spread out between our campsites and disappeared into their trailer. Steph didn't move. Then she helped me pick up the empty glasses and followed me inside.

I set my eyes on her. "What do you want to know? And or, what do you want to tell me?"

"I didn't want to say anything, but I've heard things. About Mac, and not just from others at work, but directly from him as well. I think he's going to be trouble." Steph's facial expression had worry painted all over it—narrow eyes, dipped eyebrows, and tight lips that canvased her usually happy face whenever she was uneasy about something. "There must have been more to your working relationship with that man than you've led me to believe. For you to be so uncomfortable about him being here tells me it's more than just the crappy little things he did."

"When Annie was found at the bottom of the gorge, I think he could tell I knew her. He harassed me for weeks and somehow he found out I had been her partner. He told the captain that I kept valuable information from them at the scene of her death. I was almost fired. I spent an hour in the captain's office explaining my situation and he put me on suspension for a month. Mac was happy until I returned to duty and found out I'd still be with him. That was worse than the suspension. It stayed on my record and I had to explain it when I applied for the position in Rochester."

"I'm sorry. Why didn't you ever tell me?"

When I started to explain, Steph put her hand up.

"Never mind. You don't have to explain. I know why. But in case you don't already know, I need to inform you he still doesn't like lesbians, gays, transgenders, or anyone that doesn't fall under his umbrella of male, white, and all-powerful." She leaned toward me and said in a quiet voice, "And by the way, I don't think his umbrella is very large."

I giggled. "Yeah, I'll bet he gets soaked every rainstorm." I sighed. "He never did like anyone outside of his little circle of acceptable people."

"Enough to make him dangerous?"

"Nah, just enough to make him a miserable nuisance."

She stood up. "I don't know, Blake. Like I said before, assholes like that—they just don't change. They don't want to. What I didn't say before is that most of the time, those types of guys get worse with age. And that guy? Well, I think he falls into that category."

"Since when are you an expert on the subject? I thought that was my field."

"Maybe. Maybe not. But I've been working in the same place he has, for a lot of years. I hear things. I see things. I have a lot of common sense, and I also read a lot and watch several news channels. These creepy guys get off being creepy, but knowing what your line of work used to be, I know you've been aware of that a lot longer than I have." Steph headed off.

"I hope you're wrong," I muttered as she walked across the field. I had seen many instances where corrupt people enjoyed being corrupt, but I still hoped Mac Taylor would change because he truly enjoyed harassing me.

CHAPTER THREE

By the time I arrived at my friends' trailer with Mabel in tow, they had their picnic table set up for dinner and the grill smoking.

"Hey, hon, turn that down before the grease catches on fire," Myra called to Jen. "You're gonna burn the hamburgers." She grabbed a pitcher dripping with condensation and held it up. "Vodka, lemonade, and lemon-lime soda for bubbles. Are you in?"

"I'm in," I called out as I entered their trailer to put the cobbler into their fridge. As I closed the door, something caught my eye out the window on the opposite side. A man was leaning against a tree in the site next to them, watching Myra and Jen's trailer.

I didn't recognize him, and I knew he didn't belong at that campsite. The thirty-foot Avian Travel Trailer belonged to Greg, the maintenance guy, and the man watching my friend's camper was not him. He was short and muscular, with sparse brown hair and a long, scraggly beard that didn't do a very good job of hiding a chubby face. Gregg was tall and blond.

The smile he sent my way made the hairs on my legs and arms stand to attention, sending an icy chill through my veins. Then he nodded, turned away, and walked off the site and down the road toward the back of the campground. I heard the trailer door open, causing me to jump.

"Whoa, sorry I scared you. Whatcha looking at?" I heard Jen ask.

"Does Greg have a friend staying with him?"

"Not that I know of. Why?"

"There was this guy I don't recognize watching your trailer."

"Where?" Alarm filled her voice as she hurried over to look out the window next to me.

"He's gone, but he was leaning against Greg's tree. Right there." I pointed. "He saw me look out. He gave me this really disturbing leery smile and then took off toward the tent area."

"You know, I've found that some of these campers, male in particular, have become very ballsy. They do things we never would have thought about doing when we were younger."

"Like trespassing on someone else's campsite and becoming a peeping Tom?" I looked at her. "Or a peeping whatever his name is."

Jen grinned and retrieved a pot holder. "Yeah, like that."

"Do you think we should tell Greg?"

"Not this time, but if he does it again, then yes." She opened the door. "You coming? I need some help with the burgers."

"Since when?" I said with a hint of sarcasm. "You just want some company because no one will stand near you when you're grilling."

"That's not true," she whined. "I'm an expert griller."

I followed her outside. "Is that why you've been dubbed the GGQ?" I chided.

She turned to face me. "What? What does GGQ stand for?"

Realizing she didn't know, I looked at the ground and said in a low voice, "Griller Grease Queen."

She marched toward the picnic table and called to her wife, who was sipping the vodka cocktail. "Myra. Is that true? Do you call me that?"

"Call you what?" She didn't turn to face her wife, instead flashed me a warning grin.

Jen stood facing Myra with her hands on her hips. Despite her shorter stature, Jen knew how to intimidate by bringing her body to a very straight and solid posture that alerted everyone she was not to be messed with. She was in her early fifties with curly blond hair that draped on her shoulders and light-green eyes that darkened when things were serious. Right now, they were sea green and I knew she wasn't serious. Yet. "Is that what you all call me?" she demanded.

I sat down and put my palms up as if to surrender. "I didn't do anything."

"Really, Blake? You usually start it." Myra needed to place the blame somewhere else since she was the one who had come up with the name and that wouldn't look good for her where her wife was concerned.

Jen glared at Myra, looking like she was deciding if what I said was the truth, and then looked in my direction. "You made that up to mess with me," she said with apprehension in her voice.

Myra reached up and touched her wife's chin. "You need to know that you are the best Griller Grease Queen there is." Her smile was huge before she clamped her lips together to keep from laughing, and then she pulled Jen down and planted a solid kiss on her wife's thinned lips.

Jen spun and sashayed toward the back of the camper to the grill. "Not only am I the *best* goddamned griller you've got, I'm the *only* one who will do the cooking while you all sit on your asses and drink the hours away."

And at that, we all laughed, including Jen, who was flipping burgers. Steph arrived at the end of our teasing, a can of beans in her hand. She set her can and a glass filled with what appeared to be ice water on the table. "What did I miss?" she asked as she sat down.

"Jen knows," Myra replied.

"Knows what?" Steph glanced at Jen.

"That we call her the GGQ," I answered.

Steph rolled her eyes. "Who told her?"

Myra nodded in my direction, and I shrugged.

"Damn, we'll be lucky if she doesn't decide to quit cooking for us. I can tell you right now you don't want me to cook," Steph informed them.

"You live by yourself. If you cook for yourself, it can't be all that bad," I said, pouring myself another drink.

"Okay, fine. It's not that you don't want me to cook. I won't cook. Happy?" She raised her glass to me. "That's why I've got all of you to cook for me once in a while. I have my motives."

"Now that's the Steph we all know and love." Then Myra leaned forward and whispered to us, "There better be a lot of compliments on the hamburgers, or we"—she circled her hand to include each of us—"will cook from here on in. And, Steph?" She nodded in her direction as she poured herself a drink. "If Jen finds out that you're the one who named her that, she'll never cook for you again."

"Oh, no you don't. We both came up with that name," Steph countered, her face dropping.

I nudged Steph's shoulder with mine. "Hmph. You told me Myra was the one that came up with it." Myra's mouth opened to Steph's sheepish grin. The jocular argument began as I stood and took my drink and another one to the grill, where Jen had her back to us. She held the spatula in her hand and her focus appeared to be on Greg's site as if she was ignoring us. I knew damn well the teacher side of her was listening to us. I nudged her with my shoulder. "You know we love you and gave you that moniker in the name of love."

"Nice try," she said, taking the glass I offered as a peace settlement. Jen's slim face was flushed from the grill heat. A slight breeze tussled her shoulder-length blond hair and her eyes fixed on me.

"You aren't really mad, are you?"

She stood stoically, but from her smile, I knew it was only a ploy. She was cooking something up and it wasn't the burgers.

"You promise to play nice?" I asked, after taking a sip of my drink.

"Whatever do you mean? I'm just cooking the hamburgers."

"I like mine well done." I giggled.

"Duly noted. And don't worry, my payback won't be now. None of you will see it coming," she said as she tossed the cooked meat onto a plate. Her wide smile and sparkling eyes confirmed what she said. I could see her mind was already devising different scenarios, and we would never see it coming.

"We didn't mean to upset you," I said, trying to smooth over the insult.

Jen held the plate of burgers out to me. "I'm not upset." With a flourish, she turned and headed back into the trailer.

"No, just setting the groundwork for your payback." I took the burgers to the table and leaned forward as I set the plate down. "Everyone better be on their guard. She's planning something."

Jen came out of the trailer with the macaroni salad. She set it on the table, staring at the can, and then glared at Steph. "Are the beans ready?" She sat down and helped herself with the rolls, salad, burgers, and condiments.

Myra picked up the can and ran into the trailer. She was out in one minute with the beans in a plastic bowl. "Cold beans. Just the way I like them." She set it down in front of Steph who dug in.

Despite the mild anxiety I'm sure each of us felt about what Jen might be planning, we had a splendid meal with lots of chatter and laughter. I had almost forgotten about the strange man when I leaned over to give Mabel a tidbit of my well-done hamburger. I saw him again, this time walking down the dirt road, heading in our direction.

"Jen. Jen. Don't turn, but that guy is walking this way. He's going to walk by us. I'll signal you when he does. Tell me if you recognize him."

She nodded, and a minute later, I angled my head toward the road.

As the man approached, there was no denying that he was watching us. His eyes never left our table, so I matched his stare with mine. Again, his lips spread into that hateful smile, and I forced myself to keep my eyes on him as he walked by and out of my line of sight. It was a good thing no one else noticed. If Steph had seen this man's repugnant expression, she wouldn't have hesitated to shout something inflammatory. She may have lived in the shadows where her way of life was concerned, but she was a bull on full charge when it came to letting her opinion known.

I set my gaze on Jen's face to gauge her reaction. When her eyes met mine, her facial muscles twitched as if to hide what she was feeling. She smiled feebly at me.

"Hey, Blake, help me clear the table and get dessert." She stood and gathered the used paper plates.

I picked up the empty pitcher and held it up. "I don't think I have to ask if anyone wants more."

Steph pointed to her empty glass with a big grin on her face. "What do you think?"

"Coming right up." I followed Jen into the trailer and found her sitting on the couch. She had tossed the paper plates into the sink, which was unlike her. A clean freak, she would have immediately thrown them into the garbage and turned on the hot water heater to do the pans and bowls after dessert.

I kneeled in front of her. "My God, Jen. What's wrong?"

"Holy shit. That smile was more than ominous, but what's more disturbing is I think I know who he is."

"Who?" I grew even more concerned.

"We were watching the news yesterday. The police have charged him with harassing some college kids in town—Blacks, gays, and Asians. He seems to be one of those right-wing haters."

"What's he doing here?"

"Must be camping," she said.

"Ha, ha. Very funny. Why don't you make the vodka drink? I'll get the cobbler and some plates. I bet Mac Taylor won't kick him out. I'm pretty sure he's of the same opinion." I choked out a sick laugh.

"And how's that going to work? He's a cop. It wouldn't look good for him to harbor a felon."

"He's not a felon. You said he's only been charged."

"But Mac would have a hard time with all of us that are here, let alone all the friends we've made that I'm pretty sure would support us."

"Don't always count on that. With the way the world is today, you never know how people are going to react. Let's face it, our country hasn't been this divided since the Civil War. Besides, I doubt Mac knew about his campers when he bought this place, other than anything Randy may have told him."

Jen stopped what she was doing. Her head turned. "And that was?"

"That he was tired of catering to a certain kind of people."

"No. Randy said that?"

"I don't know. That's what Officer Nasty told Steph and me. Can't always believe what he says, and I'm not sure Randy would admit to it even if he did say it. However, Mac was never one to do his research. So, I don't think he knows how many of us are here and how many others we're friends with, but he does know about me. Besides, I think he's only looking for the big bucks without having to do too much work. You know—*that* kind of guy."

Jen picked up the pitcher and walked to the door. "Should we tell the others?"

"Probably. If Myra was watching the news with you, it's only a matter of time before she recognizes him, if she sees him."

Jen opened the door. "Do you think we should start looking for another campground?"

"God no. I just got here, and you gals have been here for years. Besides, it's too soon for that. We have to see how it's going to play out. But I do think we need to keep our eyes open and our ears to the ground."

She grinned. "Is that police talk?"

"No. It's just sensible talk."

She snorted and went outside. I followed with the cobbler. After refilling glasses and dishing out the entire pan of blueberry cobbler, Jen and I told Myra and Steph about the stranger watching us and their trailer.

"Holy shit." Steph blew out a breath. "Why didn't you say something when he walked by? I've got no problem confronting him."

Myra harrumphed, and I shot her a warning glance. Steph responded by harrumphing in kind.

I wasn't surprised by Steph's reaction because I knew she wouldn't hesitate to confront the man. She had become hardened to what she called "jerks" from the years of living by herself. She was in a trailer by herself. She had no one to help her fend off any crazy man. No one to get help if she got hurt. She was a medical examiner, not a cop.

I gave Steph a smile that I hoped would quell her rising anxiety. It often turned her into a crazy lady when confronting jerks like the man we were discussing because living in what was literally a tin can all by yourself with a nutjob close by couldn't be too comforting.

I too, was by myself, but my police training taught me to deal with jackasses like this. It also taught me to control my reactions to fear.

"Let that vampire come into my trailer. I'll shoot his balls off," Steph said suddenly, almost spitting on the table.

"Wow, vampire slayer," I said, referencing one of Steph's and my favorite campy shows, *Buffy the Vampire Slayer*. "But you know they used wooden spikes in the chest, not guns to the balls." Everyone laughed. "Besides, you don't have a gun."

She looked directly at me, her eyes hard with a dare. "I do. It's legal and I'll use it if I have to."

We stopped talking, our mouths squeezed shut and our eyes focused on our friend.

"When did you get a gun?" I asked.

"Last year. There were some break-ins in our neighborhood, and I decided I wasn't going down without a fight."

"Did you ever consider an alarm system instead?" Jen asked, her face twisting with worry.

"I got that too. Can never be too careful."

"Yes, that's true, but someone who breaks into your house can use the gun against you," Jen pointed out.

"Not if I shoot first." Steph's face was flushing. I couldn't tell if it was from anger, embarrassment, hurt, or all three.

My mouth opened to speak, but Steph put her hand up. "Before you all continue to berate me, I took a course in gun handling and shooting. I have a license for it, and I have it in a safe, locked place that I can get into within seconds if I need to. I'm not stupid."

"We never said you were," Myra said, refuting Steph's claim. "Just worried about you and your safety."

"Well, that's very kind of you, but none of you live with me, so your worry doesn't do me any good. I'm by myself. I have to take care of myself. Therefore, your support would help me better than your worry."

"Of course, we support you," I broke in quickly before the conversation turned ugly. "And I'm glad to know you took the safety courses and have secured the gun. If you ever go to a shooting range, I'd really like to go with you."

"What, so you can critique my shooting skills?"

I can't say I wasn't hurt, but I knew where her comment came from. It boiled in a vat of loneliness and what she perceived as an offensive putdown from her closest friends even though it wasn't meant that way.

"No, I like to go to shooting ranges. I always go by myself. Tess didn't like guns. It's way more fun to go with someone. You know, a little friendly competition." I winked.

"You're a cop. You know how to shoot," she shot back at me warily. Then she softened a little. "You'd always win. No fair."

"For the last twenty-five years, I sat at a computer more than I was out in the field. I only shot a gun when I went to a shooting range and when I had to be recertified. It'd be fun. Think about it. Call me if you go. Please?" I emphasized the last word, making an emotional plea to her, so she understood I wasn't demeaning her in any way.

"I'll think about it," she mumbled. Then a little louder, "Yeah, it might be fun. Let's do it."

"Good. Then how about we build a campfire and have ourselves a little 'Kumbaya' time," I said, jumping up from the table.

Amidst the groans, we dragged our chairs to the fire circle and watched while Steph tended to the fire for the evening since it was her turn. One evening a few years prior, when Tess and I were visiting our friends at a campground, we spent the night arguing over who was going to be fire master. After we spent one night arguing over it, we voted to take turns (guess we were all pyromaniacs). By the time we came to that conclusion, raindrops were falling, and no one got to make a fire that night. So we took our party inside and came up with a contest to see who had the most ingenious design to build a fire using only wood and one match. So far, I was the winner. I used the standard triangle design that worked every time as long as you used the three stages of wood—tinder, kindling, and fuel—in the correct order, in certain amounts, and at the right time so the fire wouldn't die out.

Mabel settled on my lap, feeling the warmth of my body on one side and the heat from the fire on the other. I giggled to myself, thinking of a pig on a spit rotating to heat all sides of it. Mabel just had to sit on my lap in front of a campfire to get the same effect.

I looked up at the sky. It was dark and clear, with countless stars that were much more visible in the wilderness far from city lights. I loved these nights with my good friends. The surrounding atmosphere was not only warm from the campfire but also from the friendship that survived through thick and thin.

As my eyes focused on the bright yellow-red blaze that Steph had successfully produced in the firepit, I hoped this summer would be filled with fun and love, and not angst and problems that might come with an over-the-top-of-the-line, very expensive golf cart.

CHAPTER FOUR

I held Mabel tucked in my arms as we prepared to leave. She always wanted to be close to the fire, but I worried that her coarse and wiry, white fur would catch a flying spark, singeing it. If her fur became hot to the touch, I would move my chair back away from the flames to much protest from my little pooch.

I was saying good night when I noticed him. The same man who had been watching us earlier walked down the road away from us. In his dark clothing, he was barely visible, but his small, yet muscular stature and thick beard could not be denied even in the dark. I breathed a sigh of relief, glad we wouldn't have to pass him.

I made my way across the open field. I held the small LED flashlight that was bright enough to light my way back across the uneven grass, but I didn't turn it on right away. I wanted to admire the quiet evening filled with nightly sounds—chirping, buzzing, soft wind through the trees, and the occasional loud cries of coyotes and foxes—without the disruption of artificial light.

The stupidity of not turning on my flashlight embarrassed the hell out of me when I stumbled into a small hole and almost bumped into the man. I didn't see him standing in the field across from my trailer because his dark clothing blended into his surroundings, and he had no flashlight. I took in a sharp breath and immediately snapped the flashlight on. "You scared the shit out of me," I said harshly.

My use of profanity in that moment struck me as funny and I almost laughed because I didn't scare easily. But my professional training told me I shouldn't laugh because this man could take offense at it. I believed the best defense was a good offense and that would be to keep this unnerving situation lighthearted. "I didn't see you standing there," I said, with as much lightness in my voice as I could muster. "I guess I should have turned my flashlight on."

He didn't answer right away, and I wondered if he was trying to turn the encounter into something more than an accidental bumping into each other. Was his hesitancy meant to send a message? If that was the case, I was pretty sure it wouldn't be, "No problem. Sorry, I scared you. I was just admiring the sky." Then his message came out loud and clear. "Yeah, you should have."

However, the message *I* also received from his reply was, "I'm watching you." Or was I being paranoid?

Then the man turned and made his way back across the field toward the side where my friend's trailers were. I pulled out my phone, mumbling, "Jackass," under my breath, and dialed Jen as I hurried to my trailer to the protest of Mabel being jostled about in my arms. Jen answered just as I shut the door behind me. I set Mabel on the floor, and she immediately jumped up onto a recliner.

"You just left. Miss us already?"

"Hey, I ran into that guy on the field. He didn't say much of anything to me. In fact, he was pretty creepy. He walked back your way. Just wanted to give you a heads-up."

"Should we call Steph?"

"God, I don't know. On the one hand, yes. She's alone. She deserves to know. On the other hand, she might pull that gun of hers out of its hiding place and shoot an innocent guy who's just weird."

"Except you know and I know he's not just some weird guy. Myra confirmed he's the guy that's been charged with harassing those kids in town. She saw me looking at him at dinner, so she checked him out too."

I sighed deeply. "He didn't harass me. He was just a jerk. There was something about the way he said, "Yeah, you should have," after

I told him I should have turned my flashlight on. It left my skin crawling."

"That's not good," Jen said. "We should tell Steph."

"You're right. She should know. I'll go over and tell her. That way, I might be able to convince her not to go to sleep with a gun under her pillow and accidentally blowing her head off."

I ended the call and turned to face Mabel. "Will you be all right until I get back?" She wagged her tail when I opened the treat jar. I tossed her a milk bone and grabbed my flashlight and some pepper spray from a drawer. "No need to go out in the dark unprepared with a lunatic walking around," I said under my breath.

I thought about asking Steph to stay over, but I knew she'd say no. The only extra bed I had was the very small and uncomfortable one the dining booth turned into. It was short with a hard mattress, making a good night's sleep next to impossible. I would offer Myra and Jen's second bed—it had a real mattress. I knew they'd let her stay there, so I took my phone and sent them a quick text while I walked across the field. I scanned the expansive, open space for anything or anyone that might seem out of place. Then I checked the road that circled it. When all appeared to be quiet and void of any inconspicuous activity, I jogged across the field. Who knew what or who I might encounter on my way? It was times like these that my profession served me well. I knew how to keep an eye on my surroundings, to recognize a possible threat, and see things that most people wouldn't see on a dark night. The problem with that was that you had to be aware you were doing it.

When I walked across the field earlier, I was playing the part of a retiree—admiring the sky. That wasn't good. Just because I retired didn't mean I should stop doing what I had learned in my profession that at one time was second nature. Besides, being conscious of one's surroundings was being smart. I had always been alert, but I realized I had become lax in my retirement. But why wouldn't I? I was at a campground, for God's sake. One was supposed to relax.

When I knocked on Steph's door, I thought it would be best to call out, letting her know it was me. The last thing I needed was to be met by my best friend with a gun in her hand. I wondered if I was once again going to be forced to take on a full-time position of vigilance. I hoped not. Being retired meant you didn't work, and I didn't want to work.

I heard movement in the trailer and waited for the door to open, all the while surveying the area for the strange man I was here to warn her about. My ears perked up at the sound of a pack of coyotes racing past the campground. With all that racket, I wouldn't be able to hear the sounds of a prowler, especially if he was any good at prowling. I shifted my weight back and forth apprehensively. I strained my ears to focus on the sounds close by, shutting out the cries of the coyote's animalistic hunger as they searched for their prey. I listened for a dry twig snap, followed by a quiet crushing of weeds.

The door flung open, and I pushed my way in, whispering hoarsely for her to shut it. I quickly scrutinized her for the gun. If she had it on her person, it wasn't in plain sight. When I turned to face her, I took a deep breath to settle myself because the uncertainty in her expression told me I needed to be calm and reassuring. Steph with a gun made me nervous. I understood her reasoning, her right, but she was a hothead who would shoot first and ask questions later. That meant, if I wasn't careful, I could end up with a bullet hole. I didn't like bullet holes, especially in my body.

That led me to my next question. How good of a shot could she be in such a short time? Steph might be as good as me at a shooting range, or even better, but I knew she wouldn't beat me in a stressful situation. Not only was I that good, but I had a knack for remaining calm under duress. I had to be.

"What's going on?" she asked, looking perturbed. She wore a tight pair of red boxer shorts and a black ribbed tank top. I recognized her pajamas—we'd been friends that long. There were no bulges, so I assumed the gun wasn't on her. My body parts were grateful.

"Sorry, I didn't mean to wake you. Got a glass of wine?"

She studied me for a moment and then asked, "White or red?"

"Whatever you've got open."

"Okay…" she drawled out. As she busied herself filling two glasses with a deep red, she asked, "Can't sleep? Scared of the boogeyman?" She handed me the wine goblet. (There were some things seasonal campers wouldn't compromise on. Wine in a plastic cup just didn't cut it.)

"Not scared of him," I chuckled. I twisted it in my hands, debating my next words that wouldn't set her on a path of lunacy.

"I already saw him," I heard her say. Well, there went my words.

"When?" I asked, with wide eyes. Had I underestimated my friend?

"I probably never mentioned it, but I have really good night vision. Got it from my dad. I actually saw the jerk in the field when you were walking home, so I watched you until he walked away. I'll tell you…I was ready for action if he gave you a hard time."

I smiled at the thought of my friend running across the field and dive-bombing a strange man. "He didn't. Not really."

"Which means he did."

"No, not really. He just scared the shit out of me because I wasn't paying attention. Too busy enjoying the night sky."

"You? You weren't surveying your surroundings like a good cop? You should get forced retirement for that lax in judgment." She put her finger and thumb on her chin and tilted her head. "Oh yes, that's right. You already are retired. Okay, so they can't force you." She laughed.

"Yeah, retirement has its downside." I laughed with her.

"So, what happened?"

"Nothing. And everything."

She cocked her head.

"I said he surprised me and I should have had my flashlight on. All he said was, "Yeah, you should have," but the way he said it was unsettling. When my eyes finally focused on him, it was his demeanor and what I could see of his expression that said it all."

"And what did that say?"

"He doesn't like us. He's definitely not a happy man."

"Ah, duh," she replied sarcastically. "Tell me something I don't already know."

"After I went inside, he headed back to this side of the field. I thought I should warn you."

"And again, tell me something I don't know."

I smiled at my friend, whom I was beginning to realize I sometimes misjudged. "Probably shouldn't have come over. I'm sorry."

"For what?"

"For bothering you."

"I don't think that's it. You've never felt sorry for bothering me. I think it's more you're sorry that you don't think I can protect myself."

She seemed irritated. I ignored her sharp tone and explained, "That's not it. I'm a cop. I've done it for thirty-five years. Even though I just retired, you can't expect me to stop looking after and protecting the people I love."

"I don't." She smiled. "But I do expect you to respect me and have a little faith in my abilities."

"I do, but you know as well as I do, you sometimes jump the gun."

She looked at me for a moment and then burst out laughing. Understanding the irony, I joined her.

"I honestly didn't say that because I expect you to pull your gun out the moment you hear someone outside of your trailer in the night. It's just that, well, you know, you sometimes attack first and ask questions after. At least verbally…"

"Thus, calling out that it was you waiting at my door was to keep me from shooting you."

I nodded, with my lips squished together. "Yeah. Pretty much."

This time, she roared, her body rolling back and forth in her chair. I giggled at the sight of her in a fit of belly laughter.

"Look, Blake, I love you, but I've learned to be okay by myself. I did hear something outside my trailer before you came over here, but I didn't go outside with my gun blazing. That's what took me so long to answer the door. I put it back. Still, I thank you for calling out to me. I will admit that you've got a point there. Just a small one, though." She put her thumb and index finger together, grinned, and raised the glass in her other hand. "To not shooting your friend."

I raised mine. "To not shooting your friend." After sipping, I said, "You know, Myra and Jen have that nice extra room with an actual bed. They offered it to you for tonight, or anytime."

"I appreciate that, but I think for now, I'll stay here."

"Okay. Just promise me you'll be careful and stay safe."

"I promise."

We took another hour to talk about general topics like when she was going to retire, how I liked retirement, and how the summer might play out with the new owner. On that note, I bid her good night before we got too far into the subject of my old mentor. I had no desire to talk about him, and I think she knew it.

She stopped me before I walked down the steps. "Do you want me and my gun to walk you back so you can play retirement and enjoy the night sky?"

I shook my head, chuckling. "You're such an ass. I've got my pepper spray."

"Hope he doesn't use that against you. That stuff hurts your eyes."

"What was that you said to me? Don't you worry about me. See you tomorrow."

"See you tomorrow."

I waited to hear the locks engage and then set out back to my trailer. I thought it was best to take the road. The dirt-and-stone road was lighter than the dark-green grass in the field, allowing me to see it better with my flashlight off as my vision adjusted to the darkness. Even though thin clouds gathered in the sky, I could still see into the campsites and the field, noticing anything out of the usual. Thankfully, my walk home was uneventful. I took Mabel for a quick walk, locked up and went to bed.

As much as I liked the openness of my trailer, the bedroom lacked walking space. The queen-sized bed was positioned in the middle with a long cubby shelf overhead, a narrow closet on either side and a small shelf that served as a night stand. There was only about a foot and a half of floor space all around the bed. I placed Mabel on the quilt in a cocoon I made of blankets and pillows to keep her from going over the edge and breaking a leg. I climbed under the covers, drew my dog near me, and turned out the light.

My biggest fear was that Mabel would fall off the bed. The bed was high with a four-inch topper, adding to the height. It was a long way down for the ten-pound dog and if she fell off, a broken leg was highly probable. She wouldn't use the dog steps, but I kept them there hoping she might. I guessed she just got used to me picking her up to put her on and off the bed.

I sat up gasping, clutching my chest as my body released a deluge of sweat. A heart attack?

I forced myself to take deep breaths, knowing full well it wasn't a heart attack. It was a panic attack. I hadn't had one in a very long time, but I recognized the affliction. *Why now?* I thought to myself. The thought of Mabel falling off the bed and breaking her legs brought back memories of the young woman at the bottom of the gorge so many years ago.

I leaned over the bed and checked the floors to make sure the decorative pillows and extra blankets I used for a landing pad for Mabel were all in place. When I saw they were, my breathing slowed. Was I really that scared that the dog would fall and break a leg? Maybe two legs? But I knew that wasn't what caused the panic attack.

It wasn't over the money that it would cost to have it fixed, or even my distress should that happen. It was the image of the young woman's broken body in my mind that blended into the image of my dog falling that sent me into a fit of panic.

Thank God, it was already fading as I continued the breathing exercises to relax my mind and my body. The crushed figure of the girl lying at the bottom of the gorge in a pool of blood was becoming a blur, except for one thing. The Tinkerbell bracelet. That was the last thing to fade from my mind as it did so every other time the vision haunted me.

I don't know what made me get up to check the door, because I wasn't afraid of intruders. I was merely…rattled by the memories. Satisfied the door was locked, I thought about how vulnerable a trailer really was—in hurricanes, tornadoes, fire, and break-ins, among other things. I could see how being alone in one could make a person work themselves into a state of panic if they heard voices or sounds outside.

But that lone person wasn't me. I was a cop. I didn't get panic attacks (a lie). Okay, I rarely got them anymore, and I never got them on the job.

I turned on the outside light, unlocked the door, and walked outside, looking across the field. The clouds that gathered on my way back from Steph's had dissipated and the night sky was clear. There was no one in sight. Anywhere. Hopefully, everyone was in bed and it would remain that way until morning light. After one last look, I went inside, double-checked the locks and went to bed. I laughed. If one of my friends were watching me, they would think I was obsessive-compulsive.

Then Mabel glanced at me from her cocoon as if to say, "What the heck, Ma? You're disturbing my slumber," and I laughed more loudly.

I stroked her fur and cooed, "Everything is fine. Go back to sleep." I kissed her head and then lay on my back, eyes wide open. Thoughts about the evils in the world rolled around in my head, not allowing me to fall asleep, but as hard as I tried, my mind couldn't quite grasp them, or define them. They just felt…foreboding.

CHAPTER FIVE

The next morning, I woke to birds singing and sunshine blasting through the closed curtains. The bedroom was at one end, enabling a good view of the rest of the trailer. A lone tear found its way down my cheek when I looked at the empty space. If Tess and I were still together, she would be in the kitchen area busying herself with preparing breakfast. I could almost hear the popping sounds of the sizzling grease in the hot frying pan and smell the tantalizing scent of bacon as if she were there cooking.

I peered out from under the covers to a mere 125 square-foot area that seemed more vacant than my empty house back home. Two gray vinyl recliners on the left, a dining booth that transformed into an uncomfortable bed on the right with the TV above it was my living room. The door to the outside was next to the table. The refrigerator was next to the recliners with the stove and counter space beyond that. My eyes drifted to the sink with light-gray countertop and dark-brown cupboards surrounding it on the back wall to the sides above and below. The bathroom was on the left and the only room not visible.

That was it. My entire living space. I didn't know why a tiny trailer would seem lonelier than a sixteen-hundred-square-foot two-story home, but it did. It seemed like a paradox to me. The smaller space should feel safe and comforting like a baby in a mother's womb especially since several rooms with a lot of square footage was a lot to navigate when it came to the feelings and memories within. But maybe in a larger house, one could separate oneself from it. But here, where my entire living space stared back at me, well...you get the picture.

I took Mabel in my arms and sobbed. Tess and I had been planning our retirement in another five years. We'd talked about traveling to places we had on our bucket lists as well as spending time with our friends here in Ithaca, maybe renting a cabin or a motel room like we always had. We hadn't talked about getting a trailer because Tess was not a camping kind of gal. It didn't matter because she cheated on me and left before I could convince her to try it.

So, when my friends suggested it, I thought, why not? It was something I didn't think I'd have done on my own, but with them, it might not be so bad. At first, I thought being in a trailer that I owned and had never inhabited with my ex would be easy. There were none of our memories made here. It was a blank canvas for me to make my own, unlike the house where every room I walked into smelled of her, had reminders of her, and echoed her laughter.

Many of her belongings were still there, but eventually, they'd all be gone. For now, the pain of knowing she had left me for someone else was festering. So, lying in bed feeling sorry for myself would be the activity for the morning. Only for the morning.

That was until a wild knock on my door interrupted my pity party.

"It's me, Steph, and I smell bacon."

"Steph must be smelling the neighbor's bacon because we ain't cooking any," I said to Mabel, who was relaxing on the recliner.

"Hang on, I'll be right there." I got up and put Mabel on the floor, knowing I had to get her out to pee. I put her halter and leash on and unlocked the door, extending the leash in my hand out to Steph. "It's not my bacon. Must be the neighbors. But if you walk my dog, I'll cook you breakfast. With bacon."

Steph studied my face and then took the leash. "Done, but not too done. And I expect eggs over easy with toast." She grinned, turned, and took Mabel for her morning walk.

I dressed and counted my steps to the kitchen. Eight. Yup, it was a tiny space. Usually, Tess would cook because cooking was not my forte. After she left I had learned a few basics—like boiling water, and cooking bacon and eggs. Steph spent the following two weeks with me and sat at the kitchen table every morning while I cooked her breakfast. She told me it was time I learned how to cook and what better way than to cook for her.

I was grateful for my friend's bullish ways of helping me deal with my grief because no one else could have pulled me out of the depths of despair that I was climbing into with free will. Tess and I had been married for twenty-five years and lived together before that for another five. To say my world fell apart when she divorced me was like saying an asteroid just landed on Earth and demolished all life. A rather exaggerated analogy, but it's how I felt and Steph knew that.

The door opened while I was scrambling other eggs and buttering the toast.

"I am not looking for a free meal, you know. I'm only looking for a cooked meal and will gladly pay for the groceries." She grinned. "There's a difference."

"I know. You don't like to cook for yourself. I don't either."

"Yes, but right now, you're cooking for two." She grabbed me from behind around the waist and hugged me tight. "I'll make it up to you. I promise." She let go and removed Mabel's harness.

"And what number promise is that? There's a lot of promises you haven't fulfilled." I grinned.

"Standing invitation. That's what you said to me. I can come over anytime I want a cooked meal."

"I did say you could come over anytime you want. I don't remember mentioning anything about a cooked meal."

"Then how about you cook, I do the dishes?" She jumped up. "And I'll set the table. Where is everything in this luxury tin can of yours?"

"Since you're doing dishes, plates and cups over there," I answered, nodding toward a cupboard. "Silverware in the drawer below. If you want coffee, the Keurig is still in the box."

"What kind of establishment is this? No coffee?"

"You're getting eggs and bacon. Don't press your luck."

"Where's the Keurig? I'll set it up for you. It takes less time than it does to get it out of the box."

"Still in my car. Keys are in the drawer over there."

She was back in two minutes and it took less than another two to set it up. When she had the water compartment filled, she looked at me. "Tell me you have coffee pods."

"In that cupboard."

The morning was bright with sunshine, so we agreed to eat outside. We carried everything out to the picnic table, followed by Mabel, who took a seat on the bench next to me after she was hooked to her lead. Yes, she was spoiled. I believed all lesbian dogs were spoiled, therefore, mine would not be the exception. I based this solely on the lesbian dog owners that I knew because every one of them had an overindulged, pampered dog. And there were a lot of them, so the odds were pretty good in Mabel's favor that she would get whatever she wanted. I would not look like the exception to the rule.

As Steph loaded her plate with bacon and toast to go with her two easy-over eggs, she eyed the scrambled eggs.

"I know I came here for a cooked meal, but I don't need all this food. I didn't ask for scrambled eggs."

"I know. It's for them."

Steph looked up to see Jen and Myra approaching, coffee cups in their hands.

"They requested scrambled."

"The Keurig is ready to go if you need refills," Steph said to them as they took a seat at the table. "But you'll have to get your plates and silverware. I thought I was the only one Blake was cooking for."

"I'll get them," Jen said.

"Okay," I answered.

Steph looked up at me. "Have you already cooked for them?"

"No, silly. I just got here yesterday afternoon."

"Then how does she know where everything is?"

"There aren't that many cupboards to look in," Jen answered for me as she climbed the three metal steps into my trailer. "Oh, Steph, did Blake have to tell you where they were?" she said with dripping sarcasm and shut the door before Steph could riposte.

Myra laughed. "You two will never give it up, will you?"

"Why would we? We have too much fun harassing each other," Steph answered before popping a slice of bacon in her mouth.

"Watch it," I said between bites. "We have a cop for our landlord. He hears of any harassing and he might arrest you."

Steph puffed out her chest. "Let him try."

Myra sat straight up and put both her hands up in surrender. "So, who really is the new sheriff in town?"

"Ha, ha. Very funny," Steph scoffed.

"Now, now, what are you two up to?" Jen said, returning with two plates and silverware.

"We were just deciding who was tougher. Our new landlord or Steph," I answered Jen. I poured orange juice, feeling a set of gray-green eyes boring through me. I tried hard not to smile, but it was no use. Steph had an air about her that exuded strength and power. She also had the prettiest eyes. She was someone you couldn't ignore, especially when her presence sat across from you, but I knew the real Steph. She was a mush, full of intense sentiment and emotion. Sometimes she felt the weight of teasing like she did now. I could see it in her eyes.

"Who are we kidding?" I said. "We all know Steph is a tough one."

She raised her glass. "And you know it." She eyed Jen. "So, did you ladies also smell the delicious odor of bacon this morning?"

"Actually," Jen began. "We saw you coming over here and assumed your stomach was growling and Blake would feel sorry for you, so she'd cook you breakfast. Knowing Blake as we do, we also assumed she would cook enough for us."

"Don't believe a word she said. I texted them while you were out walking my dog."

Steph looked up from her plate. "My stomach was not growling," she protested.

"Yes it was," I said, grinning.

Steph stood with her coffee cup. "You all remember this when you need me to cook." She walked toward the trailer.

"You don't cook," we called out in unison.

After she opened the door, she turned. "I won't cook. There's a difference." Then she went inside.

We laughed till our stomach muscles cramped.

"She's got moxie. I'll say that much for her," Myra pointed out.

"That she does," I answered.

"It's a good thing," Jen said, smiling. "Otherwise she'd disown us."

"Except sometimes I do have to scold her moxie," I reminded them.

"When you do, be gentle with her moxie, will you? I kind of like her that way." Myra grinned.

"I always am," I replied.

Steph was indeed dauntless, but sometimes she could take it too far. The relationship we formed over the years included me scolding her in those instances and had grown as a consequence. Whenever she was about to overstep, I would step in. She felt deeply, and it was usually for good reason. This morning, her stomach grumbling along with her desire not to cook was her reason, and it made me laugh.

When Steph was back at the table, Jen had to take one more jab at Steph. "You know, most people would have brought something to add to the meal."

"I'm not most people. Did you bring anything?"

Myra and Jen raised their coffee mugs and clinked them.

I coughed on my swallow of orange juice. When I gained control, I said, "You girls are too much." I looked at Steph and felt a warmth grow inside me when I caught her smile.

"Being most people would be utterly boring," she replied, locking onto my eyes for a moment that spread the heat throughout my body. Steph definitely was not most people. My emotions were null and void—neither good nor bad after Tess left. The warmth was gone. Whatever I had felt for my ex-wife had been numbed into nonexistence, but Steph's friendship was bringing me back to life. The warmth I felt from her smiles was welcoming at the very least.

I vaguely heard Steph direct a comment toward me, shaking me out of my train of thought. I didn't hear the complete sentence, but the word *lurking* made my eyes bolt to her face. "What did you say?"

She blew out a breath. "I said shorty was lurking around my trailer very early this morning, but I don't think he was interested in me. He acted as if he was hiding from someone or something."

I ripped a piece of bacon off the last slice on my plate and fed it to Mabel. "How do you know he was outside your trailer?"

"I didn't have the living room blind down all the way. I did that on purpose. So when I heard a noise, I looked out. He didn't see me at first because I kind of crawled to the living room to stay below the view of the window. I watched for a few seconds as he moved from one spot to another like he was playing a game of hide-and-seek. Then he saw me. I gave him the finger."

My mouth dropped open. "No, you didn't."

"Not like most people. Have you forgotten that already?" Myra reminded me.

"Steph, you know it's not smart to piss off these kinds of guys," I said.

"I'm not bowing or submitting to them either," Steph shot back.

"I get that. But you're just making whatever the situation might be...worse."

"I'll deal with it." She turned the coffee cup around and around in her hands, watching it intently, most likely hoping I would drop the subject.

I did not appease her. "You know I'm not going to let this go."

"Goddamn it, Blake. Leave it alone. You can't watch over me all the time."

I sat up. "Yes, I can."

She glared at me. "No, you can't."

"Yes, I can."

"No, you can't," she said with a look that dared me to keep going.

Jen's voice stopped our silly child's argument. "Well, this is a first. Usually, it's Steph and me going back and forth."

Neither of us looked at Jen. Our eyes were downcast, making us look like sulking children, which was exactly how I felt. "You can't let yourself get out of control," I said under my breath. "You know how you can be."

"And you know how you can be. You are not my parent nor my boss. So, don't speak to me like you are. You're my friend and I take insult to your criticizing me."

"I'm sorry," I said. "You're right. I know how I can be."

"Yeah. Way overprotective. You think you're entitled to be that way because you were a cop. I'm an adult, Blake. I've been taking care of myself for a long time."

"Oh, really?" I shot back, mostly out of hurt from her insult. "What about the revolving door of girlfriends? I seem to remember you telling me that everyone but one cooked for you. Where is that taking care of yourself?" I wished I hadn't said it as soon as it popped out of my mouth. One insult did not erase another—it only added to the first insult, and my insult was ten times worse. I was half hoping she'd slap me, or hit me in the arm or something. But for whatever reason, Steph didn't react.

She popped a piece of bacon into her mouth and spoke while chewing. "Yes, they cooked for me. Except the last one."

"Is that why you stopped seeing her?" Jen asked with amusement.

"That and other things."

"So," Myra began, pointing a piece of toast toward her. "What you're saying is you're looking for a woman who will cook for you, but not take care of you."

"That and other things," Steph repeated with a huge smile.

"Sometimes, I just don't get you," Jen exclaimed.

"You're not supposed to get me. At least not about everything. I keep telling you…I'm not most people," she replied, the smile still plastered on her face.

Jen shook her head in an amused response. "You can say that again."

"I'm not most…"

"Okay, okay, I think we've got it," Myra said.

Relieved we got off the subject of Steph exploding, I asked her, "What was her name?"

"Who?"

"The one you just broke up with. Normally you tell us about your girlfriends, but you haven't said much about this one. In fact, we didn't hear or see much of you for a couple of months."

A pink flush swept over her cheeks. "Lori"—she emphasized the woman's name—"and I…we were…kind of busy. If you get my drift."

"Okay. TMI," I said, covering my ears for effect.

"Plus, we ended our relationship just before your breakup with Tess, so I didn't think it was a good time to bring it up. It was really great at first. I mean, who doesn't want someone falling all over them?"

"I think it gets old after a while." Myra thought out loud. "You can lose yourself in something like that. You know, the smothering backlash."

"There is that. But I just realized she wasn't someone I wanted to spend the rest of my life with, even though it wouldn't be that long. I'm kind of on the downside of life."

We all laughed. "You still have a lot of glorious years left," I assured her.

"Okay. Fine. I just didn't want to spend what I've got left with her."

"How many is that?" Jen asked, followed by an elbow to her side from her wife.

"How many what? Years left or women?" Steph stared at Jen.

"Um, women."

Myra tried to stop her wife's onslaught this time by a kick to her leg under the table. Jen flinched.

"Aw, Jen. Not everyone can be as lucky as you and find a woman who can tolerate them for thirty years. God, I just find that an awful long time to be stuck with one woman." Steph sat upright and stretched.

"You won't know until you try it," Jen shot back, but with a smile.

I rolled my eyes, knowing where this line of conversation was headed. So, I decided to exit stage right. "Myra. Help me pick up, will you? We'll leave these two to their usual banter."

I set Mabel on the ground and attached her lead to the picnic table. As we walked to my trailer, I watched Mabel make her way over to Steph, stare up at her and whine. Of course, Steph picked her up. I shook my head, and we went inside, leaving the sarcastic teasing behind.

"You know, she has to be running out of women. Ithaca's not that big," said Myra.

"Now that's not nice." I slapped Myra's arm, laughing. "You know, I tried talking her into moving to Rochester several times. Fresh meat and all that." I grinned.

"Now, who's not being nice?"

"No, really. She has a lot of friends there and she'd have no problem getting a job. The first time I talked to my captain at RPD about her, they were extremely interested. She said no. I tried again several years after that. I think that was the time she was dating Holly, but she's determined to retire from her job here."

"Isn't that the one that cheated on her?" Myra asked while scraping food off the plates into the garbage.

"More than once. They were on and off for years. Each time Holly cheated on her, Steph kept trying to walk away, but Holly would slither back, saying and doing all the things she knew would convince Steph to give her another chance. I think Holly is the reason Steph never stayed with a woman any longer than six months." I turned on the hot water heater to prepare for dishwashing. "Maybe in her mind, if she didn't stay too long, they wouldn't have a chance to hurt her. Haven't you noticed she's the one who ends almost every relationship she's ever had since then?"

"You'd think all the women in Ithaca would know her MO by now. If I was single and someone introduced me to her as a blind date, I'd run the other way." Myra chuckled.

"I wouldn't," I said so quietly that I wasn't even sure the words came out of my mouth. But when I saw Myra's head snap in my direction, I realized they had.

"Okay, I'm not sure how to take that."

I plugged the sink drain, added a bit of dish soap, and turned on the water. "I've known Steph longer than I knew Tess. We're best friends. I...I understand her." I turned off the water and began to wash the egg pan.

Myra grabbed a towel off of the oven handle and stood next to me, leaning against the counter. "She understands you, too. I was pleased when she took that chunk of time off to be with you after Tess...well, you know."

I rolled my head as if I was doing a stretching exercise. "Yeah, she was a good friend except that I had to cook for her." I laughed as I handed the pan to Myra to dry.

We were silent for a minute or two. I washed. She dried. Trailers being like tin cans, we could hear the banter still going on outside. I walked over to the door to check on them. Seeing their laughing faces, I didn't need to go out and officiate. But I felt the need to take in the broad smile, bright eyes, and rosy cheeks produced by Steph's embarrassment.

I turned to see Myra staring at me.

"Is there something you're not telling me?"

I tilted my head and felt the wrinkles on my forehead deepen with my confusion. "About what?"

"Is there more to your feelings for Steph than friendship?"

"Oh my God, what would make you say that? She's one of my best friends. Like you." I waved a hand of denial in the air and went back to the sink, picking up the bacon pan. Realizing I was scrubbing with a fervor that the bacon pan did not deserve, I rinsed it slowly before handing it to Myra.

She dried it just as slowly as I had rinsed it.

"I just think...oh never mind. You'd tell me, wouldn't you? I mean, I thought *I* was your best friend."

Glancing sideways, I saw the hurt in her eyes. I grabbed her into a very tight hug. "You are, but I have more than one best friend. I'm lucky like that."

"I can accept that." She hung the towel back on the oven handle and opened the door to go outside. "What's on the docket for today?"

"It's my first full day. I still have some unpacking to do. How about some afternoon wine touring?"

Myra walked down the steps with me following. "Our captain is suggesting some afternoon wine touring. Any takers?" Myra asked.

Jen and Steph turned to face us. "Great minds think alike. We already decided that," Jen said.

Mabel was now on the ground, sniffing. When she heard me, she trotted over to me, and I picked her up, obliging her with scratches behind her long ears. I heard the ostentatious golf cart stop, throwing back dirt and rocks from the hard braking. It wasn't hard to miss with the clean, white leather top and interior, the polished fenders and side panels, and the extra gadgets on the console that screamed high tech.

"Well, if it isn't Officer Squeamish and her cronies. Good morning, ladies." Mac Taylor said "ladies" as if it left a nasty taste in his mouth.

Maybe I should have offered him mouthwash.

Steph raised her coffee cup and saluted him. "Mac."

She was the only one at our table with enough guts to call him by his first name. Of course, her senior role at the IPD allowed her a bit more leeway. She knew Mac for who and what he was, and I was pretty sure he knew enough not to mess with her. She was highly regarded in her field at IPD.

It surprised me that this was the second time in two days that he chose to harass us. Or maybe it was simply because I was here, and that was something he couldn't stay away from. He had made it his life's mission to harass and abuse me the entire four and a half years I worked in the IPD.

"What can we do for you, Officer Taylor?" Myra called out to him.

"Call me Mac." His grin displayed teeth yellowed from years of smoking and drinking—a habit he began when I trained with him. Salt-and-pepper stubble made his grin appear like a hole in the bark of a tree. "I'm doing my daily rounds. I plan on keeping this campground clean and respectable so it maintains a *family* atmosphere."

We all looked at each other, and then Myra replied, "Okay," after which she said nothing more, only tilted her head. I noticed a sparkle in her eyes. Then she added sarcastically, "We appreciate your attention to keeping this campground as lovely as it is."

Knowing her sarcasm, I almost choked on my sip of water.

"Oh, I plan to. Better, in fact. If anyone or anything doesn't adhere to my rules or fit in with our image of what we want this place to be, they or it will be removed."

Steph's eyebrows raised. "Removed?"

He answered quickly because he had to know the trouble he could get into talking about removing people. "Of course, anything that needs to go will be removed, but people, well, we would ask them to leave."

"I see. You certainly have a handle on things, Mac." Myra was becoming alarmingly close to setting off Mac's temper. "But if that's the case…"

I put a hand on Myra's arm. Steph nudged me in the side and I relented.

"Why is there a man wandering the campground and peeking into people's trailers when he's been formally charged with harassment?" Myra continued.

Jen and I swallowed hard at the same time, but kept our mouths shut.

"Yeah, Mac. He was outside my trailer this morning," Steph concurred.

"What are you talking about?" Mac seemed genuinely surprised. "This is the first I've heard about it."

"I saw him on the news two nights ago," Jen said. "He was outside our trailer last night. Short, stocky guy with brown hair and a beard. Round face, brown eyes. His name is Manson Smith. He's been on the news, charged with harrassing young townies. He was leaning against a tree on Greg's site, looking in our window. Maybe Greg knows him."

Mac looked very uncomfortable, but it didn't seem out of anger or like he was trying to hide anything. He was genuinely upset about our news. "I'm sorry, ladies. I didn't know. No one else has said anything."

"I'll bet if you ask around, you'll hear more complaints about it. A lot of campers don't watch television, so they may not know who he is, but I'll bet there are other seasonals who have seen him lurking around."

"Any idea which campsite he's at?" He had put his cop hat on and was now sounding like a police officer protecting the public. "Did you see which way he went?"

"It was hard to," Steph replied. "We've only seen him at night and he kept moving in and out of campsites. Mostly on our side of the tract."

"Thank you, ladies. I'll look into that." He drove off without giving us the chance to say anything else.

Steph glared at me. "Why didn't you tell him about your encounter in the field with Mr. Smith?"

"Well, for one, I didn't get the chance. For two, it would just give him one more thing to mock me about."

"What's to mock?" Myra asked. "The guy was waiting for you."

"What do you mean he was waiting for me?"

"We saw him in the field right before you ran into him. He was watching you."

"And you waited to tell me this. Why?"

Jen intervened. "We didn't want you to pack up your car and sell your trailer the first day you were here."

Steph looked from Jen and Myra to me. Then, she burst out laughing. The absurdity of that had me joining in. But as I laughed, I realized maybe they had a reason for thinking that. I had run away from Ithaca thirty years ago. However, I had never run from anything since. I hoped they knew *that* about me.

Myra said, "She's joking. We were going to tell you this morning. We just hadn't gotten to the subject yet. Thanks to our new landlord, Mac"—she said the word the same way Mac had said "ladies"—"the subject came up before we had the chance to tell you."

"So what now?" Jen asked us.

"I think we wait," I replied. "Let's see if Officer Taylor and landlord Mac come together to do the right thing about it."

"Would that be physically removing Manson Smith or asking him to leave?" Steph questioned.

We laughed again.

CHAPTER SIX

I planned to go on a reconnaissance mission of my own to see what I could find out, leaving the unpacking for later. We had agreed to leave about eleven thirty and grab lunch before we started our afternoon of wine tasting.

After our conversation with Mac (I found it very odd to call him that since Officer Nasty had been the name I used for him for many years), I wondered if we would still have to worry about Smith. I also thought about our new landlord's position on people that didn't fit into his mold. Would we also have to worry about Officer Nasty as the new owner of the campground? Or could we simply ignore all his bluster and carry on?

I was apprehensive about visiting our fellow seasonal campers. I had met a few of them over the years because Jen and Myra had been seasonal campers for about ten years. When Tess and I came down, we often hung out with them during happy hours. Still, I wasn't sure what kind of response I'd get if I dug too much into their opinion of the new owner. Most of them were very welcoming. A few were aloof, but friendly enough. I didn't want to start anything—like unknowingly drawing a dividing line between them and us.

Mabel and I walked along the road looking at the different trailers, fifth wheels, and motorhomes. On the back road, there was a section with three small cabins. Two had cars parked in front of them. The third was empty and looking rather worse for wear. Further down, there was a large tent section.

When we neared the front of the campground, we walked by the park model on the site opposite the office. It was owned by Sandy and Kevin Miller. The park models were larger and had more amenities like manufactured homes did, but they were also on wheels and could be moved if you decided to go to a different campground. They just weren't meant to pull behind a truck on a camping trip like a trailer or fifth wheel was. They had an oversized deck with added footage where a large canopy was erected to protect from the sun's rays and inclement weather. A bar, large grill, and storage cupboards filled empty spaces along the trailer.

Sandy, a woman in her forties, was kneeling in one of her gardens that surrounded their property. She was planting flowers.

"I love petunias," I said as I admired the purple and red flowers she was positioning to alternate the colors.

Sandy looked up. "Hey there, Blake. When did you get here? Is it true you're going to be a seasonal?"

"Yes. I came down yesterday because I heard there's a big party here tonight."

"It's for the Connellys' anniversary. Are you coming?"

"Absolutely."

"Make sure you bring that little cutie."

Mabel made her way over to Sandy, who gave her a few head pats. She was a bit heavy-handed and Mabel moved away from her. "I will, but we have to get going. We're heading out to lunch."

"See you at the party, then. Have a great day."

"You too," I answered and hastened Mabel along.

"Oh, and, Blake?"

I turned around to look at her. "Yes?"

"I'm sorry about Tess."

"Oh. Uh, thank you." I tripped over a rock as I hurried to get away. I now had proof that rumors traveled fast in a campground. I wondered which of my friends spilled the beans. But did it really matter? People would assume anyway since I was here without Tess, and she wouldn't be showing up. Or they would just ask me.

I finished unpacking and then settled Mabel with some treats, left the air on for her and crossed the large, presently vacant field in dire need of a mowing. My friends were already waiting in the car.

"Come on. Lunch won't wait forever!" Steph exclaimed through her rolled-down window.

"So impatient. I'm right on time." I climbed in, and we spent the next couple of hours talking and laughing while eating pizza at the Vintage Wine House. They had a great outdoor area and a large variety of red and white wines. It was the best way to start retirement, and it reinforced the decision I had made to do it earlier in life despite my single status.

After lunch, we hit a few more wineries, then returned to the campground and went our separate ways. I walked Mabel and finished unpacking and stuffing everything into the limited cupboard space. Then...I took a nap.

For the first time in my life, I took a nap.

* * *

As I approached the Millers' deck, the first thing I saw were the Connellys sitting at the bar. With my full beer bottle and Mabel, I joined the party for some gossip. It wasn't difficult to get information because many of the seasonal campers liked to drink. A lot. I had learned to take fake sips, making my glass look full all the time so that they wouldn't refill it. The other trick to stay sober was to drink from a beer bottle. I mean, who refills a beer bottle? And you were rarely offered another until they saw yours was empty. The way to avoid that was to drink from a brown bottle that was harder to tell how much you had left.

John and Renee Connelly sat in the captain's chairs at the wooden bar built to overlook the rest of the party area. In their hands were large glasses filled to the top with their drink of choice. John had whiskey and Renee super-sized martinis.

There were already two other couples seated on the deck chairs and love seat holding glasses with pictures or sayings distinct to their likes and dislikes so no one picked up someone else's glass. After greeting people as they arrived and returning hugs, I took a seat, picked up Mabel, and settled her on my lap. I purposely sat next to Sandy Miller. She was likely a trophy wife. I imagined when her husband, Kevin, first laid his eyes on her, she was a true beauty. But now, her hair looked dry and brittle from extensive dyeing, making it hard to distinguish the color, a bleached blond bordering on white. Her face was always heavy with makeup, even at the campground. The thick eyeliner made her eyes look dark and sad, as if advertising that she was cemented in a destitute marriage. Wrinkles fanned out from the corners and she always used the adage of laugh lines whenever someone pointed them out.

Sandy was a busybody, and I believed she used that to make up for her shitty sad life. Her husband was tall, dark, and still handsome—well built, a head of thick, brown hair with mahogany tints and bluer eyes than the rich turquoise color of the ocean water meeting the Cancun beaches. He was also intelligent, holding a PhD in some type of technological field. The shitty part of her life? She let everyone know he was an addicted cheater.

I felt sorry for her. She could walk away at any time, but she never did. I imagined she was too scared of losing everything—her husband, status, money, and a beautiful and very expensive Florida home. So she made up for it by keeping her nose in everyone else's business.

"So, Sandy, how's it going?" I asked.

"It's so good to see you." Then she said to Mabel, "Hello little lady." Once again, she patted Mabel's head like she was patting down dirt around a planting, and Mabel squirmed to get away from her. "Myra told me you were thinking about buying a camper and joining us. I'm glad you did." She leaned forward and, true to form, she whispered, "Sorry to hear about you and Tess."

I let that one ride off into oblivion by not commenting because she had already expressed her condolences. I wondered if she was drunk the first time she said that to me or most likely, she was inebriated now. You could never tell with her.

"It's good to see you, too. I've got a great trailer and I'm settling in. Looking forward to the summer."

She wriggled in her seat to get comfortable for the juicy and most likely lengthy gossip she was about to tell me. "Well, I heard the new owner is an old coworker of yours."

My stomach turned. I wasn't sure I could ever get used to the rumor mill there. It was always running in good condition and perhaps foolishly, I had ignored it when I decided to plop my trailer here.

"Is it true that you didn't get along very well? I can't imagine why. I mean, you seem so nice."

I smiled, thinking *nice* being the operative word here. "Thank you," I said, not wanting to offer too much personal information.

"So, was it? True?"

I wasn't ready for that question, but I answered it as ambiguously as I could, "We, um, had our differences. But..." I added, "we always got our job done."

"Oh, that's good. I was afraid we might have some problems." She leaned forward. "You know."

I took a tiny sip of my beer and answered, "No, I'm afraid I don't. What kind of problems are you talking about?"

"Well, like if you don't get along. Everyone gets along here and it would be terrible to have someone at odds with someone else, especially if it's with the owner."

"Not me," I said, hoping to dispel the thoughts I could see spinning in her brain. Right now, she would be organizing the information, and preparing it for her fake gossip about me. "We're family here," I offered. "We all need to get along. Be nice to everyone. That's my motto."

"Oh." Obviously disappointed she didn't get any juicy tidbits, she swirled the liquid in her glass followed by a long, slow drink. Yup, she was intoxicated.

I took the plunge. "I was talking with a few people and they've seen some guy lurking around everyone's campsites. Some say they've seen him during the night. Have you heard about this?"

She practically slapped her hand to her chest. "Oh my. That's right. I did hear something about some stranger walking around the campground. But everyone I talked to thought he was a weekend camper."

That might have been the case, but I was relieved to hear that others had seen him. Sandy turned to speak to Bonnie, another avid gossiper and I assumed we were finished. I picked up Mabel and made my short rounds of conversation, making sure I reached Myra, Jen, and Steph last. I explained I'd been here awhile and was heading back to get something to eat and then relax for the evening.

On our way back, Mabel decided to sniff every blade of grass, so I decided to hurry her along because my stomach was rumbling. Suddenly she pulled the leash to my left toward a thicket of bushes.

Mabel was only ten pounds of power, but when she got a mind to go somewhere, it felt more like forty. "Come on, girl. I'm hungry, aren't you?" She kept pulling, and I knew the only way to change her mind was to pick her up.

So I did.

And when I looked up, I was staring into the eyes of Manson Smith.

I hesitated a second or two, giving him just enough time to see me. He was standing in front of me, and at that moment, my cop brain was debating my options. It was Mabel who made the decision for me. She started barking and wriggling in my arms as if she thought her mere ten pounds could pulverize the approximately one hundred eighty-pound body standing a few feet inside the boscage.

I knew he could squash my dog with one slam of his foot if she was on the ground. But she was in my arms, safe even though that was a big disadvantage for me. But as luck would have it, he turned and fled.

Still carrying Mabel, I hurried toward the campground store and main office. I didn't recognize the woman behind the counter, and I wondered briefly if it was Officer Nasty's wife.

"Hi. My name is Blakely Moore, and I'm a seasonal on site forty-two. Is Officer…I mean Mac Taylor here?" Even though everyone called me Blake, my full name was Blakely Moore, and I only used it in a professional setting. However, my parents had used it whenever they were mad at me or wanted my attention because I was ignoring them. Come to think of it, my wife had used my full name once or twice and so had a few of my friends.

"Why yes. He just came in a minute ago."

She turned her head and shouted, "Honey! A camper wants to see you."

Well, she answered that question.

Mac came from a back room huffing like he'd been interrupted during a nonexistent workout. It got worse when he saw it was me. His expression of frustration turned into a sneer that clearly said, "You better have a good reason for interrupting me or get ready for my onslaught of abuse."

So, before he could say anything, I rattled off what I wanted him to know. "I just saw that prowler, Manson Smith, in that thick group of bushes across from the pool. He was hiding. My dog sniffed him out and when our eyes met, he turned and ran."

"Which way did he go?" Mac asked as he hurried around the counter and headed for the door.

"Toward the back of the campground through the campsites."

I followed him out the door and nearly ran into the back of him when he stopped and yelled for Greg, the maintenance guy. His bellow was rough and hard, bringing Greg at a full run. I wondered how long Mac had been here to instill in Greg the need to respond to him that quickly when he howled like an angry wolf.

"That guy I told you about. He's in the campground."

The two men walked as if they were in a foot race in the direction I had indicated. I followed, listening to their conversation.

"I've checked out every campsite, and I never saw him," Greg said in between breaths.

"Maybe he's staying in a trailer or tent under another name. Did you ask people?"

"Everyone who's here."

"We've got weekend campers. Did you ask them?"

"Yes. No one has seen anyone out of the ordinary."

Mac huffed, that same sound he would make when he thought I missed the boat on something, or merely because he was stuck with a stupid female for his first trainee which was something he often said to me. I felt sorry for Greg. Mac would not be tolerant, let alone as nice as Randy and Phyllis had been. I already saw the signs, and I wondered how much bad-boss abuse Greg would take before he walked off the job.

I might have followed them further down the road, but two things stopped me—I was dragging Mabel on her leash behind me and a quick glance back from Officer Nasty made me take a turn and continue straight toward my trailer, my mind and body fighting it the whole way. But it was best I stayed out of it. Mac would turn to Officer Nasty if I stuck my nose anywhere near him.

Mabel and I had dinner, after which I fell asleep on the recliner while watching television. Someone had told me once that when they retired, they slept for three months. I hoped I didn't do that and ruin my first year as a seasonal camper. I'd miss all the fun if I slept through it.

CHAPTER SEVEN

The next morning, I saw a text from Myra. They would pick me up at eleven thirty for lunch and another day of wine touring. I was eager to see them and tell them about my encounter the prior evening, but happy that I had the morning to relax, walk Mabel, and putz around the trailer.

Time got away from me, and when I looked at my watch, I had fifteen minutes until I was supposed to meet my friends. There was still much more putzing to do, but I was ready for a break. Leaving Mabel in the trailer, where she would bask in the factory ice (air-conditioning) with the television tuned to *Animal Planet* (her favorite show), I grabbed my bag, keys, and a light jacket and headed out the door. By the time I walked across the field, Jen, Myra, and Steph was exiting the trailer.

"'Bout time. We've been waiting," Steph chided as she made her way to the car. "And waiting." She opened the back door. "And waiting. Again."

I laughed. "It'll be worth it when I tell you what happened after I left the party last night. But, if you want to continue to tease me about being"—I looked at my watch—"um, five minutes late, which, by the way, is highly unusual for me, then I don't need to tell you that I saw Mr. Smith over by the pool."

The three women stopped midclimb into the car and stood back up.

"What the hell are we doing here? We need to get this guy. Let's go." Steph shut her door and started to walk toward the main office.

I stepped in front of her. "Whoa, Supergirl. Someone's already on it. Besides, it was last night. After the party."

"Oh, you did say that," Steph answered, red-faced.

"Get in the car. I'm hungry." I grabbed her shoulders, turned her around, and gently pushed her back toward the car.

She wriggled out of my grasp and turned around. "What do you mean someone's already on it?" she challenged.

I kept pushing her. "Oh, man. I shouldn't have said anything until we were driving down the road. Please get in the car. I'll tell you everything but believe me when I say someone is already on it and we need to stay out of it."

"I can't believe *you* are saying we need to stay out of it," she said after we got in the car.

Myra drove out of the campground at a very slow five miles per hour. When you were driving, that speed limit seemed ridiculous. But when you were a camper, sometimes it seemed too fast. When Myra turned onto the main road, I filled them in.

"He can't really do anything if he's off duty, can he?" Jen asked.

"Off-duty police officers can confront criminal activity. They have to decide whether or not to take action, but there are risks involved if they do," I answered.

"Do you know if he caught the guy? Do you think he took action?"

"I don't know if Mac found him, but if I go on the history I have with him, oh yeah, if he caught him, he took action. He's a real loose cannon. A strong-arm, brute-hero wannabe."

"That's quite an interesting way of putting it," Steph commented. "Let's remember you have a, shall I say, unique history with him. I don't necessarily disagree with you."

"I guess I should have said a bad cop. Mac didn't think twice about beating someone with his baton because they talked back to him, or he thought they deserved it. If he stopped one of his friends for driving while intoxicated, he let him off with a warning. And he took bribes. Being his rookie and a female on top of that, there was nothing I could do. Those are just some of the things he did."

"Didn't anyone ever turn him in for that?" Jen asked, astonished.

"Not back then. He had most of his cop buddies in his back pocket and the captain often looked the other way. To this day, I don't know why. I have no idea how it is now." I looked at Steph, expecting her to tell us if it had changed, but she said nothing.

She eyed me for a moment and then turned toward the window and said, "I think we can all agree that if he did catch up with one Manson Smith, then we won't have to worry about him roaming around the campground anymore. I think that's a good thing."

"So do I," Jen concurred.

Myra looked at me in the rearview mirror. "OMG. They actually agree on something?"

"So, can we stop talking about the new owner of Rock Creek Campground now? I really would like to enjoy my summer," I said.

Steph's gaze left the window and landed back on me. "As much as you want to put your head in a hole where Mac Taylor is concerned, you won't be able to. You know as well as we do, he might just make himself a thorn in your behind, or maybe even ours, especially since he always seems to enjoy hounding you. So, I suggest that sometime, but okay, not today, we talk about how we can keep that from happening."

"Too bad he's the boss. We can't get him fired," I said, half joking.

"No, but we can ignore his stupidity," Myra said from the driver's seat. "From the interactions I've had with him, I think we should prepare for any stupid thing he might do as the new boss of the campground."

"Fine, fine, fine," I mumbled, wanting to be done with that line of conversation. "But as far as I'm concerned, everything that man does is based on his stupidity."

The car took a sudden sharp right turn, throwing me into Steph's side. I regained my position near my window and off Steph's lap, which I kind of enjoyed being on.

"I told you to put your seat belt on," Steph teased. Then she whispered in my ear, "But I'm not complaining."

I felt my cheeks warm. "This is the wrong way to the restaurant." I complained, hoping to quell the flush in my cheeks.

"We're not eating first. I think we all need a drink to chill out. So, we're going to a winery for some heavy wine tasting and then we'll eat."

"No complaints here," Jen said, keeping her head forward.

Steph and I locked eyes, and I smiled, hoping she would return it. She did. Then she said, "No complaints back here either."

Myra guided the car into the parking lot of one of our favorite wineries. They had deep, rich reds, brilliant whites, and my favorite… ice wine. We bellied up to the long butcher block counter, ready to make our selections. When we first started, back in the '70s, wine tastings were free. Then we paid three dollars for five to ten tastings and a tour of their facilities. Eventually, the tours died out, and as more wineries popped up in the Finger Lakes, we paid five dollars for the tastings that included a free wineglass. Now we paid twelve dollars or more for only three tastings and no extras.

The four of us had agreed to take turns buying bottles of different wines, liquor, and beer at the discount liquor store in Ithaca. One of us would hold the tasting at their trailer now and then. However, there was a distinct atmosphere at wineries not captured at a campground. The ambiance of the wineries was enjoyable because of the bustle of the patrons and talking shop with the vintners about their wine processes. So, we agreed to still patronize the wineries once in a while.

Today, we chose a cabernet sauvignon, a merlot, and a blend for the reds. For the whites, we had a chardonnay aged in French oak and a riesling (my favorite white). I paid extra for a tasting of their Vidal ice wine.

The wonderful thing about wine touring was the first couple of sips in an atmosphere that was light, yet full of merrymaking. The liquor helped us to put our woes behind us and focus on the fun. I hoped I could forget about Manson Smith until another day. For now, I just wanted to have a good time.

So, we did. By four o'clock, we had finished our tasting, ate our lunch, and continued on the east side of the Seneca Lake wine trail. I suggested we head back.

"Not to be a party pooper, but I have a little pooper back at the campground who will need to get out soon."

My friends groaned.

"I never thought you would become one of *those* dog owners," Steph laughed.

"What?" I whined. "She's been in the trailer since eleven thirty. That's a long time for an itty-bitty bladder."

"Hell, I have a large bladder and can't go that long," Jen giggled.

"Naps before dinner?" I heard Myra suggest. Since she had been our designated driver, she had only tasted one wine. We had set limits for the DD, as we called it, and to be fair, we each took our turn.

"If I go to bed, I won't get up until tomorrow morning," I said.

"God," Steph blurted out rather loud. "Since you retired, you've become old. Is that what I have to look forward to?"

I put my hands over my ears. "Quiet down, you goof. We're in a small space. You don't need to yell." I lightly punched her arm.

She grabbed her arm with her other hand. "What the hell was that for?" Steph got louder rather than quieter.

Steph had too much to drink and I knew it would be best to apologize and leave it. "I'm sorry. Please just try to lower your voice."

Then, being the smart-ass that she was, she didn't diminish the volume, but lowered her voice to a very deep bass range. "Apology accepted." She laughed so hard, I thought she would throw up. At this point, it might not have been a bad thing. She needed a little sobering up.

Steph grew quiet. When I turned to look at her, her eyes were closed, and her chest rose and fell rhythmically. She had fallen asleep. I leaned forward over the console between the bucket seats. "Steph is lobbying for naps," I said with amusement. This actually surprised me. Steph was always the last one to die out from a good day of drinking, and today, she didn't drink as much as usual. "Since when did she crash before any of us? And on what little she drank?"

Jen and Myra glanced at each other and in that brief exchange, I knew they were silently acknowledging something to each other and not including me.

"What is it?" I asked, concerned.

"Don't tell her we told you, but she's not drinking as much as she used to," Myra said, not missing a beat. "I don't know if you've noticed, but she doesn't drink every time we get together. She drank a lot today compared to what she's been drinking. When she does, she crashes."

"No way. She's always been able to hold more liquor than any of us."

"When was the last time you drank with her?"

I thought for a moment. "We drank a few times after Tess left me for her bimbo." I tried to remember what we drank and how much. "Come to think of it, when she came up to be with me after Tess moved out, she didn't drink all that much. Not even when she was sharing in my misery with a bottle of vodka. I think I consumed three-quarters of the bottle."

I was about to say something when Myra said, "I'm actually kind of happy about that. We don't have to worry about her anymore."

I glanced back at Steph who was snoring softly. Her face was a conflicting picture of someone sleeping—relaxed, soft lips that showed they were at rest, but her eyelids fluttered as if she was watching a movie in fast forward and couldn't keep up with the story.

I turned forward looking out the front window again. "Why would you worry about Steph? What's going on? I've never known any of us to worry about Steph even when she was drinking. Besides, if we did, she'd shoot us with that gun of hers."

Myra snickered, but Jen answered too quickly. "Nothing."

I looked directly at Myra in time to see her head tilt to the side and then briefly look up. It was a look of pure frustration. "Later," Myra said quietly. "I promise I'll tell you everything."

I didn't want to wait until later because I was ready to explode. Steph was still sleeping, so I asked, "Tell me what?" My voice was hard, but I swallowed to keep control.

Then Steph's gruff voice from the back seat said, "It's all right. I'll tell her."

I sat back in my seat and waited. Steph repositioned herself, rubbing her neck. I swallowed hard as I watched her long, slender fingers kneading the muscles in a slow, deep motion, and I immediately looked away.

"I didn't drink much of that vodka because I got a DUI the week before I came up. So, actually, you weren't the only one wanting to drown your sorrows in a bottle of alcohol. I wanted to join you, but I realized over-drinking wasn't the best choice for me anymore."

I said nothing at first, allowing me time to wrap my head around what my best friend had just said. She was a member of a police force, and she got a DUI. She knew better. Then again, I just said that she could always hold her liquor. Wasn't that a sign of someone who drank too much?

Had she been drowning her sorrows and never once told me she was doing so? Or why? I had no idea what was going on in her life that would make her need to do that. When she stayed with me, she wanted to join me in my drinking campaign, but did she not do it because she was fighting to stay afloat? Why didn't she tell me any of this?

So, I had to ask, "Why didn't you tell me? I thought we were better friends than that."

"We are." She reached out to take my hand. Without thinking, my hurt made me pull my hand away. She flinched. "You were in so much pain. Tess left you after twenty-five years for a woman she hardly knew. She moved out. She wasn't coming back. You needed me to comfort you. Not the other way around."

"In true friendships, it wouldn't matter that we were both hurting over something major that happened in our lives, even if it happened at the same time. It's not a competition of who's hurting more."

"I didn't say it was," Steph shot back. "I thought you'd be more appreciative that I was there for you, that I put my stuff on hold so I could help you grieve your relationship. I never thought you to be callous."

My mouth opened, then closed. I took a deep breath to keep my emotions under control. It was so easy to let them gain momentum like a snowball rolling down a hill picking up more snow. I shut my eyes to sort out what I was feeling, but it didn't take me longer than a few seconds to realize what my true feelings were.

"I'm sorry," I said in a hushed voice, more from embarrassment than anything else. "You were there for me and I will never forget it. My outburst here is a combination of the alcohol today, my leftover crap from Tess walking out, and a bit of hurt that you never told me. I understand why, but were you ever going to tell me?" I reached out and took her hand. Thank God she didn't pull away as I had.

"To be honest, I don't know. I wanted to, but I was embarrassed. Even though I'm a medical examiner and not out on the streets or anything like that, I felt I betrayed my oath and the force. You know how hard they can be on a cop who gets arrested for a DUI."

I swallowed, knowing an internal probe would have taken place with stiff outcomes.

"Have they finished the investigation?"

Steph shifted in her seat as she took her hand back. She took a quick, deep breath. "I'm at the end of an administrative leave during which I've had to attend drug and alcohol counseling."

"I'm sorry." And even though I truly was sorry, those pesky negative feelings of being excluded resurfaced. I looked at the two women in the front seats. "Did you both know?"

Steph butted in and answered for them. "They knew about the DUI, but this is the first I've said anything about the disciplinary measures. You've got to remember they live in Ithaca. They're here and you're not, and I don't mean that in a negative way. You were going through a hard time."

Now, I felt like an idiot again. I realized I was acting more like someone who was mad about being kept out of the loop than caring about what happened to their friend. How selfish was that?

"You know, next time we can go iced tea tasting." I knew it sounded stupid, but I didn't know what else to say that wouldn't have sounded worse.

But my friends laughed anyway.

"I don't know if that's even a thing," Myra said.

"We could make it a thing," I said. "We could start a business since I'm retired and you ladies aren't too far off. It would give us something to do, and a little extra cash couldn't hurt. How about a tea brewery? Iced tea, hot tea, spiked tea…for medicinal purposes only."

My friends laughed even more.

"Oh, oh, oh. We could call it Teas Anonymous," Steph said, choking on her laughter. And this only made us shift into loud, uncontrollable guffaws.

Myra turned into the campground just as our laughter died down from coming up with different names for different tea drinks. I felt the car slow to the designated speed that seemed worse than a turtle's pace. It kind of was. As Myra rounded the pool heading toward our cluster of trailers, Mac and Greg were escorting (and I use that word loosely) Manson Smith on the road toward us. Myra took a left turn toward my trailer to avoid driving by them and stopped at my campsite.

"I'm more than happy to have dinner at my place," I said trying to ignore what we just saw. "My kitchen is a larger, and I have plenty of room for the four of us to eat inside if it rains."

"Is it supposed to rain?" Jen asked.

"I just checked my phone. The weather reports say there's a chance."

"What are we having?" Steph asked, winking at me. "Leftover breakfast?"

I grinned at her. "I'm ordering pizza. Come over anytime. I'll have it here in an hour."

With a unison of okays, I headed inside to prepare Mabel for a walk. I thought about finding Mac and asking why it took so long for him and Greg to find Manson Smith and what he was going to do with him, so it was a good thing I told my friends to come over within an hour because it meant I had to stay in my trailer to wait for them. Otherwise, I'm sure I would have gone looking for Mac to make sure he was going by the book.

And I knew that wouldn't have been a good thing for me to do.

Three hours later, it still wasn't raining, and we were sitting around a campfire that Myra had made with scraggly limbs, dry brush, and a good squirt of charcoal lighter fluid. It wasn't ingenious, and it was the lazy way of starting a campfire, but Myra told us, "I have no desire to win a lame contest that's going to make me work harder than I want or need to." Dusk was upon us with a smoky pink sky hiding the sun that slowly slipped into the horizon.

Mabel had curled in a ball on my lap and was settled for the evening. She nudged her nose inside my hoodie against the cooler night air, which was also my excuse to make hot chocolate. None of us were in the mood for any more drinking and warm cocoa would stave off the evening's chill. I knew we couldn't ignore Steph's drinking for long. It was a discussion we had to have with her because we needed to understand how to help without making her feel guilty that we weren't indulging in something we enjoyed because of her.

Staying off the subject of Manson Smith, we were in the middle of a heated debate over motorhome versus fifth wheel versus travel trailer versus destination trailer or park model when the familiar drone of one particular golf cart approached. My three friends turned their heads toward the fast-approaching vehicle that came to an abrupt stop. Officer Nasty was most likely doing his evening rounds and when he saw us, couldn't resist stopping to inflict his superiority over us.

I sipped my hot chocolate, wondering if I should ask about his escorting Manson Smith earlier. I waited to see how the conversation would evolve.

"Well, ladies. Evenin'."

There was no denying I was already biased toward the man, and I tried so hard to forgive and forget, but the memories, usually locked up in the far recesses of my mind, had worked their way to the surface and festered like an angry wound infection at the mere sight of him. I swallowed hard.

"Good evening, Mac," my friends responded together.

I felt his eyes on me, then I heard him clear his throat like a cat dispelling a fur ball. "Ms. Moore," he said to me.

"Good evening, Mac," I answered in a hard tone.

"Well, I just wanted to let you ladies know you no longer have to worry about Manson Smith."

"That's great," Jen said. "Would you like some hot chocolate?"

He looked at her, as if dumbfounded by the question. Then he smiled. "Ahhh, mixed with a bit of whiskey?" He tried to smile, but it looked more like pain from stomach gas.

Steph raised her cup. "Nope, just hot chocolate tonight. So, how did you rid us of our worry over Manson Smith?" she asked, without hesitation.

His smile widened, showing his yellow teeth, and he puffed out his chest as he tried to straighten up a little. "Well, me and Greg found him hiding in one of the seasonal trailers in the back. He said it belonged to a friend of his, but he couldn't give us the name. Missy called the owner of the trailer, and they didn't know any Manson Smith. We checked the door and found he'd broken the lock. He said he had no place to go because his wife kicked him out. So, we escorted his ass to the office and called in some friends of mine. They persuaded him to never set foot on the campground again and helped him to find his way home."

"Even though his wife kicked him out?" Jen asked.

"That's his problem," Mac replied.

My stomach rolled, listening to Officer Taylor spouting his "cop lingo" in such an uncivil and inappropriate way. I didn't like his friends *convincing* Smith to stay away and then *helping* him to find his way home, or Greg's involvement, but I knew we would probably never find out exactly what he meant by it, because it didn't sound like it was by the book.

"And if he comes back?" Myra had the balls to ask.

"I've alerted all my staff to keep an eye out for him, but I don't think he'll be back. He got his warning."

And again, no idea what he meant. What kind of warning? And from whom? These were questions I would have asked as a cop. But as a seasonal camper, I said, "Thank you, Mac. We appreciate you taking care of the situation and letting us know."

He stared at me like he was unsure of how to respond to such a respectful statement coming from me. So, he turned and got into his golf cart, calling out, "You're welcome, ladies," as he drove away with a dismissive wave.

"You think we've made a new friend?" Myra asked, watching him drive away.

"Please tell me you're being facetious," Steph said in a deadpan voice.

I laughed hard until Mabel became upset with being disturbed by my body shaking with uncontrollable mirth. She stood on my lap and looked up at me with wide eyes filled with annoyance. Fed up with the ruckus, she jumped off my lap and stood before Steph, pleading for another lap that might be still and warm. Steph picked her up, wrapping her inside her hoodie and whispered in her ear. Mabel settled down and promptly fell asleep. Or at least she wanted us to think that because one eye was partly open as she watched us in pure canine disgust.

God, I loved my dog. It wasn't just the unconditional love, but her expressions that ran the gamut of human emotions—only in a doggy way. She held my heart captive and brought such a feeling of joy. I couldn't be jealous that she was settling on Steph's lap because at the end of the night, she would come home with me. Kind of like a wife. The difference was my dog would always come home. Always.

The wife—not so much.

CHAPTER EIGHT

"Mmmm, mmmm, mmm." Mabel sniffed my face as she moaned.

"Mabel," I whined back at my little ball of fluff. "This is the time I'm not so sure having a dog was the best decision." I rolled over and scratched her ears. She did what she always did. She flipped onto her back and gave me her belly which I obligately rubbed.

"Mmmm, mmmm, mmm," came the high-pitched whine once again, and I knew there was no way to prolong my stay in bed, so I threw on a pair of sweats, a hoodie, and sneakers, and off we went for a walk.

The morning air was so crisp and when I took several deep breaths, I realized it truly was a cleansing feeling. I had always loved being outdoors, but waking up to it every morning was a special treat. No cars whizzing by hurrying to get to work on time. In fact, I didn't have to get in a car and drive if I didn't want to. That alone gave me a sense of tranquility. I didn't have to drive in traffic, mad it wasn't moving, while running work projects through my mind for the day as I waited for the people in their cars to find their gas pedals.

I had tried to sleep in, but Mabel and I had become accustomed to getting up by six thirty every morning. It was also the time I had risen to go to work for thirty-five years, so I still woke up at that hour, totally awake and ready for the day. I called it a routine habit existence. RHE. (Acronyms were popular in police departments.)

"I guess we're two peas in a pod," I said, smiling down at Mabel and handing her a treat. Thank God Tess didn't argue about who had parental rights over the dog. She knew from the beginning that Mabel was always my dog. I fed her, I walked her, and she often showed me more love than Tess did. It was as if Mabel had known Tess wasn't always going to be around for her. God, she was a smart dog. And even if that wasn't the case, I was pretty sure Tess believed I would need Mabel more than her. After all, the new chick-a-doo would fill her emotional void. I chuckled. Where did my brain come up with that one? Chick-a-doo. Oh well, better than calling her a home-wrecker.

Back at the trailer, I pondered over whether Steph coming over for breakfast yesterday might turn into a daily thing. Knowing her as I did, I assumed it would and set about preparing breakfast for Mabel and Steph and me. It was past seven and if Steph was still as much a morning person as I was, she would soon be over. Myra and Jen were not morning people. They were night people and when the campfire was at their trailer, they often sat by it long after we left. If they wanted breakfast, I didn't expect them to show until we were sitting down for the morning meal. Like they did the day before, if they showed up at all.

By the time I had the batter ready for pancakes, and the frying pan warmed, there was a knock on my door. I opened it to Steph's smiling face. She held up a cup of coffee as I chuckled. "Just in time to help with breakfast. I see you'll be contributing coffee to the morning meals?" I took the cup and sniffed. "Wow, this has a great aroma."

"A new Cuban coffee I'm trying." Then she held up a bag of groceries. "As promised," she said and settled on the recliner next to the one Mabel had already claimed.

"Thank you." I set the bag on the counter and continued to stir the batter. "How about we talk menus while we eat? I've run out of ideas for breakfast. Not my favorite meal. I just know you have to eat it."

"Who told you that?"

"They did."

"Who's they?" She was starting a morning round of teasing.

"You know, they. The they that tell you what to do, what not to do, what's healthy for you, blah, blah, blah."

"Oh," she drawled. "Those they. Oh, that sounded weird. Or is it that they? Or the they?"

"You can be such a turd." I snorted, and we both laughed. "How about you get the plates, silverware, butter, and syrup?"

"Oh, man, are you gonna make me work for my breakfast, too?" She stood up and started opening the cupboards.

I watched her as she bent down, stood up, turned, and reached. She wore a pair of dark-blue jean shorts with a pale-green T-shirt. Her movements were fluid yet strong, and I could see her muscles contract and stretch like a muscle ballet. The message on the front of her shirt was *Happy Camper*, and I had to laugh, she was so damn cute. I continued to watch her as she made her way back to the recliner and picked up Mabel, cooing to her and nuzzling her nose.

I almost burned the pancakes watching her, so I focused on the rest of the batter, listening to her converse with my dog in the cutest baby talk I had ever heard. "Okay, we're ready to eat," I said, carrying the plate of pancakes over to the table. Then I got the bowl of sliced pineapple, grapes, melon, and blueberries. "Is this acceptable for your breakfast, madam?"

She was piling pancakes on her plate. "Most definitely. Anytime I don't have to cook, it's acceptable."

I handed her a small bowl of fruit. "Ahh, I'll remember that. You'll still have to clean up and do the dishes."

"I can handle that." She grinned.

"There are still the pans. And silverware. And bowls..."

"Okay, I get it," she interrupted. "But it's nothing like a full-blown dinner on porcelain."

"Who uses porcelain anymore? It's Corelle all the way. The pans still have to be washed and there is no dishwasher," I pointed out by focusing my eyes on her with a *Do you get my message here* gaze.

She put her hands up in surrender. "I'm the dishwasher. I get it."

"Good. I'm glad we've got that straight." I giggled.

"So, what's on your docket for today?" Steph asked, pointing her empty fork toward me.

"Nothing. Why? What do you have in mind?"

"Well, you're retired and I'm on leave, so we're free women. Let's take a leisurely stroll through the farmers' market and then down to The Commons. We can grab lunch and then buy some frivolous lights for our trailers…"

"Oh no, I put my foot down on that one."

"Which one?" She cocked her head in curiosity. "I thought you'd like to spend the day eating and shopping."

"Not that. The one about the frivolous lights. I am not hanging any lights that look like trailers, insects, or cans of beer on my trailer. Or pink flamingos."

Steph stood up and collected the plates. "It doesn't have to be anything like that. You, Miss Snooty, can hang simple Christmas lights."

"It's not Christmas and they're not so simple anymore," I said under my breath as she carried everything to the counter.

"Oh," she scoffed. "You are no fun. Whatever. I bet if we look long enough, you'll find something you like. You need to dress the outside of this baby up to make it look like you are an actual seasonal camper, and Mabel needs a little fenced-in yard." She walked back to where Mabel lounged on the recliner and petted her. "Don't you, baby." Then she looked at me, her eyes wide with enthusiasm at the prospect of a major makeover project. "You can put potted flowers around the perimeter, or better yet, make some gardens. Just stay within Mac's rules." She laughed.

"Oh no, no, no, no, no. That's too much work. I'm not here to work. I'm here to relax and have fun." But I smiled when I said it because Steph was adorable. Her cheeks were rosy red and her eyes sparkled. How could I not smile? I still wasn't going to do it, but I might let her fancy up my site a little.

* * *

The farmers' market was located off of Route 13. Buildings housed booths that sold vegetables, pastries, crafts, clothes, jewelry, wine, beer, liquor, and whatever else anyone wanted to sell and could get a space in which to do it. It was a popular place where you could get a good cup of coffee and a pastry.

But the seasonal and holiday items were the best—handcrafted ghosts and skeletons, turkeys and Santa Clauses. Every type of decoration you could think of lined the shelves and hung from the openings of the seller's booth. With a cheese danish and coffee in hand, we strolled down the crowded aisles and found only one booth with holiday decorations solely for the Fourth of July. Steph kept dragging me toward the display, hoping I would fall in love with the red, white, and blue outdoor lights.

But it didn't happen. What did happen was a wonderful morning spent with my best friend, laughing and talking and even discussing future dreams now and then. Like travel. We both talked about traveling out west to see all the national parks and taking trips to different countries. I stole glances in her direction often, thinking that having this tall drink of water by my side while traveling would be a great way to see the world. For a brief indulging moment, my mind pictured us hiking Glacier National Park hand in hand... Hand in hand. I shook my head. Damn, what was I thinking? Friends don't walk hand in hand unless they're helping each other over an enormous boulder or something like that.

We were friends. I was mourning my marriage, and I had no right to go anywhere other than friendship with Steph. I scolded myself, and for the rest of the day concentrated on enjoying the time with the best friend one could ever have. We eventually left the farmers' market and settled on Red's Place on The Commons for lunch, where Steph and I tried the Lickin' Chicken mac and cheese and pesto bread. Not the healthiest meal, but sometimes you just have to go beyond the healthy boundaries, so we also succumbed to a beer and a very chocolaty cake for dessert. We window-shopped, entering a store here and there, sipping a cold lemonade, and finally settled on a street bench to people-watch. I was in the middle of telling Steph about the latest in my divorce proceedings when I realized she wasn't listening. Her face had gone white, as if she felt ill from eating too much. Her usually bright gray-green eyes became dark and intense. I watched her supple lips thin into hard, straight lines, and her eyebrows narrow in anger. Her complexion, no longer white, reddened.

I followed the direction of her stare and immediately felt her hands turn my head away.

"What the hell? What's wrong?" I asked, worming my way around her to see what she was staring at that disturbed her so much. Walking toward us on the other side of The Commons, and thank God they hadn't noticed us, was my ex-wife and who I suspected was her new woman. "Oh, we need to go. I have no desire to see or be seen by her," I snapped and stood.

Steph gently pulled on my hand, forcing me to sit back down. "They're too much into their conversation to notice us, but if you stomp away, I'm sure they will. Let's just be still until they pass."

So, we were. It took everything I had to sit still. I wanted to run over and give her a new asshole. I wanted to scream, "How could you?" And there was a small part of me that wanted to punch that lustful smile off of her face, if it was, in fact, a lusting expression. I really couldn't tell from where we sat, but it didn't matter. I could never hit her. It wasn't in my nature, except as a cop if the need arose.

When I chanced another look, I could have sworn the other woman was looking in my direction, sneering. I wasn't sure if I was imagining it or if she had caught sight of me. There was no way she knew who I was, so why would she sneer at me? And again, from that distance, I couldn't be sure it was a sneer.

So, I sat with my head turned away from them, holding back my brimming tears. I could see Steph struggling. I wasn't sure why because her expression was mixed. She also looked surprised. And angry. And when she finally looked at me, she looked sympathetic.

When the couple was finally far enough away from us that they wouldn't see or hear us, I watched as my friend's face fell into a look of indignation.

"That bitch!" she exclaimed. "Or should I say, those bitches!"

CHAPTER NINE

"Oh, my God. If it wasn't my cheating ex-wife with her new mistress, I'd say you were overreacting. Still, don't you think you are? Just a bit? I mean, she didn't do anything to you," I said, confused by her verbal retaliation.

She took my hand and dragged me in the other direction. She spoke while we walked. "Oh, it's not just your cheating wife. It's the hussy she's with."

"Hussy? You know the other woman?" I stopped and almost tripped over my own two feet because she didn't stop and she still had my hand. "Stop and talk to me," I insisted, yanking on her hand. I pulled hard, forcing her to turn and look at me.

She took a deep breath. "The hussy your ex-wife is with is Lori."

I stared at Steph, confusion plaguing my thoughts until the name sank in. It made sense. The woman was looking at Steph. Not me. My eyes widened. "*Your* Lori?" I asked incredulously. "The one you broke up with?"

"That would be the one." She looked off to the side and then up at the sky with her hands on her hips.

"You won't find the answer up there," I said. Then I added, "I'm sorry."

Slowly, her eyes met mine. "You're sorry. What the hell are you sorry for?"

"I don't know." My voice had a kind of whiny drawl to it. "I don't think I can wrap my head around this, but I'm not sure I want to even try."

"I knew she was cheating," Steph said.

When I looked at her, my heart broke seeing the defeat in her expression, and I wondered why she would be feeling defeated and upset. It was my wife who cheated. Of course, my friend would be sad about it, but not devastated. I put a hand on her shoulder. "It's okay. I'm okay. There's no reason to get so angry over it."

"You don't understand."

"What's there to understand? My wife cheated on me. Not you. And I'm okay. I'm getting over it. Shouldn't you?"

"Walk with me," she answered.

She didn't wait for my answer and began walking again. I wasn't sure where we were walking to because the car was in the other direction. I hoped she wasn't searching out a bar. We walked for a while without speaking. Pressing her into speaking never worked. It only made her frustrated and sometimes angry like a bull staring down a red cloak, if you forced her to discuss something before she was ready.

"That's why I broke up with Lori," she finally began. "When we first got together, she was great. We had a lot of fun. She seemed smart and kind." Steph nodded her head toward me. "She even cooked for me. But then…"

"Then what?"

"Then I saw the signs of a cheater. You know—when they're on their phone and they don't want you to look at it. They stumble on their answer when you ask who it is."

"Or they tell you it's none of your business," I added sullenly, remembering the day I walked into the bedroom, and Tess was on her phone speaking in hushed tones. I asked her who it was, and she jumped. Plainly, I had surprised her. She said, "It's none of your business," and I knew…I knew my wife was cheating. Our marriage was heading for a big drop over Niagara Falls and neither of us would be in the barrel.

"Yeah," said Steph. "They stop calling as much and they have excuses why they can't spend time with you. I just never in a million years would have even entertained the thought that the woman she was cheating with was Tess."

I sighed. "Yep. It does kind of suck." I put an arm around her shoulder. "But there's nothing we can or I want to do about it. I'm sorry that your ex is with my ex. It hurts all around."

We walked another block when she finally said, "I'm not so much hurt for myself as I am for you. If I had known that Lori was seeing Tess, I would have told you. I would have reamed her out." She pulled away from me. "Damn it, I wish I had known."

"It wouldn't have changed anything. I hate to say the saying that I really hate, but…" I stopped Steph, turned her to face me, and put my hands on her shoulders. "It is what it is. And what it is, is that we need to move on. We've got our friends. We've got each other. What more do we need?"

She hugged me and I felt the soft shake of her shoulders as tears ran down her cheeks, wetting mine as well. "Mabel," she said through muffled cries. "We need Mabel too."

I smiled. "Yes," I said. "We need Mabel too."

* * *

Back at the campground, we joined Myra and Jen on their deck for happy hour. Myra had mixed a light margarita for us in glasses rimmed with sea salt and a wedge of lemon.

We explained our afternoon adventure in The Commons to exclamations of "Oh my God, no way, and I don't believe it." The consensus all round was to let it go, move on, and don't focus on the negative, but on the positive.

I believed that as well, but something stuck in my craw. It was the look that Lori had thrown our way. It had to be directed to Steph, but why would she have such negative feelings toward her? Lori was the one who cheated. I also believed she didn't know who I was unless Tess had shown her a picture of me. But that was doubtful. I hadn't seen Tess since she walked out the door three months ago. For me, it was done and over with.

Still, Lori's expression bothered me. I was well aware that Steph broke up with Lori and the sneer might have been toward her for that reason. It just had the feeling of more than you-broke-up-with-me anger. The look sent prickles all the way down to my bone marrow, and I wondered if there was something more to it. I didn't know why there would be. She got the girl. There was no reason to taunt me because I made no move to get Tess back. I let her go. (Not that I had any choice in the matter.)

"Tell me more about Lori," I said. I was petting Mabel absentmindedly, which allowed me to think more clearly, to put thoughts together logically and come up with an answer or a solution. It was a process I had used all the years as a profiler, and it worked ninety-nine percent of the time.

"What do you want to know?"

"Everything. Her full name, where she comes from, her job, her education, and her parents. Everything."

"I don't know that much. Her full name is Lori Smith."

"Lori Smith," I repeated, using a tone that said "Are you kidding me?"

Steph looked at me questioningly. "Yeah, why?"

I shook my head. It wasn't just the profiler in me that was always skeptical about the name Smith. "The guy lurking around the campground?"

"You think they're related? No way. I mean, not that I know of."

"Okay, I'm sorry. Go on."

"I'm embarrassed to say I don't know as much as I should have. We only dated for about four months, but she was never forthcoming with me. She held a lot back, and I didn't force it. I thought it might be because she had an awful childhood or something like that. She did say she was from a small town in New York. I never asked which one. She said she didn't go to college. She worked from home as a customer service rep for some Internet company. She didn't offer up the name and I never questioned it. It was too early in the relationship to discuss how much money she made, or if could we combine our lives. That's all I know." She stared at the deck floor. "Maybe that's always been the problem with me and relationships. I spend too much time having a good time and not enough trying to get to know the woman I'm dating."

I reached out to Steph, and she took my hand. "You don't have to apologize for that. You don't always know if the woman you're dating is being upfront and truthful with you."

"None of us always do the right thing when it comes to relationships," Myra said. "You do the best you can do."

"You got a beer for your landlord?"

My stomach lurched. I was not interested in entertaining our illustrious campground owner, Officer Nasty.

Steph immediately dropped my hand. It surprised me because it wasn't like we were in a relationship or anything. We were sharing a warmhearted moment between friends and that shouldn't have made a difference. But it did, and she dropped my hand anyway. But I knew Steph didn't like to display physical contact with another lesbian in public. One time I had tossed an arm around her at a crowded winery. She gently pushed me aside, so I was careful about touching her in public. It bothered me and I hoped she had gotten over it. Obviously, she hadn't.

Jen pulled a beer out of the cooler that sat behind her chair and handed it to Mac.

"So, how you ladies doing today? What? You're not good enough to join the rest of us for happy hour at Frank's place?" Frank and his wife, Mona, had the park model that faced the camp store. They had added on decks, canopies, a bar and grilling station and were hosts to happy hour every day.

"It was kind of crowded when I walked by," Myra answered. "And we hadn't eaten yet. So we decided to just lie low here for the evening. There will be plenty of happy hours at Frank's for the rest of the season."

Mac took a sip from the Genny beer bottle. He choked and almost spat it out, swallowing hard and grimacing, trying hard to to give away his distaste of the beer. I kept my eyes down to keep from laughing or making a derogatory comment. I had to keep control because I still wanted to talk to him about escorting Manson Smith from the campground. Part of me didn't want to know because if what he had done pissed me off, I wouldn't be nice about it. That scared me. Scared that a small part of me that wanted revenge—to have concrete proof that he had been and still was unfit to be on the police force. But getting angry would do nothing for me, and was it worth it thirty years later?

"So how's landlord life treating you?" Steph asked.

"I think I'm gonna like it here. Nothing like the fresh air to keep you going. Did you lovely ladies get a chance to read the new rules?

There's a few that will apply to your campsites, so make sure you read them. I'll start enforcing them next week."

We looked at each other. Yup, being lord and laird over a bunch of people was definitely making him happy.

Myra leaned forward and whispered, "Did you read them?" She directed the question to all of us. In response, we shook our heads. Myra looked over at Mac, who was tapping the steering wheel while leaning slightly to the outside of the golf cart so he could inconspicuously pour the beer out of the bottle onto the side of the road. Talk about no manners.

"Yes, sir, officer. We're all set," Myra answered him, tipping her glass toward him and nodding once.

Mac jerked up straight, most likely afraid he had been caught. Now he leaned toward the side closest to us with both arms on the steering wheel. "If that was the case, you wouldn't have those potted plants along the road. You better read them. There are consequences for breaking the rules. Always are." He turned on the motor and looked at us again. "Consequences." He grinned. "Night, ladies. Thanks for the, uh, beer." He drove away, his cockiness lingering in the air.

"I'll bet you he's levied fines on his rules," Jen said. "Guess we better read them."

Myra stood. "Well, I'm in for a good laugh. How about I go get the new landlord's rule sheet and we can read them together?"

I nodded. "Sitting here reading them and critiquing his directives will be much more fun than having to read them as bedtime material."

"Yeah, it might give you nightmares," Steph said.

I stuck my tongue out.

Myra walked out of the trailer, reading the paper in her hand. "Oh, here's what he was talking about. We can have potted plants, but they have to be three feet back from the road."

"Where did you get a copy of his rules?" I asked.

"It was stuck in our trailer door. Didn't you get one?" Myra held it out so I could see the bold and large lettered title that announced Mac's Rules.

"He must have skipped me."

"Yeah, he probably planned that. Mac is most likely wringing his hands together in anticipation of you not following the rules so he can fine you." Steph chuckled.

Again, I stuck my tongue out. "So, what else does the lord and master want of us?" I asked.

Myra continued reading. "Only two cars per campsite. Any stone or mulch used must be approved by filling out a form on the website. No new build, like decks, unless approved through the same form. No cooking in the campfires."

"What?" Jen sat up in the front of her chair. "This guy is bordering on, on…"

"Stupid? Control freak? Killer of camping activities?"

Steph laughed. "That's a good one, Blake."

"We all cook in the campfires. What? Is he banning roasting marshmallows? No more s'mores? That is the foundation of camping. What is he, a camping God?" Jen was on the verge of a total camping meltdown.

"Calm down, babe. I guess we're going to have to ask him to clarify that one," Myra said.

"Is there more?" I asked, curious about this jerk's rules.

"Most of it is the same rules we've always had. Quiet time at ten, pick up after your dog, and this new one: no using picnic tables for firewood…"

"Really? He added that about the picnic tables?" Steph asked.

"Oh God, will we be able to put up with this guy?" Jen asked.

"We don't have a choice this year. But next year…" Myra said, her voice trailing off, most likely thinking about the logistics of having to move to a different campground, but it was too much to think about on only the second day of our season.

"Ya think there's any way we can all get along?" I asked sarcastically.

Steph spit out the drink she just put in her mouth, and Jen and Myra laughed.

"Okay. That's definitely the pot calling the kettle black," Steph said through her laughter.

"I know," I moaned. "But I just got here. I was looking forward to a nice, quiet summer of fun and frivolity."

Everyone laughed and then Myra said to me, "You can still have that kind of summer, you know. We all can."

"Maybe. Maybe not," Steph replied for me.

I looked at Steph and she shrugged her shoulders. Maybe. Maybe not.

* * *

I left my friends' campsite feeling apprehensive. I didn't want Mac, a.k.a. Officer Taylor, a.k.a. Officer Nasty, to pull me back to the defeated, miserable woman I was when I was his rookie. I hated my job back then. I hated myself. But I fought hard to keep reminding myself that he was in charge of me and because of that it wasn't me I really hated. I hated how he treated me, his opinion of me, his superior attitude toward rookies—especially female rookies. Things were different then. I was different. Women hid in the shadows, afraid to take a stand because they had seen the outcome time and time again and it wasn't in our favor. But now, we didn't hide anymore. We stood tall and fought for our rights.

After I left Ithaca, I had put in the effort at my job every day to excel—sometimes at the expense of my relationship. Then I spent years working hard to get degrees in the field I chose taking more time away from my relationship. The result was respect, promotions, and a decent salary, giving me more than an adequate pension for retirement. And the end of my marriage. If I had to admit it, which I would, I was pretty sure that contributed to my wife getting disillusioned with our union.

After I retired, my commanding officer had asked if I would be interested in being a consultant for the department when they needed help. I agreed, but not until the summer was over. I wanted time to decompress, time to figure out where I was in my personal life and where I wanted to go. I believed I wanted a relationship in my life at some point. When I was ready. But the dating scene? Scared. The. Shit out of me. Would I be happy just being by myself, filling my emotional needs with friends and the few relatives I had left? Steph often told me about her experiences with dating websites. The horrors she described scared me more than a lot of the criminals I profiled.

With Mabel, I might be all right. If anything contributed to my emotional well-being to a point that kept me from total depression, it was my dog. Her short tail, which wagged like a tree branch in hurricane-force winds every time I arrived home, was a beacon in the darkness. Talking to her in the baby doggie talk most dog owners used brought me out of any bleak mood I was feeling. Every time I looked at her cute salt-and-pepper ears and head, and her big blue eyes, there was no way I couldn't smile. It was instinctive, innate. It was cause and effect. Mabel was the cause. My smile was always the effect.

Mabel and I made our way slowly across the field for her last walk of the day. I stopped when I noticed a car parked at my campsite. I swallowed hard because I knew the vehicle and I knew who drove it.

Why was she at my campsite?

CHAPTER TEN

Why would Tess just show up like this?

I took a deep breath. If she was sitting at the picnic table, she would see me coming. I needed to prepare myself to see her. I took a few more deep breaths and picked up Mabel. "Time to work, girl. Do your thing. Keep me grounded. Okay?" She licked my nose, and I did what came naturally. I smiled. Despite the twirly things my stomach was doing, she calmed me enough to enter my campsite instead of bolting in the other direction. Tess leaving me had taken my self-confidence and instilled a fear of confrontation in my personal life. I wasn't afraid of seeing her, I just didn't want to.

Her head popped up from her phone when she heard me. *Probably texting her girlfriend.*

"Hey, I wasn't sure you were coming back. I thought you might have seen me from Jen and Myra's place, but your back was to me. I didn't want to interrupt, so I waited here."

Had Jen and Myra noticed Tess's car? Did Steph? If any of them did see Tess or her car, why didn't they say so? In the long run, I guessed it didn't matter, except it might have given me a little more time to prepare for the confrontation.

"Why are you here?" It was abrupt and impolite, but I didn't care. I needed her to go.

"I want to talk to you."

"If it's about the divorce, anything you have to say can come through the lawyers."

She gestured to the picnic table. "It's not. Please. It won't take long."

I put Mabel down and sat opposite her, even though she gestured to a spot on the bench next to her.

As Mabel walked by, she reached out to pet her. "Hey, girl. How've you been? I miss you."

My stomach churned. I didn't want to hear how much she missed Mabel. Mostly because I didn't want the next statement to be she missed me too. But it came anyway.

She looked at me with that gentle smile that had melted my heart the first time I met her. "I miss you too."

I felt my lightweight margherita trying to conga up my esophagus. I sat down and picked Mabel up, settling her on my lap. Then I lifted my head and focused on Tess's face. She looked the same, but different. I couldn't put my finger on it. "I saw you today. At The Commons," I said. Her face grew as white as the quarter moon, matching the contrast of the moon's bright surface against a black sky. I added, "With your new woman. Lori, I think her name is?"

"I'm no longer with her. She called me to talk and suggested we meet there. She's having a hard time accepting our breakup, and I felt sorry for her. I think I used her. She didn't deserve it, so I came down to talk. That's all we did."

"I don't care."

She swallowed hard. "I really do miss you. I'm so sorry for what I did to you. To us. I was so disillusioned with our relationship, but you didn't deserve that."

I had nothing to say, so I simply replied, "Okay. Is that it?"

She flinched, which made me feel a tiny bit guilty for being so insolent, but it passed as quickly as it came over me. Her face twisted in what appeared to be a struggle over what her next words would be.

"Do you think you could forgive me?"

"That'll take some time," I replied. "Probably. Eventually. Definitely not now."

"But what if I said I wanted to come back? To work on our relationship."

"That would be a no." I watched as her face dropped, but I didn't feel any remorse, and I knew I would never change my mind. I believed there was no going back. How could I?

A tear fell down her cheek and her voice cracked when she said, "Don't you love me?"

I adjusted my butt on the hard bench and looked down at Mabel while I scratched her head, thinking how I wanted to answer. When I looked back at Tess, she was staring up at me with sympathetic eyes. At least, that was how they made me feel. "I did, more than anyone, and I think you know that." I sighed heavily. "But you broke that love and it's dissipated over time with the thoughts of what you did and what I've had to go through with the impending divorce."

"We can stop the divorce. I'll do whatever I have to to make it up to you." Now the soft and tender facial features I had fallen in love with that held me captive for twenty-five years fell into a look of despair.

I took a moment to study my ex-wife. She wore a pair of jeans that looked baggy. She never wore baggy jeans, always choosing clothes that showed off her voluptuous curves—probably because I told her how sexy she looked every time she wore a pair of tight pants. It suddenly dawned on me why she looked different. Loose fitting pants and hollow cheeks screamed major weight loss. Should I feel sorry? Maybe I would someday, but I couldn't muster it today. "Look, Tess. I'm okay where I am, and I want to stay here. I can't go back. Ever. You made sure of that."

I knew my words stung her. I watched her body stiffen, and then her throat moved as she swallowed her next words.

"Besides, you've got a new woman." I hadn't wanted to say that, but I did, even though she just told me they broke up. I had no idea what I expected from it except I knew the reason I said it. The professional part of me—the cop, investigator, profiler was searching for information. Had she loved this new woman? If not, why did she do it? Had it been worth it to break up a twenty-five-year marriage? The why would nag me for a long time. I could have just asked her, but maybe I didn't want to hear the answer.

She got up, now a run of tears streaming down her cheeks. She took her keys out of the pine-green, lightweight jacket I bought her on the last birthday we celebrated together. Then she looked at me, not holding back her weeping. "I…really am…sorry. I still love you. If…you change…your mind. You know where I am." She choked on the last words.

I took a slow breath. "Actually," I replied. "I don't." She started to speak, but I cut her off. "And I'd like to keep it that way."

Tess didn't reply, and she didn't hesitate. She got in her car quicker than a chipmunk speed-crawling into their hole when it was being chased by a predator. Even in the darkness, I could tell she was fumbling with her key to get it into the ignition. I waited until she pulled away, knowing how hard it would be for her to keep her vehicle at the five-mile-per-hour speed limit.

I felt sorry for her. I felt sorry for myself, and it made me mad. I didn't care that she broke up with Lori. Part of me screamed it served her right. But did the part of me that still clung to a lost love care about her current relationship status?

I couldn't let it.

* * *

I sat in my recliner with Mabel on my lap and watched a movie. Mabel's head popped up, and she whined as she looked at the door. She may not have been a large watchdog that would bite a chunk out of an intruder's leg, but she was a great foreseer. I never knew how she did it, but she knew when someone was about to knock before they ever did. Her senses were one hundred times better than mine and, as a cop, I thought mine were pretty damn good. True to her alert, there was a knock on my door. I rolled my eyes, hoping it wasn't Tess returning for another round. Then I heard Steph's voice.

"It's Steph. Let me in, please?" That wasn't the usual way of greeting, but Steph had a slight urgency in her voice.

I opened the door. She wore a pair of sweatpants with a pullover sweatshirt and her indoor slippers. Her clothes were wrinkled, looking as if she hurried to dress putting on whatever was in the dirty clothes hamper. Then there were the slippers. Steph never wore her slippers outside. She rushed past me and I closed the door, debated a second, and locked it.

"Hey, what's going on?" I asked.

"Didn't Mac say his cop friends showed that guy the way home?"

"Yeah, why?" I drawled out the word *why*, not wanting to have the answer I knew I was going to hear confirmed.

"Someone was outside my trailer tonight. I heard them, but I didn't see them well enough. I can't say for sure it was that guy again. Whoever it was wore dark clothing and moved too fast into the shadows for me to tell."

"Damn. We'll need to tell Mac tomorrow. You want to stay here tonight?"

"I can protect myself," Steph said, with her arms folded around her.

"I never said you couldn't, but it's always nice having someone else there to help if need be. Look at me. I'm alone, and I wouldn't mind the help. Besides, then I won't need to find a lawyer to defend you from shooting someone. Even if it is in self-defense. And…" I didn't finish my sentence because the last thing I wanted to do was to make her angry at me.

"You don't have to say it. I'm on probation right now. Shooting someone, for whatever reason, would probably end my job. So, yeah, I'd like to stay here if that's all right."

"Of course it is. I won't even make you sleep in the booth. We can share the bed." I turned off the outdoor lights and sat in the recliner. Mabel jumped up on my lap once again, keeping her eyes on Steph. "You can crash or finish watching the movie with me."

Steph made herself comfortable in the other recliner, pulling the fleece blanket off the back and covering herself up. "What movie are you watching?"

"The last *Avengers* movie. *Endgame*. I never got to the theater to see it. I'd rather see it on a big screen, but it's a bit late for that now."

"Oh, man. You missed a good movie. It's much better on the big screen. There's one particular scene toward the end when the whole theater whooped and clapped."

I put my hand up. "Don't tell me."

"Oh, no way, you have to see it."

I pressed play, and the movie came to life on the small television set in a cabinet above the booth. We watched in silence. I was pretty sure her thoughts were the same as mine. Was that guy back? And why was he lurking around Steph's trailer? I hadn't seen or heard anything around my camper, but I knew we'd have to speak to Mac in the morning.

Steph fell asleep before the movie ended. I knew how much she liked the Marvel movies, making me wonder if she was having sleepless nights because of this guy. I didn't want her to sleep in the recliner all night. She'd have kinks in every joint when she woke, so I gently shook her shoulder. A grin appeared on her lips, but her eyes remained closed.

"Come to bed," I said. "These recliners may be comfortable for watching television, but they aren't for sleeping."

"Mmm, mm," was all I received. She tossed the blanket aside and walked toward the bed. "Which side?"

I pointed to the far side, and she walked around the bed, pulled down the covers, and climbed in. She rolled on her side facing the center of the bed. I lifted Mabel onto the comforter, and she immediately settled into the crook of Steph's stomach. I watched, smiling. I missed having another woman in my bed. Someone to cuddle with. Someone who, when you woke from nightmares, would comfort you. I missed the feel of a woman's body—curves at every turn where soft skin ran down the length of limbs and torso. Steph had those curves and soft skin. She had a sweet smile and kindness that made your heart feel safe and valued.

And then I hit myself in the head. I was looking at Steph, not Tess. Steph was my friend, and I was still working through a divorce and my negative emotions toward my cheating wife, who was just here a few hours earlier. What was I thinking? I took a deep breath and released it slowly. It would be nice to sleep next to a woman even if it was only my friend and only for one night, and I couldn't touch her in the way I wanted to.

And then I realized she hadn't seen Tess's car because she didn't ask about it. And Steph would always ask.

CHAPTER ELEVEN

I woke to the smell of coffee. And bacon. I flung my arm over to the side of the bed Steph had slept in, hoping it was empty, because if she was there, then I was still in the bad dream that had plagued my sleep. I dreamt that Steph was in bed next to me while Manson Smith was cooking us breakfast. How warped was that? When my fingers felt the cool, empty spot, I knew it was Steph who was cooking. I was so relieved.

Not only had Steph vacated the bed, Mabel was gone, too. I opened my eyes to see Steph busy in the kitchen, stirring something in a bowl. Mabel was eating. Wow, I realized there was more I missed than just sleeping with a woman.

"Good morning," I called to her.

She looked up. Her hair wasn't combed and the clothes she had shown up in the previous night and also slept in looked like a car had run over them several times. But it was the best sight I had seen in a long while.

"Good morning. Your coffee is ready, sleepyhead, and I'm about to make the omelets, so you better get your ass out of that bed."

"Yes, ma'am," I teased.

She went back to stirring. "Oh, and Mabel has been out and, as you can see, is eating. Do you want orange juice?"

"That would be great, but let me get it." I changed quickly into a pair of shorts and a pullover, socks, and slippers. I was pouring glasses of orange juice and setting the table to Steph humming "Tomorrow" from *Annie*. It made me chuckle, and then I joined her in the chorus. We sang at the top of our lungs, throwing our arms out to the side like two Broadway divas. And then we laughed.

We sat to a deliciously prepared breakfast—tasty cheese and mushroom omelets with toast—and discussed what we should do about the prowler near her trailer. We agreed to speak to Mac together. With Steph by my side, he might reveal a little more about the man's exit from the campground. And Mac might also know the current status of Mr. Smith. But something deep inside made me nervous. What if it wasn't Manson Smith? What if someone else was roaming around the campground at all hours of the night? Or maybe it was just a large animal.

When we finished, I offered to walk Steph back, using the ruse that I had to take Mabel on her morning walk, even though Steph already had, but she would have said no if I simply offered to walk her back. "Mabel likes a lot of walks and she also likes to go that way."

Steph folded her arms. "I was just going to cut across the field."

"Oh, okay," I answered, a bit dejected. "What time do you want to go up and see Mac?"

"It's Monday. I'm not sure he's here. From what Greg told me, he'll only be here on the weekends and a few nights during the week until he retires and is here full time."

I raised my arm and twirled my index finger. "Yay for us." I knew my sarcasm was my specialty and sometimes, my escape, but sometimes I just couldn't help it. She slugged me in the shoulder and walked out the door with me and Mabel following. "So, do you know what nights he's going to be here?"

"He's coming back tonight for happy hour. It's the Millers' fortieth anniversary and you know how Sandy is about celebrating."

"If I remember from previous visits, it should be a superb drunken fest," I said.

"You got that right, but it will make it easier to talk to him in a crowd. He won't be able to be as rude as he usually is. Remember to bring your own glass of liquid or you'll be handed several with very strong alcoholic drinks in them."

"Got it." At the road, I turned left and waited for Steph, but she continued across the field. "I'll see you later?" I called to her, kind of asking if that was a possibility.

"As you can see by my appearance, there is a much needed shower and some clean clothes calling to me. After that, I've got errands to do. So, I'll catch ya later."

"Sounds good," I answered as I proceeded with my morning walk, feeling my heart sink in disappointment.

"Thank you," I heard from behind me.

I didn't turn. I waved a hand and called back, "Anytime. And thank you for breakfast."

I kept my eyes open as I walked. Although I knew stalkers didn't usually do their thing during the daylight hours, I was being cautious remembering catching sight of Smith the other day in the bushes. I felt the leash pull and knew we weren't far from Steph's trailer, where a clump of thick bushes and trees caught Mabel's attention. She dug her paws in so she couldn't be budged from her exploration with her nose unless I forcefully yanked her away. If I did, it deflated her Napoleon complex.

Peering into the brush, I couldn't see far and wondered if this was where Manson Smith had spent time hiding. And if it was, why? Did he know two of the trailers on this side had lesbians in them?

Not seeing anything unsettling in the bushes, I began walking again. When we passed by Steph's trailer, Mabel pulled in that direction, but I kept her on the road. "Come on, girl. We can't stop. She didn't seem to want to spend the day with us. We'll see her later." I briefly wondered if Steph was experiencing any of the same feelings I was feeling toward her. If she was, she wasn't showing it. Or maybe she was running from it. Maybe it was time I checked out the dating sites she had suggested to me.

The third trailer from Steph's was Jen and Myra's, and it surprised me to see Myra outside sitting in a chair on their deck. She must have heard me coming because she looked up. "Good morning, girl. Come have a seat." She lifted one of the two mugs sitting on a small table. "And a coffee."

"No thanks," I replied as I walked over to the empty chair.

"I just poured it. It's nice and hot. Cream and sugar. Just the way you like it."

I took it from her hand and cocked my head.

She smiled. "I saw you leave your trailer with Steph."

I sat down and waited for Mabel to jump in my lap, but she settled at my feet. The coffee was rich and hot, comforting in a warm consoling kind of way.

"So what's up? You're normally not outside this early," I asked her.

Myra's grin was always slightly crooked. She had broken her jaw in high school during a basketball game. The result was the cutest grin I had ever seen. Because of its slight slant, you never knew what kind of smile it was that always kept you guessing.

"Jen and I woke up to some noise outside the trailer."

"Steph said the same thing happened late last night near her place."

Myra swallowed. "I know you've kind of banned real life…" I was about to interrupt, but she held a hand up. "For now. You just need to give it time. It will happen. I just want to make sure you're…okay and not doing anything stupid."

I wasn't sure what she meant, so I answered, "Okay," as I felt my throat close and tears water my eyes. God, what was wrong with me? I always dealt with difficult situations in a strong, noncrying manner. She saw me leaving my trailer with Steph, so was she warning me to stay away from her? Or was I reading too much into this. Even when Tess left, I didn't cry. Now I felt like the mere mention of my life's choices or future direction brought tears to my eyes.

I think Myra noticed because she hurried on. "Even though I mentioned it, that's not what I wanted to talk to you about. Jen and I couldn't go back to sleep last night, so we watched the news all morning. Apparently, Manson Smith is missing."

"What? When?"

"Sometime yesterday. He didn't show up for some court-appointed meeting."

I set my mug down and put my head in my hands. "God, even though I thoroughly despise Mac, I sure hope he and his friends had nothing to do with it."

"Whether they did or not, I'd be happy if he wasn't stalking anyone around here."

I looked up. "Just because he's missing doesn't mean it wasn't him last night. He could have come back here, and that's who you both heard. But if something has happened to him, then we have a new problem. If this guy has been gone since yesterday afternoon when Mac and his cronies saw him off, who was lurking around your trailers?"

"You could be right. Maybe he just skipped his court date and came back here to cause trouble. Either way, this isn't good."

"I'm going to have to get more information about Manson Smith's disappearance. Then we'll have a better idea if the person hanging around last night was him or someone else," I surmised.

"That's not all. Yesterday, they found a woman's body in the gorge at Upper Taughannock State Park."

I felt my stomach flip like a gymnast doing a tumbling run across the mat. No way did I want to relive a time in my life that had such a profound effect on me and I wouldn't have to, since I wasn't on the Ithaca police force. There had been no deaths in the gorges of Ithaca for a long time, and the place where they found the body was nowhere near the bridges that college students had jumped from in the 1990s to 2010. So this death was most likely something else.

"What did they say about it on the news?"

"Which one?" Myra asked matter-of-factly, her head tilted slightly and her eyes intent on me.

"Start with Manson Smith," I said in my official profiler's voice.

"There's not much more. He didn't show up, and they went looking for him at his home. They found evidence that he had been there in the morning, so they've put out an APB on him. His wife wasn't there either, so they're looking for her to find out if she saw him."

"Steph and I are going to the happy hour for the Millers' anniversary tonight. She heard Mac will be there and we're going to try to see if we can get any information from him about his altercation with Manson Smith yesterday."

"Do you think the police know about that? Will they question him?"

"I think the only police that know what happened to him are Mac and his buddies. I'm pretty sure they didn't give up any information on Mr. Smith. I also can't imagine they would give each other up even if they did do something illegal."

"Then what makes you think he'll give you any information about getting rid of that guy?"

"He may, he may not. But if there's something he's keeping to himself because it could get him into trouble, I think I'll be able to tell." I asked the next question despite the part of me that didn't want to hear the answer. "And…" I swallowed. "The woman?"

"Again, not much. They know it's a woman, they think, middle-aged. They haven't given a full description." She paused. "I think you know why they're hesitant. I'm guessing they'll have to resort to fingerprints or dental records. They did say she was wearing a pair of faded jeans, black sneakers, and a black sweatshirt. Of course, they aren't saying how she fell."

"Maybe Mac will have information on that as well."

"And then what?" Myra sat upright. "I thought you were retired. Besides, you can't just do your own investigation," she scolded.

"Watch me," I replied.

* * *

After promising Myra I wouldn't do anything that might get me into trouble with the law, or with anyone for that matter, I went back to my trailer. I took a shower, changed into a pair of jeans, and a casual shirt, and gave Mabel her *I'm leaving, but I'll be back* treats on her favorite recliner. I drove out of the campground at exactly five miles per hour. Thank God, I wasn't that far from the main road.

I made my way into the commerce area and parked in the Walmart parking lot on Route 13. I looked in my contacts for my old friend from the IPD, Captain Maddie Spinner. She wasn't a captain back then, but she had worked her way up over the years. I always wondered how she survived the torment of some of the male officers who felt the force was no place for a woman. However, over time, things did change, and I was proud that she was part of those changes.

Maddie, who had been another rookie cop too, helped me through those four years. If it wasn't for her, I would have quit the field and found something else to do—as long as it was not within the law enforcement specialty. She kept me grounded, and when I left, it wasn't because I was disillusioned with law enforcement, only the Ithaca PD. It meant more to me than I could ever tell her because it was she who convinced me that not all police officers were like

Mac Taylor and it would be my love of the work that would keep me from totally walking away. Maddie made me believe that if I worked hard enough, I could find my place in law enforcement. And I did. With much success. She helped me to keep my dream and my father's dream alive.

I tapped Maddie's phone number and waited.

"Oh, my God. How long has it been?" Her voice was just as smoothly baritone-deep as it had been thirty years ago. It was such a contradiction in such a beautiful female. A tall body, courtesy of long slender legs, and long, silky blond hair. She was the portrait of a runway model. She always kept her hair in a bun, but when she let it loose, it framed a picture-perfect face with the smoothest skin I'd ever seen. But the most intoxicating thing about her was her deep-green eyes with specs of light in the irises that made them look like a marble I had when I was a kid.

"Too long. I'm sorry I don't stay in touch better."

"Christmas cards and an occasional call were fine. We both had our lives to live and if yours was as busy as mine, totally understandable." Her reply was monotone, faraway as if there was something else on her mind.

"How's Jim and the kids?" I asked.

"Jim is getting ready to retire, Jason is married, and I have a grandson, and Shelly is deep into her career. No husband or boyfriend."

"You have been busy. Me too, but that's still no excuse after everything you did for me."

Then she lightened up. "That was a long time ago and you don't owe me anything. So, what do I owe this pleasure to? As if I couldn't guess."

Leave it to Maddie. For the short time we actually worked together, she knew me well. "I just need some information."

"Of course you do. I heard rumors you retired."

"I did."

"So," she drawled, "how's retirement treating you?"

"I haven't decided yet. Look, Maddie, I need to know about this guy that's been charged with harassing kids in town, Manson Smith. I heard he's missing. When was it reported?"

"Are you in town?"

"I'm actually in town for a while."

"Ohhh…" She dragged out the word. "Is there something I should know about since, if there was, I should know about it?"

I laughed at her vague statement. She expected me to tell her why I wanted to know except I couldn't tell her about the prowler at the campground. Not yet. She was excellent at putting two and two together, and she would pull Mac in for questioning. Then Mac would come for me. I had to be careful.

"Let's just say if it plays out to be something that you should know about, I promise I will tell you. I just prefer not to unless there definitely *is* something to tell you."

She laughed. "I forgot how much fun it is to go around in circles with you. I just happen to have his folder on my desk." I could hear her rustling through papers. "He was reported missing around nine p.m. last night."

"When was he supposed to appear in court for his harassment charge?"

"Oh, you know about that, huh?"

"It was on the news that he didn't show."

"Does that have anything to do with whatever it is you're calling about?"

"Circles, Maddie. Circles."

She chuckled while in the background, there was more rustling of paper. When we worked together, I used to say "circles" if I didn't have enough information about a case to give to someone. It meant I was still running around in circles, trying to connect the dots. When I did, I reported it.

"I just love journalists. No, Manson Smith didn't appear at the courthouse late yesterday afternoon. We're still looking for him."

"My next question will seem odd, but I need to know. Which cops are on the case? Would you be able to find that out?"

"I take it you have a reason for this question?"

"Let's just say curiosity for now."

"I shouldn't be telling you this since you're not on my payroll, but I'll give you this one. Officers Reynolds, Hampton and, your favorite…"

"Mac Taylor."

Maddie paused a moment. "Should I be concerned?"

"No. Not yet anyway. Thanks for the information."

I could hear her sigh over the phone as if she was deciding whether to tell me something. "There is one more thing. Officer Reynolds said Smith's neighbor saw him go into the woods last night. He believed he was hunting because he was carrying his rifle."

"Did you buy it?"

"No reason not to, but I'm a little concerned. His neighbor said he had a black eye. When he asked Smith what happened, he said he fell over a rake in the barn. You're not involved in this in any way, are you?"

"No, and I promise," I said, cutting her off, "to tell you if anything comes of this. No need to if there's nothing there. Thanks, Maddie. I appreciate it."

"You owe me, Moore."

"Yeah, I know. I'll be owing you until the day I die and then some. Thanks again." I pressed the end button before she could say anything else and then drove off. My mind worked to sort out everything Maddie had told me. Was Manson Smith wandering the woods near his home or in the campground? And was his black eye the result of his encounter with Mac and his buddies?

I chuckled to myself, remembering what Maddie had told me. She asked if she should be concerned because she was waiting for me to give her more information about it or react to it. Boy, she had always been a good interrogator. Thank God, I knew her techniques, so I rarely fell into her trap. But she wasn't ignorant. Me calling and asking about Manson Smith, she asking me if I was in town already would make her suspicious of why I was asking. Knowing Maddie, she'd keep an eye on me to make sure I didn't get involved in any police business, especially since I wasn't on her payroll. I sighed wondering how long it would be before she pulled *me* in for a chat.

So where was Manson Smith? Did Mac and his buddies do more than give him a warning? I wondered if they volunteered to look for him because that seemed like more than a coincidence. But at this point, anything was possible. He could be hunting. Or he could have been hurt. Then there was the possibility he was hiding out near the campground and still prowling around for whatever reason he had to do so. He could have packed up and left the state. If Smith had a wife and children, he might have been worried about the effects a trial and possibly jail time would have on his family. Better to run than to deal with disgracing his wife and kids. Except men like that didn't usually think about doing the morally right thing like protecting his family from public scrutiny.

The question my mind wrestled with was if Smith wasn't the prowler, who was wandering around the campground? I was positive he was the one stalking the campground on Sunday night. I saw him. Twice. But last night I didn't see the person stalking my friend's trailer.

It was imperative that I attend the Millers' gathering. I needed to speak to other residents of the campground. Did they see anyone last night wandering around in the shadows? I wasn't so sure I wanted to touch the rattlesnake den especially since Maddie would probably find her way to Manson Smith on her own. I also couldn't afford to get Mac pissed at us. However, if I discovered that it was still Smith that was roaming the campground, then I would have to tell Maddie about the thing that she said she should know if there was something she should know. But should I tell her about Mac's warning to him?

I drove to Home Depot and stopped to get fencing supplies and then back to the campground where I took Mabel out for a short walk. Afterward, I worked on erecting a fenced-in area for Mabel that I purchased so she could run free. It wasn't permanent and easy to install. Camping meant you had to take your dog for every potty walk. Glamping meant you opened the door and let the dog out to a fenced-in area. As I was pounding in the last stake, I heard Steph behind me.

"Did you check the by-laws to see if that's okay?"

I stood up and stretched my back. "Nope, but it looks great, doesn't it? And Mabel loves it." I turned back to see her sitting alone in the middle, unhappy. Turning back to Steph, I chuckled. "She will once I put her water bowl and a bed inside."

"And when you're inside there with her. A few treats might help," Steph added.

"I was just going to make some lunch. Want to join me?"

"I'll have a quick bite to eat with you, but then I have to leave for the afternoon."

I picked up my hammer—the new house gift my dad gave me when I got my first hefty mortgage for my first new home. My mother gave me a plant. Dad said plants could die, but you would always need a hammer. He was right. I opened the gate and stepped back to let Steph enter. Mabel ran to her, and she picked her up.

"You know you're not going to get any points for this," Steph said as she petted and cooed to my dog.

"Traitor," I whispered to Mabel as I went inside to prepare lunch.

Twenty minutes later, we were sitting outside on two chairs with tuna melts and lemonade on a small table between us so we could be under the awning for shade. Steph graciously took a bowl of water and one of Mabel's beds outside. "Anything for sweet baby girl," Steph said in a soothing voice to Mabel, to which my dog responded by wagging her tail.

"Traitor," I whispered.

Steph chuckled.

I told Steph what I had learned earlier in the morning concerning Manson Smith. She was shocked that I had called Maddie, but she agreed with me that Smith could be the one still stalking the campground. We talked about the possibility of Mac and his cronies' warning to Smith being more physical than verbal, and that they not only gave him a good talking to, but possibly a beating to make sure he stayed out of the campground. Neither of us wanted to think Mac would go any farther than that, but he had before. I remembered the time a Black student was driving a little too fast down a back road at night that Mac and I were patrolling. Mac stopped him and was more than rough with him. When the young man got back in his car, he had a broken arm and a black eye. I actually told my captain about that. Mac was called in and put on a two-week suspension. That was it.

As Steph questioned me, I watched her mouth move, her eyes open and narrow as their color ran across the spectrum from light green to dark gray with each emotion. Today, she wore her long brown hair tied back which was the way she wore it most of the time. I liked it that way because it left her eyes more visible and I always loved watching them because, with Steph, her eyes truly were the window to her soul.

I needed to get off the subject of Mac, so I asked her, "Why don't you cut your hair?"

"Excuse me?"

"Why don't you cut your hair? It's always tied back which tells me you hate it when it gets in your face."

Her look of astonishment was humorous, but not unexpected because my question was totally out of the blue. I was taking her in like a cool drink of water and felt a warmth run from my stomach to my cheeks. I quickly took a drink of cold lemonade, professing how hot it was outside. Hopefully, she would take my rosy cheeks as a result of the warm day.

"I never thought about it. Just used to it, I guess." She smiled, her chin slightly lifted, and she studied me with raised eyebrows. "You had long hair that you kept tied back. Then you cut it when Tess left. Why?"

I smirked when I answered, "I loved my hair long when I was younger, but like you, I always tied it back. It kept getting in the way. I kept it long because Tess used to say she loved my long blond locks. So, when she left, there was no reason to keep it long. I'm really glad I cut it."

"Actually, I am too. You look adorable with that short haircut."

"Adorable," I repeated. "Not so sure that was the look I was going for."

She leaned forward and I could see the top of her cleavage down her pale-yellow V-neck shirt. I felt my already rosy cheeks heat to a fire-engine red.

"Adorable is what you got. But seriously, you look great. Tess would be jealous."

I leaned back, forgetting the chairs were lightweight, and almost fell backward. Steph jumped up and grabbed my hand, pulling me back.

"Shit!" I exclaimed, not just because of my klutziness, but at the piece of news I hadn't yet shared with her. "I totally forgot, although now I don't know why. Maybe that's a good thing," I mused out loud.

"What?" she practically yelled at me.

"First, thank you for catching me before I fell. Second, Tess was here last night when I got back."

Her eyes widened at the same time her mouth opened. Then closed. Then opened again. "No way. What was she doing here? Better yet. How did she know you were here?"

"I can answer the first question, but not the second one. In a nutshell, she apologized and wanted to get back together. I have no idea how she found out I was here."

Steph's demeanor changed in an instant, and I struggled to read the emotions that ran across her face like a ticker tape. I waited for her to process what I had just told her, and I thought I saw her face settle on questioning concern, but there was a tinge of something else in her eyes. Jealousy? Okay, that was me being stupid. "Oh, come on. We saw them yesterday in The Commons. There was no way they didn't see us." She was right. Lori had seen us. Maybe, she told Tess, maybe not. Steph hesitated a few moments. "You're not considering it, are you?"

Her question took me by surprise. I had talked about this more to Steph than anyone. I said from the beginning there was no going back, but I understood why she asked. Tess and I had been together for almost thirty years. Still, I put my hands on my hips. "Really?" I glared at her.

"I know you said you wouldn't go back, but that was before she hunted you down, apologized, and begged you for your forgiveness." She kept my stare.

"I meant it when I said there was no going back, and that's what I told her. And I don't think she hunted me down. Tess never went the extra mile. It was a half-assed apology. She didn't even beg." Steph was about to protest, but I beat her to it. "But..." I looked out over the field. "Even if it was a heartfelt apology, and she did go the extra mile to find me and then beg, there is still...No. Going. Back." My voice sharpened on the last three words. "Besides, I've moved on. I'm not sure where I've moved to, but I've moved on."

Steph took a deep breath and blew it out. "Thank God."

I said nothing, wondering exactly what made her so relieved. It made me wonder something else. "If I did decide to go back, it sounds like you wouldn't be supportive."

"If it was what you really wanted, of course I would. On the outside. But I'll be honest with you. My insides would not be supportive because I know she would hurt you again, and I wouldn't want to see that. Again."

I snickered. "I'll keep that in mind."

"Why would you..."

"I said, there's no going back. If you're the friend you say you are, believe me, and let it go. If anything, I can't believe she came back and asked."

"Well, that's obvious. Lori probably drove her nuts like she did me, and Tess realized the grass wasn't greener on the other side."

"That's a hard-learned lesson," I considered. "But it's likely the truth. She did tell me that Lori wasn't dealing with their split very well. She called Tess and Tess came down to talk to her. That's why she was in Ithaca yesterday and insisted that's all they were doing."

"If that's what she said." Steph rolled her eyes. "Let's just hope Lori doesn't do it to the next woman she's with…if there's another one. What's that saying? Once a cheater, always a cheater."

"I'd like to believe people can learn from their mistakes."

"Didn't we just have that conversation the other night?"

I laughed. "That we did, but it was about men." Then I remembered the other thing I wanted to ask her. "Have you heard anything about the middle-aged woman found at the bottom of the gorge in Upper Taughannock Falls Park?"

Steph swallowed, then squished her mouth. "I was hoping you hadn't heard."

"You know I would have, eventually. Are you bummed you're not there to do the autopsy?"

"Not really. I did quite a few of the young folks that jumped off a bridge over the years. It's too depressing."

I nodded in acknowledgment. I had only seen one of those victims, but that one thirty-four years ago was enough for me to understand what she meant. "Will you let me know what they find out?"

"Why?"

"I have a feeling. They never found out the cause of Annie's fall back then, and until yesterday, she's been the only one to go over that spot on the cliff."

Steph looked out over the field where the thick green grass was tall and needed mowing. "She went over pretty much in the exact same spot," she finally said.

Shit, there might just be something to my feeling and it can't be good. "Do you think the police are thinking the same thing I am?"

"I'm not sure. What are you thinking?"

"That even though it's thirty-plus years between the two deaths…I know, it's stupid, but my gut wonders if there's any connection. Maybe Mac might know."

"And that's something you can't talk to him about even if he isn't on the case. It doesn't concern you. You're a retired cop, and he does not like you. Besides, they never solved Annie's case, so there's no way you can prove if there even was a connection. You can, however, ask him about Manson Smith because it does concern you. You're living here for the summer. Leave the other to me. I'll ask him."

My investigative instinct was running on full throttle. My body and mind were going into major overdrive, wanting to probe every aspect of a possible connection if only to finally solve Annie's death. I felt that intense need to profile it, especially because I hoped it might close her case.

It was times like this I wish I hadn't retired.

Steph left for the rest of the afternoon to run more errands. I wondered how many errands you could have living in a trailer in a campground for the summer, but I was new at this. So, I mowed my small lawn and then settled into my zero-gravity chair with my computer to do some investigating. There wasn't much other than a very general statement citing a middle-aged woman who was found dead at the bottom of the gorge at Upper Taughannock Falls State Park. Her identity was unknown, and they hadn't revealed the cause of death (however, anyone with a brain knew it was from the fall).

I knew the area would be closed off with the standard yellow police tape. An officer would be on patrol for a few days while the forensic team collected evidence. Footprints would be cast. Any garbage or debris in the area would be bagged and tagged and markers with the number of the evidence bag would be placed where it was found, and then photos taken of everything.

All that had been done thirty-four years ago, and still the question of suicide or murder had never been answered. After a year, the story of Annie's death was whittled down to whatever could fit into a cardboard file box marked with her name and date of death. It was placed in a small section of the IPD—toward the back of the cement-blocked basement designated for the storage of cold cases. There, the boxes holding the lives of the dead unsolved cases sat on metal shelves.

I remember watching Mac pen the name Annie Wilson in black marker on the outside of the box and following him to the basement where he set the box on a shelf. I remember taking one last look at her name before I left her there to remain for—I had no idea how long she would be there, but I knew how much I loved her.

CHAPTER TWELVE

Jen texted me late in the afternoon that dinner would be served at five thirty. We were having cabbage, and kielbasa stew made in tomato broth. It was one of her specialties and one of my favorites, thus the reason I was invited over to share a bowl. I took a bottle of red wine and Mabel. She was excited to go. Plus, she really liked kielbasa. However, Mabel was like a lot of us females. Too much of a good thing, in this case, kielbasa, put way too many pounds on her little figure.

They informed me Steph would be over for dessert. In fact, she was bringing the dessert from one of our favorite bakeries in town. While we ate, conversations continued on the latest topic, one that I didn't want to have when Steph was around. "If it wasn't Manson Smith roaming around your trailers last night, who do you think it was?" I asked.

"I'm curious," Myra began. "You didn't see or hear anyone around your trailer?"

"Nope. Just the screaming coyotes and foxes."

"Oh, so the gentle sounds of nature." Myra laughed.

"I actually slept pretty good."

Myra grinned most likely thinking she knew the reason why I slept so well. She had seen Steph leave my trailer.

"You'll get used to it soon enough and then you'll miss it when you're gone," I heard Steph say from behind me. She set a box on the table and then plopped down on the bench next to me and took a deep sniff of the pot of stew.

"Did you eat?" Jen asked her.

"Never got a chance to. Did you save me some?"

Myra already had a full bowl served and set it in front of her with a spoon before she finished her sentence. Steph dug in greedily, acting like she hadn't eaten in days. She really liked her food, and she had the metabolism to eat a lot of it and never gain a pound.

"Blueberry pie. Oh, my favorite. I love you, Steph," I said as I pulled the box closer to me. I noticed I had just made her uncomfortable, so I added in jest, "Just give me a fork."

Steph answered without a pause. "Not until you cut a piece for all of us. This stew is sooooo good, and I'm not saying that just because I don't have to cook."

"Thank you," Jen said as she grabbed the pie tin from me and cut four pieces. Then she took it inside, saying, "We'll have the rest of this tomorrow. If I don't hide it, Blake will eat it all."

"Aw, that's not fair," I whined. "Guess this one tiny piece will have to do."

Myra stretched her body up and leaned over the table. "Doesn't look like a tiny piece to me."

"No piece is big enough when it comes to Murray's blueberry pie."

We finished our dessert, cleared up, and got ready to go to the Millers' gathering. Steph and I went back to our trailers to get our glasses filled with whatever liquid we wanted for the evening and met back at Myra and Jen's.

We walked to the front of the campground where the Millers' large park-model trailer greeted everyone with its elaborate decorations, gardens and oversized deck as they entered the campground. On the deck that spanned the length of their trailer was a bar and a cabinet filled with enough libations to supply the whole campground. Lots of people either sat or milled about. The crowd was growing and so was the party noise. Laughter and loud conversation could be heard all the way to our side of the campground, so we knew before we even got there that the party was in full motion.

Myra and Jen bellied up to the bar with a few other couples. Steph made a beeline to Mac. I found Sandy to see if she had any gossip about sightings of another stalker. Sandy was deep in conversation with Deanna, who with her husband, Rick, had joined the Rock Creek Camping community this season.

As far as I could tell, Deanna and Sandy had a lot in common. They were both rather attractive women whose aging over the years was not due so much to age, but to arrogant, self-righteous husbands. I didn't know if Rick was a cheater, but as I sat and observed the interaction between their husbands, I assumed he was too. I could see it in the way they tilted their heads toward each other to speak quietly so no one else could hear, then sat up and laughed over a very private joke. I felt sorry for Sandy. I liked her. To a point. That point was when her gossip took over whatever chat we were having, and I would have to devise some excuse to leave. But not today. Today, her gossip might come in handy. I also hoped that Deanna was on the same wavelength as Sandy. Two gossipers in a situation like this were always better than one.

I grabbed an empty folding chair and set it up across from the two women. I put my glass down on the wood table in front of them loudly enough to penetrate their in-depth tête-à-tête. That seemed like the perfect word for their jabber session since their heads were together closer than their husbands

"Why, Blake? So nice of you to come."

I picked up Mabel and set her on my lap.

"Oh, what a cute little dog," Deanna said. "May I pet her, him?"

"Absolutely. *Her* name is Mabel, and she loves all the attention she can get." Deanna reached over and patted Mabel, who lifted her nose to the air, giving her permission to scratch her neck.

"I would love a dog like this."

"Probably not a good idea, Deanna," Sandy warned.

Deanna didn't reply. Instead, she scowled in the direction where her husband stood.

"Happy anniversary, Sandy. How many years is it?" I asked.

She sniggered. "I stopped counting at ten."

Deanna and I laughed. Deanna put her hand on Sandy's thigh. "Oh, come now, honey. Thirty years. Right?"

Sandy waved her hand in the air as if to dismiss the comment. "Something like that." She took a very long swallow from her glass and then proclaimed, "I need a refill. Be right back."

I quickly engaged Deanna in a chat before she too, got up and left. "So, do you like it here?"

"Oh yes," she answered. "Everyone is so nice. It's pleasant enough and close to so much, but…" She trailed off.

"What's wrong?" I asked with as much concern as I could muster.

She leaned forward. "Well, I'm sure you heard about that brouhaha yesterday with Mac and his buddies throwing that nasty man out of the campground."

"No," I exclaimed. "Do tell." *I could get an Emmy for this performance.*

"The man was lurking around people's trailers."

I put my hand to my heart and feigned surprise. "Oh my. Did you see him?"

"I thought I heard rustling around our trailer in the middle of the night, but Rick, well, he told me to go back to sleep. Just wild animals, he said. But I know it was that man and I'm so grateful Mac and his friends disposed of him."

"Disposed of him? How'd they do that?"

She leaned even farther forward and whispered, "Rick told me Mac and his officer friends put him in the back of their car and drove off with him. He said he asked Mac where they took him, and Mac said it was no one's business and that all we needed to know was that he wouldn't be bothering anyone here again."

"Now, Deanna, we mustn't tell stories." I looked up to see Mac's wife, Missy, standing over us, grinning. Deanna immediately closed her mouth and sat up.

"Well, all I can say is thank God we have those gentlemen looking over our campground," I said, swallowing so as not to choke on my words.

"You can all rest assured that my husband will make sure this is a safe haven for all of you." Her smile was stiff, her eyes hard. She extended her hand to me. "We didn't get time for you to introduce me to this adorable creature?" There was a slight, awkward Southern accent like she was trying to hide a thicker one.

"Hi, Missy. This adorable creature is Mabel."

She reached down and gave Mabel's back a few quick strokes. "You know, feel free to come to the office whenever and bring this little cutie for a visit. I never get the chance to talk to everyone at these gatherings. I have so much work to do getting this place put back together. That's why I have to leave now, but it was nice to talk to you, Blakely." Her words were now melancholy, seemingly in a dream state as if her state of mind was on a roller coaster ride.

"Nice talking to you, too."

I watched her go as Deanna leaned forward again and confirmed my thoughts. "That one is a little off. I never know what kind of mood she's going to be in which changes as fast as the flick of a light switch. But I think she and her husband will be good owners. She is on top of things as far as managing the campground goes, and Mac, well, you know it's a good thing he's watching over this place. I'm just worried."

"About what?"

"I'm not so sure they got rid of that man for good," she said as she sat back in her chair.

"Why is that?"

"I heard the same noise last night around our trailer. I didn't bother to wake Rick. You know how men can be. Miserable when you wake them out of a deep sleep that turns out to be nothing."

I smiled. No, I didn't know how men were when they slept, but I wasn't about to tell her that. However, if I could believe Deanna, and I didn't have any reason not to, she confirmed that there still was a prowler lurking around the campground.

I looked up at Steph. She and Mac were in a very animated conversation. Hands were going this way and that. Their expressions went from serious, to amusement, to what I sensed was some anger on both sides. Steph's height went head-to-head with Mac's, but he had bulk that she didn't. Mac also knew how to use his mass in a threatening way. They taught that at the Academy, but Officer Nasty had figured out ways of throwing his size around that could quickly deflate a taller, larger, and angrier person as fast as letting air out of a balloon. But Steph was holding her own, and it made me smile.

Sandy came back, so I continued in their discussions that ranged from the best nail salon in Ithaca to which of Mac's officer friends was the hunkiest. Fortunately, Jen and Myra joined us and carried the conversation to other topics.

Every now and then, my eyes shifted in Steph's direction, and I grew nervous that they were still at it. Part of me wanted to go over and save her, but I knew that was unwise.

Mabel stood up, sat down, and turned around, letting me know she was getting fidgety. I had my excuse to leave. She had had enough and so had I. I stood and said, "Good night," so that all could hear me. Good nights rang out behind me as I started walking back to my trailer. I would be happier watching television for the rest of the evening with hopes of Steph stopping by before she went back to her trailer. But she didn't show.

I fell asleep to a movie and woke in the dark to total silence after the television had turned itself off around midnight.

I picked up Mabel and apologized. "I'm so sorry, baby. You've been holding your pee for far too long. Let's go." Her short tail wagged while I hooked her up and we went outside for her last walk of the day. I strained in the dark to see Steph's trailer across the field and thought I saw movement come from behind it, and then a human shape entered the woods.

Quickly, I shoved Mabel back inside, grabbed a flashlight, my phone, and the pepper spray I kept on the counter next to the door, and ran across the field. All the trailers on that side were dark except for the far end, where a fire was glowing in front of a large fifth wheel. With the flashlight off, I stealthily made my way to the woods near the back of Steph's trailer and entered the brush. When I was far enough in that I didn't think Steph would see the beam from my flashlight, I turned it on and began sweeping the area, looking for clues of an intruder. Several freshly broken branches at shoulder height told me there was one, and they were in a hurry. Further inspection produced a piece of material hanging from a bush that had prickers. There was no blood that I could tell.

I heard a noise and looked up to see a figure dressed in dark clothing with a hood pulled down, concealing most of their face. The person grabbed the fabric, turned, and ran. I followed. They ran faster. So did I, but the distance was increasing between us. I was never a fast runner. Maybe that was what the universe was trying to tell me when it steered me toward a desk job—you can't run fast enough to catch the criminals. I tripped, falling face forward.

In pain, I scrambled to my knees and took a few deep breaths. I struggled to get to my feet as quickly as I could and swept the flashlight beam all around me. I couldn't see anyone.

"Blake! Blakely! Where are you?"

I started walking in the direction of Steph's voice.

"You answer me now, Blakely Moore." Now she sounded angry.

"I'm here. I'm okay."

"Oh my God, I'm going to kill her, goddamn it, what the hell is she doing? She better not be hurt…"

The last five words made me stop. I brushed my clothes off. She sounded more than genuinely concerned. She sounded…

Steph plowed through the bushes and trees and stopped in front of me, shining a flashlight over my body and then at my face, blinding me. Agitated, I turned away. "I said I'm okay." I wasn't angry at her—well, maybe at her for shining such a bright light directly into my eyes, but more at myself for being stupid and clumsy.

"Come back to my trailer. You've got some cuts on your arms and face. Let me clean you up and you can tell me what the hell you were doing. I hope you weren't watching over me. How many times do I have to say this? I can take care of myself." She turned and began to walk.

So, I followed, but not without replying, "I wasn't stalking around your camper to look after you. I saw someone lurking in the woods behind your trailer. I went in to investigate, and they took off. I was following them. Until I tripped and fell."

She stopped and spun to face me. "Who? Did you see them? Man or woman?"

"No idea. Just a dark figure. I couldn't tell."

"Oh," she said as she started toward her trailer once more. "You can fill me in while I tend to your cuts."

Inside her living room, I sat nursing a glass of water while Steph rummaged through her bathroom for the supplies she needed. She came back out with ointments, Band-Aids, tape, gauze pads, and a small bowl with water and a cloth. I sat patiently explaining what I saw from outside my trailer while she cleaned the cuts and applied antiseptic ointment and bandages.

"I look like a freak," I said, surveying the wounds on my arm now with Snoopy Band-Aids on them. I lifted one arm and stared at her. "Really? Don't you have adult Band-Aids?"

"Nope. You're stuck with those. Really, Blake, what were you thinking?"

"That I saw a stalker and wanted to catch them. Maybe Manson Smith is back here. Maybe he's hiding out here. Or it could be someone else. We need to know either way."

Steph sat down next to me and took a deep breath. "Do you know if this person was just hanging around a few trailers, or roaming all over the campground?"

"Deanna told me at the Millers' that she thought she heard something the night before and then again last night outside her trailer. She's a big drinker, so it's hard to tell if she heard it for real or if it was a figment of her drunken stupor."

Steph studied me for a moment and then said quietly, "You know, you're awfully sarcastic lately. Is everything all right?"

"Yeah. I'm sorry. I just thought it would be a quiet, relaxing summer." Well, that was partly the truth. The rest of the truth lay somewhere between that and my retiring. It was times like this I wished I hadn't. I couldn't be officially involved in anything that might require police attention and I had to tread lightly with whatever I did. Obviously, there was no way I'd be able to stay out of it.

She giggled. "Well, I can see why you expected that. It's always been quiet and relaxing here. Until…"

"Until I came?" I suggested half teasingly.

"You're not the only new person on the block." She nudged me with her shoulder.

"Are you going to tell me what you and Mac were talking about that was so intense?"

She smiled. "Of course, but not until tomorrow. I didn't get back until almost midnight. I hadn't gone to bed yet so that's probably why I heard you outside."

"You didn't hear anyone else?"

"No, I had the television on while I got ready for bed. I turned it off just before I heard you. Look, I'm really tired so I promise I'll tell you over breakfast."

"Okay, I guess I can wait." I lifted my arms. "Thanks for this. I'll have breakfast ready for you in the morning."

"I'm going to walk back with you."

"There's no need. I've got my pepper spray."

"Look, I can't let you walk back alone with someone roaming the campground, and if you'll let me stay over again, I would appreciate that. I'm not sure I want to be here by myself with the possibility that someone might be checking me out. I'm afraid that I'll get too scared and pull out my gun." She swallowed. "I just bought it to feel safer. I'm not sure it's a good idea to have it with everything going on. You know."

I smiled. "Of course you can stay. In fact, Mabel told me to bring you back. She told me you make a better doggie bed than I do."

That got a laugh out of her. She grabbed a jacket and her keys and followed me out the door, locking up. Our walk back was quiet as I surveyed our surroundings and was glad for only the calm sounds of the outdoors. It would allow me to hear anyone approaching. I stole a glance in her direction and saw a look of cautious concern on her face. My heart went out to her. It had to be disturbing to know someone you didn't know was lurking around your trailer.

Inside my trailer, Mabel was all over Steph who, after lavishing much attention on my sweet dog, climbed into bed and assumed her half-moon position. I lifted Mabel onto the bed and she immediately tucked her little body inside of Steph's. It was the sweetest thing and it brought such joy to me seeing both of them in my bed. They were asleep within minutes.

I lay awake under the covers, listening. And I lay awake watching. Watching Steph lying next to me with my favorite little critter curled up next to her. She was one of my best friends—maybe even more. But I couldn't address that right now or even think about it.

Right now, I had to protect her.

CHAPTER THIRTEEN

I woke before Steph even though I had a restless sleep riddled with nightmares of someone breaking into her trailer. I couldn't make out who it was—woman or man. I woke profusely sweating and panting, making it hard to go back to sleep. I gently lifted Mabel from her Stephy cocoon and got her outside for her morning stroll. We walked directly to the back of the campground to see if anyone was outside the trailer where I had seen the campfire the night before.

A man was sitting in a chair with a Genny beer in his hand. I hoped it was the hair of the dog that bit him and not his usual morning breakfast. When he saw me, he nodded and smiled.

"Cute dog you got there," he said in plain English with no slurring.

I blew out a sigh of relief. "Thank you. Her name is Mabel."

He sat back and laughed. "Cute name."

"Thanks

"What kind is she?"

"She's half poodle and half Pomeranian." I paused a moment. "Did you see anyone roaming around the woods behind your trailer last night?"

He studied me inquisitively. "That's an odd question."

"It's just some neighbors have told me they heard noises around their campers during the night."

"Lots of animals roam around here. I thought I heard a huge one in the woods last night. I don't think it was a person."

"Are you sure?"

"Can't be sure, but I'd hate to think someone is sneaking around our campground."

"Yeah. Me too. Well, have a nice day."

"Uh-huh." He took a swig of his beer and as I walked by. When I glanced back, he had gone inside.

I detected a delectable aroma, and followed the smell of bacon back to my trailer. Another morning of not having to cook was bringing me morning bliss. I never liked cooking, although after Steph's lessons, I was beginning to enjoy it. However, Steph cooking for me now was the best thing that had happened to me since I arrived at the campground. Now I knew why Steph liked being cooked for so much.

"I'm not doing this every day," she said without turning away from the stove. "That's your job."

Chuckling, I watched as Mabel turned in circles, waiting for Steph to put her breakfast bowl down. "I don't expect you to, and I promise I've got breakfast tomorrow. Also, if you keep this up, you're going to totally spoil my dog."

"As it should be, but don't you think she already is? And you are correct—you've got breakfast tomorrow. I'm only supposed to be buying the groceries. Remember?"

Her dark hair was sleep-tousled, and her sweats and T-shirt were askew as if she had just crawled out of bed and immediately begun cooking. I walked over to the stove and took the fork out of her hand. "Here, I'll take over. How about you set the table, get yourself some orange juice or something, and tell me what Mac said last night?"

Without a word, she did as I instructed. She sat in the recliner and put her feet up, patting the space next to her. Mabel jumped up. I should have said if she kept this up, my dog would disown me and go home with her.

"You know, a girl could get used to this," she pondered as she scratched Mabel's ears.

I turned over the bacon. "I thought you already were," I jested.

"Yeah, but I'm single right now. Having you cook for me is the best of both worlds."

My heart sank a little. But only a little, because if all I ever had was my best friend beside me while I cooked her breakfast, I considered myself one lucky woman.

"Mac didn't come out and say it," she began suddenly, "but I believe he and his buddies roughed up Smith. As far as I can tell, they drove him somewhere south of here, dropped him off, gave him a beating, and left him."

I got the eggs out of the fridge and decided on soft-boiled with toast. I filled a pot with water and placed it on the stove. As I put bread in the toaster, I asked, "Did Mac say anything about the female body found yesterday in the gorge?"

"Nope. But remember, I'm on leave. He won't talk business to me."

"Sorry."

"It's okay. I'm just mad I can't do the autopsy. I don't trust Bevel to do a good job. Or the right thing."

I sat down on the table bench. "Bevel's your temporary replacement. Right? Are you saying what I think you're saying?"

"Yes, and probably."

"Are you going to tell your superior?"

"Captain Spinner is familiar with Bevel's work. That's why she only gave me a month's leave instead of more. I also have to finish the drug counseling and the IPD course, which is totally boring. That's where I was yesterday." Her eyes penetrated mine with a go-ahead-and-say-it kind of dare.

"I'm sorry," was the only thing I wanted to say. Nothing could be gained from reproaching my friend for something she already knew was a big mistake.

"Fine, then you might as well know everything. I got drunk after I dumped Lori, because I wasn't sure I wanted to break up. I mean, I really liked her, but she just got too weird for me." She took a deep breath. "The sex was great."

"Okay, TMI," I said, laughing.

"Anyway, I went out to drown my sorrows. Another failed relationship. Every one I've ever had has ended in a very short time. I finally realized I might be more to blame than they were. Isn't that sad? That's why I went out drinking."

"Okay. Can I ask a possibly tough question?"

"You can. Can't promise I'll answer it."

"In your counseling sessions, are you exploring why your relationships fail, since I can tell it's bothering you?"

"Wouldn't you be bothered by it?" Her tone was soft, yet it sounded wracked with disappointment at being a failure.

"I'm bothered by my relationship failing, so yes, of course." I put the bacon and toast on the table. "But I'm worried about you."

"Well, don't be. I'm handling it." She grabbed a piece of toast. "Breakfast smells delicious. I'm starved."

We had talked about it all once before. The previous summer, Tess and I were renting a cabin at this campground to hang with our friends. Late one night, Steph showed up and began to cry. She told us that it wasn't that she minded being alone, in fact, she kind of liked it that way, most of the time. She had learned to live with being single because all her friends made her feel a part of the family. But she found she was the one calling her friends all the time. At first, she would invite herself along, but that got old fast.

I knew she wanted someone in her life who would love her and she could love back. Someone to play with, share life's events with, and not feel like the odd wheel every time she went out with friends. Not because she hated feeling like that, but because she wished she could have what they did. But Steph also had problems with long-term relationships and commitment. She couldn't do it, no matter how hard she tried.

After she finished crying, she insisted she wasn't telling me all of that to guilt me into calling her every day. She didn't know why she was telling me, and in the end, she wished she hadn't. I promised confidentiality, but I couldn't leave it alone. So, one day I confided in Tess and Myra even though by doing so, I broke that promise. From that day on, we made it a habit to call Steph a few times a week, hoping not to be too obvious. Jen and Myra invited her out to eat, go hiking, or see a movie since they also lived in Ithaca. Tess and I did the same when we were in the area. I knew she was grateful, but one day she joked she would be even more grateful if we could introduce her to a nice woman who was sane with little baggage. I laughed and said I never met or had known a woman like that.

The timer dinged, and I tended to the soft-boiled eggs. While we ate, she filled me in on the rest. Mac had harassed her about her

DUI. I knew how much it angered her because I saw it during their conversation the night before. I had no doubt she shoveled it right back at him with her accusations about what he may have done to Smith.

We needed a change of subject, so I asked, "Did Mac say if he knew that someone is still running around the campground at night, lurking around trailers?"

Steph picked up a piece of bacon and waggled it in my face. "Here's the interesting part of the story. He shrugged it off."

"Shrugged it off? Like how?"

"Like he knew, and maybe he isn't going to tell anyone or do anything about it."

"Okay, I don't get that. He took him off the property, and then maybe pummeled him as a reminder of what would happen if he returned. Then the guy goes missing. So why would he think there's another stalker? Unless..."

"Unless he knows there is still a stalker," Steph finished for me.

"What are we going to do with all of this?" I asked.

"Nothing. You're retired. I'm on leave. There's nothing we can do."

"Seriously? It might be the one time we can prove that Mac is a bad cop. And there's someone prowling around the trailers at night."

Steph put her fork down and placed a hand over mine. "The past is the past. It's done and over with. Let it go. Vengeance will get you nowhere but into trouble. Let the system work. It's time for the police. I'll put a call in to Maddie, but I have to approach this with sensitivity or I'll be out on my ass before I get to retire. I won't let that happen. My job is everything to me."

I turned my hand over and squeezed hers. "I'm sorry. I get that. Handle it how you think is best."

She cocked her head and studied me. "And what about you? I've known you to go off the deep end on a case when you're sure you're right."

"I know I'm right that Mac Taylor is the worst kind of cop. I don't know if he's the reason for Manson Smith's disappearance, but I promise I'll let the system do its job on that one."

She breathed a sigh of relief. I would never jeopardize her job, and I hoped she knew that. What I didn't tell her was that I was still going to investigate who was roaming around our trailers in the middle of the night. I could do that without doing any professional damage to her or myself. After all, it was my home for the summer. I had the right to protect it and my friends.

I heard my phone ding and saw a message from Jen. "Myra and Jen want us to join them for the day. A little hiking, a little eating, maybe a little shopping."

Steph smiled. "And you can all say a little drinking. I am not an alcoholic. I had one terrible incident and believe me when I say it will never happen again."

"We know that. Did you ever stop to think *we* don't want to spend every day drinking?"

She stood. "You're no fun. I have to run and clean up. Are you okay with doing dishes?"

"You owe me." I smiled.

"I know. I'll buy you lunch."

She was out the door before I could protest. I shook my head. "She sure knows how to get out of cleanup," I said to Mabel. My pooch just glared at me, if a dog could glare. "Really? It's not my fault she left."

After finishing with the breakfast dishes, I changed into a decent pair of shorts and a nice pullover. I hooked up Mabel and took her for a walk. I wanted to go into the woods behind Steph's trailer to examine the area where I saw the person, but there was no way I could do that until she was gone, so it would have to wait.

By the time Mabel and I got back to the trailer, Jen's car was waiting for me with all three inside, their windows rolled down, yelling at me to hurry. To their surprise, I picked up Mabel and got in the car. I had expected this, so I had everything I needed when I left for my walk with Mabel—money, license, charge card, jacket.

"It's about time," Steph said, chuckling.

"Mabel needed a walk before our outing. It's not like you have anything else to do."

She elbowed me. "You're such a turd." She grinned when Mabel immediately jumped onto her lap and snarled at me.

"Oh, my God! What have you done to my dog? *You* elbowed me. Why is she defending you?"

Steph lavished hugs and produced a treat from her pocket that Mabel gobbled in two chomps. "You gotta know how to treat your women," Steph said in a very serious manner. "Obviously, you and I have problems with that." And then she whispered to me, "I'm trying to do better."

I couldn't help but laugh.

"Hey, babe," Myra directed to Jen. "You got some treats for me?"

"Later, babe. Later," Jen replied coyly.

We all laughed.

The rest of the day was light and fun, just like I wanted the summer to be. We hiked the trail at Buttermilk Falls and had lunch at our favorite Mexican restaurant in the mall, followed by some shopping. We were back at the campground by late afternoon, and I settled into one of my recliners for a nap. Mabel stretched up, paws on the chair, whining. I looked down at her.

"You're a little traitor. Why would I lift you up here to sleep with me when you snarled at me? You. Snarled. At me." Then the puppy eyes, big round blue balls made me give in and I picked her up.

We agreed to fend for ourselves for dinner and spend the evening inside, since the forecast included heavy rain. Rainy days could be a nice change once in a while. Several rainy days in a row, or thunderstorms, not so much. Still, I welcomed the peace and quiet. I fixed Mabel's evening meal

I had a TV dinner. I was the queen of microwave cooking when I was by myself. I completed the evening ritual with Mabel's walk just before small drops of rain turned into a torrential downpour. By the time we got back inside, Mabel looked like a drowned rat and was none too happy about it. I scooped her up in a towel and lovingly dried her fur the best I could. After that, we settled into bed, I had another night of restless sleep filled with dreams of people in dark cloaks walking around my trailer and then standing motionless, watching. Just watching.

I didn't expect to see Steph at breakfast, so, I dressed and took Mabel out. Sometime in the night, the pounding rain had stopped, leaving the grass and dirt roads waterlogged. Puddles accumulated where there were potholes and new divots appeared in other areas. Mac would have to add dirt and stone to the road and then tamp it down sometime soon before people began complaining about getting their rigs stuck in the muddy holes. Mabel didn't like the rain, but she disliked the rain-soaked ground even more. Therefore, it was a short walk.

I fed her breakfast and cooked for one. I planned to spend a relaxing day reading and finding a news station to see if there were any developments on the woman in the gorge. After that, Mabel and I would take a long walk around the campground, talking to whomever I could find outside for any information on prowler sightings.

I got nothing on our late-morning walk, so we went back to the camper, and I found a local news station and learned that the dead woman, Marie Sanfield, was a thirty-eight-year-old professor at Cornell University's College of Veterinary Medicine. Investigations were ongoing, but when they showed the area of the gorge that was taped off, I sucked in a deep breath. The woman had indeed gone over a cliff in the same place as Annie. Did the Ithaca police catch this? Did they even think about the cold case lying in the basement of their building? Could this death be connected to Annie's?

I believed Annie had been pushed, but to this day, there was no proof. Nothing. In Annie's case, the area had been wiped clean, including the dirt on the ground. DNA analysis wasn't developed at that time and I had no idea if the police went back into cold cases now to look for some. There were no footprints of anyone else but the victim—no evidence whatsoever that alluded to a killer. The police wanted to mark it as a suicide, but there was one thing that kept them from doing so. They found scuff marks in the dirt at the edge of the cliff, some appearing to be digging into the ground as if to get solid footing. They were from Annie's shoes, and it appeared as if she was fighting against an unseen force that sent her over the edge. The police said this could have been her final attempt at saving herself from a suicide or a murder.

When I learned of this, my heart fell apart. In my eyes, whoever pushed her cleaned and disposed of any sign that they were there, but left Annie's prints as if a tribute to her will to resist.

I had just entered the IPD. Annie was graduating from Ithaca College with a bright future in front of her. She studied environmental science and had received a job offer from the state of New York Department of Environmental Conservation. We were planning our life together—deciding when I would move to Albany to join her. She was to leave in a week, and I wanted to quit and pick up as a recruit in Albany. They didn't have any openings, so Annie convinced me I should stay to complete my training under the guidance of

Officer Mac Taylor. When I finished, I could search for a position in Albany. She reassured me that completing my program in Ithaca, despite my misgivings about working with Officer Mac Taylor, would give me a better chance of gaining a position with the Albany Police Department.

And then she was gone. Dead.

We were supposed to celebrate the night before she left, but Annie never showed up at the restaurant. I called her several times. Went to her dorm room. There was no sign of her until I went to the gorge the next morning on my first dead-body call. To this day, I don't know how I got through it. Then again, I didn't recognize the battered body of my love because I didn't look closely enough. I stayed in the background because it was too difficult for me to see any woman's body in that state. And because Mac told me to. It wasn't until I found the charm that I knew who she was.

I didn't tell the police, letting them find out her identity through the usual police procedures. I guessed part of me didn't want to believe it. Anyone could have that charm bracelet. I was afraid of being interrogated and having my lifestyle come to light and on top of losing Annie, I might also lose my job. So, I stayed quiet. I knew they would find out who she was. All I had to do was wait. And live with the guilt.

We had kept our relationship a secret. Back then, you didn't shout out that you were in a same-sex relationship, but we had talked about telling our families when we were back together and settled in Albany. Until then, we were keeping it quiet. Even now, I wasn't sure if I did the right thing, keeping my involvement with her a secret. I told no one until I finally confided in Steph many years later. She had kept my secret even to this day. I never understood why she did, especially being in a law enforcement area herself. But she did, and it had become my cross to bear.

Maybe that was why I needed to know more about Marie Sanfield's death. I couldn't let another woman's fall off the ledge at Upper Taughannock Falls go unsolved.

I was ending my call to Captain Spinner when there was a knock on my door. "Hey, Blake. You in there? It's Myra."

I struggled out of the recliner, repositioning Mabel back on the seat once I was up and then opened the door. "I know your voice. Is that a standard greeting whenever you knock on a trailer door? Tell the person who you are?" I opened the door and let her in.

"I'm here to invite you to dinner and a campfire."

"We have phones nowadays. You could have called or texted."

She sat in the empty recliner but didn't recline. She remained forward in the chair and absent-mindedly petted my dog. "I needed the walk. Plus, Jen has been driving me nuts all day."

"Oh, oh. What's going on?"

"She was in a cleaning frenzy, and she wanted me to help."

I picked up Mabel and sat down. "Oh, the joys of being single." I laughed. "You only clean when you want to and hope when you have visitors it's not too dirty."

"There are pros to being in a relationship. Like sex with someone you know."

Again, I laughed. "And that's it?"

"Let me think on it."

"Boy, she sure put you in a mood." I watched Myra for a minute because she appeared to be struggling with something. Her cute and easily styled bob was one reason I cut my hair. When I complimented her on it, she would say her looks were standard. I found that an odd word to use. She was of medium height and a bit taller than me with no striking features. Her skin was bleached white, making her face look washed-out, emphasized more by dark hair and contrasting brown eyes. But her beauty was in the peacefulness and calm she exuded, with a kind and caring personality. She never got too excited over anything, so when I saw her eyes moving around as if searching for an answer, I knew something was off.

"What's wrong? Something's happened that put Jen in her cleaning frenzy and has you all in a tizzy. That doesn't happen often."

"Someone was outside our trailer again last night. They didn't stay, just passed behind it and then headed down the road."

"Toward Steph's."

"Yup."

"When?"

Her head cocked, and I waited for her to say, "Duh," because of the look on her face, but she merely said, "Last night."

"I know last night. What time?"

"Around one in the morning."

"Have you seen Steph today?"

"She went home."

Now that surprised me, and by the look on Myra's face, she could see that. Her eyebrows dipped slightly and the corners of her lips were quivering, as if she was fighting a smile or a frown. I never knew which it was. "She didn't tell me. Is everything okay?" I asked, hoping to skirt any direct inquiry about my feelings toward Steph.

"Depends on how you look at it. Remember that girl Lori that she was dating?"

"You don't have to remind me."

"Sorry," she said. "Anyway, this is strange."

"What's strange?"

"Steph said Lori wants to talk to her about getting back together. Steph was going to meet her at some restaurant in town."

My heart sank. But then I laughed because Myra was staring at me. When I felt the bitter laughter fade, I explained, "Tess came to see me the other night. She was here after our campfire. She broke up with Lori and wants to come back to me."

"Ohhh," Myra drawled out the word as her upper body leaned back in a half roll. Then she placed her folded hands on the console in between the chairs. She swallowed. "And what did you say?"

"No, of course."

"Uh-huh."

"Uh-huh, what?" I said, frustrated at the ambiguity of the conversation.

"That kind of explains things, doesn't it? Steph broke up with Lori and then Tess broke up with Lori because she wants to come back to you. It didn't take Lori long to search Steph out."

"And I would care. Why?"

"I don't believe you care in the Tess department,"—she leaned forward—"but maybe in the Steph department?"

I jumped up and went to the fridge. Taking out two beers, I handed one to her. "I don't care if Tess stays with Lori or not. We're done. There's nothing more to say on that subject. But, yes, I do care about Steph. She's one of my three best friends, and I don't want to see her get hurt. She broke up with Lori for a reason. Why would she go back?"

"I don't think she would."

"Then why did she go see her?"

"You'll have to ask her."

I took an angry swig of my beer. "Fine. I will." Every time I thought I could put my previous life with Tess to bed for good, it crept out of the woodwork, so to speak, and knocked me down. I thought all I had left to deal with was to sign the divorce papers, which included me buying Tess out of the house. Everything was almost complete, and I wondered now if Tess would get angry at me for refusing to take her back and make the divorce more difficult—like demanding more money, or the house, or the dog. No way would I let her have Mabel.

"Are you sure that's all it is?"

"I don't know what you're implying, but yes, that's all it is. I love my friends, and I would do anything for any of you."

Myra sat back. "Okay, fine. Now that we totally went off subject, what do you think we should do about this psycho running around the campground at night?"

"I guess we tell Mac. But I think it better be you."

"I can do that, but you know what's weird? I thought Mac ran him off the property."

"He did, but the guy is missing," I said after taking a drink.

"Missing? Okay, but that doesn't necessarily mean anything. He could still be here, just not wherever they think he should be."

"You have such a way with words, but yes, you're right. He could still be the one roaming the campground. It's just…" I didn't finish the sentence because I didn't want to alarm my friend, but she persisted.

"It's just what?"

"It could be someone else."

Her eyes widened. "As in, he's got a partner?"

I looked at Myra in mild astonishment. "I never thought of that."

"Maybe in my next life I'll be a cop," she said, beaming. "So, you think last night was someone else?"

"Might be. I saw someone behind Steph's trailer, and I chased them, but I lost them. I didn't get a good look, because it was dark and they wore dark clothing with a hood pulled way down over their face. Couldn't tell if it was a man or a woman, but whoever it was looked taller and thinner than Manson Smith, but again, it was hard to tell."

"When I talk to our illustrious leader about it, should I share that information with him?" she inquired.

"I'm not sure. On the one hand, I say no. Just let him know people are still seeing someone roaming around the campground after hours

near their trailers. Then again, him being a cop, well he might get...
um, verbally rough with you in order to get all the information he
can to help him figure out what's going on, but..."

She lifted an eyebrow when I didn't finish. "You don't think Mac
deserves our help."

"We should help him for the benefit of the residents here. I just
don't think he should know I'm chasing down possible suspects. It
could get me into a lot of trouble."

"I don't see how. You're a civilian, only trying to help."

"I'm a retired cop and was his first recruit whom he hated, and I
think still does. Better you don't tell him, or you tell him that *you* saw
the person."

"Okay. I'll tell him I saw the person last night. I promise to keep
you out of it."

"Thanks, Myra."

She squeezed my hand. "Now, back to the other subject."

I cringed. "What subject?"

"The one where you have feelings more than friendship for
Steph." Her eyes penetrated mine, and I felt myself shrink from them.

Damn it.

CHAPTER FOURTEEN

By midafternoon, I decided I needed a hobby, or I'd be bored silly. I had already walked Mabel twice since Myra's visit—both long walks, and she wasn't happy with either. She didn't like doing the exercise I asked of her. She preferred to lie on the recliner on her back, feet in the air. My friends nicknamed her "slouch on a couch" because that was her position every time they visited. There was no doubt ten-year-old Mabel enjoyed her naps, so she gave me the side eye when I hooked her up for another walk to go up to the office and "chat" with Missy as she had suggested to me the other night at the Millers'. I decided getting out of my tin can and talking to people was what I needed, especially since Steph would go back to work soon, as would Myra and Jen.

My life had always been my work and my wife. Now, I had neither and I knew it was time to get moving on to the next stage. I just wasn't sure what that was, and it was making me nuts.

Mabel tugged on the leash and I looked down to see she was sitting on the road—her way of telling me she had had enough. I chuckled when I picked her up. "Wuss," I said, tucking her under my arm. It was a warm day at the end of May with clear skies that screamed blue. The grass was as green as it always was at this time of year from the spring rains. The seasonal residents who were here were already planting flowers and putting out their pots. Many campsites looked like they were vying for the cover of *Better Homes and Gardens.*

I opened the door to the campground office to find a cheery Missy behind the counter, helping a customer with purchases from their small, but thorough, camp store. It had two or three of everything you might need, but at exorbitant prices. Highway robbery, you might say, but I had patronized their retail establishment once or twice when I just didn't feel like driving to the store. The one thing campground stores had going for them—convenience.

"Hi, Missy," I said once the customer left.

I guessed Mac and his wife were in their late sixties, but Missy looked more like his grandmother. Her hair was already sour gray, and her wrinkled face screamed dry, old and…angry, which was odd. I imagined a lack of moisturizing and a lot of hard, sad times gave her the face of an eighty-year-old.

I didn't know Missy. Mac had never spoken about her, but when I worked as his recruit, lackey, punching bag—whatever you wanted to call me—I sometimes overheard him talk about his wife to his buddies. He never seemed to have anything good to say about her. So maybe Missy had a good reason for her aged look.

"Blakely. Right?" she answered while counting money and then putting it into a register.

"That's right. But please call me Blake. And I'm sure you remember Mabel."

She closed the register and looked up. She didn't appear to remember Mabel because she acted surprised to see a dog in my arms.

"This is my dog. You met her last night."

"Oh," she exclaimed. "That's right." She reached out and patted Mabel on the head harder than my little dog liked because her head kept dipping down with each smack of her hand. Mabel sank into my arms to avoid the petting.

"She is a cutie-pie," Missy said, leaning her forearms on the counter. "I've never had a pet. Mac felt it was too much work."

"Kind of like kids," I replied and at seeing the look of bewilderment on her face, I added, "It all depends on your perspective."

Missy changed the subject quickly. "How long have you camped here?"

"This is my first summer, but my friends have been coming here for years, and I used to visit them during the summers. Thought I'd give it a try now that I'm retired."

Missy looked me up and down. "Kind of young to be retired, aren't you?" It sounded more like an accusation, as if she meant to say, "How dare you retire so early when the rest of us have to work until we're old and decrepit."

"I've got a good pension, saved and invested well. I believe you should go when you can and enjoy every minute," I answered, feeling a bit unsettled that I felt I had to defend myself.

She turned and ruffled through some papers on a desk. "Is that what you believe? Good for you." Then she sat down and tapped on the computer keyboard as if she was dismissing me.

"Well," I said, turning the doorknob to leave. "You have a wonderful day."

She looked up at me. "Thank you for coming to visit. It was so nice of you. Have a good day too." She looked back at her computer screen.

I left the office and put Mabel back on the ground. "You're rested. You can walk. That was one strange visit. So, what would you like to do now?"

As if to answer me, Mabel kept sniffing.

"Fine. But you better not feign fatigue so I have to pick you up again and carry you the rest of the way."

"She's got you wrapped around her little paw, doesn't she?"

I looked up to see Steph coming toward us.

"Hey there. How…" I stopped myself before the words fell out of my mouth. I wanted to ask her how her visit was with her ex but knew better. It would come out sarcastic and not caring. As much as I hated to stay silent, it was better to wait and let her tell me where she had been and how her visit was. If she would tell me at all.

"Can I walk with you?"

Her question took me by surprise. "You never have to ask if you can walk with me. What's up?"

"Sorry, I missed breakfast. I had to go to another one of those classes."

"Uh-huh. How was it?"

"Like I said. Boring, but that's not what I wanted to talk to you about. Afterward, I met Lori. She called last night and wanted to see me. I almost didn't go, but I was kind of curious. She's still kind of messed up. Did I tell you I thought she was messed up?"

"Not in so many words," I answered. "I just kind of figured that out myself from everything you told me about her. Which wasn't much."

"There wasn't much to tell. It was a weird conversation. She talked about her new girlfriend. Then she talked about us as if we were merely on a break from our relationship and how it would be when we got back together. Then she talked about how her new relationship was the best thing that had ever happened to her. I finally got a chance to get into the conversation and told her it was nice to see her, but I had to go to work."

"That is odd. Are you going back to her?"

She didn't answer right away. I glanced at her out of the corner of my eye and saw her looking up at the sky, a smile of contentment, or something like that, on her face. Then she sighed deeply and turned to face me. She put a hand on my arm to stop me from walking.

"That's not why I'm telling you this. I could say my relationship woes with Lori are none of your business, but that's never been true. It's just that I'm tired of talking about this woman that I prefer to have nothing to do with."

Well, that answered that question. I studied her face, but I couldn't read what she was feeling, so I asked. "Then why *are* you telling me this? Why did you meet her?"

"I told you. There was something about the tone of her voice that made me curious. Look, Blake. We both know her latest girlfriend was your ex-wife. I don't think she's been involved with anyone else since then."

"Maybe she has. Remember Tess told me they had broken up, and she was only there to talk to Lori."

"And maybe that was all a lie, like the ones Tess told when she was cheating on you."

I looked away and scrunched up my face, ready to keep from exploding, but Steph took my chin in her hand and gently turned my face toward hers.

"The reason I'm telling you this is if you really loved Tess, and I know you did, you just need to warn her that maybe Lori isn't the best choice for a girlfriend, partner, wife, or whatever she has in mind. She's messed up. That's why I wanted to tell you about it.

Tess did a lousy thing, but she doesn't deserve to be mixed up with someone like Lori."

The tear that had settled in the corner of my eye was spilling onto my cheek. "You know damn well I loved Tess, and I would never want anything to happen to her either. But as you said to me, it's not my business what you do and it's no longer any of my business what Tess does."

Steph let go of my chin and wiped away the tear with one gentle swipe of her finger. "It is if it means she's doing something that might not be in her best interest."

Mabel was sitting patiently on the grass. I looked down at her and then started walking again. "Steph, she chose this. She's a big girl. She can make her own decisions. She can take care of herself."

"Yeah, but sometimes people get caught up in things they have no control over. They're blindsided and taken over by someone that can convince them to get involved. It's beyond their intelligence or common sense that tells them to stay away. They begin to believe that it could be a good thing, but you know as well as I do that it's usually not."

"When did you become a philosopher?" I chuckled. "Look, if you like Tess so much and you're concerned about her, call her. Talk to her about it. I just know I can't."

We approached the makeshift dog park, a large fenced-in area in the back of the campground where you could let your dog run free. I steered toward the gate with Steph following me and Mabel hopping like a bunny in anticipation of being let off the leash to run free to sniff, and sniff, and sniff. Once inside, I shut the enclosure and unclipped Mabel's leash. Surprise. She was off and sniffing. Steph began to stalk my dog, a game we often played with her. She loved, loved, loved to be chased. So, for the next fifteen minutes, we ran after my little ball of white fluff with a gray-and-white striped head all around the play area. Her four little legs carried her faster, helped her to dodge sharper and turn on a dime in order to elude our every effort in capturing her.

I loved watching Steph laugh as she tried desperately to outsmart Mabel. At one point, the two of them turned the same way and took off at a full sprint to the other side of the enclosure, ending in a standoff at which point Mabel ran between her legs throwing Steph off balance. "That's not fair," Steph cried out as she lumbered over to where I stood, her breathing labored. She bent over and put her hands on her knees.

Noticing Mabel had also stopped and was panting, I said," I think you two have had enough. You don't want to kill my dog, do you? She never knows when to quit."

"She plans it that way. She knows I'm close to catching her, so she feigns fatigue knowing you'll stop her by giving her a treat. Like I said, she's got you wrapped around her little paw."

I dropped Steph off at her trailer, reminding her about dinner at Jen and Myra's, and then returned to our little abode. Mabel took her position on the recliner, and I sank into the other one.

My phone chirped some time later, causing me to jump out of a very restful late afternoon nap. I saw Myra's name pop up with a reminder that dinner was in fifteen minutes, and I was missing happy hour. I hurriedly prepared Mabel's dinner and took it with me. Steph was there with a can of Coca-Cola in her hand.

"That stuff will kill you." I nodded toward the can.

She chuckled. "Nowadays, everything will kill you."

"True. I guess we all just have to pick our poison," I answered. I took a chair next to her. "Where are the girls?"

"Inside getting you a drink."

"What are they bringing me that takes two of them?" I laughed.

"No idea. Myra said they had a new cocktail they wanted you to try."

I placed Mabel's food on the ground and watched her eat. Then I said quietly, "I'm sorry."

Steph put her Coke on the small table in between us. She folded her arms and snapped her head in my direction. "Really? I told you not to do this. I am not an alcoholic. You know that. I made a mistake. Believe me when I tell you it won't happen again. The only reason I'm having a Coke is because their new cocktail has whiskey in it, and I don't like whiskey."

"I don't like whiskey either," I retorted. "They know that."

"They seem to feel you won't taste it in this drink."

And just then, Myra bounded out of the trailer with a glass in each hand. "Wait until you try this. Best cocktail ever. Steph says she doesn't like whiskey. Do you mind giving her a sip of yours if she wants to try it? I…" she said, handing me a glass and then sitting in a chair, "am not sharing." She took a long drink.

I sipped mine, expecting it to be bitter. But it wasn't. I handed the glass of slushy alcohol to Steph. "That's not bad. What's in it?"

"Apple whiskey, lemon juice, pineapple juice, berry-flavored seltzer water, and a cinnamon stick. We just love that new distillery on Route 86. We only go when their mixologist is there. She's introduced us to a lot of new cocktails."

Steph took a small sip and held the glass out. "It's okay. I can still taste whiskey. I'll stick with my Coke."

"We can make you something else. Rum and Coke?"

"I'm good," Steph answered.

Jen came out, holding her drink in the air. "What do you think? It's good, isn't it?" She answered for us. Steph and I nodded. She looked at Steph. "You liked it? Great. I'll make you one."

"No, thank you. For a drink made with whiskey, it's okay, but I can still taste it. I'm just not a whiskey drinker."

"Oh." Jen's face fell. "I'm sorry. I forgot about that."

"Okay. Enough with the I'm sorrys. I will drink if I want to drink. I just want my Coke, so can we leave it at that?" Her tone was edgy, and I knew underneath there was something else bothering her. Was she still upset about Lori and Tess?

I hoped not. I didn't want that to come between our friendship, and it might hurt the probability of anything else possibly happening in the future. Then, I stopped my train of thought. How could I think anything could flourish between us when we had already tried it once? After Annie died, I was a wreck and Steph came to my rescue. She always came to my rescue. It was what Steph did.

When I finally got to the other side of my grief, we felt a pull toward each other. We thought it was more than friendship, so we made a play for something more. It didn't work, and thankfully we ended up laughing about it, because how could you ruin such a wonderful friendship with sex? And then we drifted apart, maybe because neither of us wanted to deal with our almost sexual encounter. So, when Steph called me years later, and we rekindled our friendship, I vowed never to do anything to ruin it.

I jumped from my chair and handed Mabel's leash to Steph. "Could you watch her? I have to go back to my trailer. I'll be right back." Not waiting for an answer, I ran to my trailer, up the steps, and closed the door behind me. I threw my hands to my head. "Stop it, you idiot. Just stop it." I sank into one of my leather recliners and put my head in my hands. Crying, I told myself over and over, "You can't go there again. You can't."

When I gained control, I realized I had to come up with a reason for rushing away. I went into the bathroom and splashed water on my face to clear the tearstains and dim the redness of my eyes and cheeks. Then I turned circles in the trailer, looking for something, anything I could use as an explanation. My eyes fell upon the paper with notes from my conversation with Captain Spinner concerning the woman found at the bottom of the gorge.

I walked back. They stopped talking, and I sighed heavily. Waving the paper in the air, I said, "I almost forgot about this." I sat down and extended my arms out to Steph.

She looked at me nonchalantly, Mabel on her lap. When I glared at her, she said, "What?"

"My dog?"

"She's happy here."

I leaned over, lifted one of Mabel's ears, and whispered, "Traitor."

Jen and Myra laughed. "Looks like you might lose your dog," Jen said.

"No way. She's devoted to me. She just knows Steph is lonely and needs her healing company."

Steph nuzzled Mabel and responded, "I won't take insult to any of that, because this little bugger absolutely has healing powers." She looked up at me. "I mean, look at you. You've come a long way, baby."

I lifted my glass. "Yes, I have thanks to all of you and my little creature with healing powers."

"So, tell us what's on that piece of paper."

"I called Captain Spinner about the body in the gorge. She was nice enough to oblige me—to a degree."

"I'm sure she was," Steph interjected, and giggled. Then she said with all the seriousness she could muster, "You realize that you are no longer an official, working policewoman. She doesn't have to and probably shouldn't be answering your questions. I don't know why she puts up with your bothersome ways."

"I am not bothersome. I have questions. They need to be answered."

"That's just a polite way of saying a pain in the ass," Jen chuckled. My friends laughed with her.

I slammed the paper on my leg. "What is this? Pick on Blake Day?"

"Yeah, it kind of is. We made a decision while you sprinted across the field,"—Steph leaned forward to make her next point—"without you." She leaned back and finished, "That the third Thursday of every month will be Pick on Blake Day."

"Seriously?"

"Absolutely," Myra agreed, nodding her head.

"Do you want to hear what I found out or not?"

Steph moved about in her chair. "Maybe you shouldn't be doing this." She looked awkward and unsettled, and I wondered if this was something I should have kept to myself.

"I guess I still can't leave my job back in the police station," I said, looking down at the paper.

Myra looked at me sympathetically. "You were always so good at what you did. The thing that won't let you walk away from your work is that you loved it."

"Maybe you should open up a private investigator's business. You could still do what you love, but on your terms and in your time," Jen said, smiling.

"So *what* did the illustrious captain say?" Steph asked.

I explained that the Ithaca police still didn't know if it was a murder or a suicide. There was no evidence to either claim. Everything had been wiped clean. Everything. *Just like it was when Annie died there.* The woman was married—rumored to have been having an affair. She was a professor at Cornell Vet School and reported missing when she didn't show up for her classes. I looked up after reading my notes. "That's all she would tell me."

I glanced at Steph to see her reaction. She knew the details of Annie's case, and I was pretty sure she picked up on the similarities with this one. There was something about the similarities between the two that bothered me. I felt it in my bones.

"Why are you researching this?" Myra asked. "What's your interest in this case? Did you know the woman?"

"No, no. It's just that ever since that case I had to deal with when I first came out of the Academy, I've just always monitored this area. I was born here, grew up here—even worked here." I looked at their faces, and was pretty sure I had convinced Myra and Jen it was nothing more than I couldn't let go of my job. "What's that saying? You can take the girl out of Ithaca, but you can't take Ithaca out of the girl."

"More like you can take the job away from the policewoman, but you can't take the policewoman away from the job." Steph smiled at me. It was a knowing smile. One that told me she was going to grill me at some point when we were alone.

I smiled inwardly to myself. I could handle that.

Dinner was uneventful in the serious-conversation way. Instead it was filled with lots of laughter. We expected Mac Taylor to visit us on his grand golf cart, but he was a no-show. It was a relief that I didn't have to fake niceties to a man I knew I could never be nice to. We sat around the campfire long into the night. The stars were beacons of light on a black canvas sharing it with a crescent moon. The air was chilled, but the flames that stretched upward from Steph's fire kept the cold at bay.

Before we bid each other good night, Steph handed off Mabel to me. Then she walked down to her trailer to spend the night alone, which disappointed the hell out of me.

I sat with Myra a while longer. Jen went to bed, and I believed Myra didn't want me sitting at their campfire all alone. What I really wanted to do was to keep an eye out on the area. Maybe I was being paranoid, but I had that feeling I got when I knew something was amiss. The prowler was here. I could feel it. Now, I just had to get Myra inside so I could do a little investigating. But she wasn't budging. I told her I was tired, so she helped me put the fire to bed. I walked across the field to my trailer, with Mabel in tow while taking the opportunity to survey my friends' campsites. I put Mabel inside on a recliner, grabbed a warm jacket, and went outside to sit on the picnic table where I had a good view of their trailers and the sky. But nothing happened. No shadows lurking in and out of trailers or bushes. No unusual noises—not even the coyotes who seemed to hunt often in the early summer. Just crickets.

Eventually, I finally gave up listening and started nodding off. I went inside and got ready for bed. Mabel gave me the evil eye. I'm sure it was because she would have to snuggle up to me tonight and not Steph.

I gave her a wan smile and said, "I feel the same way."

CHAPTER FIFTEEN

Steph didn't show up for breakfast, again, so I settled for a bowl of dry Honey Nut Cheerios and yogurt. I sat in the booth and opened my laptop to begin a search on Marie Sanfield. I wanted to know more about her. Mabel wasn't interested in what I was doing. Her butt was facing my direction, and I was pretty sure that was her way of giving me the finger for Steph not being here during the night. "It's not my fault," I pleaded to her butt. Mabel didn't move, instead continued to ignore me. I picked up my phone and weighed in the pros and cons of calling Steph and inviting her to lunch. Then I set it down. Was I being too pushy? Could long-term friends become lovers? Wasn't that a song?

I scrolled through Marie's social sites. She had a Facebook page, but there wasn't much on it. She had no Twitter or Instagram accounts. I knew Maddie's department would already be delving into Marie's life and background, but there was something that tugged at me. Annie Wilson tugged at me. She was begging me to find the answer to her death, to let her family know so they could have closure. They, like me, did not believe that Annie jumped off the cliff, but there was always that nagging in the back of our minds that wouldn't go away until we knew for sure.

I had no idea if solving Marie's death would lead me to an answer about Annie. But the fact that it was in the *exact* same place bothered me. Most of the college-student suicides back in the '90s and early 2000s were off bridges closer to the university. There weren't many other similarities between the two women. Annie was twenty when she died. Marie was thirty-eight. Annie was a college student and Marie was a senior academic at an elite university. Annie was involved with me. Marie was married, but she was cheating on her husband.

There was a knock on my door, followed by the "call of the camper" as I had come to name it.

"Hey, girl. It's Steph. I'm late for breakfast. Is there any left?" She opened the door without waiting for me to answer. Mabel, that little traitor, jumped down off the chair, tail wagging, and ran to Steph so she would pick her up and lavish her with affection.

I didn't turn around. Those two were starting to irritate me with their mushiness. Where was my share of the sappy attention? I felt my body being nudged hard and realized Steph was using her body to push me over in the booth. I grabbed my laptop and pulled it along with me. Steph scootched in with Mabel on her lap, now curling up in a ball.

"You just love me, don't you, little girl?" Steph rubbed Mabel's ears, generating a low-pitched moan of contentment. "Whatcha doing?" she asked, observing me while avoiding the subject of what was going on between her and my dog.

I didn't answer. Instead, I kept surfing.

"Oh, no. You aren't jealous, are you?"

"My dog is now ignoring me. She lies with her butt to me."

"Oh, that's bad," she laughed. "That's a dog's way of giving you the finger."

When I turned to look at her, she was smirking.

"Yes, I know that, thank you very much." I went back to my computer screen, but I was chuckling because I had thought the same thing. I pushed her with my hips toward the end of the seat. "I could use a little room."

She placed Mabel on a recliner. Out of the corner of my eyes, I saw her slip her a treat, and I heard her whisper, "You stay here. Your mommy is mad at us." Then she plopped down into the other booth seat across from me.

"Who are *you* stalking?" Her hands folded on top of the table as if waiting to admonish me when I answered.

Without looking at her, I replied, "Marie Sanfield."

"You know you could piss off Maddie."

"Not if she doesn't know I'm doing it."

"Be careful," she warned. "And I'm hungry. What's for breakfast?"

I looked at my watch. "Breakfast is long gone. Wanna go to lunch?"

"Only if we can take Mabel."

I tilted my head and glanced at her. "Would you two prefer to go alone?"

"Who's going to pay?"

I closed the websites I was perusing and sat back. There was no comeback. Nothing. I shook my head. She won this round, I mused. I'd get the next one. "Fine, but then it's my choice of where we go."

"You're not going to pick somewhere I don't like, are you?"

"My choice," I said in a singsong voice, getting up from the booth. I hooked up Mabel and extended the bright-red nylon leash to Steph, but instead of taking the leash, she picked her up.

"You know, if you keep handing her off to me, she'll think you don't want her anymore."

I grabbed my dog and went out the door with a chuckling Steph walking behind me. We enjoyed a leisurely lunch at a small diner on Route 13, followed by a walk at Robert Treman Falls. The trail along the water was long and uphill. Coming back was downhill—easier on the lungs, but tougher on the knees. Still, it was a cool walk on a hot, summer day, the path shaded by the trees lining it.

When we got back to the campground, Myra and Jen were walking along the road. I slowed the car and Steph rolled down her window. "Hey, girls," she crooned.

"Well look who it is. Went off without us, huh? Who's doing dinner tonight?" Myra inquired while they walked alongside my car.

Steph's head turned in my direction. Her lips squeezed together, her eyebrows raised, and she gave a very slight tilt of her head. I knew what it meant.

"I've got dinner. See you around six?"

"Sounds like a plan. We'll bring the drinks."

"See ya later," Steph said and rolled up the window. Her posture was stiff like an ironing board.

"What'd I do?" I asked, afraid she had indeed noticed my reaction despite my efforts to hide it.

"You are my best friend. More than my best friend, so I'm only going to say this once more. I. Am. Not. An alcoholic. Since after graduating from college, I have not gotten drunk except for that one night. I was"—she turned her whole body to face me—"stupid."

"I know. I'm sorry if you thought I was judging you."

"You're not judging me. You're trying to steer me away from alcohol in a way that won't seem controlling. But it is."

"I promise I won't do it again."

"If you do, I'll have to take your dog. I don't want her to be raised in an atmosphere where she is told what to do. She has a mind of her own, ya know."

I chuckled. "That she does.

When Steph got out of the car, she turned away and stuck her butt in the door. I laughed hard all the way to my trailer where I dropped Mabel off and drove back out of the campground to Walmart. I bought a cooked chicken, bagged salad, corn on the cob, and a few sweet potatoes. I got back in plenty of time to boil the potatoes and the corn before my friends showed up.

Myra set the table with my white-and-blue speckled plastic dinnerware. Steph, of course, fed my dog. Jen filled the glasses with her latest drink mixture and I served the uncomplicated but sumptuous meal.

It wouldn't have been dinner without the sound of Mac's golf cart approaching. It didn't matter where we ate, he always seemed to find us. He was like the prowler, except he operated out in the open in daylight. "Ladies, ladies, ladies. How are we today?" There was a glint in his eye that looked more like he was up to something than he was happy to see us.

Steph held up her drink. Tonight's refresher was a raspberry slusher with raspberry liquor, and it was as tasty as fresh raspberries off the bush. Just colder. "Well, Mac, we're doing just fine. How are you?"

"I'm so glad you asked."

I got up and began to clear the table, not wanting to know why.

"We made a killing last weekend. The campground was full, and Missy did a great job of organizing all the events. I can see the reviews coming in now."

I rolled my eyes as I climbed up the steps into my trailer. *Let them deal with him. I did it for almost five years, four years and three hundred and sixty-four days too many.* I turned on the pump and scraped the food from the dishes into the garbage. The water would be warm in a matter of minutes and I would wash the dishes, grateful I had a reason to leave my three best friends to entertain Mac.

I heard the door open and looked over to see Steph. "You okay?" She walked around me and leaned her back against the counter, folding her arms.

I turned on the hot water and added soap. "I'm sorry to leave you three out there with that rat, but I just couldn't listen to him."

"I get it. I know better than anyone what you went through during your rookie years, but it's in the past and you can't let that rat..." She leaned backward and met my eyes. "Have so much influence over your life."

"He hasn't for a long, long time," I shot back.

"Then why now?"

"Maybe because his is literally staring me in the face." I washed the plates one by one. She stood by me in silence while I rinsed them and then tossed the silverware into the sink. "How do you do it?"

"Do what?"

"Interact with him in a way that gives you the upper hand and makes him look like an idiot, even though he doesn't realize it."

She grinned. "I've had thirty years of practice. I can teach you. It might come in handy with other people you meet along the way."

"Huh. Something to consider. I can see you and me in a battle of wits."

She picked up a towel and started drying. "I would win."

"I'm a fast learner," I said, handing her a pot. "You think Myra and Jen will be mad at us for leaving them out there with him?"

"No way. They play like I do. They enjoy harassing him without him knowing they're doing it."

"Does everybody know how to do that but me?"

"Why yes, young grasshopper. I already taught them." She laughed as she dried the last pot and then put the towel over the oven handle. "Shall we?" She swept her arm toward the door. "I'll give you your first lesson."

I groaned as I walked outside to see Mac deep in an explanation of something. Steph came up beside me and whispered, "Look at Myra and Jen's expressions."

I glanced at them feigning interest, their eyebrows slightly raised, a minimal smile on their lips, a look I had never seen on them. So, I copied it. *My first lesson.*

The evening sun was just at the horizon and the sky was that grayish blue that happens right before the evening blackness takes over. I scooped up Mabel and sat in one of the chairs placed around the fire pit, waiting for Mac to leave and Myra to prepare the campfire.

I felt his eyes on me. "Don't know where that asshole went. But I made sure he wasn't comin' back here. He got the message, all right. A real cop knows how to do that." Still eyeing me, he puffed out his chest. "Shouldn't be any more trouble around here. If there is, you ladies just call on ol' Mac."

Myra lifted her glass to him. "Absolutely. Will do. Thanks for stopping by."

He started his golf cart as he looked us over like he was weighing what he might say next. Something past us caught his attention. He slammed the pedal of his golf cart down to the floor so hard I thought his foot would fall through, and tore off, leaving a dirt cloud in his wake.

"What do you think got him so riled up?" Myra asked.

I kept my sight in the direction Mac was speeding toward, wishing he would give himself a fine for speeding. I saw a shadow moving quickly in between trailers in the distance. Standing, I placed Mabel in Steph's lap and grabbed my flashlight. Steph put a hand on my arm.

"Where're you going?"

"I don't trust ol' Mac. He saw someone, and he's headed over there to cause trouble."

"Please, Blake, sit down. He's probably checking out someone who looks like the prowler which he has the right to do. It's his campground, not yours," she pleaded, keeping her hand on my arm.

"But it's my war," I spat out, not realizing how stupid it sounded until I said it.

"We're camping, for God's sake," Jen said. "There's no war here that I know of. You?"

I gently pulled my arm away and said to Steph, "I'm pretty sure she's directing that to you."

"Nope, no war here," Steph answered through hard lips.

Myra's head was cocked with one raised eyebrow, trying not to look sympathetic. "Maybe you weren't ready to retire." She held my glass out to me. "Sit and drink with us and we can discuss how best for us to handle your retirement."

I could have sworn there was a twinkle in one of her eyes, but it didn't relax me or soothe the profiler beast within. "We? I don't think *we* are going to discuss that. I'm fine. There's a stalker still roaming the campground. I think Mac might have hurt Manson Smith. I want to know what happened to Marie Sanfield, and that's just all in my nature. I will always be this. Retired or not, and I will take that drink as soon as I get back. Steph, please take good care of my baby."

"Will do," she answered. "Be careful. Don't do anything I wouldn't do. Oh wait, that's a moot point. Try not to do anything stupid." Her eyes remained downcast on Mabel who was curled up in her lap. She stroked her back as she sighed deeply.

"I'm not afraid of a stalker," I shot back.

"I didn't say anything about a stalker."

That left me speechless, so I trotted down the dirt road toward the back of the campground. I saw Mac's golf cart parked in the small empty field next to the three rental cabins. Cars were parked in front of two of the cabins, indicating they were rented. I made a wide berth around those two and hurried into the woods behind them.

If truth be told, Steph was right. There was no war. I was making it one and it made me angry that I didn't seem to care that she was right. But I couldn't help myself. I had to make sure if someone was stalking the campground, Mac caught him. I was just worried that Mac might discover I was following him. His anger was something I didn't want to face, but I couldn't, I wouldn't let this go. I had a flashlight and my can of pepper spray in my pocket—I now carried it every day, everywhere—so I wasn't worried about getting hung up in the woods in the dark.

The trees and vegetation grew thicker and closed in on me as if to swallow me whole. I stopped to turn on my light, knowing it would alert anyone who might be out here, possibly Mac. Then I heard a noise. Faint at first, and soon I realized it didn't belong to the catalog of nature's sounds. I moved toward it and heard a deep-throated groan of...pain. Someone was in pain.

I hurried, not caring about the noise I made as I broke branches and bushwhacked through like an Amazon explorer. No matter how careful I was, I still tripped over rocks and vines. Finally, a figure lying on the ground came into view. I could only tell it was a man. His head was down and turned to the side, but his face was away from me. I circled him to get a better look and saw Mac's scruffy beard and hard face. I bent down and felt the pulse in his neck. He was alive. I checked for injuries and found his head was bleeding. When I touched the wound, he stirred and grunted and then struggled to get up. I helped him to a sitting position, and that's when he said gruffly, "Did you see him? He hit me with something."

"No," I replied. "Come on, let me get you back to the office. You were knocked out. You need to have your head checked. You're bleeding."

I imagined Mac was steaming because it was me who found him. It made me smile as I put my shoulder under his arm and got him to his feet. He said nothing else. He didn't fight me as I assisted him to his golf cart, where I managed to ease him into the passenger seat. I drove him back to the office. If Missy wasn't there, I'd take him to the house. Luckily, she was inside, visible through the large windows in front. She looked up when we got close. Noticing I was driving Mac's vehicle, she dropped whatever it was she was doing and ran out to greet us.

"Oh, my Lord. What happened? Why are you driving his golf cart?"

I found the question quite odd and rather comical, but I knew better than to laugh. "He's not fit to drive," I answered, trying to keep a straight face. "He's hurt."

We each took an arm, listening to Mac mumble under his breath as we helped him hobble into the office. Missy steered him around the counter, where we lowered him into a stuffed chair that had seen better days. She disappeared into the back room and returned with a large official-looking first aid kit.

"What happened?" she growled at her husband.

Mac shot me a glare that plainly said, "Keep your mouth shut," and then answered his wife. "I was piling some wood in the back storage lot and tripped. Must have hit my head on something."

I also received a look from Missy that seemed to doubt his ability to tell the truth. Caught in between the two, I came up with an excuse to leave before they dragged me into the middle of a couple's spat. "I need to get back to my friends. I know he's in good hands now," I said as I hurried out the door and back to my campsite. I wondered who was wandering around in the woods and if it could turn dangerous for campers. My shoulders slumped when I saw the chairs empty and the campfire out. Were my friends mad at me for leaving so abruptly?

Mabel! I ran into my trailer to find Steph sitting on a recliner with Mabel nestled in her lap, a bottle of beer in the cup holder, and our favorite sci-fi series on the television. *The Grimm.* I thought it was rather apropos at this point. I took a deep breath and shut the door behind me.

"Sorry," I said.

She didn't look up, but took a long swallow from the bottle. When she finished, she turned her head in my direction. "I'll say two things. One. That was kind of rude of you. This is Mac's campground. You really should let him deal with it."

I walked over and sat in the other recliner, putting my feet up. "And the other?"

"What happened?" Followed by a tiny grin and a nod toward the table across from where we sat. I picked up the open bottle of beer.

"How long has this been sitting here open?"

"You should be thankful I stayed here with Mabel and had one ready for you when you got back."

After a swallow, I answered, "I am. And again, I'm sorry. Really."

"*So?* What happened?" she repeated.

"I'm pretty sure the stalker was roaming the campground again. I saw Mac pull into the end-cabin driveway, but by the time I got there, he was gone. I found him a good ways into the woods toward the cliff along the creek. He'd been hit on the head, knocked out cold."

"Holy shit. Is he okay?"

"Not sure. There was a lot of blood, but I know head wounds bleed a lot. His wife is tending to him now. I just hope she takes him to urgent care or something."

"Did he say anything? Did he see who it was?"

"He said he didn't see who hit him. He said nothing else. Someone whacked him, but we just have no way of knowing whether it's the prowler, or a hunter or a teen being a jerk. But here's the weird thing. When I got him back to the office, he gave me a look that told me to keep quiet about how he got hurt. He told his wife he was stacking wood and fell. Then his wife shot me a look that said it better be the truth, and I'm sure she was waiting for me to either verify or nullify her husband's story."

"Did you?"

"Nope. I hightailed it out of there."

"Huh. Now what?"

"Now, you stay here for the night, just in case the stalker is still around." I took a sip of beer. "And…I'd rather not be alone," I lied, hoping she'd take the bait.

"Shouldn't we call the police?" Her eyes were on the TV, and they were sparkling. Her lips were slightly upturned.

"Mac *is* the police, and he's also the owner, as you have pointed out. That's his job to call the police. I just don't think he will because he doesn't want to. I think he's been convincing everyone that the stalker has gone for good, so no one needs to call the police. If we call now, it could have some repercussions. He might kick us out of the campground. Especially if the police realize he's been dealing with this on his own and maybe not by the book."

"Kind of like you, huh?"

I rolled my eyes. "No. I went to help him. Good thing I did."

"Okay, so I'm back to now what?"

"I'd like you to be with me when I confront him."

To Mabel's dismay, Steph picked her up and set her on my lap. Then she stood. "I'm okay to stay at my trailer tonight. Thank you for the invite, but if I've told you once, I've told you a hundred times. Maybe a thousand. I can take care of myself."

"Then why did you stay here the other two nights?" And I immediately wished I hadn't said it.

Steph walked to the door and opened it, beer in hand. "I knew you didn't want to be alone. I think you'll be okay tonight." She grinned. "As for talking to Mac with you. I'll think about it. Good night, Blake." She shut the door behind her.

I called out, "Thanks for watching Mabel." And I realized there was one thing I was getting very good at. Pissing people off. I had run out on my friends and they weren't too happy with me. Jen and Myra didn't wait for my return and Steph made it clear that running off after Mac wasn't a very nice thing to do. I wiped at a tear vacating my eye and running down my cheek. And now, the sudden change in Steph's mood. *I'm not going to cry over this.* The wet path down my cheek was now a steady stream.

Yeah, right.

CHAPTER SIXTEEN

The next morning, after taking Mabel out for her walk, I had an urge to make eggs Benedict. It was maybe because I considered it comfort food and right then, I needed me a little comfort. I'd never be able to stop my curiosity, and I decided while walking, I wasn't going to try. It was who I was, but I was afraid I could jeopardize our friendships if I kept up my investigations. I had to work on my covertness.

I was humming while preparing breakfast when there was a knock and a call of the camper interrupted me.

"Hey, Blake. It's me, Steph. Can I come in?"

I opened the door and then turned away, going back to my cooking. "There's extra, but you've got to set the table." She didn't answer me and I said nothing else. I watched her out of the corner of my eyes as she took plates out of the cupboard, silverware out of the drawer and placed them on the table.

"Mabel girl. Did you miss me?" She picked her up and settled her on her lap. She stroked the dog's head, whispering what I thought might be sweet nothings to her, but I couldn't hear any of it. I was a tiny bit jealous she wasn't whispering them to me and then scolded myself for that line of thinking.

Finally, Steph spoke. "I'm sorry about last night."

I carried the first pan over to the table and placed two helpings of eggs Benedict on each plate. Then I brought the pan of sauce over. Steph moved from the recliner to the booth. I placed the warm pan on a pot holder and handed her the spoon.

"Now I really am sorry." She spooned a general helping of hollandaise on her eggs, then put the rest on mine. "Did you hear what I said?"

"I did. But I'd like to know what you're sorry for."

"I was kind of rough on you."

"Over the decades I've known you, I have learned that sometimes it's best for all, including me, if you are."

Steph stared at me. Then she said, "I appreciate you recognizing that. Now, let's eat. This is so yummie." We discussed possible leisure activities for the rest of the summer. Memorial Weekend was over, which meant the campground and the town would be less crowded, making entertaining ourselves much more enjoyable. Steph picked up our plates and took them to the sink. "I've been thinking." She turned around. "You're approaching this the wrong way."

"Approaching what the wrong way? Entertaining myself?"

"Ha, ha. I don't think talking to Mac is going to benefit anyone. Maybe we should work together on this. The stalker seems to be around my side of the campground most of the time. No idea why, but I sure would like to know. What if you stay with me tonight and we do some surveillance together? Two are better than one—safer that way."

I cocked my head in surprise. "I haven't asked you to help because I don't want to get you in trouble. You'll be on probation when you go back to work. You can't risk your job or your pension."

"I won't do anything to put my job in jeopardy. You can count on that. So, what do you say?"

I studied her a moment, debating if this was a smart thing to do. I definitely was leaning toward a yes. "On one condition. That Mabel can stay at your place, too." I kept my facial expression as straight as a con man, but I wanted to smile and sing to the world.

She folded her arms. Her eyes twinkled and her lips tilted in a half-smile. "The only reason I'm inviting you to stay is because I know Mabel will have to come too." Then she got up and walked over to the dog, who was wagging her short tail and looking dreamily at my friend.

"You two are such traitors," I chuckled. "If I didn't know any better, I'd say Mabel was cheating on me and had this whole thing planned. Just great. Three cheaters in my life."

Steph turned to look at me, a serious expression on her face. "First, I can't believe you tossed me and your dog into the same barrel as Tess. Mabel is not cheating. She just wants both of us in her life. There's plenty of room in that little heart of hers." She petted my dog as she said to her, "Isn't there, wittle girl?" Mabel's tail never stopped wagging. "Second, you and I are not in a relationship. I am not cheating on you."

"Sorry," I said as my face flushed with remorse mixed in with embarassment.

She winked at me and went to the sink to do the dishes. I helped Steph finish the dishes, rather, I finished and she went back to lavishing affection on my dog. We agreed to go over to Jen and Myra's and force them out of repose to partake in some frolicking for the day. But first, we took a long walk with Mabel. The weather couldn't have been better if we had ordered it. The sky was cobalt-blue dotted with a large yellow ball, making it look as if an artist had painted it in the exact position where it hung. There were no clouds, but the temperatures were moderate, with a hint of humidity that told us the day would be hot and sultry.

We discussed things we could do for the day and agreed on renting kayaks. We could paddle on the Cayuga Inlet that was easy paddling on a quiet stretch of water with a few places to put in and a kayak rental store on one of the tributaries. When we arrived back at the campground, we walked directly to Myra and Jen's trailer and performed the call of the camper.

Jen poked her head out with her index finger on her lips. "Myra's on an important call."

"Okay. We'll wait out here for the two of you," I told her. Steph dragged two of their chairs out from under the trailer, and we took a seat and waited. Mabel got a drink from the water bowl Myra and Jen always made available to her and then settled down on the deck at my feet.

The familiar sound of Mac's golf cart made both our heads snap to see him driving down the road, thankfully, at a slower pace than usual. I smiled. Maybe the bonk on his head had been good for him. Then again, if it's too good to be true, it usually isn't. It was the first time he rolled to a stop instead of abruptly braking, but he didn't turn toward us. He stared straight ahead. "Hey, Moore."

"Good morning," I answered, not knowing what else to say. His greeting wasn't sarcastic, and there was no teasing or condescending tone in his voice. He seemed uncomfortable.

"Um. Wanted to say thanks." He started the engine of his little throne on wheels and continued down the road.

"Will you look at that?" Steph said, grinning. "Not sure what to make of it."

"Me neither," I said, watching him drive down to the end of the campground, around the bend, and back up the road that ran in front of my trailer. He made another turn and headed back to the office. That was the advantage of our friend's campsite. From here, you could see everyone come and go. You couldn't see the office, but all roads led to the parking lot in front of it and that was in full view.

Steph got up and banged on the trailer door. "Come on, you two. Quit screwing and get out here. We have a plan for the day."

Heavy footsteps went the length of the trailer and the door swung open. "We are not screwing," Jen said in defiance. Her hands were on her hips and she looked at us with her teacher's face that she used when she was annoyed with us. "My wife is working."

"Tell her to stop. It's the weekend."

"Um, Steph?" I interrupted quietly.

"What?" She whipped around and scowled at me.

"It's Monday, a workday."

She backed up, a bit of redness flooding her cheeks. "Whoops. Sorry. We'll just be going now. See you gals later." As soon as Jen shut the door, Steph said, "Definitely screwing."

I laughed. "Then, we'll go kayaking. Meet me at my place in fifteen?"

"Sounds like a plan."

Mabel was already standing, looking up at me. "You want to go kayaking, girl?" This time, her whole butt wagged with the beat of her tail. I chuckled, and we walked home to get our PFDs.

I packed a small cooler with snacks and water and put it in the trunk with the life jackets just as Steph crossed the field. I couldn't help but smile. My stomach twittered with butterflies at the thought of spending the day with her alone. I hadn't felt like that in a long time, but I held it at bay, wondering if she felt the same, if just a little.

"Hey there. Is Mabel ready to hit the water?" She tossed her life jacket into the back of my SUV. Steph trotted to the gate, opened it and Mabel went right to her, getting up on her hind legs and resting her front paws on Steph's legs. On the cuteness scale, it was a ten-plus. I locked up and we took off for an afternoon on the water. I was going to spend the night in her trailer, where we would be doing one of the things I liked best. Surveillance. I should have worn my happy camper T-shirt that also said, "Life is good." Today it was indeed. Retirement was looking better and better.

After kayaking, Steph and I decided to have dinner at a local restaurant near where we rented our kayaks. The establishment had an outdoor seating area, allowing us to have Mabel at the table. She curled up on the patio floor and went to sleep while we dined on broiled seafood and salads. Two glasses of chardonnay topped off a delicious meal, but the best was yet to come. We took Mabel for a walk and visited a local ice cream shop a few blocks away. I would have stayed out all night with Steph if I could. We were relaxed, enjoying each other's company and…well, having the best time I'd had in ages. I would have loved to take a leisurely stroll in the park that bordered the river we just kayaked in, but Mabel needed to be fed.

We skipped the nightly campfire and curled up on Steph's couch to watch more of *The Grimm*—she on one end, me on the other, and Mabel happily in the middle. Mugs of decaffeinated green tea were the drink of choice for the evening, making life in Steph's park model peaceful and happy and I wished never-ending. Despite the fact there was more room in her trailer, it felt cozier like a home whereas mine felt more like a decorated tin can. Her furniture was larger, like what you would buy from a furniture store. Mine was made smaller to fill smaller spaces and looked like what you would buy from an RV store. The park models had actual rooms—one or more bedrooms, a larger bathroom, kitchen and living room with space to move around. I could get used to it, but it just wasn't meant to be unless I decided to upgrade from a twenty-nine foot trailer to my own park model.

Hoping to hear any human movement outside the trailer, we kept the volume low. After two episodes, I took Mabel out one last time around ten and surveyed the area while Steph remained inside, snoozing. As I passed the three cabins, I could have sworn I saw the shadow of a person walking down the steps of the cabin that had been empty for a while and into the woods. Mac was probably happy to have rented it. He was always about the money. I continued on my walk back toward my friends' trailers. A few minutes later, I thought I saw movement in the woods near the edge of the ravine that ran along the side of the campground behind their campers. I gathered up my dog in my arms and tried to be nonchalant. When I reached Steph's camper, I went inside but remained near the door, listening.

"Steph," I whispered loudly. "Steph, wake up."

Her eyelids fluttered and then slowly lifted, exposing two exhausted green eyes beneath her slitted lids. A few seconds later, she realized I had my ear to the door. She sat bolt upright.

"He's out there?" she mouthed.

I nodded.

Very quietly, she got up and walked over to get closer to me. "Shouldn't we go after him?"

"We wouldn't catch him. He's closer to Jen and Myra's site, moving along the edge of the ravine. I want to wait and see if he comes this way," I answered in a hushed whisper. "Get my pepper spray and flashlight." I brought my arsenal with me except for my gun, and I told Steph hers was to stay in the locked box. She did as I asked and came back, handing me the pepper spray. She held the flashlight, ready to bolt on my command. If there was a security camera outside, the footage would have been comical to watch, with the two of us leaning toward the door listening and Mabel sitting up at attention, ready to spring at a moment's notice.

Steph started to say something, but I shushed her. "He's close. Are you ready?"

She nodded.

"Make sure you shut the door behind you. We don't want to lose Mabel."

Again, she nodded.

I threw open the door and jumped down the two steps to the deck, scanning the area. I saw movement and started in that direction. He was going too fast to be quiet which was in our favor—until we gave chase. Then, all I could hear were the sounds we were making as we smashed down weeds with our feet and broke branches with our bodies. My eyes quickly settled into the darkness of the night, helping me see a shadowy outline of somebody running toward the bank of the creek at the back of the campground. So, I sped up, not caring what damage I did to my clothes and skin as thorns and limbs grabbed at me. I could see a light in front of me, so I knew Steph was close behind. Then she was by my side and soon she was ahead of me. As we had discussed, she, being the faster runner, would try to get ahead of him so we could at least outflank him, if not cut him off.

I was startled when Steph jumped in the air, and I heard low-pitched groans and growls. I was on them in seconds and she was taking some hard punches. I jumped on the assailant's back and pulled him off her. We soon had him pinned. Having enough sense to put zip ties in my pocket before I went to Steph's, I put them on his wrists before he knew what was happening.

He still tried to stand, so I yanked on his feet and pulled him back to the ground. Then I placed a hard foot on his back. "Move and I'll make you a paraplegic."

The man stilled.

I looked at Steph. "Are you all right?"

She was sitting on the ground, doubled over, holding her stomach. "You want to hold him while I return the favor?" she grunted under her breath. Slowly, she stood. I surveyed her face. Lots of ice and tenderness would be needed tonight. She was bleeding from a cut on her cheek. Her lip was swelling, and a trickle of blood ran down her chin. From the labored breathing, I knew she had taken at least one punch to the stomach.

"You want to do the honors?" I asked her.

She leaned over and ripped the full-faced ski mask off of the prowler's head. It jerked his head upward, and I was pretty sure wrenched his neck because he cried out. "I bet that hurt," Steph spat on the ground, most likely to get the taste of blood out of her mouth.

I handed the very large zip tie used by my police department to Steph. I had confiscated "a few" before I retired for um…emergencies. Steph took it and bound his feet. Then we rolled him over and I stomped my foot on his chest as a reminder not to move. Steph shone the light on his face. Both our mouths opened at the same time.

Manson Smith lay on the ground.

CHAPTER SEVENTEEN

"I thought Mac had got rid of him permanently?" Steph said, half serious, half joking.

"He didn't do a very good job of it, did he?" I answered her wryly, wondering why this man was taking such a chance. If it had been Mac who caught him, I was sure he'd take him out somewhere and finish him off because he'd be so pissed off that the man came back after his warning. I had seen Officer Nasty do it before, so Smith was lucky it was Steph and me who caught him. I looked down at the man's face, a mixture of anger and…something else. It was almost as if he was being tortured. "Why are you running around the campground in black clothes and a ski mask harassing the campers?"

He didn't reply.

"Look, either you can answer us, or we'll take you into town to the police station, or better still, we'll turn you over to the owner of the campground. I'm pretty sure you've met him already."

Smith turned his head and spat out of the side of his mouth. "'Cause of my kid."

Steph caught my eye, and I shrugged my shoulders. "What about your kid?"

"She's one of you," he said vehemently.

The light went on in my head. He meant she was gay. "So because your daughter is a lesbian, you thought it was a good idea to harass us like you did those college kids in town?"

"Was," he said, glaring up at us.

"What do you mean was?" Steph asked.

"She's dead because of you lot."

I wasn't sure I wanted to continue questioning him out there in the woods. He didn't have a lawyer present and the two people questioning him were a retired criminal profiler and a medical examiner on probationary leave. Not a good combination for protecting Steph's job.

It was time to call Maddie. She had asked me the first time I called her, "Is there something I should know about since, if there was, I should know about it?" I had told her if there was something to know, I would tell her. Now, there was something she needed to know.

I stayed with Smith while Steph went to the front parking lot and waited for Maggie. I knew that if she came in a cop car with lights blazing, Mac would be outside demanding what was going on. As he should be. Just for all the wrong reasons. Thus, I had asked Maddie to come in an unmarked car. She agreed but informed me that Mac would have to know at some point. She just didn't say at what point.

I tried talking to Smith while we waited. I helped him sit up and asked him about his daughter.

"Her name was Marie."

In the dim light of a thin moon penetrating the trees above us, I could see his tearstained face, and I swallowed hard. "Marie Sanfield?"

He nodded.

"The woman the police found at the bottom of the gorge."

He nodded again.

"But your name is…Oh. Sanfield was her married name." I heard a car approaching and knew it would be Steph with Captain Spinner and possibly Mac.

"Yes. She left her husband for a woman. That woman is the reason she's dead." Even though his eyes narrowed with loathing, I understood why he was doing what he was doing. I didn't agree with it, but I understood.

"Is that why you're harassing us? You're looking for the other woman?"

He didn't answer, avoiding my eyes.

"You think she's here, don't you?"

And then he looked up at me.

"Blake? Show me the light," Steph called out.

I shook my head, smiling at her reference to a movie, show, or a song (I didn't know which) and clicked on the small penlight. I would have loved to hear her say that to me in a different time, different situation except this one. Holding the flashlight in front of me, I glanced at Smith who was once again staring at his legs. Steph appeared with Maddie behind her. I breathed a sigh of relief upon seeing the uniformed officer behind her was not Mac.

"So, who do we have here?" said Maddie in her most authoritative work voice.

"Manson Smith," I answered, not taking my eyes off him.

"Nice ties."

"Thanks," I said to Officer Hampton, recognizing him as one of the men who helped Mac give Smith a warning about not coming back. Now, I definitely knew Mac would find out about this sooner than later. My shoulders slumped. I had thought my only saving grace was calling Maddie, but she had brought one of the cops that was with Mac when they escorted Smith off the campground. Did she know about Hampton's part in Smith's off-the-books removal? If she did, why did she bring him? Or did he just happen to be the only cop on duty that was free. I might as well pack up my camper and sell it.

"Officer Hampton, would you please take Mr. Smith to the car and wait for me there?"

"Yes, ma'am." He shot me a sideways glance as he hauled him up to his feet. He cut the zip ties on his feet and then he walked him out of the woods to the car. Maddie waited until he was out of earshot before she spoke to me.

"You want to tell me why a retired cop and one on probation took it upon themselves to run this man down?" She stood with her arms folded while we explained about the stalker, including Mac chasing him down and taking him out of the campground with the two other officers. I told her about Mac chasing him again the night before and getting injured. Then I told them both what Manson Smith said to me before Officer Hampton whisked him away.

"Did you know he was her father?" I asked Maddie.

"Yes, we knew. But it wasn't something you needed to know. You're retired. Remember? However, if you had told me there was a stalker here, and what had happened the first time he was caught, and you knew it was Manson Smith…"

"We waited for Mac to call the police, but I guess he never did," Steph said.

Maddie gave her a disciplinary look and Steph swallowed.

"I know. We're sorry. Look." I shifted my weight to my other foot. "I came to this campground because this was where my friends have been for years. If I had known Mac was going to buy this place, I wouldn't be here. But here I am, and I just thought if I could get to the bottom of why this guy was stalking the campers, especially this side of the campground where a lot of the lesbians are, then…"

"You should have known better," Maddie began. "I'll have to talk to Mac since he owns this place, but I can't promise anything. He has a right to ask you to leave. You went behind his back. And you know from experience how things like that go over with him. You just better hope that when I tell him I know about his escorting Mr. Smith off this property, he doesn't take it out on you. I won't be able to help you. You're lucky I'm not dragging you in." Maddie turned to leave but stopped. "Blake, you need to stay out of it. Now."

"But…"

"No buts. I don't want to hear a word about you putting your nose into this case again, or anything related to it. Got it?"

"Yeah," I finally answered, frustration filling my voice.

"I will say thank you for getting this guy, but you should have told me sooner. It was something I needed to know." She left without another word.

Steph took my hand. "She's just mad that she has to smooth this over with Mac. Although, she won't be at the receiving end of the worst of his blowup. It'll be you. So, I think she feels more like I do—sorry that you'll have to experience his wrath like you did so many years ago."

I let go of her hand and let my head drop back with dread. "I should have told her."

"*We* should have."

My eyes widened and I looked at her. "I'm so sorry. What's this going to do to you?" I turned, and ran out of the woods. "Maddie," I called out. "Wait." Steph ran after me, and when I got to Maddie's car, I put my hand up behind me to stop Steph. "Maddie, Steph had nothing to do with it. I am telling the truth. When I saw Smith in the woods, we were inside watching television. She followed me out. That was it. I've been investigating all on my own."

Steph protested, but I turned and shot her a don't-you-dare look. When I turned back to Maddie, she was sitting in the car.

"I believe you, Blake. This time." She closed her door and drove off with Manson Smith slumped in the back seat.

"Well, that was a fun night," I heard Steph's mocking voice say behind me as I watched the car turn the corner toward the office parking lot. I waited to see if it stopped, but the sound of the vehicle told me it was now on asphalt and driving toward Ithaca.

"Let's get you fixed up," I said. "Then Mabel and I will go home."

She studied my face, then shook her head. "By all means. After you." She swept her arm toward her trailer.

"We got the stalker. You don't need me to stay with you. Right?"

"Yeah, right." She turned and walked toward her deck, and I could have sworn her shoulders dropped with the weight of everything that had just happened.

I was at a loss as to what to do or say. I followed her, not wanting to assume she wanted me to stay and wondering if that was the right thing to do. She trotted up the stairs, and opened the door to Mabel just sitting on the floor patiently awaiting our return. Steph picked her up and handed off my dog to me. She took one step inside, leaving me on the stairs.

"I can take care of my wounds. Thanks."

"Um, okay," I said, taking my dog. "And thanks for helping me. We were quite a team." I hoped that was enough to get some response from her indicating to me what she wanted me to do...or to say.

"We always get our guy," she joked. "I can sleep better now. And thanks for covering for me."

She closed the door, and I felt... No idea what I felt. I just knew I didn't feel good. And then I realized I didn't have Mabel's leash. I looked up at the door, waiting for Steph to open it and hand it to me, but she didn't. The light went off, so I carried Mabel back to my trailer. I grabbed another leash and took her for a short walk. Then I made a campfire and sat in a chair letting the warmth run through me while I berated myself for not insisting on taking care of Steph's injuries.

With my dog on my lap, I watched the sky, void of clouds, play its nightly dance with twinkling stars. I found the Big Dipper and eventually the Little Dipper. I smiled. That was all I knew about the stars and constellations. I would Google so I could find more because the night sky was truly beautiful in all its glory, and it reminded me that there was so much more to life than being a cop. Suddenly, I found Steph's face in the sky and she, too, was beautiful. And that made me think that now I had to find out how to understand women, relationships, and my own stupid head.

I had sat at my little campfire late into the evening pondering every little thing that happened that day. Possible mistakes with Steph and maybe even a few things I did right. Of course, it was all from my point of view. When I finally climbed into bed, it didn't take long for me to fall asleep. I didn't wake until the next morning when I heard the call of the camper. My watch displayed eight thirty, and I couldn't remember the last time I had slept that late. Of course, I couldn't remember the last time I'd gone to bed so late.

My foggy brain didn't recognize the muffled voice calling from outside. I climbed out of bed and opened the door to see Myra holding two steaming mugs. She held one out to me. I took it and backed away from the door so she could enter.

"Are you going to tell me what the hell happened last night? People are buzzing and Steph won't talk. What's going on?"

Mabel trotted down her little steps from the bed and jumped onto Myra's lap. My mouth opened in surprise. "Oh my God, she's never gone up or down those steps before. Have you got a steak bone in your pocket or something?"

"Hey, girl. Wish you could speak," Myra said to Mabel. "She probably came down to tell me how stupid her mommy and Steph are being." Myra grinned at me as she stroked Mabel's back.

I'd bet my trailer that Myra was right. I could hear it now. "My mommy is an idiot when it comes to women. And being retired." I went into my bedroom and changed. "What do you want to know?"

"How about everything? Hey, I also heard you two were skulking around our trailer yesterday. You know I still work."

As I pulled a T-shirt over my head, I answered, "We were hoping we could take a day off and go have some fun."

"I would have liked that, but you know how Jen is—a stickler for work ethics."

I grabbed a pair of shorts. "Maybe you should live by your own work ethics and not hers once in a while," I teased. "You are the one working."

"What? And disrupt our happy home? Besides, she works, just not in the summer."

I slipped into a pair of flip-flops and returned to the living area. Myra eyed me suspiciously. "Why'd you sleep in so late? Usually, you and Steph are done with breakfast by now."

I chuckled. "Are you spying on me with binoculars?"

"You know we are," she admitted.

I shook my head as I opened a cabinet and grabbed the box of Cheerios. "I made myself a campfire and contemplated the stars last night. Among other things. When I realized I couldn't identify many constellations, I ordered a book on Amazon. Then I went to bed. It was pretty late." I sat down at the booth, poured some Cheerios into a bowl and began eating them with my hand.

"Blah. You don't put milk on your cereal?"

"Nope. Don't like it mushy, and I can't eat it fast enough to keep it from getting mushy." I held up a little circle of goodness. "Honey nut. Don't need milk."

"Alone?" Myra asked, and I wasn't sure if she meant the Cheerios without milk or something else since she said no more.

Then it hit me. "Yes. Alone. I was at my campfire by myself. And in bed with only Mabel."

"So that was after you and Steph caught Manson Smith and turned him over to Captain Spinner," she recounted what she obviously knew.

I blinked. A couple of times. "If you already know, why are you asking me? And how do you already know?"

"I wanted to hear your side of the story."

"Oh," I said, realizing her information came from Steph. "It's pretty much the same story as Steph's." I popped a handful of Cheerios into my mouth.

"If that's really true, why isn't Steph here and why is she so cranky this morning? Did you two have a fight?"

I thought about that for a moment. "I don't think so."

"Huh. Something went down between you two."

"What makes you think she's not mad at someone else?"

"Probably because she told me you two had a disagreement."

"Geez, Myra. Why didn't you just say that to begin with?" I got up and stomped over to the fridge, taking a long swig of orange juice.

"I don't like to get into yours and Steph's business."

I choked on the liquid, forcing me into a coughing fit. When I gained control, I stared at her. Then I walked over to sit again. "But that's exactly what you're doing only in a circumvented kind of way."

She leaned back and folded her arms, with a smug look. "I knew there were brains inside that head of yours." She pursed her lips. "Now tell me what's really going on."

Tears filled my eyes. This time, I didn't fight them because I knew I couldn't. "I thought I was still getting over Tess, but I have these feelings. Feelings for Steph that I shouldn't have. It's too soon, and we've been friends since childhood. I think she might be aware of my feelings and she's getting upset with me. Besides, if it hasn't happened by now, it probably won't happen at all."

"If you mean that long-term friends can't find their way to romance or survive a romantic relationship, I'm here to tell you that you're wrong. They can if they know how to survive a relationship to begin with. If you mean it's too soon after Tess to feel anything for anyone, you're wrong about that, too. I think you were falling out of love with Tess a long time ago."

She cut me off when I began to object. "And she with you. It was only a matter of time. Blake. You deserve that kind of love that stays with you no matter what. If you think it's Steph, then tell her."

I sighed, turning my head to look anywhere but at Myra because everything she was saying was right. Then I looked down at my hands I was wringing together. "What if she doesn't feel the same way?"

"Then at least you'll know, and you can open your heart again for someone else to come charging in."

I smiled wistfully.

"Now, fill me in on what happened last night and what your police-captain friend said to you. Steph said she was angry in a nice kind of way, if there's such a thing."

I laughed. Steph always knew how to explain bad things by downplaying them. I told Myra everything, except the range of emotions I felt throughout the night.

When I finished, she asked, "Do you think that's the end of it?"

"Yeah, I do. He admitted he was stalking us. He was looking for his daughter's lover. I don't know why he thought she was here. I asked him, but then Maddie arrived. Smith said he blames her lesbian lover for his daughter's marriage falling apart."

"Sounds possible."

"Maybe so, but it wasn't his marriage, and she's his daughter. You're supposed to support your kid, not do criminal things for them."

"What do you think he was planning to do with his daughter's lover? And why would he have thought she was here? Did his daughter stay here?"

"I have no idea, but he had a look in his eye. He probably blames this woman for his daughter's death, too. But as far as I know, they haven't deemed her death a murder yet. They're still looking into suicide. It's possible."

"If she did commit suicide, what was he going to do? Rid the world of lesbians because one turned his daughter's eye? Starting with us? And why us?"

"It wouldn't surprise me if that's what he had in mind. He's not quite right—you know, the light is on but nobody's home. However, I think that last question is one they need to look into if the investigation does head that way."

"Then I'm glad you and Steph got him, and if Captain Spinner gives either of you a hard time, I'll give *her* a hard time."

I laughed. "Good luck with that. Hey, on a different subject... then again, maybe not. I've got a question about those three cabins in the back of the campground."

"What?"

"How come the one on the very end looks empty most of the time?"

"Greg told me they can't rent it. The foundation is sinking, and they have to decide between knocking it down or repairing it. Mac wants to fix it. Greg keeps arguing that it won't be safe no matter what they do so it needs to come down. However, rebuilding is more money than Mac wants to spend, therefore it remains empty. Why do you ask?"

"I could have sworn I saw someone walking down the steps last night."

"Probably just an onlooker. Greg told me they need to circle it with that yellow caution tape to keep other campers from peeking in the windows and walking on the deck." She stopped a moment, and her eyes brightened as if a lightbulb had turned on. "You don't think Smith was hiding in there, do you?"

"If he was, he won't be now." I smiled at my friend, who was petting Mabel with the acrimony she must have been feeling at that moment. Mabel was arching her back to get away from Myra's hard stroking, and finally jumped out from under her hand and off the chair.

"Oh, I'm sorry, girl." Myra looked at me in alarm. "Did I hurt her?"

I picked her up. "She's okay. Your emotions on the subject got the best of you." I giggled. I need to go for a walk. I can't make Mabel wait any longer."

"I'll come with you."

Just as I opened the door, I heard the wheels of a golf cart skid on the dirt road. Myra looked at me.

"You think you can hang onto those emotions for a while longer? I may need some help with this one," I said to Myra.

"Moore! Get out here."

Boy, his mood sure had changed from the last time I saw him. Mac jumped off the vehicle and marched toward my fence. He had parked his electric cart cockeyed, half on the road and half on my grass. I swore if he left divots, I'd be after him to fill them in and insist he give himself a fine as was written in his own campground by-laws. I laughed to myself as I walked outside, knowing that was the least of my problems at that moment.

I put Mabel down and hurried to the gate to keep him from opening it. Thankfully, he stopped when he reached it, arms folded, most likely so he wouldn't punch me, and waited.

"Mac, what a nice surprise." I tried my best to sound pleasant.

"Really, Moore? You've got some…" But he stopped when he saw Myra walk out of the trailer and stand next to me.

The best defense is a good offense. I had read somewhere that the quote was attributed to a Chinese military general. "If you're here about last night, I'm sorry we didn't come get you. I was kind of busy, and I don't have your phone number, so I couldn't call. The only thing I could do…"

"We could do…" Steph was walking toward us. I didn't see her cross the field, but I was glad she showed up. "Was to call 911. You would have done that, anyway. Right, Mac? Besides, Captain Spinner said she would keep you informed. She must have done so, or you wouldn't be here to…To what? Why are you here? There's no need to thank me. I was just doing what anyone would do."

I smiled at Steph, and to my relief, she smiled back. Mac, on the other hand, sneered unattractively while he seemed to be thinking of a comeback. It took him a while longer than I would have liked. Whenever Officer Nasty had to think about how he was going to berate you, it was usually worse than when he just spat it out on the fly.

"We didn't have time to get you," I continued. "We saw Manson Smith outside of Steph's trailer and ran after him. After we subdued him, we called 911 because we knew we couldn't leave just one of us with him." Obviously, I left a few things out. "Captain Spinner took the call. We thought she'd stop and get you or stop after she picked him up to let you know what happened."

Myra stepped forward. "I, for one, am happy it's finally over with. We're all glad that someone like you,"—she was looking at Mac—"bought the campground. We feel a lot safer. I mean, you took care of the guy when he first appeared. Just unfortunate he came back."

I watched her put a feminine sucking-up-to-a-male-jerk smile on her face. *Lesson Two.* I felt a little bad for the guy. He was up against three very determined, accomplished, and shrewd women, and there was nothing he could do. I was also grateful that my two friends stood by me because if it was just me, he would have made me suffer. He stood no chance against the three of us.

Mac puffed out his chest a little and seemed to relax. "She wants to talk to me about my little confrontation with him. What did you say to her?"

"Nothing. I told her nothing about you and Mr. Smith, and that's the honest truth," I answered.

He looked at each one of us. Mabel was close to the fence with her back to him and was pooping. I wondered if she was giving him the ultimate doggie finger. I fought to keep from laughing out loud.

Seemingly satisfied with my answer, he said as he turned away and walked to his golf cart, "Next time, you come to me."

I wanted to mock-salute him and say, "Yes, sir, absolutely, sir." But I refrained. Mac backed up his vehicle and drove up the road.

Steph walked through the gate. "There's no way that'll be a good meeting."

"For him, or Captain Spinner?" I asked, trying to hold Steph's eyes on mine so she could read that I was sorry for whatever it was I had done.

"Both." Then she noticed the leash in my hand. "Taking Mabel for a walk?"

"Yes. She hasn't been yet."

"Kind of late for you, isn't it? Oh, yeah, and I forgot to bring your other leash." Before I could answer, Myra grabbed the leash from my hand, hooked up Mabel and handed it to Steph, who looked at the ground and said, "Better pick that up."

"No problem," I answered, feeling the awkwardness between us, and did what she asked.

Myra grinned at both of us. "Shall we?"

I immediately spoke to cover the uncomfortable silence. "I sure got away with that one thanks to you two."

Steph smiled at me. "Yes, you did."

With that one smile, I felt the awkward mood replaced with a warm feeling—like a cloud that evaporates, letting the warmth of the sun find its way through. At some point, Steph and I would have to talk. For now, I basked in the glow of my friends while we walked my dog under a very blue and cloudless sky.

CHAPTER EIGHTEEN

Over the next few weeks, the four of us took many afternoon road trips. We did everything from wine, beer, and spirits tasting to hiking and shopping or a movie. We found a craft fair and music festival where we laughed and sang along with every song, although none of us knew the words. Steph joined me for breakfast most days and things seemed back to normal. I had come to accept that I didn't really know what the definition of normal was between us and that was okay.

I had never felt so relaxed and that feeling affirmed that retirement was the best thing I had ever done. Mac refrained from stopping at our campsites and life at Rock Creek Campground was finally settling down. There were potluck suppers and happy hours for the residents, and I was relieved not to hear about any more stalkers hiding in the woods from other seasonal campers.

I combed the news every day for any breakthrough in Marie Sanfield's case as well as for information on her father. The only thing I found was that Manson Smith was charged with trespassing and stalking in the third degree. It was possible he'd have a hefty fine and some jail time. Steph and I still hadn't spoken about the night we caught him, and I didn't dare ask her if she heard anything about it. I sure as hell didn't call Maddie. I was just happy Maddie wasn't calling me. Or Steph.

One morning when I was walking Mabel, I heard a vehicle approaching from behind. As always, I pulled my dog off the road and stood aside to let the car pass.

It stopped, and Steph rolled the passenger window down. She leaned over. "Hey there."

"Good morning," I replied. "Interested in doing something today? Hiking? Shopping?"

"No can do. I got a call to come back to work."

I was happy for her, but at the same time, sad for me. "That's fantastic," I managed to say, sounding enthusiastic.

"I suppose. I've been having a lot of fun and it's made me think I might go see a financial planner. The time I've had away from the job has given me a glimpse of retirement and I have to say, I like what I see."

I couldn't stop the grin that spread on my lips. "That would be awesome. I really enjoy playing every day."

"If you can afford it. I don't think I could play every day, but knowing I could if I wanted to even though I might not have the money to do it is incentive enough."

"Hey, even if it gets you closer to retirement than you thought possible, it's something to look forward to. I'm curious, though. Is there a reason they asked you to come back before your disciplinary period ends?"

"What else?" She shrugged her shoulders. "Another dead body. I think Captain Spinner is tired of Bevel botching the autopsies." From what Steph said, Bevel came from another town, looking for upward movement. He sounded good on paper and gave a first good impression. But that was it. Apparently, he sucked at his job. The department only used him when they could find no one else.

I felt my anxiety rising. "You know I have to ask."

"No, you don't. The only thing I can tell you is that it's not another woman at the bottom of the gorge. I can't tell you anything more."

"I appreciate what you have told me. Will we see you for dinner?"

"I'm working again. You don't think I'm going to come home and cook for myself, do you? I expect a hot meal when I return." She winked, rolled up the window and proceeded at the turtlelike speed out of the campground.

As I watched her leave, I knew the days would now be lonely once again until she got some time off, or until the weekend. "Well, Mabel, it's just you and me." Mabel didn't wag her tail. Instead, she looked longingly after Steph's car. I gently tugged on her leash to coax her to start walking, but she wouldn't budge. "I know, girl. I know."

* * *

Myra and Jen prepared a meal fit for a celebration. I wasn't sure going back to work was something to celebrate, but I knew Steph was happy to still have her job. While the two of us sat at the table nursing a raspberry lemonade, Jen brought out mashed potatoes and steamed broccoli. The smell was intoxicating, especially since I had eaten little for lunch. Then Myra carried a plate over from the grill with a mouthwatering aroma of seasoned filet mignon. "Jen is taking a short hiatus from grilling." She winked at us and we knew it was the beginning of Jen's revenge for her title of GGQ.

Steph's eyes glowed, and she fell upon it like someone who hadn't had lunch *or* breakfast. We laughed and then delved into the meal ourselves. It was a peaceful meal with no golf cart screaming to a halt while we ate. Only the birds called out now and then, followed by the crickets as the sun began to shift to the horizon, making room for the moon to take its place. When we finished, Myra shooed us away. Part of the celebration, she told us, would be her and Jen doing the dishes. Then she winked at us, so we knew there would be more than dishwashing.

Steph took Mabel's leash, and we walked leisurely while she told me about her day. She autopsied the victim of a firearm incident, a gun collector who accidentally shot himself in the chest with a Spitzer bullet. She further explained that this bullet was invented in 1898, and historians claimed it changed the face of warfare when it was used in the first machine guns. Thanks to her explanation, I didn't have to Google Spitzer bullet.

"It really messed up his insides. I'll bet his wife will gladly sell his collection of antique guns and bullets," she mused.

I was about to give my opinion on the matter when I heard a familiar female voice behind us.

"Ms. Moore."

We turned to see Missy hurrying toward us. She bent down and petted Mabel who shied away. "She's so cute," Missy said as she looked up at me. "You should bring her to the office more often. It will be the only time I get to interact with one so small."

Steph raised an eyebrow.

"My husband is a police officer. They love their German shepherds. He says a small dog is a poor excuse for a dog."

"Whoa, that's harsh," Steph said.

Missy stood and smiled. "I know. He can be like that. I don't tell him I disagree. I just let him go off on his rantings. It's easier that way." Then she turned to me. "I wanted to say thank you for helping Mac. I'm sorry it's taken me so long to get back to you. I took him to urgent care. He had a mild concussion and a few stitches, which I think embarrassed him. I also want to thank you for not calling him that night they arrested that bad man in the campground and letting the on-duty police do their job. He didn't need another clout on the head, especially since we had a full weekend coming up."

"You're welcome, Missy. Happy to help."

She leaned forward and said in a quiet voice. "I just wouldn't do it too often. You know how he can be." She turned and began to walk away, ending with, "Thank you again. Have a great night. Bye, Mabel."

"Well, that was nice," Steph said when Missy was out of earshot.

"I'm kind of surprised. She was really standoffish the day I visited her in the office."

Steph leaned into me. "Remember who her husband is." She chuckled.

"Have they come up with anything on Manson Smith's daughter?"

She looked off into the distance, as if debating whether she should talk about it. Finally, she did. "It's been kind of like Annie's death."

I cringed. If that was the case, we would never know what happened.

"They haven't found anything conclusive, so her death is still undetermined. Manson Smith continues to rant and rave that his daughter was turned to the"—she air-quoted the next two words—"dark side, and that 'one of them' killed her in a jealous rage."

"Interesting. Men like him give girls like us a bad name." We walked a bit in silence. "We'll probably never know," I mumbled, not wanting to accept it might be the truth.

Steph stopped and placed her hands on my shoulders, turning me to face her. "Annie was a long time ago. Things are different now. They'll figure it out. It's just going to take some time."

I didn't answer her.

"Look at me, Blake."

I did.

"You've been hanging on to this for far too long. Is that why you're so invested in Marie Sanfield's death?"

"It just seems too coincidental to me."

"Yes, but it's been over thirty years."

"You know what I do. Or did. Right?" I sounded demanding and immediately felt bad.

"Of course. A criminal profiler. But thirty years?"

We started walking again at the insistence of Mabel pulling on her lead. "There've been other women at the bottom of gorges throughout the years. I've kept tabs."

"Most of those were suicides or accidental falls," she persisted. "And not in the same gorge."

"So, they say."

"Have you talked to Maddie about it?" she asked softly.

"Not really. I ask her things now and then but try to go around it without offending her or making her feel like I'm sticking my nose in where it doesn't belong. She also doesn't know what Annie meant to me. Besides, she already warned me to stay out of it."

"Look, Blake. I think it's time you walk away from this one. Enjoy retirement. Let it be someone else's problem for now."

I didn't say it, but I didn't have to. She knew I couldn't let it go. It was who I was, and I realized I wasn't ready to let that go. For once, after all these years, I believed there was more than a slim chance I could find out why Annie was found dead at the bottom of that gorge.

When we got back to my campsite, Steph lit a fire and we sat close to it, feeling the chilly air on our backs. Mabel curled up in my lap tonight, which surprised me since Steph was there. We talked now and then, sitting in silence in between conversations, listening to the crickets and coyotes on the prowl for their evening meal. After a while, I saw Steph's eyes close and knew that was my cue.

"I think Mabel is getting cold, and I'm kind of tired."

Her eyes opened, and she smiled at me. "Sorry."

"No apologies. You should get to bed, since you're the one who has to work tomorrow."

"Sounds like a plan. Thanks for tonight. It was nice." We both stood, and she took me in her arms, hugging me close and tight and it felt so good. I stayed in her arms, letting her be the one to release the hold. When she finally did, she stroked Mabel on the head, who was sitting in my chair, looking dreamily up at her. "Night," she said in a whisper that lingered in the air as she walked away, turning on a flashlight.

"Good night," I answered and went into my trailer, happy we had time together, but disappointed I didn't try to talk to her about my feelings, or at the very least, put my big girl pants on and make a pass at her.

In time, I thought as I closed the door behind me. *In time.*

* * *

Early to bed, early to rise. I had the second part of that quote down, waking once again shortly after six. Mabel was sitting next to my head, staring at me since five thirty. I tried to ignore her but by six o'clock, I couldn't stand it anymore. It was time for her daily walk. The grass was wet with dew which meant her legs had to be towel-dried when we got back. She hated that so I told her it was payback for staring at me for a half hour.

I was antsy afterward, so I settled Mabel in her recliner (Yes, I now deemed it her recliner, and I thought about making a sign for it.) and went out for another walk with a goal of two miles in a half hour. I liked speed walking. It was a challenge to go fast without breaking into a jog while using a full foot placement.

When I got back, Steph was waiting inside my camper, sitting in Mabel's recliner with the dog on her lap. She looked up at me, and I noticed her eyes were bloodshot, and her cheeks were wet with tears. She slid Mabel onto the seat and stood in front of me, looking me square in the eyes. Her mouth twisted as if she was struggling to find words.

"What's going on?" I tried to take a step back from her, but she put her hands on my arms and held me there. Her gut-wrenching emotion alarmed me. "You're scaring me, Steph."

"I got a call from Maddie while you were out walking," she managed to say in a choked voice.

"Oh, no. There's another body, isn't there?" Why would that have her in so much despair?

Steph sniffled and turned her head. She swallowed and looked back at me. "Yes."

"Where? In the same place? Do they know who it is?"

This time, she swallowed hard as tears ran down her face. For a moment, I thought about Jen or Myra and panic took hold. "You know who it is! Tell me, goddamn it," I said, more loudly than I wanted to. But I was terrified, as if her own fear and sadness were spanning the distance between us and planting themselves into my already hysterical mind.

She said something, but when she said it, she looked down and her head was shaking back and forth as if she was trying to convince herself it wasn't true.

"What? Is it Myra? Jen?" I asked, trying unsuccessfully to keep my voice down. She shook her head.

Finally, she looked up at me. Now she was full-force crying. "Yes, to your first two questions," she rasped.

I didn't know why, but the validation that there was another body at the same place as the last two calmed me, but because Steph wasn't pacified, dread washed over me again. She was crying harder now while mumbling repeatedly that she was sorry.

I took her in my arms. "It's okay. What are you sorry about?"

Then I heard a tiny whisper close to my ear. I struggled to hear it correctly, I think because at first my brain could not, did not want to accept what she breathed out. Then my mind latched on to Steph's three words within her inconsolable sobbing.

"It was Tess."

The world spun in all directions. Steph wasn't making sense.

I remembered Steph holding me as we both sank to the floor. I remembered crying, and not really knowing why, because even though we were over, Tess couldn't be dead. I remembered Mabel squeezing her little body in between us, trying desperately to get to my face. When she did, she licked Steph and me incessantly.

I don't remember how long I remained in Steph's arms or when she gently lowered me onto the bed sometime later. But I remember feeling the weight of the patchwork quilt on my body and Mabel settling next to my head and neck. And the last thing I remembered was my dog's breathing next to my ear, so soft and reassuring as I grappled with the death of my ex-wife.

CHAPTER NINETEEN

When I woke, I didn't know the time or how long I had slept. It was a chore to open just one of my swollen eyes, but eventually I could see Steph sitting in the recliner. She was talking quietly on her phone. I tried to hear what she was saying, but her voice was too hushed to make out words, and my mind was fuzzy. Mabel was lying on my pillow next to my head.

"Hey, girl." I petted her and she licked my fingers.

Finally, I dragged my body, that felt as if a Mack Truck had slammed into me, to a sitting position and grabbed some tissues on the night shelf next to my bed. A few minutes later, Steph tapped her phone off, and looked out the window. I didn't know what to say. I didn't even have any questions because I knew I hadn't really accepted the news yet.

"Hey," I said.

Her head snapped in my direction. "Hi." Obviously, she didn't know what to say either. "How are you feeling? I'm sorry, that's a stupid question."

Nothing seemed right or appropriate, or stupid, for that matter.

Finally, I broke the barrier of incertitude. "It's really true," I said, not asking a question, but just stating the fact.

"Yes, Blake. I'm so sorry." She walked over and positioned herself on the bed next to me. I handed her two pillows to put behind her back. She took my hand, and we sat in silence. Mabel settled on my lap, obviously sensing that something was wrong.

There was a knock and Myra and Jen walked inside without announcing themselves. I almost laughed at this because I expected the call of the camper and part of me wanted to scold them. Maybe someone dying was an exception to the rule. They came directly over to the bed and crawled on the mattress, finding a spot on either side of us, giving me hugs before they settled in. With my friends surrounding me, I felt strong enough to ask more.

"What do they know?" I directed this question to Steph.

"Not much. It happened during the night. The police only found a few footprints that matched her shoes. They were near the edge where they believed she fell. They couldn't"—she choked on her next words—"find any sign of a struggle."

"Then why was she there?" I laid my head back on the pillow and felt more tears roll down my cheeks. Did she really do it? If so, did she do it because I wouldn't go back to her? Was I the reason?

As if Steph heard my thoughts, she spoke sternly. "It wasn't your fault. They're not ruling out murder, given the similarities to other recent incidents. They have to finish the investigation. And even if they deem it a suicide, it...Is not. Your fault."

Myra was squished next to me, and she hugged me. "Steph's right. You can't control what others do. It's not your fault."

I simply nodded, knowing that their support would not take away my guilt. Suddenly, I sat up and asked, "Do I need to go down and identify the body? Maybe it's not her. You know how beat up these bodies are after falling into that gorge."

Myra guided me back down as she answered my question. "Steph already did." She went while you were sleeping. I stayed here."

I fell into uncontrollable sobs once more, knowing how damaged Tess's body would be. I cried for her parents, who would be devastated and for my best friend, who had to see her body in the state it was in. She was Tess's friend, too. It was different seeing a dead body when it was someone you knew. And even though Steph had performed countless autopsies, performing one on a friend was quite different.

"We're still married," I said. "The divorce isn't final. I don't want an autopsy done."

"I told Maddie that. But you know as well as I do it has to be done. As a cop, you know it might help find the answers as to why she died."

"Did anyone call her parents?"

"Maddie did."

"My phone. Where's my phone? I'm sure her parents have called. I need to get a hold of them."

"That's who I was talking to when you were sleeping. I told them you would call them later. Wait to call them. You all need to process this before you speak to each other. They're going to have a lot of questions that you need to think about. Like why Tess left you. You said you weren't sure if they knew about the divorce. It won't seem fair, but they're going to grasp at straws for answers."

Relenting, I settled back on the bed and soaked in the love of my friends and my dog. I would need all the strength I could find for what I had to do over the next few weeks. I closed my eyes.

Why, Tess? Why?

* * *

The next morning, I spoke to Tess's parents, the Anglers. My heart broke, listening to them sob as they asked me questions I couldn't answer and others I didn't want to. Just like Steph said they would. They knew Tess and I were having problems, but Tess hadn't filled them in on everything, and I felt it wasn't my place to tarnish the reputation of their daughter. Besides, I didn't want to.

Her parents were wonderful people and had accepted me as their daughter-in-law from day one. So, I lied about why Tess left, and I made them believe I was all right with it. That I understood her decision and who knew what the future would bring? We might have found our way back to each other. I hoped the lies gave them a little comfort. But my heart broke knowing the truth—that Tess and I would never have reconciled if she were still alive. They just didn't need to know that.

I packed a few things, closed up the trailer and gave a set of keys to Myra and Jen. I told them I hoped it would only take a few weeks to have the funeral and get all our affairs in order. We were in the middle of divorcing, and now the process would stop. I had to find out what would happen from here. We all hugged, and I promised to let them know about the funeral, and to text them when I got home.

I hugged each of my friends who told me to call if I needed anything. I loaded Mabel into her car seat and promised them I'd be back. After all, this was my life now, and I didn't want to desert it. It seemed more important to me than it had been before.

I drove away, waving to my friends in the rearview mirror. I convinced myself that I felt nothing because I couldn't let myself fall apart anymore. I had to be strong. I had to be strong for Tess's family, to make the hard decisions that would bombard me, to find a way to say a final goodbye to the woman I had loved more than life itself.

The drive home was as if I traveled in space—endless, undefined, lost, remembering little of it. I stepped into the house and stood still. Our home had felt different when Tess left, but now it felt haunted—empty and full of ghosts. Rather than unpack, I took Mabel for a walk. Walking always made me feel better. It emptied my head and allowed me to think positively—to piece things together and make a list of what I needed to do.

However, when I got home, Mabel and I became slouches on the couch together, and I turned on useless television hoping to block out the sorrow. I didn't know how long it would take up residence in my heart. I did know it would get better. It just would never be gone. Until then, I had to feel it and do what I could to get through it—thus my dog and the TV.

* * *

Tess's parents stayed with me during the funeral, even though they lived in Rochester too. Tess had two siblings who lived out of state, but they stayed at their parents' house. I knew then Tess hadn't told any of them about the divorce and that I was buying her out of the house. All they knew was that we were "temporarily" separated.

I went through Tess's things with her mom and helped her pack up what she wanted to take. Most of Tess's belongings were still there. Just her clothes were gone. Her mom needed the pictures and mementos more than I did. She had more than they could fit into their car, so we agreed to set a time for her to come and take the rest at a later date. I had already separated myself emotionally from our material possessions, but they still meant something to her mother.

Steph, Myra, and Jen arrived on the day of the funeral. Steph looked beautiful in a pair of black pants and a matching black suit coat. A silk blouse in lazy stripes of black, tan, and gray accentuated her outfit. She hugged me tightly, and I clung to the warmth and shelter of her strength.

During the calling hours and at the cemetery for the memorial service, she stayed by my side. She replaced my parents, who had died many years ago. I was an only child, so Tess, her family, and my friends had become my family. Yet I didn't stand with Tess's family. She had left me and I felt separated from them as much as I did from her. So, I felt blessed to have my friends—my true family—there on that day. I knew Tess would be happy about that.

During the ceremony, Steph tightened her grip around me. Her solid body next to me was a physical rock to lean on, especially since I felt I might pass out. My heart and my soul had the emotional support of all three of my friends, and I could never put into words how much their presence held me together and kept the loneliness at bay during that time.

Tess's parents hosted a luncheon at a local restaurant. I sat at a table with my friends. I had no desire to talk to people, but I responded to anyone who approached me. My friends patiently stood by while I spoke to other mourners. When all was said and done, it had truly been a beautiful service and my ex-wife, the woman I loved and adored for many years, was laid to rest beneath a large pine tree. With my consent, her parents had bought the plot next to theirs so she would be close to them. Tess and I had talked about buying cemetery plots together but had never got around to it. I had to believe that things happened or didn't happen for a reason. Now I wondered where my final resting place would be when my time came. I ached with loneliness. It was a thought that overwhelmed me, and I almost passed out from the vastness of the loneliness and uncertainty that spread within my soul, afraid my soul might be alone in the afterlife as well.

The day following the funeral, Tess's parents squeezed their suitcases into their already jam-packed car and promised me they would keep in touch. They lived in a suburb a half hour away, but something inside me whispered I wouldn't see them. I loved her parents, but I wondered if seeing me would only remind them of the daughter they lost too early. They did arrive a week later to remove the rest of Tess's belongings as we had agreed upon. If having all of Tess's belongings would bring her parents comfort; it was the least I could do for them. That's not to say I didn't keep anything. I did. Before the funeral, I boxed up the items I knew one day I would want to look at again to remember a wonderful time in my life with a woman who still had a place in my heart despite our separation.

I watched them drive away, and I felt arms circle my waist. "What do you want for dinner?" Steph said, keeping me in a warm embrace.

"You don't have to stay. I don't want you to think you have to babysit me. You did it the first time Tess left. You don't have to do it again."

Myra and Jen were now in front of me, looking stern. "If Steph wants to stay, then she stays," Myra scolded me gently.

"Okay, okay. How about I treat you all to pizza? I don't think any of us feel like cooking," I said. "And we know Steph never cooks."

They spun me around and steered me toward the house, and I heard giggling behind me. "Sounds like a plan," Myra said. "But we will order the pizza. We also have beer and wine and no place to go. So, we're going to drown our sorrows and then tomorrow morning, after the hangovers fritter away, we move on. And Steph stays."

Jen, Steph, and I stopped at the same time and looked at Myra.

"Fritter away? Where the hell did you get that word?" I asked.

"From the dictionary, of course," she replied, pulling me toward the door.

Myra did the best thing for me without even knowing, or maybe she did know. She brought me humor, if just for that moment, because we all broke out into loud laughter as we teased her.

"Then we'll fritter away all the beer and wine," Steph said through her guffaws.

"Oh, oh, pizza, wine, and beer aren't going to help me fritter away the extra pounds I put on this year," Jen exclaimed, and we laughed harder.

I watched each of my best friends walk past me into the house, making fritter jokes and laughing so loudly, I was pretty sure the neighbors were snooping through their window shades. And I thought that maybe I could fritter away all the horrible feelings I was holding on to with pizza, wine and beer, and my three best friends.

CHAPTER TWENTY

Mabel was curled up into a ball in her car seat. I smiled at the tiny creature that kept me sane without even knowing she was doing so. Or maybe she did. We were a few miles away from Rock Creek Campground, and I was excited to get back to my summer. I wanted to enjoy life instead of constantly trying to put it back together. It had taken longer than I thought to do everything I needed to do. It was the beginning of July and I realized I had missed most of June at the campground. Myra and Jen had stayed with me a day after the funeral, returning to the campground satisfied Steph was staying to take care of me. And she did. She stayed a few more days and then returned on weekends. With someone to lean on, it enabled me to take care of the rest of Tess's affairs. I worked with the lawyers and banks to finalize everything—closing credit cards, taking her name off joint bank accounts, transferring the house deeds to me alone, and so on. Because we were still legally married, and to my surprise, everything went to me as specified in Tess's will. It just was a lot of paperwork to get it done.

The Anglers never asked if I needed help. I couldn't blame them. They'd lost a daughter. That wasn't the logical order of things.

Their grieving was exacerbated by not having the cause of death determined. If my dealing with Tess's estate meant relieving them of difficult reminders, I would have done it even if we had been divorced.

There were some things I needed to do on my own that I didn't want her parents to know about and Steph not being there during the week allowed me to do them. The first was finding out where Tess had been living. After fruitless searching, I called in some favors from my friends at the RPD. That led me to a small apartment in the back of a house. There was no paper trail because Tess was paying with cash. The utilities were included, so there was no record there either. I wondered if Tess did this because she was unsure about what she was doing. After all, she had wanted to come back to me.

Her sparsely furnished living space—only a couch, table, television on a stand, and a bed—startled me. There were minimal kitchen supplies, and I wondered if that too was because she planned on coming back home. Or she was waiting for the divorce to finalize after which she would get all her stuff—or half of our stuff.

I found nothing to explain why she'd gone over the cliff. Nothing to suggest either murder or suicide. And even though her footprints at the scene didn't suggest a struggle, I firmly believed she would not jump off a cliff. She wouldn't hurt her family that way. That, I was sure of. Deep down, I believed she wouldn't hurt me that way either.

I left it as it was and paid the next month's rent, telling the landlord she had died, and it would take a month to settle things. I was exhausted. So, when the thick forest that surrounded the campground came into view, I opened the window despite the hot and humid air outside and breathed in the scents of nature. I turned into the entrance, slowing my vehicle to the aggravating designated speed and slowly made my way to my trailer. I smiled when it came into view. The awning was out, and my friends were sitting on the blue-and-yellow folding chairs, drinks in their hands and lunch set out on the picnic table.

Steph was at the passenger door before I stopped my car. She lifted Mabel out of her car seat. "Oh, I missed you, you little bugger." My dog was wagging her tail, her butt, her front end, and licking every inch of Steph's face. Time away from Steph only seemed to have heightened my dog's backstabbing antics with her. It didn't bother me, though—it made my heart swell.

Myra opened the trunk and lifted out two bags of groceries. Jen was behind her getting the other bags.

"Wow, if I get this kind of help every time I come back, I'll have to go away more often."

"Oh no. Don't expect this treatment if you plan on coming and going like nonseasonal campers. We don't help the weekenders unpack. We won't help you," Myra stated while climbing the three steps up into my trailer.

I smiled as I pulled Mabel's things out of the car, including her outdoor bed that I tossed over the fence where it landed upside down. Steph had put her down and Mabel jogged over to her bed and, seeing it turned over, gave me a dirty look. "Just a minute, Mabel," I said to her in frustration. Steph was there before I could get into the enclosure and moved it next to the chairs, putting it upright. Mabel turned her back to me and trotted over to Steph. "If you keep spoiling her…"

"Too late," Steph informed me while grinning. "She knows who's got her back."

I smiled back at her because I knew she also had my back, and then I carried Mabel's bag into the trailer. Jen and Myra were putting away my groceries. They stopped what they were doing and took me into a warm embrace.

Then Myra went back to unpacking my groceries. "How are you? I know. Terrible question, but I'm going to ask it."

"I'm okay. Really. I'm looking forward to communing with nature and clearing my head."

Jen chuckled. "You? Communing with nature? This I gotta see."

"Ha, ha, ha," I replied with a grin.

"Jen made us a great lunch," Myra informed me. "Come out and commune with us and the food."

So, I did. Right into Steph's waiting arms. "We're so glad you're back," she whispered in my ear.

And I was so happy to *be* back. I did notice Steph said "We're so glad you're back," and not "I'm so glad you're back." Then again, I had three wonderful friends who had done more than I could ever ask of them and *all three* were happy I was back.

We lunched on egg salad and tuna sandwiches. I had one of each. A bowl of fresh fruit, a bag of potato chips and homemade chocolate chip cookies finished the lunch. We each had their newest cocktail—a

Smirnoff Kool Spritz made with Smirnoff Pink Lemonade, watermelon juice, club soda, and a watermelon slice on the glass.

I started the conversation in order to avoid anything Tess. I was working through it, but not ready to talk about it. "So, how's it going here? Any changes from the new owner?"

Jen rolled her eyes, Myra laughed, and Steph started right in. "He's as arrogant and demanding as he is on his job. You should know all about that," she said.

"What'd he do now?"

"Well, for one thing, your grass can't be higher than four inches," Jen offered.

"Four inches," I repeated. "Are you serious? At least they mow it for you while you're gone."

"Not anymore," Myra jumped in. "We found that out when we came over to check on your trailer and saw a notice on your door. If you didn't mow your grass by the next day, you were getting fined. So, Jen went up to the office…"

"And you know what they said?" Jen interjected with her part of the story. She was bouncing up and down like a little kid who couldn't wait to have their say. "They said it was in the new set of rules, and if you want your grass mowed while you're gone, you'll have to pay twenty dollars for each mowing."

"No way," I exclaimed. "This little patch?"

"Way," Myra said. "So, we mowed it for you and we're only charging fifteen dollars. We gave you a break." She grinned, followed by Jen slugging her in the arm.

I laughed.

"You don't owe us anything, but do you believe that?" Jen asked.

"Actually, I do," I answered. "He always was about the money. What else has the jackass been doing?"

"He still comes by on that hot-rod golf cart of his and puffs out his chest while he boasts about being the owner and how he's going to whip this place into shape," Steph said in between bites of her sandwich.

"What about security?"

My three friends stopped chewing and drinking and looked at each other.

"What security?" Steph asked.

"I read Manson Smith has an alibi for his daughter's death but still has to face charges of harassment as well as stalking and trespass at the college *and* the campground," I said and could plainly see it was a sore subject. "I also read that he got out on bail. If Mac knows that, what's he doing about security? Or maybe Manson Smith hasn't been around?"

"Oh, Mac's a regular protector," Myra said under her breath.

"Is there something you're not telling me?"

"There's been some rumors," Jen said hurriedly, like she wanted me to know but wasn't supposed to say.

"What kind of rumors?"

Steph took a deep breath. "People are just talking nonsense..." She looked at Myra, who shrugged her shoulders.

"She'll find out sooner or later," Myra said to her. "Probably sooner."

"Come on, what's going on?" I felt myself reaching the end of my tolerance rope.

Steph took a bite and put the rest of her sandwich on her plate. "There are rumors that Manson Smith is pounding on the outside of trailers in the middle of the night, throwing chairs around, messing with the campfires, and lurking in the shadow of the woods. Mostly on the sites of PLUs."

I sighed. "People like us. Does Mac know?"

Myra answered, "Yeah, he does. People are a bit out of control reporting anything they think is out of the ordinary, especially if it happens at night. For all we know, it could be kids. There's a few in the area that have been labeled troublemakers. I think Mac's been looking into that."

"What about you? Have you experienced any of this?" I stared at Steph and held her gaze, challenging her not to lie about it.

She took a sip of her drink. "Some. Not every night, but whoever is doing this is really stealthy."

"I go for the kids in the neighborhood," Jen said. "Why would Manson Smith come back here? Again. Especially after he had his confrontation with Mac and his friends, was arrested by the police and now both parties of the dynamic duo who captured him the second time are here. It sounds more like something teenagers would do. I was talking to Sandy the other day. She said their campfire circle was

destroyed and their picnic table turned upside down. Although..."
She stopped when Steph gave her a warning glance. She didn't finish.

I crossed my arms. "Although what? Come on, give it all up."

"It seems the person is around Steph's camper more than any others," Jen said, her eyes down, most likely to avoid Steph's dagger stare.

"That's not necessarily true," Steph countered. "I've seen shadows around your trailer, too, Blake."

"Mine? Are you sure?" I was surprised since I had been gone for a month.

"That's what I meant by stealthy." Steph sipped her drink. "There's been complaints about it all over the campground, so I've been talking to people. I think they're seeing something else, like an animal, or a regular camper cutting through campsites. And you know that happens a lot, especially around yours. Your site seems to be a major thoroughfare when you're gone."

"Great, just what I need. Isn't that trespassing? I mean I do pay rent for the summer," I asked.

"It was when Randy and Phyllis ran the place. Not so much with Mac," Myra said. "I've lodged complaints about both things with Missy. The only time you can get near Mac is when he shows up in his glorified golf cart. And we can't even do that because he avoids us now."

"Oh, wait till you see how he's got it decorated. All red, white, and blue for the July Fourth weekend," Jen exclaimed.

"Yeah," Steph said. "You came back just in time for the festivities. But Maddie is looking into the neighborhood teenagers. One boy was arrested on a few different minor counts. So, we'll see."

"Maddie's involved? Good thing. Maybe I should call her. I want to get an update on a couple of things."

Steph met my eyes and her stare was different. It wasn't the friendly, caring, soft eyes I usually looked into. This time, they were hard and almost cold. "Stay out of it, Moore."

I flinched. Steph had never called me by my last name. She sounded more like Mac than the friend who held me up during Tess's funeral. Myra and Jen looked down. I was flabbergasted by her outbreak and dumbfounded as to what to say or do next. Myra solved that problem. She stood up and announced she had some work to finish up. Jen said she had errands to do. They invited us to meet at their place for dinner. Grilled chicken with Jen's seasoning that usually made our mouths water at the mere mention of it. Today, not so much.

Steph remained nursing the first drink Jen had given her. By now, it had to taste more like warm, diluted watermelon juice. "So, how are you really doing?" she asked me.

"I'm okay. You want to tell me what that was all about?"

"Look. Captain Spinner doesn't want you involved in any of this."

"Is that what she told you?"

"Yes. And I have to say I agree with her. You're retired. Let the police do their job. If you're bored, get a hobby."

I couldn't understand why Steph was being so cantankerous. Something was off, but there was no way I was keeping my nose out of it. Sadly, I realized this was coming in between Steph and me. Whatever this was between us seemed to be bouncing back and forth more than a Ping-Pong ball during a game. "Yeah, sure. I was thinking about gardening."

Steph said nothing as she watched Mabel, who was walking toward her and looked up with saddened eyes. "That's okay, you widdle baby waby. Everything is okay."

I was silent for a moment. How did I tell her what I was really feeling without sounding…pathetic. I sighed heavily.

"Wow, that's a deep sigh. Must be pretty bad," she finally said.

"No, just describing what I'm feeling might sound really bad."

"Try me."

Before Jen left, she had poured the last of the drink in my glass and its cold felt good on my fingers. I swallowed and dove in. "Tess was already gone for a couple of months. I was getting used to it, and yes, I was still sorting through those feelings, but part of the jolt of her not being around was already in motion." I looked from my glass. "Do you know what I mean?"

"Yeah, I think so."

"I've always had this ability to leave things in the past. I can't change them, so I accept them and move on. It's not worth getting all emotionally charged over it after all is said and done because all it will do is get you…"

"Emotionally charged?" Steph lifted one eyebrow.

I chuckled. "You know what I mean. I'm the type of person who doesn't want to live in negativity or turmoil. I sort through it and let it go. So, I was already letting go of Tess cheating and leaving. It's not her being gone from my life I'm having difficulty with. I accepted that a while ago. It's that she'll no longer walk on this Earth, and I never expected that to happen. Never in my life did I want that to happen. Not now. Not like this."

I swallowed down a deluge of tears that were pushing against my emotional dam. And then it broke. "I need to know what happened to her," I said between hard sobs. "When she left me for Lori, as much as I hated it, I knew she was alive—with another woman. But I don't know what made her go over that ledge, and I need to know." I cried like a little baby. "Why did this happen? I can't"—my voice quavered—"let go of this."

"I promise you," Steph said pleadingly. "The police are doing everything they can to answer that question."

I cried, with Steph sitting across from me for what seemed a long time. Eventually, my sobs turned to simple tears. "They didn't do such a great job with Annie. What makes you think they will with Tess?"

She handed me a napkin. I wiped my eyes and then blew my nose at which she exclaimed, "You sound like a foghorn," and we both broke out in laughter. My laughter was raw and sad. And my pain was magnified because Steph didn't come to me and comfort me like she usually did. I picked up my dog and hugged her. I realized with great sadness that something had changed between us, and it was just Mabel and me now.

"How about we take Mabel for a walk? I don't know about you, but I could use a good walk," Steph suggested. The next sentence she directed to Mabel, who was curled up on my lap. "You'd like to go for a walk, wouldn't you, girl?"

And, of course, her tail wagged furiously.

It was a glorious afternoon for walking. The bold sun on a background of solid, flawless sky blue beckoned us to go. The temperature had dropped into the low eighties and there was a cool breeze that caressed our skin. It was the best medicine I could have asked for. Steph and I talked about mundane things—the latest Netflix series we had watched, gossip slinging around the campground—anything except the campground stalker and Tess, or her and me. It seemed to ease her mood. For me, the fresh air and walk relaxed me, but my insides were stirring with the confusion about Steph.

Afterward, we put Mabel in the car and drove to town to pick up ingredients for salad and a dessert for dinner. We ended up at Walmart where I carried Mabel into the store, placing her in a cart. She was always a hit wherever I took her. I stood by, listening to Steph explain Mabel's rescue history, and my heart melted at how much my best friend loved my dog.

Would she ever, could she ever love me that way? Right then, I would have said the answer was no.

Steph returned to her trailer, and I went to mine to make the salad and feed Mabel. I sat down on a recliner to watch the news, which I hadn't done since Tess's death. I didn't want to hear anything about it from newscasters. Any information I needed, I would get from Captain Spinner.

I noticed one report about a stalker at a woman's home on the outskirts of the city. She kept seeing someone standing where the edge of her yard met the woods behind her house. When she called out to them, they turned and ran. So, she called the police. The only description given was someone around five foot seven, or eight, or nine, with black clothing, and a hood over the face. I chuckled, knowing that was almost nothing to go on, but that was often the public's standard MO of every stalker and criminal when they didn't get a good look at the perp. However, this one had the same vague MO as the one in the campground, and the caller was a woman.

I decided the only thing that could keep me sane at this point was to launch my own investigation. Without telling anyone. Without anyone else's help. Were the three cases—the disturbances at the campground, Marie Sanfield's death, and Tess's death—connected? There was nothing concrete to connect them, and I didn't believe Manson Smith had anything to do with the two women's deaths. He was a disgruntled father who wanted Marie's lover to pay for breaking up his daughter's marriage, so why would he kill his own daughter? And Tess was not Marie's lover. I truly believed that Manson Smith had nothing to do with them. Therefore, my investigation would center on just the two deaths.

Over at Myra and Jen's trailer, I gave Mabel's leash to Steph, who was comfortably seated in a chair on the deck and then took the salad and dessert inside. I was handed a glass of freshly squeezed lemonade from Jen as I walked back out the door. Myra was lighting the grill, preparing to cook. I sucked in a breath of clean, fresh air with a hint of pine and campfire coals and then sat next to Steph.

The meal was better than we could have asked for—proof in every piece of chicken gone from the pan, with a few tidbits left for Mabel, followed by peanut butter chocolate pie. After we moved our gathering to the campfire, it wasn't long before the quiet hum of a golf cart grew louder, announcing Mac's arrival. He pulled up alongside their lot and turned in his seat, leaning his arm on the steering wheel with one leg propped up on the seat. He looked... ridiculous.

"Well, well, well. Haven't seen you around in a while, Ms. Moore. Thought you might be having second thoughts about staying here with us fine people. Maybe you're too good for us."

My head turned the same time as my stomach, and I mouthed to Steph, "Does he know?" I didn't think Mac Taylor knew I was married to Tess. But he would now, if he saw Tess's police report. My name would be on it as her next of kin, her wife. She nodded, and my stomach dropped. The last thing I wanted to do was explain my love life to this asshole.

"I had a family emergency to tend to," I replied, hoping not to have to take this conversation any further.

But I didn't have to worry about that. Mac Taylor did it all by himself. Unfortunately, he also knew my parents were dead. "I thought you didn't have any family," he said with a twinkle in his eye and a smug grin.

"Aw, Mac, you only knew me years ago during my stint with you as my mentor, if that's what you want to call what you did. I've got plenty of family." I smiled at my friends.

"You know, Officer Taylor, you can be such an ass," Steph said loudly enough for him to hear.

He shifted in his seat, putting his leg down and his other arm on the steering wheel. I actually thought I saw him look embarrassed before he leaned forward, turned away and looked down the road. "You ladies have a good night." He sped away at more than the posted five miles per hour.

No wonder people don't like cops, I thought. Some of them believed they were above the law as displayed by Officer Nasty.

"Was he always such a jackass?" Myra asked, watching him roar down the dirt road.

"That was him being nice," I scoffed. "I can't speak for anyone else, but any interactions I have with that guy reinforce my belief that he was and still is a permanent asshole."

Jen laughed. "What about you, Steph? You must have other interactions with him at work."

She lifted her can of soda. "Asshole," was the only word she said.

"That only leaves one question." Each of us turned our heads to look at Myra. "Does that mean we should start looking at different campgrounds for the coming years?"

I was not ready to find another campground or even talk about it, so I bid my friends good night and moseyed across the field with Mabel.

CHAPTER TWENTY-ONE

Missy had filled the coming weekend with all sorts of Fourth of July celebrations, from scavenger hunts to a seasonal campers' potluck dinner. There would be a bonfire in the open field, fireworks to follow and kiddie games both days. She had a food truck coming the second night, with music in the large building, a mini carnival with a fortune teller, more games and a few rides that would be placed at the end of the field. From this, I learned if you wanted peace and quiet, you needed to leave on the weekends.

Mac went all out to please his campers, yet his security methods were wanting. I had had conversations with other seasonals, but learned little. None of them had anything more to say about it other than what my friends had already told me. Mac wasn't doing anything, but people weren't too concerned about it, because as Steph told me, there was nothing substantial, only brief sightings and rumors and the banging on trailers had stopped—most likely kids.

I had no desire to be around the campground for the celebrations. Steph stopped showing up for breakfast, making me all kinds of irritable. Her work hours were nine to five, and that would have given her plenty of time to have our usual start-up meal, so it felt as if she was ghosting me.

The next morning, I received a call from Maddie, who asked me to come in. They needed a little more information about Tess. I loaded Mabel into the car and drove to town. I stood in front of the dull concrete building and took a deep breath before entering. At the front desk, the greeting officer recognized me. "Well, look who's back." He pointed at me, his finger shaking up and down as his brain worked to bring back the memory of me. "Moore. Right?"

I smiled and extended my hand. He took it and I said, "It's nice to see you, Officer Gentry."

"I never thought I'd see you back here again. What are you doing in this neck of the woods? Must not be here for work cause that ain't no police dog." He snickered, looking over his desk and down at Mabel, who promptly turned and gave him her butt.

I smirked. "I've got a meeting with Captain Spinner."

"Oh, sick of the big city? Coming back here to pick up where you left off? If that's the case, you better leave that little mutt at home." There was a hint of sarcasm, but he said it with such a genuine smile, I knew it was more teasing than being mean. I wasn't sure Mabel thought that way because she kept her butt facing his direction.

I grinned. "You couldn't afford me anymore, Gentry. And Mabel, here, she's Napoleon through and through."

He nodded to the stairs. "So, an intruder might lose a finger or a toe." He chuckled.

"Something like that." I picked up my dog.

"Go on up. She told me you were coming."

"Of course she did," I mumbled under my breath and then said to Mabel, "You could take him."

I heard him chuckle again as I took the steps two at a time and smiled at the door with Captain Spinner's name stenciled on the glass. She had worked hard to get here, like I had to become a profiler. Maybe that was why she always agreed to talk to me, not just because we were friends.

We were in the Academy together and rookies in the same department, but she had a different mentor, and had been able to take a different path to climbing the proverbial ladder. She had seen how Mac Taylor was, and she knew how he treated me. She wanted to report him to our superiors, but I wouldn't let her. There was no way I would let that man ruin two careers. Times were different then. She had told me once she was grateful that I refused to let her report him for his treatment of me, but I knew how disappointed she was in herself for not doing so.

I put Mabel on the floor and knocked softly. Her strong, deep voice called, "Come on in." She came toward me, smiling, and threw her arms around me. "All these years and we've only talked on the phone. I hate that we've only met in person because of crime. I couldn't say this at the campground, but God, it's good to see you."

"You, too." I squeezed her back, but it wasn't nearly as binding as her hug was. The woman was an Amazon, built like a brick shithouse, as my mother would have said if she were still alive.

"I'm so sorry for your loss," she whispered in my ear.

I released myself from her hug only to keep the tears at bay. Maddie observed me with her soft eyes and a gentle smile, all of which turned to hardened steel when the need arose. She looked down at my dog. "And who is this?"

"Mabel. She's in training to be a police dog."

"Right," she drawled as she walked back around her bulky wooden desk and sat in the ergonomic cushioned chair, a contrast to her elaborate mahogany tanker of a desk. She refused to get a newer modern one because it had belonged to a long line of policemen in her family since the early 1900s. It was a magnificent antique and something to be revered.

I sat down in a chair positioned in front of her desk, placing Mabel on my lap.

"I really am sorry for your loss, and I hate that this is the reason we're sitting together."

My mouth went dry, making it difficult to swallow.

"And here comes the question we all hate in situations like this. How are you doing?" She shook her head. "Yup, still a stupid question, I know. But I have to ask it."

"It's all right," I answered. "Everyone asks and I know it's because you all care. I'm doing okay, but there's something I haven't told you yet. I guess I was waiting until my heart really caught up with it, but now…well, I guess there are no more reasons not to."

"What is it?"

"Tess left me earlier this year for another woman. We were in the process of getting a divorce."

The look that took over her facial muscles was expected. They squeezed and tightened as her eyes widened, and her mouth formed a small circle. "So, it's true. Oh, I'm so sorry."

I said nothing. With a heavy sigh, Maddie fell to the back of her chair. I said, "I thought that might be the reason why you wanted to talk to me. You found out about it."

"We heard rumors. I wanted to confirm it with you and ask you about it, if it's okay."

I nodded.

"Who was she seeing?"

"The only thing I know about the woman is that her name is Lori, and she actually was involved with Steph before she met Tess."

"Steph?" She said the name as if not believing what she heard.

"Yes."

"Your friend Steph?" Her facial muscles tightened as if she was struggling not to let a particular emotion show.

"Yes."

"My medical examiner Steph?"

"Yes." At this point, I had to smile. I could see the wheels in her mind turning and spinning, weaving stories and possible scenarios correlating with Tess's death.

And that's when I jumped into her thoughts. "Steph had nothing to do with this. She didn't know Tess and Lori were an item until we saw them at The Commons at the end of May."

"Awkward." Her one-word reply said her mind was still racing. "Are you sure about that?"

"I hope you're not implying you think Steph is involved in this. She is the best person I know. She would never…"

Maddie put a hand up. "Remember who I am."

I sat up straight at the off-handed suggestion I be careful with what I said. "I know, but I would swear on my life Steph had nothing to do with it."

"You know what happened last April."

She wasn't asking because she didn't think I knew. She was fishing and I was getting angry. "Of course I do. It's unfortunate Steph did a stupid one-time thing." I leaned forward and put my index finger up. "One-time stupid mistake. She's going to therapy and working through it. But you need to know, *she* dropped Lori. It wasn't the other way around, and Tess was nowhere in the picture where Steph was concerned."

"Okay," she said slowly as the new knowledge joined the informational cog in her brain. "Then let's focus on this Lori. What's her last name?"

"Smith."

"Really." Maddie wrote it down. "Where does she live?"

"I don't know."

"I can see why Tess might not have told you, but Steph never did?"

"I never asked her."

"Where did she work?"

"Nope. Don't know that either." I was beginning to worry about Steph and how this must look for her.

"Can you describe her looks?"

"I only saw her from a distance and despite the fact I was a cop and should remember, I was too upset to see Tess there." Realizing how bizarre this sounded, I laughed. "We didn't talk about her much. We talked more about the relationship, how Steph was feeling about it, what bugged her, what she liked. None of the women she dated were ever around for that long, so I didn't meet most of them, let alone ask the personal questions because, well, you know, it's Steph."

Maddie folded her hands on the desk and smiled. "That I do. I've already called her in so I can ask her these questions. If this Lori was the last person who was with Tess, we need to find her."

"Yes, I was hoping you would. I need to know what happened, why it happened."

"Do you think her death had something to do with this woman?"

"If you mean did she kill herself because she was distraught over cheating on me? No. She wouldn't do that. Besides, she broke up with the woman she left me for. Other than that, I really can't say if it does." Before Maddie could elaborate on that line of questioning, I said, "Steph told me to stay out of it, that I had to let the police do their job, but I can't do that. I owe Tess, no matter what she did to me. I owe her parents to find out the truth."

"You should know that Steph would be right on that."

"Look, Maddie. I really don't believe Tess would have stepped off that cliff on her own accord, but..." I swallowed.

"But what?"

"She came to me the last week of May and said she wanted to come back. I said no."

Maddie's eyes widened slightly, and I knew she was mentally taking more notes. I had the urge to put a pen and paper in her hand.

"Are you ruling it a suicide?" I choked out the words.

"You know I can't tell you that until the department finishes their investigation. I can tell you they are still undecided. So, don't ask anything else about that." She stared at me with thin lips.

"It's not a suicide. I know it's not, and I would hate for her parents to see that on her death certificate."

"You might not have a choice. So far, there's nothing to say otherwise."

"There was nothing in her apartment, either." I slipped a piece of paper across the desk with a key. "I left everything as it was, but I did go through it. With gloves. Hopefully, you won't find my fingerprints anywhere, but possibly my DNA if it comes down to that. I thought you might want one of your people to take a look. I paid the rent in cash for the next month and told the landlord she would be out by then. You've got less than a month before I need to go in and get rid of everything."

Her eyes widened more. "So, there could also be DNA in there from Lori."

"It's possible, but I have no idea."

"You understand even if we get fingerprints or DNA, we may not find her in our systems. It's still important that we talk to Steph."

"I know. I do have one more question."

"Can't say I'll answer it, but go ahead," she said dismissively. I could tell she was anxious to move on the information I just gave her.

"Any news about Marie Sanfield's death?"

"I can tell you that Steph is going to redo Bevel's autopsy. He's such a screwup. I'm surprised she didn't tell you."

"She's a little crabby about it right now."

"You might as well know. Unless Steph finds something different, it looks like they will deem it a suicide."

"Shit," I mumbled as I stood and extended my hand. Maddie took it in both of hers.

"Be careful. You're retired. You know the limitations. Make sure you stick to them. I remember how bullheaded you can be. A brilliant analyst and profiler, but bullheaded." I couldn't tell if the grin she gave me was from Maddie...or Captain Spinner. Either way, her compliment made me smile.

"I can't promise anything, but"—I put Mabel on the floor—"I won't do anything to ruin the investigation." I pulled my hand back and walked to the door. Then I turned and added, "At least I'll try."

"Go away, Blake. I've got work to do."

I closed the door behind me and when I looked up, Steph was standing in front of me. To say I didn't feel all types of awkward would be an understatement. Her stare was intense, and I almost shrank under its weight.

"What are you doing here?" Her question was accusatory.

"Captain Spinner called me this morning and asked me to come in."

"Oh. What a coincidence. It just so happens she called me, too." I wasn't surprised.

"How about you keep yourself occupied for a while? I'll text you when I'm done and we can get some lunch. Especially since I missed breakfast." She walked past me into Maddie's office without waiting for a response and with no acknowledgement of Mabel whatsoever.

I looked down at my dog whose eyes were sadder than they'd ever been. "I'm sorry she didn't pay any attention to you." As I petted her, I muttered under my breath, "Looks like her panties are still in an uproar." I blew out a breath of relief, because the last thing I wanted to do was to piss off Steph, especially since she was in a foul mood lately. At least she asked me to lunch. I just wasn't sure it was going to be a good lunch or a bad one.

Mabel and I moseyed back to The Commons, where I spent the next two hours ambling up and down the walkways, stopping for a cool drink, window-shopping, and then doing it all over again. The Commons ran a few blocks, but if you weren't in the mood for shopping or eating, there were plenty of places to sit and people-watch. Finally, I settled on a bench with my second raspberry iced tea and did just that. With my phone on my lap. And waited.

And waited and waited.

Steph's text came through close to noon, and she suggested meeting at Taco Bell on Route 13. Taco Bell of all places. I thought she'd pick a restaurant somewhere in town since we were both already there. Now I had to walk back to my car and drive. I texted back to give me twenty minutes just for that reason. Her reply? *K.* Just a K. How could you gauge one's emotions on one letter of the alphabet?

Then again, maybe you could.

It took me longer than twenty minutes because of the noon traffic. I was worried that if her meeting hadn't gone well, she might just leave the fast-food place without waiting for me. But I saw her blue car parked in the back of the lot, so I took the spot next to it and found her at a table outside, thumbing through her phone. I tried to read her face, but it was a solid no-show of emotions. Mabel lay down on the ground next to Steph's feet, and I sat opposite her. We both waited for her to acknowledge our arrival, but she said nothing, nor did she look up from her phone.

"I'm sorry, but I had to walk back to the parking garage from The Commons, and the traffic was crazy getting here. All the workers are off for lunch and looking for a place to eat." My effort at trying to sound jovial didn't budge her. I swallowed and then sighed. "I'm sorry I didn't tell you I was going to see Maddie, but she only called this morning. Maddie understands that I need to know what happened to Tess."

"Tess was my friend. You're my friend. You do deserve to know what happened. I'd want to know." She continued to swipe at her phone, and then a minute later, she looked up. I got a better view of her face and still, there was nothing. "I don't know," she said, her blank expression unreadable, yet she was as anxious as a drug addict needing a fix.

Confused, I asked, "Don't know what?"

"I only know what Lori told me. I didn't have any proof if any of it was true. She always came over to my place. I never saw where she lived. She told me she was in between living arrangements and when she got settled, she'd have me over for a home-cooked meal. I believed her, but now that I think about it, I'm not so sure. She practically lived with me, so she could have very well been in between places. I don't know." Her face wrinkled in worry. "I don't know if she was really from a small town in New York. She never told me which company she worked for. I never asked. She didn't talk about work. When I think about it, I knew nothing about her." She looked at me, unsettled. "I should have asked her. Gotten to know her better. Was I like that with everyone I got involved with? Is that why I can't hold on to a real relationship?"

After that rambling, I was afraid Steph was going to explode. "You know as well as I do, it takes a lot of dates to find out even the bare minimum about someone. And you're probably getting all worked up about nothing. They don't suspect Lori. They just want to ask her about Tess, where she was, what her mood was. You know, the usual kind of police stuff."

She relaxed a bit. "I know that. I'm not worried about that. They'll find Lori and hopefully she can give some insight about what happened to Tess. It's just that…it was Tess. And Lori. And in the end, I can't help because I didn't really know her. I never take the time to know anyone I get romantically involved with. How sick is that?"

I reached across and put a hand on hers. "It's okay."

"No, it's not. You know, this DUI was the best thing that happened to me. It's forced me to take a good look at myself."

"You're making too much of this." I tried to alleviate her growing concern. "There's no need to worry. You'll figure it out."

"I'm not worried. I'm just angry."

"At me?" I asked, afraid of the answer.

"At me. I let women into my life without learning much about them. I always enjoy the sex. Maybe I'm a sex addict. Oh, I don't know. I always get along with them really great in the beginning, so all that other stuff just gets swept under the table until the newness wears off and then we're just…nothing." She stared at me with an expression that said, "Am I stupid or what?"

So I said, "You're not stupid. You enjoy getting to know someone with the hopes of a future together. That's how it's usually done. And we all know you don't feel that for everyone you meet. So, you move on until the right one comes along."

She rolled her eyes. She attacked her phone again, swiping furiously with her index finger, tapping and swiping.

I put my hand on hers to stop her. "What's going on?"

"What if Lori did have something to do with it? Or has information that could help the police find out what happened? What if they can't find her? It could be all my fault."

"Steph, it is not your fault. Do you hear me? I don't believe Lori had anything to do with Tess's death, either. It's just a coincidence that your ex-girlfriend ended up with mine."

Steph angled her head at me. She didn't have to say anything for me to see she wasn't so sure. "You don't understand. I live here. Lori and I dated here. In Ithaca. You and Tess lived in Rochester. What was Lori doing up there?"

"I can answer that. Back when Tess confessed to me, she told me they met at Josie's Bar. Lori was in Rochester for a job interview. That's all she said, but it didn't matter. What mattered is what happened between them afterward. At some point, they must have had problems. Why else would Tess end it and want to come back to me? I don't know what their issues were and I can't confirm who dropped who, even though Tess said she ended it with Lori."

"The answer to your question is guilt. Maybe Tess never really wanted to leave you to begin with. She just, oh I don't know, maybe it was a midlife crisis. She felt guilty for leaving you instead of talking to you about it. That's what made her think twice. You were her world. No one could deny that."

"I appreciate that. But if that were the case, she wouldn't have cheated, and she wouldn't have left, asking for a divorce. She would have talked to me about having a midlife crisis."

Steph sat up straight. "Wow, you're rough. But like I said. Guilt."

"Come on, Steph. I'm not rough. It's just how I feel. You don't cheat on the love of your life if she's really the love of your life."

Steph grinned. "That's a good one. Should be on a Hallmark card."

"No. I mean it. If there's a problem, you talk about it and work it out. Guilt has no place here. You just don't run to the other side where you think the grass is greener because you're having a midlife crisis. 'Cause, believe me, it's not. You buy a fancy car or skydive or something silly like that. You don't mess up everybody's lives. And you sure as hell don't go back because of guilt."

"You've been there, huh?" She was challenging me and I knew it.

"Whether I've been there or not, it's what I believe." I was done talking about my breakup with Tess, so I said, "Look. It's not your fault. The only thing that's important here is that they find Lori and talk to her. They'll find her, and hopefully she can give us a clue, any clue, as to what happened."

Steph looked off into the distance, a tear running down her cheek. "And what if that clue leads to suicide?"

"Then I'll have to live with that."

After a few seconds of silence, she spoke. "Let's order."

"Now that's an excellent change of subject."

She got up and turned to me, saying with as much sincerity as I had ever seen her muster, "It's not your fault either." She started for the door.

"Hey, would you order for me? I've got Mabel here."

She spun, a look of surprise on her face. "Where?"

I nodded toward the ground.

She hurried to Mabel, whose head perked up. Steph took her little head in her hands and kissed her and crooned how sorry she was for not paying her any attention. Then she went inside and came back out with two five-dollar meals. We discussed what she had told Maddie, which wasn't much more than what she told me. "If anyone can find her, Maddie can. She'll get answers." It sounded as if Steph was making the promise for Captain Spinner.

"I know she will. Until then, how about we just enjoy the summer? Or at least the weekend."

She smiled. "I'll bet Mabel's pretty mad at you for making her tag along all morning."

"Yup. One more reason for her to turncoat on me," I chuckled. "So, on that note, I better get going." We walked out to the parking lot, and she followed me to my car. I put Mabel in her car seat and as I closed the door, Steph threw her arms around me into a very bearlike hug. I did the only thing I could. The only thing I wanted to do. I hugged her back, but then she moved as if uncomfortable with my action and took a step back.

"There's something else I need to talk to you about." Her hands were in her pockets, and she shifted her weight as she looked away from me toward Route 13 like she was studying the traffic patterns, deciding on the best way to go back to the campground.

This was not going to be good. Whatever this was.

"Ever since Tess left, and you came down to the campground, we've been getting, um, closer."

I sighed in relief. Finally. She looked at me for a brief moment in which I saw a flicker of a smile on her lips and a speck of glimmer in her eyes. I was wrong. This *was* going to be good. Then it disappeared, and her eyes were dark. Nope, this was going to be bad.

"I, um…I need to take a step back from…From this. From whatever this is."

I gulped. Okay. This definitely wasn't going to be good. "What do you mean? We're friends."

"We have been. Yes. For a long time. But lately, I've felt…It seems you feel something more. Tess was my friend."

I felt a wave of anger wash over me, and I swallowed to keep the tidal wave that could engulf us in rage in check. "She was *my* wife." My voice was hard.

"Exactly."

"I don't know where you got this stupid idea. We're friends. I think we agree on that. Like you said, we've been friends for a really long time. Longer than anyone else I'm friends with."

Steph sighed. "Yes, we have been. But I can't cross that line."

"What fucking line?" I said, feeling the wave rise within me. "Are you telling me we can't be friends because you think I'm feeling something more?" My voice rose in volume and I saw Steph cringe as she looked around, most likely hoping no one was within earshot. I didn't care. "Well?" I practically shouted.

"Yes." The word swooshed out between her lips in barely a whisper.

"Wow. I'm so glad you think you know how I feel." I put my hands on my hips and turned to look away, not knowing what else to say. Not knowing what all my feelings were that swam inside the tidal wave of my anger. Hurt. Disappointment. Regret. Rejection. And… guess I did know after all.

"Blake. There's more. It's not just that. But I'm back at work, and I can't jeopardize my job. I know if you ask me to play detective with you for whatever reason, I will. But Tess's death is still an open case, and I can't get involved except for whatever is expected of me in my job, and you know I can't talk to you about that. It will be too hard not to if I'm around you."

"Great. This is really great," I choked out, forcing myself to look back at her. I leaned slightly forward. "I *have* a right to know, and I'm not leaving Ithaca until I do."

A lone tear fell down her cheek. I didn't feel bad about causing it because I was about ready to sob myself, and that was her doing.

"I understand. I don't expect you to leave. I'm sorry, Blake. I hoped you would understand and not be mad, because I really hope you find out what happened." She bowed her head and the words that came next cut me to the core. "I'm just not sure finding out either way will be the best thing for you. But I know it's not my choice or my place to…"

"You're right. Not your choice. Not your place. Goodbye, Steph."
I got in the car and pressed the ignition button. Steph stood outside
my door for a few moments. I stared straight ahead, but I could see
out of the corner of my eye she was crying. It only made me angrier.
It didn't have to be this way. It could have been so different, and I
knew what was making me so angry. Everything Steph said was right.

I put the car in reverse and pulled out of the spot, mindful that
she hadn't moved. After all, I did love her. Maybe a little too much.

CHAPTER TWENTY-TWO

The drive back to my trailer was another hard one, like heading back to Rochester after the news of Tess's death. This time, however, Mabel glared at me the whole ride back. I was grateful to make it back to the campground in one piece, hoping I didn't piss off too many other drivers on the way back.

I hooked Mabel up and took her for a walk, but toward the other side of the campground, away from Steph's trailer. I had always faced challenges and difficult times with the strength to move beyond them. But now I felt as if I had mono or chronic fatigue syndrome. Not only was my mind shutting down, but my body was following its path, closing down to the past months of loss. So much loss.

And now my best friend was stepping away from our friendship because she believed I was feeling too much for her. But I was. So why didn't I talk to her about it like I said you were supposed to? Would we have been able to avoid this if I had? Now I was walking in circles around the campground and trying to figure out how the rest of summer might play out. It had been the four of us going places, having fun, eating dinner together every night.

Now... Now what?

My phone vibrated in my pocket. Part of me wanted to whip it out and see if it was Steph saying she was sorry and taking back everything she said. Part of me knew it wasn't and I didn't care who was texting me. It was a message from Myra informing me dinner was at their place at five thirty. My tears made it difficult to see where I was walking, and I tripped in a rut in the road that Mac hadn't fixed yet. I noticed Mabel looking up at me with her sad eyes screaming pity...and unconditional love. I picked her up and held her close, letting the tears fall. I wished it were a weekday when the campground was close to empty. But now, the holiday campers were here and I felt the campground closing in. Maybe I should only come here during the week when no one was around including Steph. Or maybe find another job to give me a reason not to be here.

Would Steph come to dinner? Should I go? Should I tell Myra and Jen what was happening, or just go and play it out facing whatever the evening presented? Either Steph would be there or she wouldn't. How much worse could it get? The Fourth of July weekend was about to begin and there would be plenty of celebrating around the campground. I just wasn't sure what I was going to do. Spend it with my friends? That depended on Steph.

I walked back to my trailer, went inside and locked the door. I grabbed the box of Kleenex and settled into a recliner, mindlessly clicking through the TV guide. Mabel jumped up and gingerly climbed onto my lap, curling into a ball. I wanted to shut my mind off for a while. I wanted happiness, instead of feeling like the whale of disappointment and sadness had swallowed me whole. Like Geppetto in *Pinocchio*.

Three hours later, I woke to the buzz, buzz, buzz of my phone vibrating on the table. It was five o'clock, and I was due for dinner in the next half hour. Maybe the afternoon had been a dream. Maybe Steph would have forgotten about it. Myra had left a message to bring some butter as they had run out.

While Mabel ate dinner, I grabbed my usual paraphernalia for the evening, and a stick of butter. Halfway across the field, I noticed only three chairs on their deck. Myra and Jen sat in two of them with beers in their hands. My lungs quickly deflated, and I felt as though

I couldn't take another breath. Maybe Steph not being there was a good thing. I'd have a better chance of getting through the evening's festivities if she wasn't there.

I felt sad for myself. I felt sadder for Steph. If she stayed away because of me, that wasn't fair to her. She had been at this campground with Myra and Jen for years. This was my first year. I knew I would have to find a solution that worked for both of us. After all, Steph was working again, so I wouldn't see much of her, not cooking breakfast for her anymore. However, the evening meals would need to be dealt with. We could go every other night. God, that sounded like a divorced couple and we weren't even a couple. Mabel pulled on her leash, bringing me out of my miserable problem-solving.

"Hey there," I called out as I approached my friends. "Here's the butter." I tossed the stick to Myra, who caught it with a softball catcher's finesse.

She smiled at me, but it was a different smile. Kind of like the one Mabel gave me earlier on the road when we were walking. "She's not coming to dinner," Myra said. "Something happened. You want to tell us what it was?" That was Myra. Straight to the point. She didn't pull any punches. When she struck, she hit dead-on, bullseye, right in the middle of a dartboard.

I sank into the chair and sighed heavily. There was no sense denying anything. "Remember the conversation we had at my trailer the other day? Well, it appears Steph had already figured it out, and she doesn't want any part of it."

"What conversation?" Jen asked.

"You know, hon. The one where I believe Blake is feeling something more for Steph than friendship."

"So, what's wrong with that? They've been friends for so goddamn long. Maybe they *should* be feeling something more," Jen exclaimed.

I actually had to smile at that. "That would be great if it was reciprocated, but it's definitely not," I said, gazing out toward the tree line and the blue sky above it—so separate yet so connected. I had thought that Steph and I were like that. Today, I learned I was wrong.

"It's really okay," I continued. "It's just that, well, things like this— dinner together, playing together. We won't be able to do that. At least for a while, if not forever."

"Oh, come on. That's a bit dramatic, don't you think?" Jen looked alarmed.

"I don't think it is, Jen," Myra answered for me. "Steph was pretty adamant when she called me about not being around when Blake is."

I felt the bullet go right through my chest as if Steph was standing in front of me, holding her gun, and had pulled the trigger. What had I done to deserve this?

"Blake, have you spoken to her? Let her know that you're okay with just being friends?" Myra suggested.

"Yes, and no. She told me this afternoon and didn't give me a chance to say much of anything. Then my anger prevented me from saying anything. Besides, I don't think she even wants a friendship now…and I'm not sure either of us can be. Right now."

"Why, for God's sake? How can she destroy a friendship she's had since childhood? You two have always been there for each other," Jen insisted.

"I believe Steph is going through something larger than a friendship. She's doubting her ability to be in relationships which is probably why she's running from our friendship—so she doesn't kill that too. I think that's what's behind all of this."

"What would give her that idea?" Myra asked.

So, I told them. I told them how upset she was about never really getting to know any of the women she'd been involved with. I explained that because her latest ex was the one my wife left me for, and because Tess and I were both her friends, she felt responsible for our marriage ending.

"No way. She had nothing to do with that," Jen said adamantly.

"You're right, she didn't. But in her mind, she did. Nothing is going to change that. She has to work through it. I just hope when she does, our friendship survives." I opened the cooler on the deck and got a beer. I noticed Mabel was facing Steph's trailer. Her head was on her paws, and I knew she was waiting for someone who wasn't going to show.

"Now what?" Jen asked, irritated. "Are we going to make schedules so when we see either of you, the other isn't there? Pick a side?"

Myra slapped Jen on her thigh.

"Ow, what was that for?" Jen shot her wife dagger eyes.

"You know what. This isn't about our inconvenience. It's about our friends, and we will do what is necessary to help them through this. We are Switzerland. We don't choose sides."

I gave Myra a thank-you smile. "And I can help with that," I added. "When dinner is ready, how about you give me my share to go. I don't think I'll be feeling very social for a while. That way you can get Steph over here and feed her. You know she won't cook for herself, and I'm sure she'll be hungry after working a full day. As far as when I cook, I'll send you home with Steph's share, and since Steph doesn't cook…" My smile was bittersweet.

"Sure. Jen, honey, would you go pack up some food for Blake?"

Without a word in response, Jen went inside the trailer.

"Don't mind her. She's just really upset about this. She thinks it's going to end our friendship with one of you. Or both." Myra looked toward Steph's trailer. "She was really rooting for you two."

Jen came out with a large Tupperware container and handed it to me. "She wasn't the only one," I said to Myra. Then to Jen, "Thank you. I'll see you gals tomorrow."

I gathered up Mabel and headed back across the field to my trailer, noticing the evening's activities beginning. Thanks to the excellent event planning and organizing by Missy, there would be campfires, parties, good food and fireworks. The campground was filled to the brim with holiday campers, and the July Fourth bonfire was to begin at dusk.

Mabel and I ate our dinners inside the trailer to the sounds of happy campers outside. I wasn't in the mood to be among the happy throng. I didn't feel what they were feeling, and neither did my dog. She wasn't even taking nibbles from the tidbits I tossed in her bowl. When I took her outside for a quick walk, I stopped dead in my tracks when I saw the flames shooting high above the pine tree not fifty feet away, like a dragon breathing fire up toward the sky. Feeling a mild breeze picking up, the size of the fire made me nervous.

I was awake most of the night—worried about the fire, more worried about Steph. I was awake in the early morning hours when they finally doused the bonfire, leaving a pile of gray, white, and black ash with a few pockets of bright red. When I got up, I used my small blower to remove the ashes from everything, including my car, not caring how early it was because they had kept me up most of the night. I was washing down the outdoor furniture when Myra showed up, an arm outstretched with a mug in her hand.

"You're up early. I'll bet you pissed off a lot of campers with that blower." She smirked. "That's what woke me. Mac will probably be here sometime today to give you a fine."

"Too bad. They want to put a dangerous fire right over there near our trailers, then they can listen to me clean up after it." I stood up, stretched my back, took the mug and sniffed. "Mmmm. You can come more often."

"So, why did you start cleaning so early? I know you're a morning person, but this is a bit much." She picked up Mabel, found a dry chair, and sat with her in her lap.

I ceased my incessant cleaning and sank into the chair next to her. Then I jumped up and looked at my behind. "Great," I mumbled, seeing the wet spot, and then sat back down. "Nothing like a wet butt."

Myra was chuckling to herself. "Boy, you sure are in a tizzy."

I looked down at my folded hands hanging over my knees. Then I looked at her. "Wouldn't you be?"

"Wouldn't I be what?"

That just got me mad because she knew damn well what I was talking about. She just had this way of making me say it. "Mad that I messed up our summer, our friendships."

"*You* did not mess it up all by yourself. Steph had a good hand in this one."

I sat back in my chair. "And how do you figure that?"

"She's been messed up for a long time and never did anything about it, never took responsibility for it until she got that DUI that threatened her job. Kind of sad, don't you think? If she had taken care of her commitment problems long ago, she might be a happily married woman."

She was right, and I was mad at her for that. Or should I say jealous because if Steph was a happily married woman, there never would be a chance for me to be with her.

"Of course, then there wouldn't be an opening for you." Myra winked at me.

My cheeks flushed, and I worried that she could actually read my mind. So, I slapped her arm and Mabel jumped down.

"Now look what you did. No wonder your dog is getting attached to Steph."

"Stop. I know you're trying to cheer me up, but that line of teasing won't work."

"No, huh?"

"No. No, it's not, because I don't know what to do now." I looked up to the sky as if an answer would fall from the clouds and hit me on the head like golf-ball-sized hail.

"How about you come with Jen and me today? We talked about doing a little hiking and then some errands. Take your mind off of all of this."

"I appreciate it, but I'm going to stay here for the day. I've got to figure some things out."

Myra stood. "Well, don't go making any major decisions without telling me first. Promise me."

"I'm not going to…"

"Promise me."

"Okay. Okay. I promise." I got up and continued to wipe the chair I had been working on when she arrived.

Myra hesitated for a moment. "See you later." And then she walked away.

"See ya." I watched her cross the field and then noticed movement down at Steph's trailer. She was standing by her car looking this way. I waved. Steph got into her car, and I watched her drive out of the campground, knowing Mac would also be at her door this evening giving her a fine for driving too fast.

I looked down at Mabel. "What do you say, girl? I've got some things to do and some decisions to make." We went inside, where I spent the morning on my computer. I had to keep my mind occupied, so I fished around for information on Marie Sanfield's case, Tess's case, and Manson Smith's case (just for the fun of it). I made some calls to a friend of mine back at work and asked them to do a little digging on the same thing. A close colleague, Officer Tony Grant, was apprehensive at first but agreed to do what he could. Then I looked at used campers that were comparable to mine, to see what they were selling for.

Meanwhile, the festivities continued on with kids running around and riding on the big water slide and small merry-go-round that Mac had brought in for the weekend. I didn't have to see it to know the pool was full from the sounds of splashing water, kids yelling and laughing, and parents talking. It was as if everything was being broadcast through a megaphone directed toward my camper.

I took Mabel for brief walks now and then, not straying too far from my site. The campground was just too busy, and I wasn't in the mood for it. The evening was no better. Fireworks went off in the field and I turned up the television so the loud noise wouldn't disturb Mabel. They didn't terrify her like so many dogs, but she was on alert. The next day was quieter until noon when a parade of campers and trailers headed out of the campground, signifying the end of the holiday weekend. I was happy about that. Just not about much else.

The following week, I watched Steph drive off to work in the morning and come back in the early evening. I ate with Myra and Jen only one evening, begging off the other invitations. After several days of me staying holed up in my trailer, they said if I didn't come over, they would come to me. So, I gathered up Mabel and made the trek across the field to eat a delicious dinner of grilled chicken, salad, and baked potatoes. I was glad I relented since I had eaten every brand of frozen dinner at Walmart. Twice.

When I took Mabel for a walk one evening, I saw Steph sitting on their deck, deep in comical conversation. I was happy to see her happy. I was sad that I was sad. I felt my heart going through a paper shredder. I hurried my dog along, which meant pulling her away from where she wanted to sniff.

That night, after a lot of inner struggle and debate I made the decision to put the trailer up for sale. I had to tell Myra and Jen before I put the sign up, but I didn't know how. They would try to talk me out of it, but it didn't matter, because I didn't know how long it would be before Steph and I could be at the same campsite at the same time. Right now, it hurt too much just watching her drive off to work. It was for my own good—time to move on. Move forward. Find a new purpose. As for finding a new love? It was something I had no interest in. Losing love twice in one year was just too much. So, until I sold my trailer, I would work on the two cases to keep myself busy. If that wasn't enough to occupy my mind and my time, I would simply go home.

The next night, I noticed that Steph's car wasn't at her camper. I checked again before I went to bed and in the morning when I took Mabel out. As far as I could tell, Steph hadn't come back after work. All that week, I kept an eye out for her like a crazed woman in love whose partner was acting suspiciously, but I also likened it to being a policewoman on a case. I was just doing my duty. She was still my friend even though our friendship was dead in the water. I would always love and care about her. After a week of her being absent from the campground, I started to worry.

I invited Myra and Jen to my place for dinner, hoping that by filling them with good food and alcohol, I could get them in a relaxed mood and tell them of my plan to sell and maybe get information as to where Steph had been. And maybe how she was doing. Dinner was going well until I dropped the bombshell. My plan of wining and dining my friends to ease the blow of my decision did not pan out.

"You just got here," Myra said a little too loudly, telling me I had done okay on the alcohol part of my plan.

"You can't sell. Steph needs you," Jen added.

"No, she doesn't. She hasn't spoken to me. She hasn't been here for over a week. I'd say that's someone who doesn't need or want me."

Myra and Jen stared at each other, unspoken words flowing between them.

"What is it?" I asked, having seen that unarticulated action between them before which meant there was something they didn't want to tell me, but struggled with not doing so. "Go on, spill it."

"Steph helped the police find Lori. She came down to talk to them from Rochester. That's where she's been. She…"

"Why didn't Steph tell me that? She promised she'd tell me anything about Tess's case."

"Because there's nothing to tell other than Lori and Tess stopped seeing each other weeks before her death. Lori said she only saw Tess once after they broke up. To talk. It was that day at The Commons. You already knew this. As far as we know, she didn't give them any more information that would help to determine the cause of Tess's death."

I couldn't respond to what they were saying. My heart sank a little lower, knowing that the suicide stamp was getting closer to making its mark on my wife's death certificate. It would not only be her parents who felt they failed her, but I would too.

"We were going to tell you," Jen said, as if pleading their case for keeping silent. "Um. There's something else."

"This is why I need to get out of here. This isn't going to end if I stay here. So, what else is there?" I heard whining and looked to see Mabel's paws on the bench beside me. I picked her up. "It's okay, girl," I said as I petted her.

Jen swallowed hard. "While Lori was down here being interviewed by the police, she contacted Steph. I think they're going to give it another try."

"We don't know that," Myra snapped at Jen. "The only thing Steph told me was that they talked."

"Good for them," I answered as sharply as the pain I felt. "I'm happy for them."

"Blake." Myra reached across the picnic table to take my hand.

I drew it back. "Really, I am. Now you've got another couple to hang out with, and I won't be a third wheel."

"Ouch, that's not nice," Jen said, glaring at me. "We haven't treated you like that. I thought we meant more to you than a mean insult."

"I'm sorry," I said, dropping my eyes to my plate that still had half the piece of homemade lasagna on it. "I didn't mean that. It's just…" I dropped the level of my voice involuntarily. "It hasn't been a really good summer for me. Strike that. Year."

"We understand," Myra answered. She took Jen's hand and squeezed it. "Don't we?"

Jen nodded, but said nothing, her face drooping with sadness.

"I'll clean up. You girls go on home. I need to be alone." I said, dismissing them, which made me feel bad because they had been nothing but wonderful friends. "I really am sorry. You've been so good to me. Once I get my life back on track, maybe I'll give this camping thing another try. But for now, I need to go back home. I need to figure everything out. Steph, Tess. Everything."

Myra and Jen came over and took turns hugging me. "We love you," Myra said. "You know where we are if you need us."

"Just across the field," I said, adding a little chuckle.

"Just across the field," Myra repeated softly.

"Good night, Blake. Thanks for dinner." Jen's eyes were full of disappointment.

"You're welcome. I'll bring you some leftover lasagna tomorrow. Good night." Mabel stretched up, putting her paws on my arm, and licked my face. I petted her as I watched my friends stroll across the field. Then my gaze shifted to Steph's camper. "I know, girl. That's part of the problem," I said, rubbing her ears. "Steph's just across the field too."

CHAPTER TWENTY-THREE

I put the For Sale sign up the next day. I made myself not look across the field while I pounded it into the ground. To stay occupied, I mowed the lawn, trimmed the weeds, and made lists of what I needed to do when I sold the trailer.

Then I sat in the chair with Mabel on my lap with the hot summer sun beating down on us, wondering if I was making the right decision. Maybe I shouldn't sell it. Just close it up and go home. That way, I would still have a place to come to next summer. I mean, I could figure my life out by then, couldn't I? I enjoyed it here. Maybe I'd meet someone by then and we could come down together. One thing I knew—I didn't want to be down here alone or end up being a third or fifth wheel. Again.

Even though Jen and Myra assured me I was not a third wheel, no one ever understood that feeling until you were one. No one made me feel that way on purpose. I made myself feel that way, and it was difficult not to do when everyone around me was coupled. That now would include Steph and Lori. But if I sold my trailer, I might not get a spot for next year. But selling was the right thing to do. It was time to let go. It was also time to get me and my little girl out of the sun.

We went inside to cool off with the factory ice blowing over us and I made lunch. We went back outside to eat, but this time under the awning with Mabel sitting in between my legs, waiting for a small piece of lunch meat. I settled back onto my zero-gravity chair, using relaxation techniques I employed whenever I couldn't sleep. The warmth of the day felt good on my skin, and the natural scent of pine trees, clean air, and freshly mowed grass filled my nostrils.

It worked, because my phone ringing woke me. "Hey there," I answered Maddie as cheerfully as my mood would allow.

"Blake. Let's just pass the formalities. We found Lori."

"Yeah, I heard. Steph told my friends who told me. What did she say?" I asked, even though I already knew, but hoping Maddie might have more.

"She said she stopped seeing Tess several weeks before Tess's death. They had a mutual separation. She said Tess seemed fine, and she only saw her once to talk."

"That corroborates what Tess told me when she stopped at the campground to see me at the end of May." I felt my stomach turning, anxious to hear what Maddie was going to say next.

"We're still investigating, but I have to be honest with you, Blake. That's why I called. We're running into too many dead ends, including Tess's apartment, and I'm sorry to say this, but it looks as if it will either be determined suicide or become a cold case."

"A cold case," I repeated, "If you're thinking a cold case, then you have doubts about suicide. There's something that's leading you toward murder, but you can't find anything more. So, what's suggesting murder?"

"Her footprints. The investigators are baffled by them and don't ask me any more about it. I'm sorry, Blake. I'll let you know when the final ruling is made after the inquest."

"Thank you, Maddie."

I sat for a while, determining my next move. It only took a minute for me to pull the sign out of the ground. I couldn't sell. Not yet. I could ignore Steph, her trailer, her coming and going—whatever I had to do to find out what happened to Tess. Besides, Steph wasn't around anymore, day or night. Maybe she was at her home with Lori. But, I had to stay and try. However, I accepted that when Tess's cause of death came in, I might have to go home. I would need to see her parents.

My phone dinged, and I looked at a text from Myra.

You're a crazy woman. How many times are you going to hammer that sign in and take it down?

Followed by a laughing emoji.

I chuckled, realizing there was no way I could hide what I did outside. They had a window to my site. I texted in return. *You want to have dinner together?*

Thought you'd never ask. But it's our turn. Come at four for cocktails.

Mabel had jumped off my chair and was roaming around her confined area, sniffing various blades of grass. "Attagirl. You tell everyone who owns this place." I laughed at my dog when she turned her head slightly, giving me an evil sideways glance. Then I looked over at Steph's trailer. Part of me half expected Steph to be there, and part of me accepted she wouldn't be. I was usually a hopeful person, positive. I wondered if I should shelve that line of thinking for a while. I should at least stop looking at her trailer.

After dinner, the three of us sat around their campfire drinking their latest concoction. Mabel sat in my lap, seeming a little under the weather. She missed Steph's lap. I missed Steph. My friend. I realized I couldn't live without Steph in my life, so I needed to find a way to make her see that we could be friends and only friends. We talked about how things had calmed down. I also asked if either of them had heard anything more about Manson Smith or his daughter, Marie Sanfield.

Myra answered me. "There's been nothing about it on the news. I asked Steph last week, but she couldn't say. You know the whole thing about confidentiality. 'If I tell you, I'd have to kill you.'"

I giggled. "That's a little overdramatic, but yes, I understand."

While we talked, a familiar sound approached. There was no way you could ignore the whirr of Mac's motor as he drove up in his chariot. I envisioned him wearing a crown and a long Roman gold-trimmed cape, sitting on something that looked more like a throne than a leather bench.

"Haven't seen him in a while," Myra said, watching the vehicle approach.

"Wished it was a while longer," I added.

"Hey, girls," Mac called out to us. "Thought I'd stop by and give you some good news. Sorry I haven't been around to check in on ya, but I've been kind of busy."

"Would you like a beer?" Jen asked him, and I glanced at Mabel. I could always announce that I needed to take her for a walk.

"No, just had one. But thanks."

"So," I began. "What's the good news?"

"I'm always lookin' out for my people." He grinned and puffed out his chest, but his stomach extended much farther than his chest could ever do. "They convicted that Smith fella today for assault, trespass, and harassment. They haven't sentenced him yet, but I don't think he'll be around here again. I hear they might try to pin a murder charge on him for the death of his daughter and if they do, well, let's just say he won't be seeing the light of day anytime soon."

I almost broke out laughing at the irony of him stopping by with this news. It was like that saying, ask and you shall receive. I asked, and I was receiving the answer from Mac. Of all people. But his information was surprising. Maddie had told me a while back that Marie Sanfield's death was going to be declared a suicide. What did they find that changed their minds? It might give me more insight into Tess's death. Now I had to adjust my plan of action.

"And I'm sure," Myra started in, "that you had a lot to do with saving us from this despicable man."

I wondered if Mac was aware of her sarcasm. When he answered her...let's just say he could be a really stupid man. "I sure did. Might get a medal for turning that one in. Anyways. Got to be off and let the rest of my people know everything's okay now."

"Thanks, Mac," Jen said, waving as he drove away.

"Do you believe that?" Myra asked me.

"If you're asking, do I believe him about Manson Smith? The answer is yes. If you're asking, do I believe he had anything to do with it? The answer is twofold. Yes, I do, but not in the way he was implying."

Myra reached out her glass toward mine, and we clinked. She got my drift.

"Do you mind if I join you?"

I would have jumped up, but Mabel beat me to it, jumping off my lap to greet Steph who bent down and picked up my little pooch. Mabel licked her face as if her tongue was a washcloth and Steph had taken a dive into a peanut butter jar. Myra was up and back with another chair, plopping it down between mine and hers, then planting herself back into her seat.

"I didn't know you were back," Myra said.

I was kind of speechless, not sure of what to say, but knowing I had to stay cool. After debating several greetings and policing them through my brain, I settled on, "Glad you could join us. You just missed the king of the forrrest." I sang the words "king of the forrrest" like the lion in *The Wizard of Oz*.

Everyone laughed.

Steph sat down, whispering to Mabel, "I missed you," and "You're such a love."

"She missed you too," I said, but knew my dog had already implied that.

Steph smiled at me. It was a welcome sight, but it was a smile I couldn't read. I wouldn't try, either, because I was grateful she came. I hoped this might be the beginning of a new friendship.

"So what did that scumbag have to tell you this time?"

"He bragged about Manson Smith getting convicted and a possible second charge for murdering his daughter. He made it seem as if it was all because of him. He's expecting a medal," Jen explained and then asked, "Would you like something to drink?"

Steph rolled her eyes. "A medal, huh? That's a good one. Got any soda?"

"Coming right up." Jen scurried over to a cooler that sat on the deck and pulled out a Coke.

"Thanks. Actually, he wasn't responsible for Smith's conviction, although he had a hand in it. He testified at the trial about Smith harassing his campers. They called me as a witness, too."

"They did?" Bewildered, I wondered why no one else at the campground was called to testify.

As if she knew what I was thinking, she added, "They called me because I camp here and am part of the police department. Despite my DUI, they deemed me a credible witness. But…" Steph took a drink.

"But what?" Myra coaxed her to finish her sentence.

"The DA is pushing for the murder conviction. I heard that Mac told the police that Smith told him he was going to kill his daughter. She shamed him and her husband because of an affair with a woman. However, I'm not sure that's true. Manson denies ever saying that, but I think Mac is out for a big finish before he retires. To be the hero." She winked at Jen. "Or that medal he mentioned." She laughed.

"A hero to who?" I asked rhetorically. "You and I know, and I'm sure a lot of other gays and lesbians know that Mac feels the same way about us as Smith. He's a homophobic prick," I said.

"Maybe he's just not looking for a medal, but also a raise to fatten his pension," Steph said. "I've heard him say he wants to retire soon to put his energies into his campground. I just know that he's got his nose into this so deep I'm surprised he can breathe."

I chuckled at her analogy. "I'd like to see them pin a medal on his chest."

"I hope the pin goes in deep," she replied, earning her a thumbs-up from all of us.

"How have you been doing?" I asked cautiously.

"Doing okay. I've been busy at work cleaning up Bevel's mess." She leaned over and said in such a quiet voice I had to strain to hear, "He did Marie Sanfield's autopsy. Maddie asked me to redo it."

Maddie had told me, but I whispered back, "Do you know why?"

"His reports were sloppy and confusing. There was something off about his findings and his deductions. Even though some of the information seemed insignificant, when you put the complete picture together, it didn't fit. Like a puzzle that has a piece missing."

"If that isn't cryptic, I don't know what is," Myra scoffed.

"Make of it what you will, but you know I can't give you any more than that."

We didn't ask her where she had been all week or what she was doing. We didn't ask her if she was going to stay. As difficult as it was for me, I pretended none of that mattered and treated her like an old friend you don't see for long periods and when you do, it's as if that time in between never happened. You pick up seamlessly where you left off.

I think I struggled with it a little more than Jen and Myra. There were times I had to catch myself from not saying, "Hey, do you want to go wine touring?" or "Hey, how about a hike?" Instead, I told her about the hikes I had taken and the gossip I heard from and about the other seasonal campers like Sandy and Kevin having a screaming match inside their trailer that was heard throughout the campground. Or the Millers having to drag Greg's ass back to his camper because he was stumbling over all the patio furniture after having downed several large beers with whisky chasers.

When we all agreed it was time to turn in, Steph handed my dog back and gave me a quick hug. Her hugs to Myra and Jen were longer and closer, but that was okay. Baby steps. I hooked Mabel to her leash and ambled across the field. I glanced back to watch Steph make her way back to her trailer. She got in her car and drove off. I turned away because I didn't want to make her feel I was watching her. Which I was. I wanted her to feel that it was okay to be here when I was here, and it was okay to leave. Tonight, she took a small step in that direction.

Maybe Steph and I could find that road to friendship after all. If that destination truly was where we needed to be.

CHAPTER TWENTY-FOUR

12:41 a.m. I wasn't sure how long it would take for me to forget that moment in time, but it wouldn't be anytime soon.

I woke with a start, hearing my phone hopping around on the booth table once again. I had forgotten to place it on the charger when I went to bed. Damn. That meant the battery still had some charge, but it was probably pretty low. I clambered out of bed, turned the light on, and fetched my phone. Who would call me at this time of night? I didn't recognize the phone number, and usually when I couldn't ID the caller, I didn't answer. If it was important, the caller could leave a message. This time, for whatever reason, I felt an overwhelming urge to answer this call. "Hello?"

"You need to go to the gorge or Steph could die."

Before I could rebuke the person for playing such an awful joke on me, or ask them what gorge or why Steph might die, the call ended. I hadn't recognized the voice. I honestly couldn't distinguish between a male or female. It was low, hoarse, and hurried. I didn't care, and I was taking no chances. I threw on some clothes faster than Superman changed in the phone booth. After putting Mabel on the recliner, I kissed her and gave her treats. Then I left with my gun, my pepper spray, my dying phone, and a flashlight. Last were my keys and license. I drove fast out of the campground not caring how fast I was going.

I *knew* where I had to go. Only one gorge came to mind. When I got out to the road, I hit fifty-five faster than the vehicle's commercials bragged about. I'd have to write a letter to Ford telling them they needed to revisit that. It only took me ten minutes to get to the parking lot at Upper Taughannock Falls Park, but it was the longest ten minutes I had experienced on the darkest of nights I had seen in a long time.

There were no cars in the parking lot, but I knew this had to be the place. It made sense, since this was the gorge where Marie Sanfield's and Tess's lives had ended. And Annie's. I quickly assessed my surroundings. I didn't expect to see anyone because the park was closed, but thought it better to keep my flashlight off.

It was an eight-minute walk to the spot where Tess and Marie went over the ledge. The hard dirt path wove through the woods, over a small bridge, and then opened up to the high cliffs that surrounded Taughannock Creek. The path continued along the cliff edge. At this time of year, the creek was low, and sometimes in very dry summers, Taughannock Falls was known to dry up. There were tiny waterfalls and whirlpools along the upper creek, and I could hear water making its way to the long drop a mile down the path.

I approached the path cautiously, taking in the chain-link fence lining this side of the gorge. In certain areas, there were a few feet of ledge on the other side of the fence. The area where Tess had fallen was about four feet wide for about twenty to thirty feet along the cliff. Wooden benches dotted the trail here and there so one could sit and enjoy the view. However the view was obstructed by the fence, so people often jumped the fence there and sat on the other side. Then a park ranger would help them back to the trail side and hand them a ticket for trespassing. Obviously, though, the fence didn't deter everyone, I thought as I made my way along the path, keeping an eye out for Steph and whoever called me.

There was more light along the top of the gorge than in the woods, and I was glad I didn't need to turn on my flashlight. However, anyone could see me coming as I was in the wide open. There was no way to stay hidden unless I approached the area I needed to get to through the woods, and that meant bushwhacking. There was no trail through the forest in this part of the park. I had one more hairpin turn on the trail before I would be visible to anyone in the area where Tess went over the gorge. I stopped and listened.

Voices.

I heard voices. More than one. They were faint, and I strained to hear them.

Female. Two. Maybe three. One of them was Steph, and my heart sank.

I was about to make the turn when I heard a definite third voice. Steph was quiet, but the other two women's words were escalating in volume and intensity, inciting one nasty argument. I needed to get closer to hear what they were saying and I needed to know which side of the fence Steph was on. The intensity of the argument told me I had to get there fast, especially if Steph was on the wrong side of the chain-link fence.

I couldn't let them see me coming as I might startle them. And that could be deadly. I had to assume they were near the ledge, along it somewhere. There were a few spots with only one or two feet between the fence and death. I had to hope if they were on the wrong side of the fence, it was in a spot with four feet between them and the edge.

I headed into the woods. It was to my advantage that it was very dark which meant I didn't have to go too far into the forest. I could stay close to the tree line and still not be seen. Their yelling would hide any noise I'd make as I approached, and if I stayed in the shadows enough, they wouldn't be able to distinguish between me and an animal. I felt like a sloth moving ever so slowly, but I was so worried I might not get to Steph on time, I had to fight the urge not to burst out of the woods like a bullet shot from a rifle. I continued to listen to the voices while I slowly made my way through the bushes and trees.

Steph was trying to calm the other two women, but every time she spoke, one of the other two women erupted into a fit of rage, blaming Steph and Tess and Marie and… Annie. Annie. A woman continued to blurt out other names I didn't know but I had to assume they were all lesbians.

Who was shouting these names? What was she blaming these women for? I dug deep to remember some of the other women who had fallen into different gorges over the years. I had kept a list at home, and my brain could see it on my natural wood desk in the room I had designated as my office. Ainsley. Yes, she was on the list. Becca was another.

I stopped dead in my tracks, realizing I had been right all along. There *was* a connection with the women's deaths and it was here. Right now. Screaming. I had felt all along that there was a serial killer, but there was no evidence. In the '90s and early 2000s, most of the deaths had been just sad and horrible suicides. They were all college kids, males and females, and when their friends and families were interrogated, the same theme came up every time. The students were overwhelmed with school. They had feelings of guilt over disappointing their parents. Annie was a student, but Tess and Marie were not, and I bet if I dug into Ainsley's and Becca's pasts, they wouldn't be either. So was Marie's father here?

No. The voices were clear now, definitely all female, making me glad I didn't have to confront Manson Smith. The two women were yelling with such fervor, constantly interrupting each other, making it difficult to understand what they were saying. I did, however, have a clear view of the three women from where I was hiding. Steph was among them.

Shit. Damn. Fuck.

They were on the wrong side of the fence.

My heart dropped as I surveyed the ledge they were standing on. A mere three to four feet from the fence to the edge and only about eight feet in length. On either side of the outcrop where they were arguing, the ledge tapered off to nothing.

A large, clear opening stood between me and the fence. No grass or weeds, just dirt. It was a distance that made reaching them before they saw me almost impossible, but I had to get to them without them knowing if I was to have the advantage. I watched as Steph slowly, ever so slowly, moved sideways toward the fence. Speed wasn't always the answer, and it looked as if she could either climb over it or grab onto it for safety.

I studied the other two women. One was about my age, maybe in her mid or early fifties. She had short black hair and was of average height and build. Her voice was filled with fear and rage. The other woman was taller, but I couldn't get a good look at her since her back was to me. I surveyed the ground I had to cross to get to them and noticed a small, black surveillance camera had been smashed on the ground. I looked around and saw the tree nearby where the metal holder was bolted to the trunk, and realized the police must have installed the cameras.

Good for them, I thought. And then, *bad for me*. They wouldn't see this, unless there were others nearby and intact. I prayed that there were more surveillance cameras, but even if there were, I had no idea if they were constantly monitoring them or just checking video now and then. *Please at least let there be someone monitoring the camera feeds and they notice there is no picture.* But even if they did, they might not send someone right away. I shoved my hand into my pocket and pulled out my phone.

Shit. Damn. Fuck. *What a dummkopf!*

My phone had died and I hadn't even thought about charging it in the car. Where was my head? I knew where. It was on the ledge. With Steph.

I knew then I had to make my move. I convinced myself the police would be here, sooner or later, hopefully sooner. The picture of Annie's Tinkerbell charm bracelet popped into my head, and I knew I had to hang on to hope. I didn't know if anyone else was lurking in the woods, possibly Manson Smith, so I had to take my chances. More importantly, the two women were now frantic, waving their arms, pointing to Steph who was almost to the fence. I was running out of time to get to her before one of them pushed her over the ledge.

Then the unthinkable happened.

The taller woman lunged for Steph, taking the other shorter woman by surprise. She rammed into Steph, pushing her toward the edge of the cliff. Steph was silent as she fought her off and tried to get away from the precipice, but the taller woman had surprise on her side and had taken Steph off guard.

I jumped out of the woods. And I ran.

The taller woman kicked at Steph's legs, knocking her feet out from under her. Steph fell, the bottom half of her body dangling over the ledge. I saw her hands scrape along the dirt and rock as she tried to find something, anything, to hang on to. She dug and clawed her fingers into the earth as the weight of her body pulled her over the edge.

Thirty feet away.

The shorter woman did a side tackle, knocking the taller one back. Then she lunged for Steph, dropping herself onto her stomach and grabbed Steph's arms, tugging her back.

Twenty feet.

Steph dangled off the cliff, trying to pull her bodyweight upward. Her fingers were still clawing into the ground, frantically searching for anything to hold on to as the shorter woman tried to pull her back up off the edge.

When I saw Steph's body jostle as the taller woman grabbed the shorter one by the legs and violently pulled her away, trying to dislodge her hold on Steph, I dug deep to find every molecule of power within my body.

Ten feet.

"Let me go!" the smaller woman yelled.

"I. Will. Not. You will not go down this path!"

"I won't let her fall," the shorter woman screamed back at her assailant.

"Hang on to her, Steph!" I shouted as I launched my body into the air toward the fence, hoping I could get my feet close to the top and clear it like a side vault in gymnastics. I kept hold of the top railing to keep from going into the gorge myself. I used to be really good at those. I was just a lot older now.

The two women turned in my direction, giving the taller one a quick advantage. She yanked with all her might and the other lost her grip on Steph. They stumbled off to the side and an ugly, physical struggle ensued.

I was over the fence, landing hard on my legs. The solid ground sent a surge of pain through my body, throwing me off balance. The whole time, my pleading eyes were on Steph to do everything she could to keep from falling. She had nothing to grab on to, no tree roots or rocks protruding from the dirt, no footholds in the rock face to get her feet into. I knew because I had studied this area several times.

I would not let Steph be one of those women who fell to their death in the gorge. Even though my legs screamed "Pain!" I fought with everything I had to stay on them, to use my leg muscles to propel my body toward Steph. I fell onto her arms and my bodyweight stopped her from sliding. I reached for her arms, taking one in each hand, and shifted my weight off of her limbs.

"No!"

A man's voice. Had the police finally arrived? I felt a tiny bit of relief, but just tiny because we were far from being safe.

"Stop it. Please," he pleaded.

Mac?

I was shaken to recognize Mac's voice. Just my luck, he'd be the cop to show up. I hoped there were others with him who would want to help me and not leave me here with Steph's life literally in my hands. I couldn't look back without losing my grip on Steph's arms, because she was thrashing in an effort to get back up on the cliff ledge. There was too much of her weight hanging over the cliff, making her body gravity-bound for the bottom of the gorge, and I felt myself losing ground.

"Steph, stop. Someone is coming. I've got you. I promise. Just stop moving."

Her body relaxed slightly, but I knew it wouldn't last for long, and I didn't know how much longer I could hold her. But Mac was coming. He was a cop. He would put his opinions of me aside and help me because right now, I was only a citizen trying to save a life.

The whole time, the two women continued screaming at each other, pushing and shoving, engaged in a bitter altercation. I glanced to the side where they were grappling with each other and realized they, too, were precariously close to the edge.

But it was the recognition of the taller woman that rocked me to my core. Black-and-gray peppered hair framed a worn and wrinkled face, making her look more like an eighty-year-old. I understood in that moment that her timeworn face was more from life experiences than time itself and she dyed her hair to hide it.

Missy.

"Lori, no!" Mac yelled.

What the hell! Lori?

My head was spinning, but I fought to stay with Steph, gripping her arms with everything I had. I heard the fence rattle, alerting me that Mac had to be climbing over it. At the same time, Lori screamed at the top of her lungs, "I hate you both!" just before she threw herself into Missy's body with all her might.

The sound of Mac's feet hitting the ground next to us was a fraction of a second too late. Missy lost her balance and fell backward in slow motion. A blood-curdling scream split the night air. It was silenced in an instant at the sound of a faint thud.

The woman I now knew was Lori, rushed past him and grabbed Steph's arms, helping me to pull her up and onto the stone ledge. When the bulk of Steph's body was safely on top of the cliff, she fell into my arms, the weight of her pushing me onto my back. I wrapped my arms around her and held her tightly, feeling her body shake with adrenaline and the aftermath of being so close to dying. Mac stood still, his head drooped.

I mouthed the word *thank you* to Lori, who stood watching us for a few seconds. Then she looked at Mac. He lifted his head and met Lori's gaze.

"Lori," he choked out.

Lori stood frozen in place. She looked over the edge.

"Lori. Look at me."

She turned to Mac. There were no tears in her eyes, in fact her expression was blank. "Mother said she killed all those women. Why would she do that? She used to always bring me here as a child but she stopped after Annie died. Here." She looked over the edge again.

"Lori, honey, come away from there."

"She didn't bring me here anymore because she said she didn't want me to be sad about Annie, but she killed Annie, and Marie. And Tess. Why would she do that?" Her voice grew louder.

"No, honey. You must have heard her wrong," Mac said.

Steph and I didn't move. We held on to each other and I knew I felt dread in my heart and I was pretty sure she did too.

"No. She told me so. She said she killed Ainsley and Becca too, that they were bad for me. But I didn't even *know* them."

Steph and I remained frozen in place. I held on to her, not caring that we were supposed to be just friends, because I knew I could never be that to her again. We lay there in silence, listening to Lori as my mind raced and scrambled for answers as to what just happened. But I began to piece everything together.

"Your mother wouldn't do something like that, honey. Oh God, Lori, where have you been? We missed you."

"Bullshit!" she yelled with such anger and contempt. "She said she did. And you missed me?" She spat on the ground. "You didn't love me. You both abhorred me because I was a homo. And all that time, all that time, I thought Mom was on my side, but it was her who sent me away, not you. She found me in the cabin on your stupid campground. She tried to convince me to go back. I will never go back there." Lori's head tilted back and she laughed. Short, sad and defeated. "*She.* Killed them all."

Then Lori looked at me. "Annie. Tess," she whispered. "I'm so sorry."

She turned in circles, moving precariously close to the edge. Then a loud pitiful wail escaped her lips as she threw her hands up to her face. Mac lunged for her, but before he could reach her, she took a step backward.

And she was gone.

Mac fell to his knees, head in his hands. The word *no* escaped his lips in a loud roar like the coyotes on a nightly hunt. He was a broken man without ever falling over the edge.

Steph let out a small scream as I stared into the blankness where Lori had just stood. Shock and frustration made me yell, "Goddamn it, where are the police?" I held on to Steph as she wept, but knew I couldn't wait any longer. "Steph, have you got your phone?"

With her head buried in my shoulder, she said, "Pocket," in between sobs.

I found it in a side pocket of her jacket and, keeping one arm tight around Steph, dialed 911. Steph's head lay on my chest. The dispatcher told me the police were two minutes out. They must have noticed the dead camera to be that close. Still, I explained that one cop car would not be enough. They would need more and they would need an ambulance.

Mac remained on his knees, silent.

"Missy disabled all the cameras," Steph finally said.

She pulled away from me and we both inched our butts back to the fence and leaned against it. The clouds were separating, evaporating and glimmers of random stars came into view. It was peaceful and serene despite everything that had just happened.

"Did Missy really tell Lori all that?" I asked Steph.

"Yes."

It almost seemed apropos because death had happened under a layer of clouds in darkness and now the life that was saved sat against a chain-link fence under a clear and magical, starry sky. The only words that came to my mind in that moment were *unintended consequences*. I believed if Missy and Lori knew the outcome of their actions all those years, their dead bodies might not be at the bottom of the gorge. But we'd never know.

I took Steph's hand in mine. "Tell me what happened? How did you get involved with this?" I studied her face and saw anguish, pain and sadness.

"It's a long story, and I don't think we have much time. I hear sirens." She squeezed my hand. "Do you mind if I explain it to you at the same time I'm going to have to explain it to Captain Spinner?"

I chuckled. "Sure. I never liked repeating a story either. You do know, though, that you *will* have to repeat it."

"Yeah, but only to Jen and Myra. I can live with that."

The police cars arrived in exactly two minutes, but it took them another five by foot to reach us. I stood with my hands up—expected in situations like this since they would not know me and have no idea how I was related to this situation until I told them. So, I did.

"My name is Captain Blakely Moore. Retired criminal profiler with the Rochester, New York police. I'm armed with a registered firearm that I'm licensed to carry, and pepper spray."

When Steph stood up next to me and faced them, the approaching police officers lowered their guns. Apparently, they knew her. After taking custody of my weapons, one asked, "Dr. Davis. Are you all right?"

"Yes, Sergeant Fuller, but the two women at the bottom of the gorge are not. And neither is Officer Taylor."

One policeman kept an eye on us while the sergeant hopped the fence and peered over the edge. Then he knelt beside Mac. "Officer Taylor. Are you all right?"

Mac didn't move or lift his head. The sergeant looked up at us.

"Their names are Missy Taylor, Mac's wife. The younger woman is Lori Smith. However, I think you'll find Lori Smith is not her real name. I believe you'll find her last name is really Taylor," Steph informed them. "She's Mac's daughter."

My head snapped in Steph's direction, whose head tilted in a very slight nod to me. It was true, and I never knew about it. My mind was swimming in questions and when that happened, my brain went into overdrive to find the answers. I needed to know. "Did you know?" I asked, my stomach turning as I waited for the answer.

Steph moved closer to me, and I felt her take my hand in hers. She squeezed it, reassurance that she wouldn't let me go crazy searching for answers in all this madness. She would be beside me. "No. not until Missy showed up here."

"When I heard Lori say *Mom*, I didn't believe it. He never once told me he had a daughter when I worked as his rookie. I thought she might be Manson Smith's daughter."

"That thought crossed my mind too, but there was no reason to think that other than the same last names," Steph said.

"You're right. I think at that point I was just reaching for answers."

Sergeant Fuller led us to an ambulance where the medics attended to our minor cuts and bruises. Another climbed the fence and was trying to help Mac. Both of us insisted we didn't need to go to the hospital, but we waited sitting on the back doorway frame of the ambulance for Captain Spinner to arrive.

"How did you know I was here?" Steph asked me, still holding my hand.

"I got a call. It was a private number. I don't know who it was or even if it was female or male. I wonder if it was Lori. They told me I had to get to the gorge, or you would die. They didn't say which gorge, but I assumed it was this one after everything that's happened."

She rested her head on my shoulder. "It couldn't have been Lori. I was with her the whole time. But, it's a good thing you're good at what you do. You always knew who, when, what, and where before anyone else did. Good deducting, Sherlock."

"Why thank you, Watson." We both chuckled with a quiet, relieved, and thankful laugh.

"Well, well, well. I didn't expect you both to be here. You want to tell me what went down?"

We looked up to see Maddie in her role as Captain Spinner, standing before us, hands on her hips.

Steph took a deep breath. "Before I get started, you need to know that the two women at the bottom of the gorge are Mac Taylor's wife and daughter. I think he's over there with an EMT. I was here with Lori when Missy showed up. They got into a huge fight and Lori shoved her mother who fell over the edge. Mac didn't get here in time to keep it from happening. Lori lost it and just…" Steph's voice cracked.

"She stepped off the ledge," I answered. "I'm pretty sure he had nothing to do with any of it."

Maddie put her hand up. "Sergeant Fuller!" she bellowed.

The sergeant was giving orders to other police officers. He stopped midsentence and jogged over to where we were. "Yes, Captain."

"Where is Officer Taylor?"

"He's in pretty bad shape. Mentally, not physically. They're loading him onto a gurney."

Maddie snapped her fingers close to his face a couple of times. "Pay attention, Fuller. I need you to get this crime scene under control. Fast. Tape it off. Up here and in the gorge. Get officers down there and get forensics here, and send two officers to the hospital with Officer Taylor. Tell them to let me know when I can talk to him."

"Yes, Captain." He was off like The Flash.

I smiled at the authority Maddie commanded over her officers. It was not only impressive, but it was welcomed by the females under her command. They knew where Captain Spinner was concerned that there would always be fairness. Case in point—I saw Sergeant Fuller leaving with a policewoman instead of a man.

She looked at Steph. "All right. From the beginning."

Steph was tired. I could see it in her drooping eyelids and hear it in her slightly slurred speech. Her recount to the captain on what happened was briefer than an author's blurb on the back of a book cover. I added a few pertinent pieces of information that would help with the investigation while Steph leaned against the door frame of the ambulance and closed her eyes.

Realizing Steph would need rest before she continued, Captain Spinner told her to be in her office at ten a.m. the next morning for a formal interview. "I don't usually let my witnesses leave until I get every detail from them because it's fresh in their memory. But I know you, Dr. Davis. I know you'll tell me everything." She gave Steph a stern look. "Tomorrow morning. Ten. Don't be late."

Her head fell back, her eyes looked up toward the sky, and she took a deep sigh, followed by a tiny smile I could tell she was fighting from growing into a larger one. Without a word, she walked back into the throng of police milling about, shouting orders to secure the area and begin their investigation. I watched as the familiar yellow tape was strung from tree to tree. By now, police would be at the bottom of the gorge and soon the area would become a fully-fledged investigative crime scene.

I extended my hand to Steph. "Where to?" I asked, expecting her to ask me to take her home to her house in Ithaca.

"I'm pretty sure Mabel is waiting for me. Take me to your trailer."

I grinned.

When we got back to my trailer, I went outside with Mabel even though it was three thirty in the morning and knowing I would not be waking at the usual six thirty. I hoped this would sustain her tiny bladder until a later wake-up time. Steph had to be as tired as I was, and getting up at our normal early hour seemed like a real impossibility.

Before I left, I told Steph to take the bed and decided I would leave Mabel with her since I knew my dog would rather sleep with her than me. When I went inside, she was already under the covers, propped up with a few pillows. I set Mabel on the bed next to Steph after which my pooch circled her wagon and with an overactive tail, settled down next to Steph's midsection. Both appeared extremely satisfied, and that made me happy. I opened the cupboard door and pulled out a set of sheets, a blanket, and a pillow and set about making the dining booth into a bed.

"What are you doing?"

I looked up to see Steph grinning at me.

"I'm making my bed."

"Why?" She dragged out the word.

"So, I can get some sleep. I only like napping in the recliners. Long-term sleeping in them doesn't agree with me."

She patted the mattress next to her. "There's a perfectly good bed right here with lots of room. Besides, we've slept in this bed together before."

I couldn't argue with that.

CHAPTER TWENTY-FIVE

The next morning, I woke to Steph in my bed with Mabel snuggled beside her. I felt my entire body smile at the site as I quietly got out of bed and prepared breakfast. Soon the trailer was filled with the tantalizing aroma of bacon.

"That smells really good right about now. What time is it?"

"Eight thirty. You have enough time to clean up and eat. Then I'll take you to Maddie's office."

"Will you stay with me while I speak to her?"

"She asked me to come too because I was there. But even if she didn't, I would go whether she liked it or not." I smiled at her.

"Good. I'll get ready and take Mabel out."

We ate breakfast outside since the dining table was still down with bedding on it from the night before. Afterward, I settled my pooch with treats for the time we'd be gone, and arrived at Maddie's office five minutes early.

We sat in front of the large mahogany desk. Captain Spinner placed her phone on the desk and tapped record. "I am informing you that I am recording this interview. It will be typed up as your formal statement."

We both nodded. Steph took a deep breath, sighed and began. "I knew I was taking a risk. Actually, I was taking several risks. I risked getting myself into a situation that would be, um, difficult to get out of. I was also risking the possibility of never having a relationship with Blake. I've loved Blake since we were kids. But I never knew if Blake felt the same and stopped wondering when she met Annie in college. I was happy that Blake had finally admitted who she really was. I had only wished it had been with me and not a college student she had met through me while I studied premed.

My mouth dropped open, but I remained quiet as she continued.

"When Annie died, I thought I might have a chance, but I needed to give Blake time to mourn, to figure out what it meant. And then, before I knew it, she had left the IPD and moved to Rochester to take another job with their city police force. And my chance was gone. We kept in touch. We remained friends. Best of friends and that was okay.

"I was so happy for Blake when she married Tess. But I could never find that kind of happiness for myself. Instead, I lived vicariously through all my friends' relationships and supported them no matter where I was in my own personal life. I realized a few months ago that was not a good place.

"Woman after woman left my life just as quickly as they had entered it, and I wondered if maybe I was never meant to be with anyone. So, I kind of gave up on relationships, instead continually pursuing romance until it fizzled out because a relationship was the only thing left waiting for it to fail. Which it always did.

"When Tess died, I saw Blake's pain, and I didn't want her to feel the kind of loneliness I felt. I knew she would never find happiness again until she found out what happened to her wife, and she couldn't do it herself. She was retired. And you, Captain Spinner, told her to stay out of it. Blake would never stop looking and probably get into all sorts of trouble for it. So, I had to find out exactly what happened to Tess. I needed to find the truth. I had to do that for her.

"Blake was too emotionally involved. I backed off from her because it would be harder if I allowed her to work with me. She was too close to getting herself into trouble, and she would only impede any progress I could make on my own. It hurt her. I knew it, but it had to be done. And it was all because of Lori."

I looked at her in surprise, but still said nothing.

"I suspected something was off about Lori. Really off. I still had her phone number, and thank God, she hadn't changed it. So, I called her and arranged a dinner together after which she stayed the night at my place in town. I hated it, but I had to make Lori feel comfortable enough so she might tell me something useful. Anything. She was skittish and I knew she'd run if she had any inclination that I was fishing.

"No matter how hard I tried, Lori wouldn't give up any pertinent information. She was vague in details or professed she didn't know. She did admit that Tess and she had broken up, but she did not say why or who left who. Except for the one day Tess came to Ithaca to see her at Lori's request, they hadn't seen each other since the breakup. Tess had said a final goodbye to her. Lori was hurt.

"I believed what she said but I didn't give up. I continued to spend time with Lori because I had a feeling—a feeling that there was still something she knew that might shed a little light on Tess's death, and it ate at me. Lori remained a closed book with lots of secrets. I could only sense the depth to her misery. During this time, I experienced a profound sympathy for her, yet I didn't know her any better than an acquaintance. Then one evening while we were having dinner at my house, Lori opened up about an affair she had after Tess. A married woman with an out-of-control religious-nut father was all she said. I wondered if it might be Marie Sanfield when she said the woman's father was hunting her down for ruining his daughter's marriage. She told me the affair ended when the crazy father almost found her."

My profiler mind went crazy. Was Lori in the campground all that time and did Manson Smith know that? It sure fit what Steph just told us.

"She asked if I wanted to take a night stroll," continued Steph. "Lori explained that 'The sky is littered with stars and you can see them so much better if we go to one of the parks out of town. It's a really great place to view the sky. My mother used to take me there when I was a child.'

"This was the first private thing she had told me and I then knew that she grew up somewhere around here. I told her the parks were closed and you couldn't park your car anywhere because they barricade the lots at night. Lori grinned mischievously and said she knew a park we could get into and a place where we could leave our car. Then she said, 'Live on the wild side for once. It'll be fun. We can have a great make-out session under the most romantic sky you'll ever see.'"

"If she had asked to do that when we first dated, I would have jumped at the thought of romance under the stars. But now I was skeptical, so with a bit of dread, I said yes, hoping it would get answers for Blake.

"Lori drove me to the exact place where Tess, Marie, and Annie had died. That was more than a coincidence, and I began to get the feeling that Lori had something to do with their deaths. And I was getting scared. She parked in a field down the road, hiding her car in a clump of trees. We walked through the forest without a flashlight, and she did it with such ease. She must have walked that way through the woods on more than one occasion since she seemed to know where every rock, tree root, and hole was which didn't surprise me since she said her mother had brought her there often.

"We sat on a bench behind the fence for a while, looking out over the gorge and watching the stars. I noticed clouds beginning to form, and I could hear water quietly flowing below. We talked about life. Nothing specific. Mostly, I listened to Lori talk about her dreams. She wanted to find long-term love. She said she had had to move too often and it didn't give her time to find any permanence in her private or her work life. I asked her if she had a passion for anything. She looked out to the other side of the gorge and said she didn't know. She talked about finding a woman, a partner who would love her for who she was no matter what. She wished she had parents who were alive and understood what she was going through. Then she asked, 'Have you ever heard that if you throw a penny into the gorge and make a wish, it will come true?' She walked to the fence and climbed over it.

"I warned her not to do that because it was dangerous. She said she had done it more times than she could count. At that point I was getting really nervous. Then she looked over the edge and said, 'I'll bet there's a hundred dollars in pennies at the bottom of that cliff.' She fished in the front pocket of her jeans and pulled out two pennies, holding them up. She urged me to come over telling me she was pretty sure I had a wish just burning to be made.

"I don't know if it was the fact that I did have a wish, or if it was a push inside me that said I needed to do this if I was to find the truth that made me climb the fence. But I did, and she handed me the penny. We closed our eyes and whispered in our minds our greatest desire. Then, just as we looked at each other and tossed the pennies, I heard a noise behind us.

"Lori turned and spat on the ground and shouted 'What are you doing here?' I was completely dumbfounded, surprised, confused, and flabbergasted...well, you get the picture. Mac Taylor's wife, Missy, was standing behind us. On our side of the fence. Neither of us had heard her climb over. I wondered how she did that without us hearing her. Let alone at her age. The chain-links made a lot of noise when you climbed them.

"When Missy spoke to Lori, her tone was exact, demanding, and pleading all at the same time. She said, 'Please. Let me end this.' I contemplated her sentence. I didn't understand what she meant by ending this and why Missy would be there pleading to Lori to end something?

"Lori said, 'My parents gave up on me. They're dead.' That's what she told me when we first met. She refused to say anything more on the subject. So, I was pretty confused by what was happening.

There seemed to be an anger brewing inside Lori I had never seen before, and I was definitely getting more scared by the minute. She seemed on edge and unstable, but so did Missy. Lori told her to get the fuck out of here.

"When I saw Missy give me a very ugly dismissive look, I took a step sideways and away from the ledge. Then she told Lori she wasn't leaving. She was her mother and Lori had to listen to her. Needless to say, I was shocked."

That one definitely caught my attention.

"Then it got heated between them. Lori took a deadly step toward Missy and again told her mother to get the fuck out of there. Missy scolded her about not speaking to her mother that way, and told her she was leaving with her. Missy said they would finish it once and for all and that she would take her back to Change of Heart because she needed help. Missy said she had to send her there because she was sick."

"Lori was breathing fast and heavy. I also noticed Missy had made tiny and very discreet movements in my direction while keeping her eyes on Lori. That was when I decided to make my own move back toward the fence and get out of there.

"Missy kept talking, telling Lori they had looked for her for a long time and thought she was dead. When she found Lori in the cabin at the back of the campground, she was so happy to see her. And then she mentioned her father and Lori lost it. She got really loud and said she had stayed away from both of them for a reason. She said she didn't want to be around them, or to be connected to them in any way. They were dead to her. That fit with what she'd told me.

"Missy stopped moving. So, did I. She kept her eyes on me but asked Lori if she thought she could carry on with the likes of me? Then Missy said, 'Haven't you had enough? Every one of them betrayed you. That's all they know how to do. Annie, Ellen, Ainsley, Becca, Monica, Tess. I took care of them for you. I took care of them all! They found the Lord by my hand. And now this one.' Missy pointed at me. She was so full of hate. She called me a poor excuse for a female and told Lori that she was not perverted like me. She then told Lori that she needed to go with her because she would not let these wretched, sick women ruin her."

I was horrified by what Missy had done and angry they had put Steph through such a terrifying experience.

"Lori yelled at her mother, 'You killed them? All who? Who else did you kill?' Her mother smiled and nodded and that's when Lori said she was leaving and made a move toward the fence. At the same time, Missy bolted toward me and caught me by surprise. We struggled, but she had the upper hand, and she pushed me hard. I tried to dig my feet into the ground to force her back or to get around her, but my sneakers just slid on the dirt. I thought if I got my body on the ground, she'd have a harder time throwing me over the edge, but she kicked my feet out from underneath me before I could do that. And I fell. Like I had intended to do. Just not in the direction I had wanted. My body slid over the edge, and that's when I thought I was a goner. Then Lori lunged at Missy. I think she shoved her into the fence, and I felt Lori grab my arms. She held me while I tried to get a foothold so I could climb back up, but there was nothing to get a foothold in. Just solid, smooth rock. I remember thinking that this was not the wish I had made, and I wished I had that penny back."

I chuckled quietly as I took Steph's hand.

Steph went on. "I was hanging on to Lori's arms, but I felt her grip weakening. The bulk of my bodyweight was hanging over the edge, and there was nothing I could do. That's when I heard Blake." She was looking at Maddie when she squeezed my hand and smiled. "She saved me." Then she looked at me. "The story is yours from here."

I shook my head several times as her account of what happened began to sink in and my mind worked on overdrive to draw conclusions instead of making assumptions and formulating theories. There was one thing that stood out above all others. Steph loved me.

"Mac didn't help you?" Maddie, or Captain Spinner (I couldn't tell which persona was speaking), asked me incredulously.

"He didn't have to," I replied. "Lori helped me. I truly believed he would have, but when Lori pushed Missy to get away from her, Missy fell into the gorge. He seemed paralyzed. His wife had just died. He was…in agony. And then there was his daughter who pushed her. Don't fault him for that. Then Lori stood up and saw her father.

"By the time we were safe against the fence, Mac tried to reason with Lori," I explained. "Then she looked at me and said Annie's and Tess's names and that she was sorry. She backed off the ledge before Mac could get to her. She didn't fall. She took a step. She knew what she was doing. Mac fell apart, and then I called the police on Steph's phone. Mine was dead."

Maddie looked at Steph. "You said you heard Missy mention the names of women that died in this gorge and in others. And she said she killed them?"

"Pretty much. She said they found the Lord by her hand. When Lori asked if she killed them, Missy nodded."

"Oh, God," Captain Spinner said. "And Mac knows all this?"

"Yes, he does."

"Damn," she said as she ran a hand through her hair. Then her phone rang and she answered. "Right. Okay. I'll be there in about an hour. Keep me posted." She looked at us. "The doctor said that Mac wanted to talk to me. Will you be all right?"

"Yes," Steph said, and I echoed her answer.

Captain Spinner stood and extended her hand. "Thank you for coming in. You know the procedure. Go home. Get some rest. But don't leave the area until we release you. You're definitely going to have to come in for more questioning and to sign your formal statement."

I saluted Maddie. "Got it, boss."

Steph smiled as she shook Maddie's hand. "I got it too."

Still exhausted, we went back to my trailer and took Mabel for a short walk. Inside, Steph picked up the pooch and plopped down on the bed once again. Not wanting to overstep my boundaries, I sat down in a recliner and closed my eyes, deciding to nap there. I heard soft thuds and looked in the bedroom to see Steph patting the bed beside her in an animated way. "*What* are you doing?"

"I'm going to take a nap."

"Over there?" I could have sworn she had a mischievous grin on her face.

"But I thought…"

"You thought what? Didn't you listen to what I said earlier? Because of how I feel about you, I *had* to push you away. There were a lot of reasons, but the greatest was I had to get close to Lori. She was watching me."

My head snapped in her direction. "What? You didn't say that."

"I forgot to tell that to Maddie, too. Damn. I'll have to call her tomorrow. Yeah, Lori told me she had been watching me for a while. I think she was the second stalker, after Smith came looking for her and got his marching orders. I just don't know how he knew she was here. You also need to know that I am not, nor will I ever be serious about Lori. There was no love between us. I've always had and still do have feelings for you. I did all this for you."

I didn't know what to say.

"It took a lot for me to admit some of that in front of Maddie." She lowered the volume of her voice. "I wanted to tell only you, but the extenuating circumstances forced me to do it differently."

"Neither did I ever expect any of this." I looked down at the bedding.

"You can put those permanently away later," Steph said with a grin.

"Sounds good to me," I replied as I stripped down to my underwear, put a T-shirt on over my bra and then slid my bra off from underneath it.

"I could have helped you with that." Steph's eyes and mouth softened, making my mouth dry and a shiver run up and down my spine.

I leaned against the pillows she had arranged for me. "I'm not going to lie to you. The way you treated me really hurt me, because it was the way I thought you actually felt, so I had to understand and respect that." I turned to meet her eyes. "Now, you're saying something else and I'm…confused?"

She tilted her head and her lips squeezed together in a smile that reminded me of when my mother realized I had just done or said something that made her happy, even though I had no idea what it was. "Are you *asking* me if you're confused or telling me?" Then she leaned forward—slowly—watching my eyes the entire time. Her lips softened once again, her cheeks flushed, and there was a gleam in her eyes.

"We have a lot to talk about," she whispered as she got closer.

"We do?" I said in a cracked voice.

"We do."

"Do we have to do it now?"

"No," she breathed out.

And then *I* kissed her. And *she* kissed me back.

CHAPTER TWENTY-SIX

I woke a few hours later wrapped in a pair of warm arms encircling me. I soon realized only our upper bodies were touching, because one ten-pound mutt separated us. Mabel's butt was against Steph's hips and her front legs pushed against me. Steph was hers.

I petted Mabel's back and she fixed her eyes on me as if to tell me to go away. "Not this time," I whispered. "You do know I'm the one who feeds you." Mabel's short tail wagged furiously. "Stop," I giggled. "You'll wake her up."

"I'm already awake."

I looked at Steph, struggling to open her eyes.

"Good thing the captain gave me the day off. Don't think I could properly slice open a body today."

I kissed her forehead. "Then I guess we can talk."

"How about we go outside with some drinks and snacks and we can chat while we eat?"

"Chat. I like the cutsie word you're using for the conversation we're going to have."

"Depends on the conversation," she replied.

"Or the outcome."

She leaned forward and kissed me fully on the lips—the same kiss that led to our hour long make-out session, ending only because we fell asleep from pure exhaustion. We felt a wet nose press in between our lips and we laughed, and laughed and laughed, all the while loving up my little peanut, who I realized now was *our* little peanut.

"I'll get her settled and then find some food," I said, climbing out of bed.

"I can take care of Mabel if you want," Steph offered.

"Okay, but that's one topic we're going to have to visit."

"Which is?" she said as she put her clothes back on from the night before.

"Make that two. One is the intentional purloining of my dog." I was pretty sure she wouldn't know the meaning of purloin, but as always, Steph surprised me.

"I am not trying to steal your dog. I am merely trying to establish a relationship with her."

"You've known her since I adopted her. You already have a relationship with her," I teased.

"Not one so…so involved. I only got to see her once in a while when you came down to visit or I came up to Rochester. Now, what's the other?"

"You might want to bring some extra clothes over here. I can empty the cupboard on that side of the bed." I nodded to the built-in unit on the side Steph had slept. Her grin formed with the corners of her lips lifting slightly.

"Only if you bring some over to my place. I have a few empty drawers."

"Deal." I smiled.

"Deal." She scooped up Mabel and added, "And I still don't cook."

The grin I gave her in response felt wonderful. Had we both found happiness?

I found some dill pickles, chips, and cookies as Steph busied herself pulling out plates and glasses for the lemonade I prepared. She took it all outside and then came back in announcing she needed coffee. I grinned as I pointed to the Keurig. I had already started a cup for her.

She kissed me on the cheek before she picked up Mabel's bed and took it outside, placing it on the ground next to her chair. I watched her, feeling my body warm at the sight. We sat opposite each other and ate in silence for several minutes before she reached across the table and put a hand on mine. "You already know how I feel about you. I need to know if you feel the same. I mean, is it too soon?"

Warmed by her concern about the loss of Tess—twice—I answered without hesitation. "I do and no, I don't think it's too soon. I just don't want you to think it's not real because people might think it's too soon."

"I don't care what others think. Besides, our best friends are really the only ones that matter, and I know for a fact, they are all for it."

"They told you so, huh?"

"Yes."

"Myra told me as much, too."

"There. That one's solved. But I'm worried that with my past, as far as relationships are concerned, I'll scare you off. You think I'll run after the novelty wears off. Like Tess did."

I squeezed her hand. "I'm not scared. Maybe you were just waiting for the right woman to come along. And you've been with me for a lot longer than anyone. If you haven't run by now…"

"Damn, I sure had to wait a long time for it," she chuckled.

Then the mood turned serious, and I asked, "So, what do we do from here?"

"I don't know," she answered, as if looking for a more definitive answer.

"You know, if you think about it, we're totally doing this backward," I said.

"What do you mean?"

"Usually, you have wild sex first and then get to know the person. We already know each other. Really well, I would say."

"Then all that's left for us is to have the wild sex." She winked. "Seriously, how does that make you feel?"

"Like I want to leave the dishes and jump back into bed with you." Thinking about it made love-touched warmth travel through my body, and I felt a longing, needing and wanting that I hadn't felt in a very long time. I wondered at that moment if Steph and I would be able to hang on to that feeling.

Then, as if reading my mind, she said, "We don't have to take the time to get to know each other, because as you say, we know each other better than anyone else. Now, we can just take the time to *love* each other."

Her words made me instantly believe. And I knew. I knew we would be together, if not for always, at least for now. And for now, that would be enough.

We cleaned up our dishes, but instead of jumping into bed afterward, we went for a walk without Mabel so we could talk. We kissed. It was sweet and warm and tantalizing, and I knew I could so get used to this.

"We have plenty of time to jump into bed," she said, looking into my eyes in a way that made me shiver and melt at the same time.

I took her hand, and we walked for over an hour, rehashing the events of the night before—from Missy's and Lori's deaths to our make-out session, ending with how we felt about each other, because we couldn't deny it any longer—we felt the same. We held hands while we walked along the quiet road. Once in a while a car or a school bus would pass, but mostly, only the peaceful sounds of the empty spaces filled the air. When our walk ended, we knew there was so much more to talk about, but like she said, we had time. Lots of time and all that mattered was we knew it would be together.

Steph said she was going to run home and change, and she would meet me back at my trailer. I sat outside on my zero-gravity chair, allowing the feelings of love and longing play with my body. Shortly thereafter, I saw Steph jogging back across the field toward my trailer. I knew what she was up to by her big smile. She was going to lavish love, affection and probably a few treats on Mabel while telling her what a terrible mother I was for not letting her walk with us.

I ran to my door, fumbling with the handle so I could get in and pick up Mabel before Steph got there. I flung it open just as Steph grabbed me from behind before I completed the top step. Laughing like two kids, we playfully pushed and shoved each other—her trying to get to Mabel, me trying to keep her from doing so. We were careful to make sure no one fell down the metal steps, ending in us falling to the floor in the doorway, causing us to laugh even harder.

"Mabel, Mommy's home and she loves you," I struggled to say as we rolled around on the floor.

"Oh, Mabel, your mommy left you way too long. Come here, girl. I'll take care of you." She didn't get all the words out because I kept trying to cover her mouth with my hand while she tried to swat it away. So, I tried another tactic. I kissed her. We lavished each other with long, slow kisses, exploring lips and tongues and allowing the feeling of sexual pleasure to give us a preview of what was to come.

Suddenly, Steph stopped. "Where is she?" she asked, looking around when we finished.

It was then we noticed Mabel lying down on her recliner with her head on her front paws, eyeing us. If ever a dog's eyes could convey admonishment, it was Mabel's, and it only made us laugh harder. We lay on our backs for a few minutes. Every time we looked at my dog or each other, another round of boisterous laughing ensued. Finally, Mabel must have decided she'd had enough and jumped off the chair and began licking both our faces. It was then we heard someone clear their throat.

"Ahem. Are we, uh, interrupting anything?"

We looked up to see Jen and Myra at the foot of the stairs. "We were arguing over who was going to give Mabel her treat," I said.

"At the rate you two are going, she's probably going to starve before one of you wins the argument," Myra said, arms folded.

Steph scrambled to her feet and took a treat out of the jar. She thrust it at me. I took the mini milk bone and gave it to Mabel. "See? Would you like to join us for a drink? I was just about to put the awning out," I said.

"Sure," Myra answered. "What are we having?"

"Lemonade. Let me know if you want me to add anything substantial to it."

"Nope, lemonade will be fine."

"So, ladies. What was all that really about?" Jen asked.

Repressing a giggle outburst by clenching her teeth, Steph answered, "Blake told you. We were, uh, quibbling over who was getting Mabel's treat."

"Quibbling, was it? Looked more like an all-out takedown."

We all laughed as Jen and Myra went outside, taking a seat at the picnic table. I pushed the button and opened the awning, all the while watching Steph out of the corner of my eye. She was pulling a pitcher of lemonade out of the refrigerator—with Mabel still in her arms. I thought my lips would crack if I didn't stop smiling today. It had been a while since I felt this good, this happy, and I wanted it to last because it felt...good. So good.

I now knew Annie's and Tess's deaths were not suicides. Neither was Marie Sanfield's, and more than likely nor were all those other women. Ainsley and Becca on my list, and perhaps Ellen and Monica that Missy had mentioned. And Steph was here because she loved me, and that meant everything, even if it meant I had to share my dog. Then again, sharing Mabel with Steph also felt…good. Really good.

We sat outside for the next few hours filling Myra and Jen in on the prior evening's events. Then during dinner, we filled them in on the status of Steph and me…together.

"Oh," Jen squealed. "This will make payback for my grilling title so much more fun."

Myra, Steph, and I groaned. Now we had to be on our guard for Jen's comeuppance.

"I've only got one question," Myra said. "When do you want me to build your deck and shed?"

* * *

The next few weeks, I existed in a dream state while Steph, Mabel, and I lived between our two trailers. We began to explore our lives together in a relationship. We took walks, ate meals with our friends and slept together each night with Mabel curled up between us. Even though we hadn't made love yet, I knew that day wasn't far off. For now, we spent the time alone partaking in incredible foreplay that I didn't want to end. Steph was right. We did know each other, but not in the sexual way. So, in a sense, we were still getting to know each other.

One morning over breakfast, Steph asked me, "I know you're still not over Tess and that you may never be. I also know she will always have a place in your heart, but what about Annie? Do you finally have closure on that?"

"I don't know if I have closure yet. I think I will when they finish investigating all of this, but"—I took her hands in mine—"I closed the door on my feelings for Annie a long time ago. And I hope you know that just because Tess will always have a place in my heart doesn't mean that there's not enough room for you." I kissed her lips and was immediately filled with their warmth and welcoming feeling. "You're the one that's filling my heart now and you always will be."

Then I saw a strange look in her eyes. I wasn't sure what to make of it. I let go of her hands and said, "I'm sorry. Is that too much for you?"

Her shoulders relaxed as a beautiful, brilliant smile showed on her face. "That's just it. It's not too much. I want all of this. I want the commitment, and I want this love." When I leaned in for another kiss, she put her hand gently on my chest. "I just need you to know that I'm still going to therapy and will continue to go. I'm so happy where I am, and I want to stay that way. Therapy will make sure that I do."

It was a promise that meant more to me than her mischievous escapades in trying to win my dog's affection. She didn't need to. She already had both our affections, but it made my heart smile and swell with love.

Steph went to work every day, and I spent the alone time thinking about my next move as far as my everyday life was concerned. One day, I received a call from Maddie, except that it was officially from Captain Spinner. She asked me to come down to the station. I had already been interrogated by her and signed my statement. Still, I didn't ask why. I just went. I didn't care anymore about pursuing the case. Steph had gotten answers for me and Captain Spinner and the police force just had to put all the pieces together. I knew it would only be a matter of time before I would hear from Maddie and find out the why and what.

When the Ithaca police closed the case, I hoped to hand Tess's parents her death certificate that would not state suicide. Hopefully, it would end their struggle with feeling like failures to their child. They didn't fail her, after all. Life did.

Maddie was looking at a file on her desk, glasses resting on her nose. She never heard me enter the room. I sat in the chair that squeaked and Maddie looked up. Her smile was subdued, and I knew this case had taken a toll on her as well.

"You look good, Blake. Steph's been more chipper than normal too. Things must be working out between you two."

I beamed. "You could say that."

"I'm glad something good came out of all this." She sighed heavily. "You know everything I say to you in this office remains in the office."

I nodded.

"And despite the fact you'll go home and tell Steph, it still needs to remain in this office."

I smiled, knowing that was Maddy's way of letting me know it was all right to tell Steph, because Steph would keep it in this room as well.

"Some of us knew Mac and Missy had a daughter, but he always kept his private life very private. Lori's birth name was June Taylor. She always hated the name. Mac told me in the hospital she hated it so much, she asked her parents to legally change her name to Lori June Taylor when she was in middle school. She was an unhappy child, so they agreed hoping it might help her. No one ever met her. There was a reason for that. I knew she had run away in her teens, but I had no idea why. Until now."

She shifted her weight in her chair and grunted. I wondered if that ergonomic chair wasn't so ergonomic for her after all.

"Anyway, what really happened was that Lori had been dating girls. Both her parents were aggressively homophobic as we all know, and when they found out about Lori's sexual preferences, I heard that Missy sent Lori away to one of those religious camps that promises to delesbianize your kid. It was one of those organizations where they take the child in the night while the parents are out."

"Change of Heart," I said. "Remember Missy said she had to take her back to Change of Heart."

"That's right. I also had heard that Mac was furious when he found out his wife had sent their daughter away without telling him. He told me she convinced him to let Lori stay there until she finished the program, claiming it would be better for their daughter. He didn't really have a choice because she wouldn't tell him where Lori was. That's when he hired a private investigator to find her, but came up empty-handed. Most likely that's because Lori had run away from Change of Heart and probably changed her name then to Lori Smith.

"Mac was a great guy before that all happened—caring, friendly, always watching out for his coworkers. I think that's when he changed. He became the Mac you had to deal with, and we all know today. It was right about the time you had your first big case."

"Annie," I said quietly.

"Yes, Annie. No one ever connected the dots because there weren't any to connect. At the time, I suspected you may have been involved with Annie, as you were incredibly upset, more so than seemed likely for an unrelated suicide. But I never said anything to you. Times were…different. We never did talk about any of it, and I'm sorry for that. I wasn't a good female coworker, or friend for that matter." She sighed. "From what we know, Missy killed Annie when she found out that her daughter was seeing her."

I wasn't sure I heard her correctly. My stomach did a flip-flop. There was no way Annie would see someone like Lori. But I waited until Captain Spinner finished.

"That's when Missy sent Lori away. After that, the other women Missy mentioned were random killings. Lesbians. Lori didn't know those women and we believe Missy searched out any lesbian she could find, thinking they had turned her daughter even though her daughter was gone. Eventually she stopped."

"Man, she was pretty off. Mac never saw any of this?"

"He says no. He knew she hated lesbians as much as he did, but he was too busy being his own crappy self. We're still talking to him. Anyway, it wasn't that long ago that Lori landed back here in Ithaca, but never contacted her parents. She had changed her looks, but her mother saw her one day in The Commons and followed her to where she met Tess. We have witnesses that saw her there. Her mother must have kept an eye on her because Lori was already seeing Marie Sanfield. She killed Marie and then Tess."

My mouth opened and my heart beat faster.

"We're still investigating the connections these women had to Lori. We know from you and Steph that Tess was involved with Lori. That helps a lot. We also found out by speaking to Marie Sanfield's husband that the timing of her affair with a woman put it after Tess and Lori broke up but before they met in The Commons and before Steph started her own little investigation. But he didn't know who the woman was." She winked at me. "This is going to give me a heart attack."

"Sorry about that." I grinned.

"So as you see, this investigation will take a lot longer since both Lori and Missy are dead."

She waited for me to say something, to feel something, but right now…I had nothing. I took that back. I feared they still would rule Annie's and Tess's deaths as suicides. But how could they? Not with all they now knew.

Maddie shifted in her chair again and continued. "When Steph told me she didn't believe Manson Smith was the only stalker at the campground, we did a little investigating. We suspected someone else was hiding out in the condemned cabin, which we now know was Lori."

My eyes widened.

"Mac told me that he thought something was up with Missy a few days ago. She was acting strange. This must have been when she found Lori in the cabin. But Mac said she never told him Lori was there. He said when she got out of bed and left that night, he waited and then tracked her through a phone app that gives you the location of someone you set it up for. So whether he knew or not, he knew something wasn't right."

Maddie sighed. "Manson Smith told us during an interview that Missy saw him lurking around the empty cabin one night. He said he was looking for the woman who got involved with his daughter because one of Marie's friends told him who her lover was, and that her lover was staying at a campground. So we know from both Steph's and Smith's statements that Lori was at the campground. Mac swears he didn't know, but I'm not sure I believe him. To be honest, if he did know, he'll never let on. He's very good at hiding secrets. However, I don't know if he'll ever be able to get to the other side of this one."

"A lot of questions that may never get answered," I said sullenly.

"My next question to you, Blake, is a tough one. Did you know that Lori was seeing Annie?"

"No. Not Annie." I shook my head.

"I'm sorry, Blake, but we have information that they were seen together on several occasions."

"But that was a long time ago. How can you believe those stories?" I was getting upset to think Annie might have been cheating on me. With the same woman Tess cheated with. What were the odds of that?

"Calm down. I'm not saying they were in a relationship, but I do believe Lori wanted one with her." I started to object, but she put a hand up. "Remember the coins Lori liked to toss into the gorge?"

"Like in a fountain," I muttered. "Yes."

"There were notes in Annie's case file about pennies found near her body. It's against the law to throw coins into Upper Taughannock Creek. There's a sign at the entrance that says that. But Lori said she and her mother did it often."

My heart sank, remembering that day all those years ago.

"There were coins found near Marie's body and Tess's. We believe it was Missy who most likely tossed the coins in after them because we've been reexamining the case files of the other victims and they too had pennies near their bodies. Lori wasn't in the area when these women were killed. It appears that after Annie died, she left town and didn't return for years."

"But you don't know for sure," I said.

Maddie nodded. "We actually know a lot, but there are still so many questions. I just don't know if we'll ever get all the answers. Like how many women did Missy kill? Were any of the other women involved with Lori in any way? Because we can't be sure that Lori didn't come back at other times before now and started up a relationship with one of them? There's still a lot of interviewing that needs to be done with the victim's families and it was years ago that these deaths occurred. Memories fade and get clouded with time. I also wonder if Mac is telling the truth that he had no idea about what his wife was doing?"

I sucked in a breath, knowing Steph was almost one of those Missy killed. Why Missy didn't target her earlier, we would never know. Maybe it was because *she* broke up with Lori. She put herself in danger by making Lori think she wanted her back. Just to help me. At that moment, I thanked God, the universe or whatever or whoever was at the helm of our existence for not letting Lori find out what Steph was up to. "One more question. Who do you think called me to tell me Steph was in trouble?" I asked.

"I don't know. I believe it was Mac, but that would mean he knows more than he's telling us. We checked your phone, but the call came from a burner. We may never know. We're still investigating, so all of these cases will remain open. For now. I don't know how long it will take, but I can give you, Tess's parents and Annie's parents this. It's the main reason I called you in."

Captain Spinner handed me an envelope. Inside was Tess's death certificate. Under the cause of death was "Open Murder Investigation." Normally, a police officer would deliver it to the parents but as Tess and I were still legally married at the time of her death, she gave it to me. I'm sure as a favor. I knew in that moment that I would take a trip to Rochester to present it to the Anglers and stay for a while to help them through this news if need be.

I was about to ask her about Annie's death certificate, but she read my mind. "I already delivered it to Annie's parents. It says the same. They were grateful. Maybe one day you could call them."

I shook Captain Spinner's hand and thanked her, and then I hugged Maddie. I returned to the campground to wait for Steph to come home from work. I texted Myra and Jen and told them dinner was at my trailer and spent the afternoon preparing hamburgers, a macaroni salad and fresh fruit. I had everything ready when Steph came home. God, I loved saying when she came home because, well, home is where the heart is and Steph was my heart.

We had just sat down outside when we spotted Myra and Jen crossing the field.

"Hey, girls," Jen shouted.

We raised our glasses to them, and then I handed them each a glass of wine. While eating dinner, I recounted my meeting with Maddie, reminding them that what was said in her office stayed in her office. But I trusted my friends. I trusted Steph. I was lucky to have them in my life. Lucky and oh, so grateful.

A thought struck me and I turned to Steph. "What made you come up with your ludicrous scheme to chase Lori? Apart from thinking she was odd, why did you think she had something to do with Tess's death?"

"Remember I told you that Bevel kept screwing things up on his autopsies?"

I nodded.

"I'm surprised Captain Spinner didn't tell you. When he got Tess's body, he removed her shoes but didn't record them into his notes. He didn't bag them separately either, which is a big no-no. Instead, he put them into the evidence bag with the rest of Tess's clothes. So, no one ever checked the tread of the shoes with the footprints at the murder scene. Shoes are always bagged separately, but because he didn't record them, no one thought anything about it."

We looked at her quizzically.

"They found footprints standing on the ledge that proved someone just stood there. Nothing showed any kind of struggle. The forensic team assumed the footprints belonged to Tess. It was up to Bevel to check her shoes, but it got overlooked because of his stupidity."

Steph looked directly at me. "You said from the beginning that Tess would never jump. I found the shoes when I went back to work. I told Maddie about them and forensics compared them to the footprints at the scene. You see, the shoes in Tess's evidence bag were sandals. The footprints they found were from sneakers. After I found Bevel's mistake, I researched the sneakers. They were from a pair of Hoka 8 sneakers. Did you ever notice that Missy wore Hoka sneakers? I found that odd, because they're expensive and usually only younger people wear them. But they're good for standing on your feet all day. I noticed Missy's shoes one day and it made me remember that Lori always wore Hoka sneakers too. It was then I hatched my plan." She looked at me. "I needed to know."

"Maddie never told me. You didn't tell me!" I exclaimed.

"Maddie ordered me not to. She wanted you out of the investigation. But it gave us a lead that someone else was there. I just had a feeling about Lori, so I had to find out. That's why I started seeing her again. So I could see if she still owned a pair of those sneakers."

"Did she?" Myra asked.

"Yeah, she did."

"Did Maddie reprimand you for any of this?" I asked.

"Not yet." She smiled. Then she said in a quiet voice, "Needless to say, Bevel will no longer be our backup ME. The captain has feelers out to find someone else. I don't think she'll get rid of me anytime soon, especially since I gave them their first real lead."

"Hell, because of you, the case is on its way to being solved," Jen said. She raised her glass. "To the hero." Myra and I also raised our glasses to Steph. She blushed.

I smiled, remembering Maddie telling me we were too much alike. Then I gave her my best disciplinary look. "You took a really big risk. It was almost you at the bottom of that gorge. I wouldn't have been able to bear it if it had been," I said to her, so full of gratitude that it hadn't been and for the deadly risk she took for me.

"Like I told you. I had to do it."

I laughed. "You know what Maddie told me?"

She tilted her head.

"That we are too much alike." I took her hand and squeezed it. "And I'm so grateful that you are as much a need-to-know as I am, but even more so that you're sitting here with us now."

"You know," Jen said. "No one has seen Mac around, which makes sense since he had two funerals to prepare for and from what you've said, he's been spending time at the station being grilled about how much he knew. Greg's been running everything, but he keeps his mouth shut. He hired Sandy Miller to work in the office and even she isn't saying anything."

I was glad Jen had changed the subject. I was getting ready to pull Steph into the trailer and show her just how grateful I was.

Jen continued, "Everyone knows something's wrong, but no one knows exactly what happened."

"Until it's on the news which I'm pretty sure it will be soon," Myra said glumly.

"What I'm wondering is if Mac's going to sell this place or come back and make our lives even more miserable. You know how that kind of loss can affect a person."

And as if the universe knew the answer, the familiar sound of Mac's golf cart filled the air and soon he was stopping in front of my campsite. This time, he got out of the vehicle and walked up to my fence. He looked…different. Like a man who's been beaten down by life, which now I knew he had been. Still…

"Good evening, ladies." He leaned over the fence and petted Mabel. I was astonished that she let him and then she even gave him a slight tail wag.

"Hi, Mac," I responded. "I'm sorry for everything that has happened."

"Yes, we all are," Steph added.

Mac stood. "Thank you. And…uh…I'm sorry too. I'm letting everyone know that I'm back full time. I'm retiring from the police force." He paused. "I think it's time."

"Good for you," I said. "You'll love retirement. Gives you time to do some real soul searching." I looked at Steph and took her hand. She smiled at me, and didn't drop my hand. I smiled back.

"Well, I don't know about that. But it'll give me time to focus on making this campground a better place for everyone." This time, Mac's smile seemed genuine.

"And for you," Jen said, grinning back at him.

"And for me. Well, you ladies have a great night, and I'll see you around. Don't forget we'll be having a potluck dinner next Saturday for the seasonals. I really hope you can come. Sign-up sheet is in the office. Well, good night." He walked back to his golf cart.

"Good night," we echoed to him.

After he was out of sight, Myra said, "Well, look at that. He might have just proved us wrong. Maybe people can change. It's just unfortunate that he had to lose his wife and daughter."

Steph studied me. "Can you live with Mac being the owner?"

"I'm willing to try, but I won't promise anything until I see it."

Steph took my hand. "I'm with you all the way."

I squeezed her hand. "And that's why I can get beyond seeing him as Officer Nasty and now as Mac, the owner of the campground. Because I have you."

Her smile was the light that I knew would turn on if the nightmares returned. I wouldn't be left alone in the darkness to deal with them by myself anymore. Now, there was one more thing I had to do before we ended the evening. I cleared my throat and put forward the proposal I had been working on. "I want to open a detective agency."

Myra and Jen looked at me. "Excuse me?" Myra said, apparently flabbergasted.

Steph, who sat next to me, continued to stare across the field. "On one condition," she said.

Myra's mouth fell open. "You two have conditions? Is this serious?"

"Yes, and yes," I answered.

"So, Steph," Myra began. "Does this mean you might come out of the shadows?"

Steph was still holding my hand, our fingers stroking. After a few seconds, she met Myra's gaze. "I guess I already have. Besides, I've got a good reason to now."

Myra's grin said it all. She was happy for us because she knew all along what we didn't. That being together was not only the medicine we needed to heal our wounds, but the way it should be.

"What's the condition?" I asked Steph.

"It's two conditions. One, that I can help you set up your business. Two, so when I retire, I can join you. Be a partner. In every way."

"Oh..." I dragged out the word. "A partner. That's a lot of commitment. Are you up for that?"

Steph turned on the bench and took both my hands in hers. "Like I said. In every way." She kissed me long, her lips soft and supple and moist.

Jen and Myra stood. "Well," Jen said. Guess it's time for us to go. Besides, now that you two are officially a couple, and life is good, I can start planning my payback for the wonderful nickname you all gave me. Have a good night." She winked and they left holding hands as they crossed the field.

"How about we take this inside?" Steph suggested. Who was I to argue?

We cleaned up from dinner and took Mabel inside, closing the door behind us. I knew in that moment that we were going to finally know each other in every way possible. I knew we were ready to make love. So, we did.

Over, and over and over again.

Other Books by Nance Newman

Whisper's Series - paranormal mystery
All Alone
Bad Man, Bad Ghost
Dirty Wrong
Sound Travels
The Structure of Lies
Bad Man, Bad Daddy

Heartwood Series - young adult magical realism fantasy
Heartwood
Fractures
Dubiety

Nonfiction
Journaling Through a Heartbreak

Lesbian Fiction
The Stonewall Railroad science fiction dystopian novel

More Titles from Bella Books

Jones – Gerri Hill
978-1-64247-598-2 | 260 pages | Mystery
One weekend getaway, six friends, and a deadly secret that will wash away everything they thought they knew.

Merry Weihnachten – E. J. Noyes
978-1-64247-610-1 | 292 pages | Romance
Christmas traditions aren't the only things getting mixed up when these two hearts collide beneath the mistletoe.

Sweet Home Alabarden Park – TJ O'Shea
978-1-64247-570-8 | 362 pages | Romance
She came to restore a royal estate—she never expected to rebuild her heart.

Dr. Margaret Morgan – Christy Hadfield
978-1-64247-628-6 | 286 pages | Romance
Facing the professor on campus everyone hates is terrifying—but falling for her might be even worse.

Overtime – Tracey Richardson
978-1-64247-630-9 | 278 pages | Romance
A charming romance about second chances, found family, and scoring the goal that matters most.

The Big Guilt – Renée J. Lukas
978-1-64247-657-6 | 206 pages | Romance
What if the one who got away became the one you can't have?